THE WIDOWS CLUB

Dorothy Cannell

THE WIDOWS CLUB

BANTAM BOOKS
TORONTO • NEW YORK • LONDON • SYDNEY • AUCKLAND

THE WIDOWS CLUB
A Bantam Book / May 1988

Book Design by Nicola Mazzella.

Library of Congress Cataloging-in-Publication Data

Cannell, Dorothy.
The widows club.

I. Title.
PS3553.A499W54 1988 813′.54 87-47913
ISBN 0-553-05259-4

Published simultaneously in the United States and Canada

Bantam Books are published by Bantam Books, a division of Bantam Doubleday Dell Publishing Group, Inc. Its trademark, consisting of the words "Bantam Books" and the portrayal of a rooster, is Registered in U.S. Patent and Trademark Office and in other countries. Marca Registrada. Bantam Books, 666 Fifth Avenue, New York, New York 10103.

PRINTED IN THE UNITED STATES OF AMERICA

FG 0 9 8 7 6 5 4 3 2 1

To my husband Julian,
who need have no fear.

THE WIDOWS CLUB

PART ONE

PROLOGUE

From the Files of
The Widows Club

President:

Ladies, dear friends: Our monthly meeting having been called to order, let us offer a generous round of applause for today's pianist, Mrs. Edwina Grouse, and her rousing rendition of "All Things Bright and Beautiful." Edwina is a charter member, now living in Spain, and we are delighted to welcome her back to Chitterton Fells, if only for a short visit.

Membership:

Applause.

President:

And a big thank you to the Gardening Committee, who provided the charming centerpieces. Ah ha! I see hands waving. Yes, yes, all you horticultural enthusiasts—the chrysanthemums will be raffled off after lunch. Proceeds go to the Policemen's Benevolent Fund. Now, as always, the moment of solemnity: Everyone please rise for the recitation of our club pledge.

Membership:

Sisters in sorrow, we pledge eternal loyalty to our Founder and to each and every member of The Widows Club, past and present. Together we will mourn, console, laugh, work, and heal. We pledge to open our hands and hearts to other women soon to be likewise bereft of a life partner. And always we will bear courageous witness to The Widows Club motto: *Mors Magis Amicior Quam Inimicior.**

President:

Well done. Ladies, please remain standing. We will shortly be served kedgeree, followed by gooseberry tart and custard. Not gourmet! But the best The Dark Horse can offer. And Ways and Means has provided a treat for us today—a taste-testing of their new hazelnut fudge! Ways Chairwoman, Betty White, tells me that if we all pull our weight and sell one hundred boxes each, the proposed day trip to the Tower of London is distinctly feasible; please hold your applause, ladies.

I now have the pleasure and privilege of asking you to raise your wineglasses and offer a toast. To a new member whose husband has recently been called to his just reward. The Welcoming Committee has already introduced her. But to us she needs no name other than Sister.

Membership:

Cheers! All the very best! Welcome to The Widows Club!

*Death is more friend than foe.

Funerals are heaps more fun than weddings. My mother told me so when I was a little girl. More flowers, wittier conversation, superior food, and invariably better liquid refreshment.

Her words were, "Ellie darling, any household bubbly is adequate for toasting health and happiness, but the drowning of sorrows demands the best dry gin."

My mother, who met with a fatal accident in a railway station when I was seventeen, would have been delighted to know her funeral was the bash of the season among her intimate circle. I failed to enjoy myself, but everyone else, including my father who adored her, was still swigging back the neat gin and doing "Knees Up, Mother Brown" at 3:00 A.M. on the morning after, despite complaints from the neighbours.

More than ten years later, as I stood in the windswept churchyard of St. Anselm's on that chill afternoon of the 8th May, my mother's edict was a gramophone needle grinding circles inside my head. Funerals and weddings . . . funerals and weddings.

Only a few months ago, Ben and I had been married in this

small Norman church. And now I stood under the elms, abject with misery, waiting for the Reverend Rowland Foxworth to begin the burial service.

I was living a nightmare. Once I had been Miss Ellie Simons, resigned (if not content) with my lot as an overage, overweight virgin. Tipping the scales at thirteen stone wasn't so bad. I had my work as an interior designer, my cat Tobias, and my motley kith and kin had reduced social contact to the annual Christmas card. Then, fate had struck in the form of an invitation to a family reunion at the home of Uncle Merlin, an ancient eccentric, who had spent the last half century walled up in his castle on the cliffs above the village of Chitterton Fells. To go or not to go? Was it worthier in the mind to spend two days being the butt of familial fat jokes or to send a gracious decline, knowing full well that Aunt Astrid and her flawless daughter Vanessa would be snickering up their mink cuffs at my refusal to show my face and attendant chins? Impetuously, I telephoned Eligibility Escorts, and before I could rethink my pride and principles, its proprietress, Mrs. Swabucher, had rented me Bentley T. Haskell, darkly handsome, one-time chef, now aspiring writer of porno prose, to accompany me for the fateful weekend.

And what a weekend! Uncle Merlin was a toothless personage in a Wee Willie Winkie nightcap; the other relations were at each others' throats from sunrise to sunset. As for Bentley T. Haskell, I swiftly came to feel I had grossly overpaid for his escorting services. The man was snotty, defensive, irreligious. He immediately turned his lascivious eyes on cousin Vanessa and had the effrontery to turn nasty, when, under the extreme provocation of mounting tension, I made a little slip and hinted—okay, *announced*—that he and I were engaged to be married. Naturally, I had every intention of doing the decent thing and setting him free. A few weeks later, however, events took a tortuous turn. Word came that Uncle Merlin had died. Haskell graciously returned with me to Chitterton Fells for the funeral, and at the reading of the will we were stunned to discover that my capricious great-uncle had left the entire estate to us, jointly, upon the fulfillment of certain conditions. One was that I lose approximately one third of my weight, and another that Ben write a book containing not one naughty word, and . . . oh yes, we had to reside together in that derelict house for a period of six consecutive months. After judiciously weighing the pros and cons, we leaped at the golden ring. I thrilled to the challenge of tearing down cobwebs, sweeping out half a century of dirt, seeing Merlin's Court live again, as it had in his mother Abigail's day! We hired a housekeeper, Miss Dorcas Critchley, who became my dearest (female) friend in the world. Jonas the curmudgeonly gardener metamorphosed into Jonas the Faithful Unto Death. And Ben came to write the most scintillating cookery book ever to set sail through the post in hopes of landing a publisher. Of course, I never dared hope that he and I would experience a fairy-tale love story utterly in keeping with our turreted, moat-endowed residence; but we did. And, at age twenty-eight, I was reborn. I shed four and a half stone. The hair, the eyes, ears, nose were the same, but I got a new body.

Oh, God, why did you dangle happiness in my face only to snatch it away?

Ben had helped me end my tragic love affair with eating. Ironic, considering his profession. Because of him, I stopped feeding myself like a refrigerator, lost the stipulated poundage, learned to like myself a bit better, and at long last had the sweet knowledge that a real live man loved me. We were going to live happily ever after.

The one thing I overlooked was that I was the sort of woman who bred disaster the way hamsters breed hamsters.

A seagull uttered a plaintive cry as it skimmed aloft, over the crooked tombstones; the vicar opened his book; the buzz of voices dwindled.

The air was permeated with the mildewed sweetness of the wreaths. A tear slid down my face. Here was a funeral with even more to offer than usual. Here was the grand finale to Sudden Death, Police Inquiries, Headlines in the Newspapers, and, best of all, the Questionable Involvement of a Wealthy Young Woman.

Me.

How unfair, how wrong, that I, more than the man lying at final rest, should be the focus of the crowd's interest. I was certain I was being watched.

"Really, Ellie!" I could almost hear Mother's voice. "What can you expect? You are the star turn in a drama where the only price of admission is a wreath. You alone can provide the updated, unexpurgated details of the Event."

I am not a killer. Didn't the coroner's report clear me of all blame? No matter what people may think or say, I was only guilty of trying too hard to be the perfect wife. Biting my lip, I looked out furtively from under the brim of my black hat. Was it surprising I had gone a little mad after all the anguish of this past week? If only Ben's father had come with me, I might have done better. But he didn't believe in funerals.

I trembled and clutched the icy foot of the marble angel I was hiding behind as two elderly ladies clad in rusty black crunched by. Late arrivals. One brushed my arm and, apologising in a quivery voice, moved hastily past. I got a whiff of a sweet, primrose scent. Did she wish to be near the front in order to get a better view? Or did she shrink from the idea of being close to me?

Let people talk. Perhaps I did not deserve any friends. All that week I had refused to see anyone except Ann Delacorte. I had been unable to say no when she pressed me to visit her at the flat above her antique shop, so she could comfort me. Comfort! Nothing could comfort me!

There was a serenity to Ann that had drawn me from the first. But glimpsing her now, I thought her heavy black veil overly dramatic. Ann had an enthusiasm for the fashions of the forties, but was she basking in the poignant figure she presented as she clutched the arm of Lionel Wiseman, our solicitor? Lionel plucked a handkerchief from his breast pocket and pressed it into her hand. Death makes hypocrites of us all.

The day was the kind that has had all the color washed out of it. The grass between the headstones was sparse and coarse; the naked branches of the clustered elms were inked against a cobwebby sky. The wind carried a fine misting rain, and from far below (St. Anselm's was also known as The Church on the Cliff) came the seething whisper of the sea.

"I am the Resurrection and the Life . . ."

Dear Rowland. Ben had always been rather jealous of this good-looking clergyman with his public school background and quiet charm. My fault again. A year ago, despairing of Ben ever falling in love with me, I had encouraged him to think that Rowland harbored a restrained but abiding passion for me.

"Ashes to ashes . . ."

The brass plate on the coffin flashed in the watery sunlight. A bluster of wind shook the trees and carried a woman's voice straight to me.

"Wish vicar would get his bustle moving! I wouldn't have missed this one for nothing, but I'll have to stop coming regular if I'm like to miss the five o'clock bus. People keep saying it was the chicken that did for him but I says the mushrooms. Usually is the mushrooms, in't it?"

A muffled voice answered. "Papers said natural causes; but we all *know* what a softy Dr. Melrose is. Couldn't bear thinking of *her* in the dock, that's my bet. Not bad looking, is she? And a decent figure. Hard to believe she was fat as *butter* when she first come here."

"Dust to dust . . ."

He was inside that coffin. Dead by my hand. Dead of eating food I had prepared. Adequate to the grandeur of the occasion. The gala opening of Abigail's, Ben's restaurant. For months he and I had dreamed of the great day, but when it arrived, fate intruded, and I became chef for a day.

"And to dust thou shalt return . . ."

My mouth was filled with dust and ashes. If only I had some chocolate, preferably Swiss, loaded with almonds. Oh, how despicable I was.

Reverend Rowland Foxworth closed his book. Wind ruffled the hem of his cassock and he stood motionless in the increasing mist while two men in black coats stepped forward and lowered the coffin down into the grave. My throat closed. People were bending, picking up moist handfuls of earth and letting them fall with sickening thuds onto the gleaming coffin lid. Ann Delacorte was looking over at me. And she wasn't the only one. The crowd was spreading out. As soon as Rowland indicated the obsequies were officially concluded, I would be mobbed.

Sorry, but I couldn't give them that pleasure. Slipping the strap of my bag onto my shoulder, head bent, I hurried past the two elderly ladies who had arrived late. They were standing beside Gladys Thorn, the immensely tall, immensely thin organist of St. Anselm's. And I kept going—past drunkenly postured tombstones and unmarked grassy mounds, almost running as I reached the lich-gate.

It would take me less than ten minutes to walk along the Cliff Road to the sanctuary of Merlin's Court, away from these prying eyes. I would cross the moat bridge. I would open the heavily studded front door and enter the immense hall with the two shining suits of armor standing on each side of the trestle table against the staircase wall. My eyes would look toward those stairs, and I would fight for the courage to take that sweeping curve up to the master bedroom.

No, no! I could not do it. Not yet. I stood motionless. To my left, the battlements of Merlin's Court rose as if painted in watercolors on grey parchment. Below, the sea crashed.

"Contemplating nature, Mrs. Haskell? Or suicide?" The voice crept eerily through the mist. Seconds later, the stoop-shouldered figure of Mr. Edwin Digby materialized. Mother waddled alongside. Mr. Digby lived in The Aviary, a Victorian house situated a quarter of a mile beyond Merlin's Court. He was a man in his sixties, a man of mystery in the literal sense, being a famed writer of suspense novels. Mother, plucking at his coat, was a matronly goose with feathers of Persil whiteness.

"Please assure me that you are all right, Mrs. Haskell, and not seriously deliberating a leap into infinity. Alas, that ending has been wantonly worked to death by myself and others."

I tore my eyes from the yawning drop at my feet. "Don't let me detain you, Mr. Digby. I'm fine, really."

"Word reached me that there is to be no funeral feast. Doubtless such an assemblage would be too reminiscent of the fatal evening." He frowned down at Mother. "I regret, Mrs. Haskell, I was unable to attend the service. However, I am not sorry to have met you. Poisons being in my blood, professionally speaking, I was intrigued by your husband having been struck down at so inopportune a moment. Which is not to say I don't feel for you, Mrs. Haskell. Good afternoon!" Upon which, he and Mother waddled into the mist.

I started walking. I needed to go where I might sit quietly and sort through the debris of my life. But before I had taken a dozen steps, a bus came lumbering around the curve and drew up a few yards beyond the churchyard gates. A dozen giggling teenagers, some in school uniforms, some in ankle-length coats, with electrified purple hair, emerged. Of course —the youth group met in the church hall on Friday afternoons.

It became expedient to step out of the way. Three boys (one with a gold stud through his nose) took flying leaps off the bus. Then they plunged in among the others, who had formed a dancing figure of eight, and screeching out some current hit song, rocketed past me. None but the girl at the end looked at me. A small girl with sandy-colored plaits flying away from her shoulders and eyes too big for her face, a face too old for a girl of thirteen or fourteen. Eyes that didn't smile. But her mouth did, in a curve of shy, almost secret, recognition. I forced myself to smile back. She was Jenny Spender. A girl who knew a lot about the unfairness of life. Whenever I thought about my wedding day, I thought of Jenny.

They were gone. Their voices thinned to a wordless howl. I brushed away a dead leaf that blew against my cheek and went on. Every time I came to a dip in the road a swath of mist would engulf me and I hugged close to the right. Rocks and briar scratched my legs, but it would have been fatally easy to stray too far across the road, as a Mr. Woolpack, a local locksmith, had regrettably done the previous year. Chitterton Fells had been stunned by the tragedy. I remember showing the headlines to Ben . . .

A car motor shattered my reveries. Turning, I peered back up the hill. Out of the mist, a long dark car was nosing around the bend. Only it wasn't a car in the usual sense of household vehicle. It was a hearse.

Odd! Shouldn't it have left the cemetery much earlier? It stopped about twenty yards from me. Backing even farther onto the verge, I flagged the driver on. But the hearse stood motionless. I wished I had not read that book about the car with a mind of its own.

The mist had thickened and a pulse began to beat in my head. If the hearse would not get going, I would. There could be no question of its driver being inextricably lost because the road led directly down into the village, and its motor was running at an even purr so the hearse wasn't stalled. Ignobly, I turned. One foot in front of the other. The road twisted. The hedgerow ended and a cobbled wall began. Once or twice I was tempted to look back over my shoulder, but I experienced a growing certainty that if I did, the hearse would be stopped and sitting, looking at me.

My pace quickened. I craved the comfort of a cup of tea. Lights. At last. Street lamps gleamed palely ahead, like illuminated dandelion puffs. I could discern the crumbling Roman archway which divided Plum Pretty Lane and The Square. I pelted toward it.

A youth on a bicycle slammed to a halt smack in front of me, face livid in the glare from his lamp. Flipping an obscene gesture under my nose, he sucked in a fetid breath.

"Lady, you shouldn't be let out without a bloody seeing-eye dog!"

"I'm sorry."

"Bleeding right you are. When did Her Majesty give you the flaming right of way, Miss?"

"Mrs.," I said automatically. "Mrs. Bentley T. Haskell." The hearse was pulling to the curb in front of Pullets Jewelers, where six months ago Ben had bought my engagement ring.

Kicking down on a pedal, the youth let out a low whistle. "What! The woman with the recipes men die for! Reckon I should count meself lucky to have crossed your path and lived!"

He was still yelling after me as I entered The Square. "How rude! Know what, lady? Why don't you drop a line to Felicity Friend. You know, the woman what writes that sob page in *The Daily Spokesman*. Ask Dear Flis how to entertain the bloody town without blokes dropping dead and putting everyone off their grub!"

The fat Ellie could not have run from the kitchen sink to the refrigerator without getting winded, but now, pursued by his insults, I sprinted the length of Market Street without catching my breath.

In daylight, Chitterton Fells abounds with the cobblestone charm of a Victorian card. Now, in the dusky twilight, each facade looked secret, a little sly. All the shops were closed. Lights gleamed through grilled windows. Silence hung thicker than the mist. Reaching The Dark Horse pub, I cut a curve around Mother, feathers glistening like soap flakes, now waddling patiently up and down outside the saloon bar.

At last! There it was—Abigail's—the gabled Tudor building with Georgian bow windows on the ground floor. At one of those windows, a curtain twitched. Otherwise, the place was depressingly lifeless. A sudden bang made me jerk around.

But the person closing the door of Bragg, Wiseman & Smith, Solicitors, was no ghostly apparition. It was a solidly built, middle-aged woman. Lady Theodora Peerless, Mr. Wiseman's private secretary. As she drew near, I called out a greeting. She made no response and my silly, expectant smile slid off my face. Bracing myself, I called again, but her footsteps were already swallowed by the mist. She must not have heard me. Teddy Peerless liked me, or rather, hadn't shown unmistakable signs of loathing. But that was before . . . She *was* the one who found the body. I shoved the thought away.

Slowly I went up the red brick steps and under the dark

green awning lettered *Abigail's* in gold. Suddenly, I had no idea why I had come here.

Portraits of famous chefs hung on the wainscotted walls of the octagonal foyer. How sad to remember the day I purchased them and the night-watchmen lanterns, now electrically wired and mounted, and the gleaming library table that was to do duty as a reception desk. Despite its unpleasant, sad associations, Abigail's was sanctuary, a place where even phantom hearses could not get me.

A waiter trod softly across the parquet floor, his lips hooked into a smile, hands fluttering in a display of welcome. I could not recall meeting him before, but Ben had proved a hard taskmaster during the probationary period, and staff had come in one door and out the other.

"Out jogging, Mrs. Haskell? I perceived you from the window in the Bluebell Room while smoothing out a wrinkle in the curtains."

I undid another button of my coat, unable to speak. My eyes turned toward the Bluebell Room. I considered its remodeling and furnishing one of the finer moments of my career as an interior designer. Moss green carpet, walnut-panelled walls. The fabric that covered the chairs and couches grouped around the fireplace repeated the bluebell pattern of the curtains and valances. My favorite touch was the portraits of children rambling through local woods in springtime. Ben had been delighted with the results. Now the room was flawed in a way I could never put to rights. At six o'clock on a Friday evening it should have been crowded with sherry-sippers and cigar-puffers waiting to be summoned to one of the dining rooms. Guests should be anticipating such delights as Ben's inimitable fricassee of pheasant (to be featured in a full-colour photo on page 239 of the cookery book). Instead, it stood empty.

The waiter, whose name (according to the discreet name tag on the lapel of his jacket) was William, took my coat and folded it over his arm.

"Permit me to offer my sympathy, Mrs. Haskell. This is an 'orrible," he cleared his throat, "horrible time for you. But mustn't despair of business picking up." Removing a piece of lint off my coat, William rolled it between his fingers. I fought an insane desire to yelp.

He quelled it by adding soberly, "Death does seem to have

reached epidemic proportions of late in Chitterton Fells. Especially among the gentlemen. We have the late manager of the Odeon, gone missing, then found in the deep freeze with the ice lollies. And only this afternoon two police constables stopped in for coffee (most gratifying) and mentioned the discovery of a male cadaver down a disused well in Chitterton Woods."

Those pictures in the Bluebell Room! One of them had shown children throwing pennies down that well. A dish of chocolates sat on the rent table, and I had to squeeze my hands behind my back to stop them from lunging.

"Did the policemen say if the man was Mr. Vernon Daffy, the estate agent?"

"They did." Butler's face assumed an expression of gravity. "But I should not be keeping you, Mrs. Haskell. Would you be here to see Mr. Flatts? He is presently engaged in practicing gravies, but I know he will be delighted to see you."

"No, please! Don't even mention I am here. I would like a pot of tea, after which I will ring for a taxi to take me home." Poor Shirley Daffy, she had been so wonderfully brave when Vernon disappeared last week. And now he'd been found down a well!

"As you wish, madam." William's tone was reproving.

No matter. I absolutely would not see Ben's assistant, even though he was my cousin Freddy. After all, he had failed me in the Cooking Crisis that awful day . . .

William ushered me into a small room. The words Coffee Parlour were engraved on the brass doorplate, but the room was designed for afternoon tea as well as morning coffee. It was softly lit by brass wall lamps shaded in pink silk. Warm and rosy shadows played upon the stuccoed walls between the age-blackened beams. I wished I could get warm.

"Some hot buttered toast with your tea, Mrs. Haskell?"

"Thank you, but I'm not hungry."

I had grown adept at lies of this sort. Besides, I had been afraid to eat ever since it happened, in case I couldn't stop. Ben had never fully understood my feeling that my new, svelte body was only on loan and that at any minute I might have to give it back. He had accused me of resenting the fact that people had stopped oohing and aahing over the change in me. He had . . . but so many things had not helped our relationship and then, of course, there had been the Terrible Row.

When William left, I parted the curtains and rubbed at a

spot on the pane. Parked across the street was the hearse. My heart thumped. Dropping the curtain, I sank back into my chair. I must try to get a decent night's sleep. If I didn't, my nerves would go from bad to worse; I would end up in The Peerless Nursing Home, run by the notorious Dr. Simon Bordeaux.

William must have left the door ajar because I had not heard it open. I could feel, rather than hear, his footsteps. Ben always said the best waiters moved like burglars. I stifled a yawn. Perhaps I would sleep tonight. I couldn't even summon the energy to turn my head. A scent of rain-drenched wreaths—flowering and over-sweet—filled the air. The tea would help revitalize me. A hand crashed down on my shoulder, and my scream filled up all of Abigail's empty rooms.

"My dear, I am so sorry I startled you," said a feathery female voice.

"Really, Primrose," came a crisp admonishment. "How often have I warned you against popping up like that on people? You might have given the girl a heart attack. And we are in the business of *saving* lives, remember!"

Clutching the tablecloth, I looked upon two elderly ladies. One had dyed black hair swept into a cone on top of her head. Earrings shaped like miniature daggers sliced back and forth against her neck. Her velvet bolero and taffeta skirt were straight from a thrift shop. Her companion was more conventionally dressed in a tweed suit and violet jumper, but small pink bows ornamented her silvery curls and she sported an enormous Mickey Mouse watch. Her eyes were limpid blue in a crumpled face. She was the one drenched in toilet water. As I stared, the black-haired one delved into a carpetbag strikingly decorated with beaded peacocks.

"Here, Primrose." She held out a dark purple vial. "What a blessing I remembered to bring your smelling salts."

"How very dear, Hyacinth. But I do not believe I feel the need—"

"Not you, dear. Poor Mrs. . . . Haskell."

The bottle lay in my palm.

"Do you ladies own and operate a hearse?"

"We do." They spoke in unison. "May we"—they laid their coats on a serving trolley and gestured toward my table—"may we join you?"

I turned the smelling salt bottle over. It was at least fifty years old and rather pretty with that lattice cutwork. I remembered having seen an identical one in Delacorte's Antiques a month ago.

"Yes, do sit down. I'm interested in why you tailed me down Cliff Road and . . ." William entered with the teapot, three porcelain cups and saucers on a tray.

The black-haired woman crooked a finger at him. "Most welcome, Butler. Put the china down in front of me, please. Poor Mrs. Haskell is a little unsteady. I think it best that I pour."

What an officious woman! I didn't mind her taking the head of the table, but I did mind her addressing Ben's waiter like a second footman in the baronial hall. Unruffled, he smoothed back the curtain I had moved.

"The toasted tea cakes are delayed, madams." He inclined his head. "A minor combustion occurred in the kitchen."

"Brought under control, I trust?" warbled the silverhaired lady. "This has already been a most difficult day." Fishing a lace-edged handkerchief out of her bag, she dabbed at her blue eyes. "Not that the funeral wasn't wonderful. Exactly what one would wish for oneself, don't you agree, Hyacinth? Superbly mournful hymns and so very handsome a clergyman. A bachelor, I heard." She lowered the hanky a half inch. "Butler, would it be possible to provide some brandy for the tea?" She turned to address me. "My sister and I find neat tea rather acid-forming."

"How very—"

"At once, Miss Primrose." He picked up their coats and folded them over his arm. "The house offers an unassuming but spirited cognac that I believe your late father would not have been h'ashamed—ashamed—to serve."

My jaw dropped a notch.

The black-haired lady reached out to pat my hand, still clenched around the smelling salt bottle. I flinched.

"You surmise correctly, Mrs. Haskell. William Butler is in our employ."

The carpetbag was rummaged through again. "Mrs. Haskell, our professional card."

It lay in my hand, heavy and sharp-edged.

Flowers Detection.

Specializing in crimes with a difference.
Miss Hyacinth Tramwell, President;
Miss Primrose Tramwell, Chairperson.
No Divorce

"You're private detectives?"

"You didn't guess? Splendid." The silver-haired lady caught the smelling salt bottle neatly as it toppled. "As for Butler—when Hyacinth and I are in residence at Cloisters, Flaxby Meade, he performs those services suited to his name. In our professional engagements, he assists us in ways even better suited to his talents."

Butler made me a deferential bow. "I am an ex-burglar, Madam. And so I have an understanding of the criminal mind."

These people were strange, genteelly so, but I definitely did not wish to partake of tea cakes with them. Dragging my bag across the table, I overset the salt and pepper shakers.

"My dear, do not hurry away." The black-haired one set the little pots to rights. "I am Miss Hyacinth Tramwell, and I speak for Primrose in saying we sincerely regret frightening you this afternoon. Do believe me that until we motored into the village and saw you in speech with the cyclist, we were unaware that it was you, Mrs. Bentley Haskell, walking ahead of us down Cliff Road. It was in hopes of making your acquaintance that we attended the funeral. We were exceedingly disappointed when you left precipitously."

I gripped the table edge. "Why didn't you pass me on the road?"

Primrose Tramwell lowered her silvery head. The pink bows quivered. Her cheeks matched them in hue. "This is exceedingly embarrassing, Mrs. Haskell. I have only recently begun to drive and am still learning by my mistakes—only a couple of walls and an old gardening shed, you understand—but now before I take the wheel Hyacinth gives me a refresher course on which pedal is which and what all the little knobs are for." She fiddled with a button on her cuffs. "As for passing, I have every expectation of advancing to that stage soon."

"The important thing, Prim, is that we have now met Mrs. Haskell." Hyacinth spoke bracingly.

A respectful cough from Butler. "Miss Hyacinth, would you wish something more substantial than the tea cakes?"

"Not at the moment, thank you."

As Butler bowed himself out, she plucked at a jangly gold bracelet with a blood-red fingernail, her shoe-button eyes on me.

"We can talk quite freely in front of Butler, but alas, when he remains unoccupied too long, he gets itchy fingers. I'm sure you meant no harm, Mrs. Haskell, but leaving your bag in full view was tantamount to twirling a mouse in a cat's face."

"I'm sorry." Chastened, I tucked the bag under the table.

"Mrs. Haskell"—Hyacinth Tramwell's earring knifed back and forth—"you have been brought to our attention as the victim in a most deadly affair."

"Victim?"

"Along with the deceased; may the Lord have mercy upon his soul."

Propping my elbows on the table, I measured out my words. "You know about my recent . . . tragedy. What else do you know about me?"

In response, Hyacinth delved into her carpetbag and fetched forth a green clothbound book, the housekeeping journal sort. She stabbed it open with a red fingernail.

"Your father—Bosworth Hastings Simons—attended the Richmont Choir School and Cambridge, where he read Art History. Currently he is self-employed as a rainmaker on the outskirts of the Sahara."

I bridled at her intonation. "Needless to say, I would prefer him to be a belly dancer, but I realised long ago we cannot choose our parents' lives for them."

"How true!" sighed Primrose. "Our own dear father was, at times, a bitter disappointment."

Hyacinth trounced over her. "Your maiden name was Giselle Simons. Sixteen months ago you met your husband, Bentley Thomas Haskell, through an organization named Eligibility Escorts, owned and run by a Mrs. Swabucher. Under the provisions of your Uncle Merlin Grantham's rather colorful will, you and Bentley inherited the property known as Merlin's Court.

This restaurant is named for Merlin's mother, Abigail." The red nails flicked to another page. "You also inherited an elderly gardener by name of Jonas Phipps, and shortly after your arrival at Merlin's Court, you employed a Miss Dorcas Critchley as housekeeper. She is a games mistress by profession and a woman of independent means. She and Mr. Phipps are presently on excursion in America. You have a cousin Frederick—"

"Our dear sister Violet resides in America," interposed Primrose. "At a place named Detroit. Regrettably we have never been to visit, but it sounds enchanting. Perhaps one day under propitious circumstances . . ."

A withering glance from her sister's hooded black eyes quelled her. "My dear Primrose, we are telling Mrs. Haskell *her* life history, not ours."

I took in Primrose's crumpled face and Hyacinth's sallow one. "Why did you speak just now of my being a victim?"

Hyacinth snapped her book shut.

"Hereabouts, Mrs. Haskell, as I am sure you are woefully aware, you are being dubbed the Demon of Death. Flowers Detection, however, is convinced you have been preyed upon by a murderous organization. It wickedly decreed that a man should die, and you became the scapegoat."

"That's nonsense. I—"

William materialized. We sat mute while he set down fluted plates, filled with butter-dripping tea cakes. He tilted back the bottle he had been carrying under his arm so Primrose could survey the label.

"The cognac for your tea, madam." At her nod of approval, he set it with a flourish on the table.

"Butler, are we alone on the premises?" queried Hyacinth.

"Mrs. Haskell's cousin left a few moments ago, madam."

"Good! Please close the door behind you and keep watch in the hall."

Hyacinth tapped me lightly on the wrist with her fork as Butler exited. "It is imperative we not be overheard. The members of this organisation wear the perfect disguise: nice, kind, ordinary faces." A covert glance at the window. She lowered her voice. "It is in an attempt to eliminate this organisation that we are here."

Were these women escapees from a place like The Peerless Nursing Home?

Hyacinth was cutting her tea cake into geometric shapes,

and Primrose was placidly sousing her tea with cognac. Hyacinth reached for the bottle and angled it over her cup. "Will you indulge, Mrs. Haskell?"

I did feel a need.

"We arrived in Chitterton Fells some weeks ago," she continued placidly, "at the behest of an insurance company, whose name we are not at liberty to divulge. We *can* tell you that their computers had been bleeping out distress signals. You know the insurance company mentality, Mrs. Haskell—they want people to worry about dying but never actually do it. Thus, you can appreciate our client's chagrin on discovering that during the last few years its balance forward had been affected by a marginal, but suggestive, upswing in the number of untimely deaths among married men residing along this part of the coast. Most distressing."

"Particularly," Primrose interjected, "for the innocent people whose premiums will soar."

My heart thumped.

Hyacinth took a bite of tea cake and a sip of tea. "Not in one case was murder cited as the cause of death. Postmortems, when performed, invariably brought conclusions of misadventure, suicide, or natural cause. Suspicions of one kind or another may have been raised, but as in the case involving yourself—"

Enraged, I came up out of my chair. "How dare you accuse me of involvement with a murderous gang—"

"Shush, shush, my dear." Primrose eased me back down. "We know your participation to be entirely involuntary and unknowing."

"Let it also be said"—Hyacinth realigned my teaspoon on my saucer—"that this is no gun-hefting mob in cheap leather jackets. This deadly organisation is a women's club, highly selective, with a charter, a president, and duly elected officers. Anyone desiring admittance must be sponsored by a current member and have her application reviewed by the board. The club's function is to aid women who choose widowhood over divorce—specifically in cases where the husband has flouted the Sixth Commandment."

Primrose poured more tea. "So much more comfortable to become a grieving widow than a divorcee with a reduced standard of living. Especially when one considers that these would-be widows are spared all unpleasant details of"—she flinched—"termination. We are rather sketchy on details, but we do know that after the applicant is sponsored, she answers a telephone questionnaire, pays her initiation fee, and is encouraged to make the husband's last days on earth a pleasure to remember. No nagging. The television tuned to his favorite channel. All his favourite meals served. Allowed to stay out as long as he wants with the other woman. It being, after all, only a matter of time until he falls off a cliff or drops down a well."

Ashes to ashes. I should go home.

"After which"—Primrose removed a crumb from the front of her jumper—"the new widow receives tremendous emotional support from the group. She is kept far too busy working on items for the bazaar or growing herbs in little pots to give way to guilt."

"Who does the murdering?" My tea was a little weak. I added more brandy.

"As Primrose said, we are missing a lot of puzzle pieces," responded Hyacinth, encouraged by my curiosity. "We believe the method of each murder is planned and on occasion implemented by the club's founder. Board members are encouraged to do volunteer work in connection with the deaths."

"Excuse me, but this is laughable." To prove my point, I gave a hollow chuckle. "Other than its fiendish purpose, you might be describing a group like the Chitterton Fells Historical Association."

Primrose Tramwell looked vastly pleased with me. "On the surface, much the same style of organisation. Indeed, it would seem that numerous members of The Widows Club are also active members of the group you mention. One pictures them swelling the ranks of the Women's Institute, various old girls associations, and such circles as those that worship self-fulfillment, Chinese cooking classes, keep-fit, yoga, and so forth. Flowers Detection is convinced that infiltration of other organisations is a requirement of The Widows Club charter."

"A necessary means of sniffing out fresh blood—women who are unhappy in their marriages." Hyacinth laid her knife and fork on her empty plate. "Absolutely delicious. The tea cakes, I mean."

I had been picking raisins out of my tea cake with a fork and now with a surge of defiance ate one. "I'm not in love with The Historical Association. They recently toured my house at an extremely inconvenient time." I paused, remembering. "Even so, I can't picture one of those women writing out a check for her husband's murder or inquiring if she could put it on her Barclay Card."

"Do you perchance recall," queried Primrose avidly, "any of those ladies wearing a bar-shaped brooch, rather pretty, with a row of enamelled blackbirds?"

Her pansy blue eyes held me. "Many of them did."

Hyacinth compressed her lips. "Let us not digress. The scheme has worked splendidly, so far, because the perpetrators are those people one meets everywhere. One doesn't see the woods for the trees or the members for the club. Men especially would not sense anything amiss. The male sex never has appreciated the marvelous contribution made by female organisations providing volunteer service. The masculine mentality perceives them as social playgrounds whence the little woman can amuse herself after the housework is done, his mother visited, and the dog walked. Tragic, but perhaps it is as well that the victims do not sense their peril."

I stopped playing with my tea cake. "What of female friends and acquaintances of the widows? Wouldn't they ask questions, express interest in the club's activities?"

"Widows, I fear, tend to be the forgotten species and not nearly as amusing as spinsters." Primrose straightened out one of the pink bows on her hair. "People are relieved when they don't want to keep coming to dinner. I imagine that acquaintances of our widows merely think how nice that Maude or Cynthia keeps so busy—whist, Tuesday afternoons; committee work, Thursday evenings; out selling homemade fudge for charity on weekends."

"Mrs. Haskell"—Hyacinth drew her chair closer, setting the earrings off again—"please understand we are not here to cast stones. The Widows Club does raise a sizeable amount annually for charity. But can good works mitigate the fact that its primary function is deadly?"

I shivered, mainly because I was becoming interested in this nonsense. "What about conscience—don't any of these women break down after the deed is done? Killing a husband is—is unnatural!" A bitter pang swamped me as I recalled the first time I had felt the urge to murder my brand-new husband.

Primrose sighed. "Murder is always nasty. But unnatural? I am not so sure. Murdering one's child or parents, that indeed flouts nature. Disposing of a husband?" She shook her silver head. "My dear, you will point out that neither Hyacinth nor

I have ever married, but I can readily conceive that even the most devoted wife might be faced with the temptation to lay out her spouse rather than his clean underwear."

"Quite so, Primrose! However, we are not put on this earth to give way to temptation." Hyacinth lifted her painted black eyebrows at me. "Mrs. Haskell, you inquired whether, despite everything the support group can do, any of the widows falter under the burden of remorse. We have spoken to such a woman. Since our arrival in the area, Butler has held several positions other than the post he occupies here. He has been a barrow boy, a telephonist, a dustman. While engaged as a window cleaner, he made contact with a Mrs. X, a patient at The Peerless Nursing Home. Unfortunately the interview was hampered by its taking place in a broom cupboard, added to which Mrs. X was only partially coherent as a result of the medication she had been administered during her sojourn there. But we did make some gains. Mrs. X claims to be one of several women presently occupying the third floor, all being treated for the same problem—loose lips."

"The Peerless is run by Dr. Simon Bordeaux." Mine was a statement, not a question. I had reasons for not wanting the doctor to be a villain, but I had seen that nursing home, locked in the center of a dense wood. My heart went out to Mrs. X, whatever her sins. I grew calm, numbed by the draft from the window and the conviction that the Tramwells were not senile. Eccentric without doubt, but eccentricity was in my blood.

"Yes, my dear," said Miss Primrose Tramwell, "we know the doctor—by reputation. We have ardently endeavoured not to prejudge him, but at our ages Hyacinth and I cannot take lightly the notion that the good doctor may have curtailed the lives of elderly females for pecuniary gain. And, it must be said, it is repellent to us that he purchased a proud ancestral home (the Peerless family is almost as old as ours) and turned it into an antiseptic facility and at such cost to that hapless Lady"—she reached for her sister's green notebook—"ah, yes, Lady Theodora Peerless. A fellow woman, cast out upon the world, if not as a governess, as a typist—which is rather worse, one fears."

"Mrs. Haskell, how well are you acquainted with Dr. Bordeaux?" asked Primrose.

"We've met a couple of times. He attended the . . . our fatal affair."

Primrose looked down at her lap and Hyacinth avoided my eyes. "We had certainly planned to gate-crash the event but were forced to return to Cloisters that day. Our dog Minerva was indisposed."

My hair had loosened at the back of my neck. I pinned it back up to hide the trembling of my fingers and ate another small raisin. Dr. Bordeaux's pale, aesthetic face wove itself out of the shadows in the room. I was remembering things, incidents, conversations with people, especially Ann Delacorte. The clock in the hall struck six times. I retrieved a hairpin that had slipped under my collar.

"What information do you have about this Widows Club?"

Hyacinth picked up the green notebook. "Current membership comprises approximately thirty-five women, including eight board members and the current president. Each member is obligated to remain active for one year following initiation. Board members must retire after a one-year term of office. This, as Primrose and I understand the matter, is because these are the women who actively participate in the murders. Too much—buttering of the stairs—could take its toll. Or become addictive. Presumably The Founder would not wish any one person gaining an ascendancy."

"And you suspect that Dr. Bordeaux is The Founder?"

"My dear, we certainly do not discount him because he is a man." Primrose fussed with her silvery curls. "But, we are well nigh convinced he is merely an accomplice, not the brains."

I finally asked the obvious. "Why did this insurance company call you in, rather than going directly to the police?"

Hyacinth used her finger as a bookmark. "Not one ounce of real evidence to drop in the lap of Scotland Yard. One of the difficulties we have encountered is that the charter members, who must surely know The Founder's identity, have long since dispersed, gone on to new—and one can only trust—single lives."

"How long has the club been in operation?"

"As near as we can gauge, five years."

"Think me a flea-brain," I said, "but if you are sure of Dr. Bordeaux's involvement and Mrs. X is only one of several widows he is treating for acute attacks of remorse, what is the difficulty in substantiating your claims?"

"I very much doubt that our long-suffering constabulary would put much stock in the ramblings of bereaved women suffering from their nerves." Primrose pensively added more cognac to her tea. "And, my dear Mrs. Haskell, as we informed our insurance company employers, these unfortunate women cannot give us the one name we desperately need. They don't know it. What happens, we ask, if The Founder slips through our net? What will be achieved even if we do put this club out of operation? Chitterton Fells will become a less eventful place to live; but The Founder may simply start a similar service organisation somewhere else."

Hyacinth's ebony eyes bored into mine. "Which is why we have approached you, Mrs. Haskell. We ask that you help us unmask our villain."

"Me?"

"My dear child"—Primrose caught at me with her small fluttery hands—"recall the old saying: 'In the midst of life there is death!' How true . . . as is its reverse."

"Why should I trust you?"

"Why shouldn't you?" chimed the sisters.

I could think of a dozen responses to that, but I had succumbed to my tea cake and my mouth was full of flavoured rubber cement.

"We will, should you wish, introduce you to someone who can vouch for much of what we have said." Hyacinth flicked over a page in the green book. "We mentioned, I believe, rumblings from computers owned by our employer. But we were not called in until a certain woman had presented herself at Head Office. This person claimed to have been the Other Woman in several liaisons, each of which ended in the sudden death of her lover shortly after he had requested divorce from his wife. That woman lives here in Chitterton Fells and is anxious to see justice done."

"How convenient that all the victims were insured with the one company!" I observed, somewhat maliciously.

"That would be rather too fortuitous." Hyacinth grimaced in amusement. "But ours is one of the largest and most nationally prominent in the business. It has a vigourous local office and has been the hardest hit. After their visit from this Other Woman, our people conferred with other companies, found further significant mortality data, and agreed to head up the investigation."

"Oh, indeed!" I said. "Why did this Other Woman go to the insurance company rather than the police?"

"She did go to them first, after encountering what she termed the last straw." Primrose pursed her lips and shook her head. "The man (one certainly cannot term him a *gentleman*) whom she had been meeting each Wednesday evening in . . . a Volkswagen parked in a used-car lot, failed to turn up, which was most unusual." Primrose flushed down to her neck. "Invariably he apparently begged to be allowed to come early. This time, however, he had been permanently delayed. It seems a crane at his place of business had deposited him in some sort of metal crusher. The woman had been saddened when her other paramours kept turning into bodies, but this one being scrapped sent her in hysterics to the police station. The Inspector advised her to see her doctor"—Primrose lowered her voice—"about hormone tablets."

My tea cake buckled when I stuck a knife in it. "Do I know this Venus?"

"According to our records, you do." Hyacinth waved the cognac bottle over my cup.

I nodded assent. "Who could this inflamer of male desire be?"

Primrose looked smug. "I fear it would be a breach of professional confidentiality for us to reveal her name. We prefer to wait and let her speak for herself."

I held up my hands. "That's quite all right. If you were to divulge it now, I wouldn't be able to concentrate on what it is you want from me." The brandy tasted good now that it was no longer diluted by tea, but it wasn't responsible for the small hopeful flame that lit within me. If what the Tramwells said were true, then maybe in helping them I could make some small reparation to Ben.

"Excuse me," I said. "Before we proceed, I must make a phone call." Going out into the foyer, I found Butler dusting the chocolates in the dish on the library table. I asked him to fetch fresh tea, and as he headed for the kitchen, I picked up the telephone and quickly dialed my own number. My father-in-law answered at the third ring. After a brief conversation, I returned to the coffee parlour and closed the door behind me.

I sat down. "Ready."

Primrose pressed a scented handkerchief into my limp fingers. "We wish you to give us a history of the events leading up to the tragic event which occurred on these premises one week ago tonight."

"How much do you need to know?" The steadiness of my voice startled me.

"Everything." Hyacinth uncapped a fountain pen.

"All right," I began. "On the day of Abigail's premiere, I woke at a little after six o'clock feeling totally exhausted because all that night I had dreamt I was preparing food for the party. Ben, you see—"

"No, no! Mrs. Haskell. That is not what we want at all." Hyacinth dabbed at a splutter of ink.

"Dear me, indeed not!" piped up Primrose. "We wish you to go back to the beginning. Start, if you will be so good, with the day you and Bentley came to Merlin's Court. Your views and impressions since coming to this area are as important to us as the climax."

"Why don't I begin with my wedding? Ben and I hadn't done much socializing with the locals before then; but that day the church and later the house teemed with people. I remember hearing one of the guests say that everyone was there except Chitterton Fells's three most famous: Edwin Digby, the mystery writer; Felicity Friend, the advice columnist; and the wicked Dr. Simon Bordeaux."

"You had sent out a great many invitations?" Hyacinth was making notes.

"None."

The pen stopped moving.

"Ben and I had a very short engagement and wanted a quiet wedding. But, then again, we didn't want to offend the people we didn't invite. So we phoned the people we really wanted there and put a small squib in the Coming Events section of *The Daily Spokesman*. It appeared right at the bottom of the page and was headed 'All Welcome', giving time, date, and place. The response was horrifying. The phone buzzed day and night with acceptances to our gracious invitation."

"I am sure it was a lovely wedding." Primrose pulled out her handkerchief again.

I hesitated. "The day—it was the first of December last year—was marred by some unfortunate circumstances. The best man, Sidney Fowler, found weddings depressing. He had only agreed to do the honours in hopes of combatting his phobia. The weather was less than perfect and we were about to get the dreadful news about Ben's mother. . . ."

PART TWO

. . . "My dear Ellie, I am sure you were a breathtaking bride!" Primrose sighed sentimentally. . . .

Organ music wafted through the open church doors as I stumbled through the lich-gate and down the mossy pathway flanked by ancient tombstones. I clutched the skirt of my white satin gown and my bouquet of yellow tea roses in one hand and Jonas's arm with the other. Late again. I am always late—for dental appointments, theatre performances, jury duty—but I *had* planned to make an exception for my wedding.

"Hurry, Jonas!"

The sea breeze lifted my veil, snarling it about my face. My seed pearl tiara slipped over one eye, giving me the look of a demented fairy.

"I *am* hurrying."

Jonas was over seventy. What if he dropped dead at my feet? I would spend the rest of my life consumed by remorse. Some people might think it odd that I had chosen to be given away in marriage by my gardener. But he and Dorcas had been my mainstays during my struggle along the byways to Ben's affection.

If Jonas were taken ill, the wedding would have to be postponed, and that would be the end of me. Women have come a long way from the days when growing up to be an old maid like great-aunt Clarissa was considered a fate worse than death. Today's woman knows that the word spinster is not synonymous with pebble glasses, a long beaky nose, and button boots. The glamourous, sophisticated single woman has risen—a triumphant phoenix—from the ashes of a dying breed. But the world still harbors pockets of spineless, jelly-kneed females who believe the quality of their lives will be immeasurably improved by the acquisition of a husband. I am such a woman. Do I deserve to be stoned?

When I was six years old and was asked what I wanted for Christmas, I replied, "Something simple in gold for the fourth finger of my left hand." Nothing, nothing must spoil this day. Or better said: no further blight must be cast upon it. My mother was dead, my father was a nomad last seen hitching a camel ride across the Sahara, but I had naively hoped Ben's parents would wish to share our joy. Wrong. His Roman Catholic mother had sent love and best wishes but declined attending because the service was to be Church of England. His Jewish father spurned the invitation because three years previously he had taken a vow (on his mother's photograph) never again to speak to his only son. Ben had been stoic and I had been snarly about their childishness. And that morning had brought fresh tribulation. I had awakened to find my veil lying in a tattered heap upon my bedroom floor.

Jane Eyre revisited, except that in my case the vandal was not a madwoman, but my cat Tobias. A desperate hunt through the attic had procured a replacement. An antique lace tablecloth. Really, it looked fine and would be a conversation piece at many a future dinner party. I had then waited placidly for the arrival of my white-ribboned taxi. And waited. Jonas and I had met its driver, puffed and purple-faced, outside the churchyard only a moment before. The ancient vehicle had stalled halfway up Cliff Road; there would be no charge.

So we walked. We were but a stone's throw from the church doors when Jonas's top hat blew off. The organ music petered out as I sidestepped a freshly dug grave and pelted after that wretched hat.

"Let it go," bellowed Jonas. "Like as not there'll be a beret or two in the lost-and-found box."

A beret! A fine figure I would cut being escorted down the aisle by a man holding a beret in his white-gloved hand. I scooped up the top hat as it skimmed over a ground monument lined with that green bath-salts stuff and hobbled back to Jonas.

His heavy walrus moustache twitched in irritation. "Ellie girl, why are you pegging along at the tilt?"

"Twisted my ankle." Setting the hat back on his head, I cast a saddened glance at the stains now rimming the hem of my gown, hoisted the skirt up, and grabbed his arm again. As we mounted the crumbling stone steps, the organ music swelled once more into a joyous flood.

"A mite early for carols, isn't it?" Jonas muttered. "Close on a month till Christmas."

"The organist must have started taking requests," I whispered as the cool mustiness of the entrance surrounded us. "Poor darling Ben: He'll think I've changed my mind, that I'm not coming. Hurry, Jonas!"

"Damned lucky to be getting a rare girl like you," came his muffled comment.

"Jonas, I will not have you swearing in church." I kissed his weathered cheek. "Bless you for everything."

Past the poor box and the pamphlet table, then through the archway, to the tune of "O Come, All Ye Faithful." The pews were lined with people. I was sure my nasty relatives, having betted heavily against this day, were chuckling at the possibility of a no-show. I wanted something to eat, nothing fattening you understand, just a low-cal cracker or two.

A schoolboy standing inside the nave looked, saw us, and ran backward a few paces down the aisle. Eyes raised heavenward, he jerked a thumbs-up sign toward the choir loft. The carol tapered away and "Oh Perfect Love" surged forth.

"I never really believed this day would come. Now I'm scared witless that even at this the eleventh hour something will happen to snatch Ben away."

An elderly woman in a pink voile hat leaned out from the back pew and touched my arm. "Didn't I know he was Mr. Right?"

I knew that voice . . . Mrs. Swabucher, owner of Eligibility Escorts, the woman who first introduced me to Ben.

With a whispered "Talk to you later," I dragged Jonas past

an unfamiliar female voice sighing ecstatically: "My word, don't she look a picture. Love the veil. Real Victorian."

A rumbling male voice replied, "I dunno. For all her money she's not a patch on our Beryl."

On my left, a tall woman in a fruit-laden hat jostled a grizzly baby against her hip.

Voices, faces—a moving haze swamped by the scent of centuries, incense, and freshly cut chrysanthemums. I hate chrysanthemums, but we had an abundance of them at Merlin's Court and Ben had wanted to use them. He said they were jolly flowers. Jolly depressing, I called them.

A hand brushed my hip and I squinted round to see portly Uncle Maurice winking at me. Jerking on Jonas's arm, I almost missed seeing lovely, loathsome cousin Vanessa stick out an alligator-shod foot. But I saw it just in time and trod down hard in passing. A small triumph but a foolish one.

My eyes adjusted to the dim light provided by the narrow stained-glass windows and the flickering candles upon the altar. The three men standing on the chancel steps looked like they had been embalmed. The one in the middle was the Reverend Rowland Foxworth and on his left stood the best man. Sid Fowler had grown up a few doors down the street from Ben's family, and recently we had discovered that "Sidney," the posh hairdressing salon on Market Street, was his place. But I had eyes for only one man. The one tapping his foot, arms akimbo. My husband-to-be.

That stance signified not so much impatience as pent-up fury. I could see his jaw muscles working as he ground his teeth. Poor darling Ben! Who could blame him for being angry?

Hitching up my gown and crushing my bouquet against my side, I ran the remaining few yards down the aisle, leaving Jonas completely behind.

"What peasantry!" Aunt Astrid's voice bounced off the rafters and echoed through the church amid splutters of laughter. I didn't care a farthing. Elbowing Sid off the steps, I whispered in my beloved's ear.

"Darling, I'm sorry. You can't imagine all the things that have gone wrong. I couldn't reach your parents on the phone to beg them to change their minds. And those men who were supposed to come last week to move the harpsichord down from the attic—they arrived, but one of them sprained his back so we had to shove it in the boxroom; meaning we are stuck with records for the reception." My voice was coming out in strangled gasps; I realised I was standing on my train.

Ben's voice broke through his clenched teeth. "I thought you had stood me up, and for the devil of me I couldn't think of a way to make it look as though I had jilted you. Fifty million pairs of gloating eyes pinned on one is not conducive to quick thinking."

My dark handsome hero. I smiled worshipfully at him.

Sid fumbled in his waistcoat pocket, and Rowland Foxworth turned a page of his little black book with a silvery rustle. Footsteps sounded behind us. Dorcas, wearing a brown velvet jockey cap and plaid cape, stepped forward and removed my bouquet.

"Sat on it, did you? Not to worry. I'll tweak those petals right back to shape."

Jonas, with an austere nod at Ben, muttered, "Treat her like a queen, boy, or I'll wring your scrawny neck." He stepped back to stand beside Dorcas.

Aunt Astrid's voice rang out again. "Can you credit it? Those clodhopping boots all caked with mud. Only Giselle would have the gardener give her away."

Ben's hand closed over mine, and suddenly the world was blissful. The organ music washed to a ripple, then faded away.

"Shall we begin?" Rowland Foxworth smiled. A sense of timelessness assailed me, along with the smell of mildewed wood, polished brasses, dusty velvet kneelers, and chrysanthemums.

"Who giveth this woman to this man?"

"I do," answered Jonas at his most gruff. "And make a note in yer hymnal, vicar, if the lad gives her a mite of trouble, I'm taking her back."

Make haste, Rowland dear. Other women may wish these moments extended, every word savoured for cherishing in later years, but I couldn't wait to feel that ring on my finger, to know that I was finally Mrs. Bentley Haskell.

"Dearly Beloved, we are gathered here today . . ."

I was drowning in the brilliance of Ben's eyes, their shifting colors . . . such an incredible blue-green, flecked with amber . . . and those black lashes, long enough to rake leaves. How could I, a fat girl masquerading in a thin body, be so blessed?

"And so I caution all here present that if any of you know of any just cause or impediment why Bentley Thomas Haskell and Giselle Simons may not lawfully be joined together in the holy estate of matrimony you shall declare it now or forever after hold your peace."

Pause.

"Yoo-hoo, I do! I have something to declare!"

Gasps. A commotion erupted at the back of the church. A baby bellowed. Exclamations of horror. Footsteps. Rowland, an expression of consternation on his kind, handsome face, tucked a finger into the book and let it fall shut with a thud. Ben dropped my hand and turned to stare at whoever was pounding down the aisle. I took one look and became immobilized.

This was monstrous. Whoever the woman was, she was off her rocker. A disappointed spinster who went from wedding to wedding, causing a ruckus at each one? Perhaps I should try to pity her. Might I not have ended up the same way myself?

"There now, Mumma's little pudding cheeks. Say hello to Da-Da."

A baby! The Just Cause and Impediment she held aloft was a baby. Ben's baby. Jane Eyre's tribulation was nothing to this; she only got lumbered with a mad wife.

Closing my eyes, I took slow deep breaths. I tried to bear in mind that Ben had never claimed to have kept himself untouched by human hand until I had happened along. Yes, a baby did indicate a certain closeness in the relationship, but I would have to try very hard not to be jealous and petty.

The woman identified herself: Mrs. Bentley T. Haskell, the First. She was screeching that the louse had bunked off without even the courtesy of a divorce.

Loud bawling from the baby.

"Pack of lies, the whole lot of it!" rapped out Dorcas. From the corner of my eye I saw her lift my crushed bouquet as if to pitch it in my predecessor's face.

A sparkling laugh, which I recognised at once as cousin Vanessa's.

A menacing yowl from dear Jonas.

Ben's arm came around me. Wed, or almost wed, to a bigamist! I searched his profile and found it explosive. Exerting every ounce of will, I forced my leaden body into a half turn.

The woman, all six foot of her, was planted level with the front pew. My one, benumbed thought was: how could Ben ever have desired her enough to produce the child now dangling untidily over the arm of her black coat? The destroyer of my happiness was wearing a week's worth of greengroceries—apples, bananas, and oranges—on her hat. Beneath its olive-green brim, mangled yellowish curls bounced against hollowed cheeks caked in rouge. Her eyelids were coated with a luminous mauve, liberally sprinkled with tinsel dust, and the exaggerated bow of her mouth was outlined in glossy lavender pink.

The baby kicked out, and the black-clothed arm went into a spasm of junketing up and down. An appalling, expectant silence descended. Time went into slow motion. Among the sea of faces I saw Uncle Maurice, Aunt Lulu, my ex-neighbor Jill—a hand covering her mouth—and Ann Delacorte, who had helped me select my wedding dress from those for sale in her husband's antique shop. Could she persuade him to take it back?

"Believe me, vicar ducky, I ain't a vengeful woman. All I asks is me rights." The woman drew her free hand across her eyes and spluttered piteously.

"Wicked shame," came a cry from the rear. "He should be strung up, won't say by what on account of being in church." This theme was swiftly picked up by other voices. "Makes Dr. Simon Bordeaux look like a saint. He puts women out of their misery!" someone yelled.

Tucking the book under his arm, Rowland appeared lost in thought. "Ellie, Ben—and you, madam—I think it best that we adjourn to the vestry to discuss this unhappy turn of events."

The shadows cast by the candles made the woman look as though she needed a shave. Ben, how could you? I thought mournfully.

"To the vestry, to the vestry! I feel a lynching coming on!" Ben's arm tightened around me, and despising myself, I clung to him.

Rowland cast his eyes upward. I thought he was praying for help, then realised he was signalling to the organist. With "Rock of Ages" pouring its rousing tide of rejoicing and repentance down upon the up-in-arms congregation, Ben and I, the woman and the infant, followed Rowland into the vestry.

Drawing the door closed behind us, Rowland fumbled in the folds of his cassock, pulled out a pipe, jammed it into his mouth, removed it, and stood tapping the bowl with one finger.

"Ellie," he said pensively, "why don't you sit down in that chair by the writing desk. Perhaps you would like a glass of water?"

I shook my head dumbly and remained standing.

The woman was lounging against the wall; the baby tugged on her coat buttons.

Rowland looked from her to Ben, who still had his arm around me.

"Is what this woman claims true? Ben, are you now or were you ever married to her?"

I braced myself, but I was not prepared for what happened. For suddenly, clutching his arms around his middle, Ben backed against the wall, doubled over, and howled with laughter.

His mind had snapped under the strain. My gaze fixed on his wife.

I must have had a minibout of temporary insanity because my hand reached out, not to strike the woman, but to help myself to one of the apples on her hat. Thank heaven pride returned. I would not sully my hands or my lips with anything this woman had touched with those fingers poking through the holes in her gloves. I couldn't look at Ben. It was ghastly enough to hear his emissions of mirth.

My eyes clung to Rowland and saw his lips moving. Was he praying for a speedy end to this abomination? And whose side would God be on? If what this woman claimed were true . . . but of course it wasn't. She must be brought to see that she was indulging in a case of mistaken identity. If not, flogging no longer being an accepted practice, there had to be some equally compelling . . .

Another revolting gurgle of laughter burst from my bridegroom, and the rubber band holding my nerves together finally snapped. I was standing in a welter of butchered dreams and in the process had gone as mad as Mr. Rochester's first wife. For I could swear that Ben's first wife had winked at me.

Incredibly I beheld a countenance that, seen in better light, was uncannily familiar. My rival's expression switched to weary martyrdom. Lifting a hand to her hat, she plucked off a banana, peeled it, and stuffed it into the child's slobbering mouth.

"Perhaps we should fetch Dr. Melrose, Ellie. I believe Ben has gone into shock." Rowland's voice was deeply concerned.

So dear a man! His was a mind singularly unacquainted with evil. The baby—bonnet askew, collar jacked up because its coat was buttoned wrong—spat out a chunk of banana and, bleating miserably, banged sticky hands against its mother's rouged cheeks. And then, as I stood in frozen horror, the poor little creature was shoved into my arms.

"Here Ellie, take the ruddy little blighter. Won't hurt you to practice up on motherhood," said the woman in the masculine voice of my cousin Freddy Flatts. "Come on, Ellie, old stodge! Be a sport like your intended! He was as surprised as you were, but he's taking it on the chin."

Freddy grinned down at my fiancé, who had slithered into an ignoble heap on the vestry floor. "Glad you enjoyed the joke, mate. Been toying with the idea of pulling this stunt for years. But I can tell you, I couldn't come up with any couple that meant so much to me that I was prepared to shave off my beard, bleach my hair, and bribe old Alvin into lending me his soggy kid. Not until you two. Something to tell the grandchildren, eh? But I tell you, my girdle is killing me."

From the Files of
The Widows Club

29th November

The Gardening Committee did unanimously elect to change the date of the dried-flower Christmas ornament project, from 3:00 P.M. on the 1st of December (a Friday) to 7:00 P.M. on the 4th of December (a Monday).

The meeting place to remain at the home of Evelyn Jones. As previously arranged, Mary Phillips will bring the cheese and biscuits. The Gardening Committee will provide the coffee and wine.

This change of dates was deemed necessary due to the number of members wishing to attend the Haskell/Simons wedding. As always, the Gardening Committee fully supports the club's position that occurrences of a matrimonial nature are highly therapeutic for members. A motion was made by Maude Garway to picket the event. This was seconded by Alice Reardon, but outvoted by the membership.

The annual holly-gathering Sunday was rained out and has yet to be rescheduled.

. . . "I would have killed Cousin Frederick." Hyacinth's black eyes sparked. . . .

"On your marks, get set, smile!" Crouched behind a camera worthy of Lord Snowdon, Dorcas dropped her left arm, signalling action. Alas, one of the tripod legs buckled. The crowd closed in to proffer advice.

As the bridal party—Ben and I, flanked by Jonas and Sid—stood on the church steps, bombarded by pealing bells, and stung by the wind, I refused to meet my husband's eyes. I felt no great need to kill Freddy. My cousin Frederick Flatts was born with his brain trickling out of his ears and had attained the age of twenty-nine still believing the world hungered for his sublime wit. On Rowland's advising him to go confess his sacrilegious prank to the congregation and inform them he would be returning the infant to its parents forthwith, he had replied gloomily, "If they'll take the little monster back."

Ben was the one I longed to murder. I could still see him sagging against the vestry wall, weak with laughter, while that sticky baby tugged at my veil and yanked tufts out of my bouquet.

"I love you, Ellie." His breath brushed my face like a kiss. Too little, too late.

His hand moved up my arm. "I'm sorry, darling, but I was so unsettled by your arriving late that Freddy's stunt sent me over the edge."

I should have tossed my train over my shoulder and stormed from the church.

In years to come my children would say, "Mummy, why do you have that wicked look on your face in your wedding pictures?" And I would have to explain to those innocent mites what it feels like to have the words "I do" drowned out by the babbling of the guests. They were still at it now as they stood grouped at the base of the steps.

"Hold that pose, lovebirds! Best profile forward, Ben. Love the Mona Lisa smile, Ellie." Dorcas pegged her jockey cap on the head of a marble statue of the great local hero, Smuggler Jim Biggins, and jamming her red hair behind her ears, squared her shoulders and got down to the serious business of twiddling dials.

Click. Click.

"Looks like we have to wait for these clouds to move, so go on, make a break for it, old son." Ben's eyes were on me as he spoke. I closed mine to keep my righteous anger intact.

"Do I get to kiss the bride?" asked lachrymose Sid, and I felt my hand lifted and pressed to a pair of lips—his, presumably.

"Sidney, how gallant!" I tapped him playfully with my bouquet, entirely for Ben's benefit.

"Tall women bring out that side of me," he mourned. "I refuse to stand on tiptoe to kiss even the best of them. I suffer enough indignity having people use my ass as a door scraper." And with that he hunched off down the steps. Jonas stumped after him.

"Hold fast, Mr. and Mrs. H." Dorcas was grimacing at the clouds now rolling like dense smoke across the sky. "Should brighten any minute, if it doesn't pour first. Want some nice snaps to send Ma and Pa, don't we, Ben? Must show the stay-at-homes what they missed."

"Absolutely," he replied.

I straightened the seed pearl tiara, fanned my veil over my shoulders, and smiled for the crowd. I could see my ex-neighbor and Freddy's amour, Jill—the mystic, built like a toothbrush and with the same sort of bristly hairdo, wedged between Uncle Maurice and a woman in a busby. And there, next to Smuggler Jim's statue, stood Mrs. Swabucher, all pink tulle and gusts of ermine. Rowland was wending up and down along the edge of the gravel path, the black book clasped in his hand. A sweep of overhanging branches cast shadows in his wake. He seemed to be looking over to the lich-gate.

"I wish my parents had been here." Ben drew me close.

I addressed the buttons on his shirt. "Your mother would have thought her novenas answered when Freddy called a halt to the proceedings."

"I wanted them to see that they made a success of me—I'm happy."

And I was hungry. Would I always have that deplorable tendency when emotional?

"Here." Ben's fingers closed over mine. When he let go, he was holding my tattered bouquet and I was holding a chocolate rose.

He wasn't looking at me; he was smoothing out live petals. "Take a bite and tell me how you like it."

"Rather rude surely, with all these people watching."

"We'll pass some around when we get home. I made two hundred and ninety-one. One for every day since we met."

"Say honeymoons!" cried Dorcas.

I must have been faint with hunger because the world went all fuzzy round the edges. The wind had dropped and the bells ceased, leaving a vibrating silence.

"Are you sure you don't want me to save this one and press it in a book?" My voice came up from a mine shaft. I nibbled a leaf off the rose and, eyes on Ben's chin, handed him the rest.

"A fraction too much vanilla, do you think?" he asked.

I could have destroyed his day, his week, his year simply by saying yes.

My ring flashed between us. We were married. Really and truly married. (Did it matter that I could remember nothing of the words spoken at the altar?) A shiver of wind touched my neck. I smiled for Dorcas, then looked up as I felt a spatter of rain. Somehow Ben's face got in the way.

All the laughter had vanished from his eyes, leaving them

darker, even more brilliant, and so ardent my breath caught in my throat. I traced a finger through his hair. I loved him. Why shouldn't he laugh at Freddy's little prank? I wanted a husband with a sense of humour, didn't I? And he had been under tremendous emotional strain over his parents, which wasn't to say they weren't perfectly lovely people in their narrow-minded, bigotted ways. Ben's dark head bent over mine. The church clock chimed the quarter hour.

"Two hundred and ninety-one days, one hour and thirty-seven minutes," I whispered against the delicious warmth of his mouth.

"Good shot!" bawled Dorcas. "Should get it enlarged. Nice one for Ma and Pa to put out on the piano."

"Happy, Ellie?" asked my husband.

"Blissful!" Our marriage was stronger for having come through the fire. I curved my arms up around Ben's neck. Jonas came stumping up the steps.

"Are you two going to stand gawking at each other all afternoon, or are you going to be sociable and drop in on the reception?"

"Certainly we are." Reaching out a hand, I helped Jonas up the last step.

"Good," he snorted. "Because left alone with the family, I might forget me place and poison one of them."

Jonas went to assist Dorcas in packing up her equipment. I took my bouquet from Ben and waved it at Rowland, trying to attract his attention. But at that moment Aunt Astrid, resplendent in a pale mink and a black hat with spotted veiling, accosted him. Poor Rowland, no wonder his shoulders looked so tense. Aunty was directing a gloved paw toward darling daughter Vanessa, artistically posed against a backdrop of tombstones. I snuggled my arm through Ben's and indulged in momentary smugness. Would mother and daughter never learn that a woman needs more than a stunning figure and flawless face to attract a man of true worth?

The crowd was beginning to disperse, heading toward the line of cars parked against the railing. Coming through the lich-gate were five or six laughing teenagers, members of St. Anselm's youth group, I supposed. I had heard they met on Friday afternoons. They must be the reason Rowland kept glancing—

"Ellie, Bentley—my precious children!" Mrs. Swabucher swept up to us in a flourish of gauzy pink and swirls of ermine.

"Dear, dear Ellie! So beautiful! Although possibly a little too thin! And Bentley, handsome as ever!"

"Hated to take me off the books, didn't you?" He grinned at her and received another squeeze.

"I cannot tell you how delighted I was to be included in this joyous culmination of that day, Ellie, when you came to Eligibility."

Everything about her—the grandmotherly perfume, her energetic kindness—brought back the rainy afternoon when I had sat in her powder puff office and begged her to find me Mr. Right.

"We must have a long talk at the reception."

"I wish, dear, but I've a granddaughter expecting a baby any second and have promised to be available to boil water. No choice but to leave at once and . . ." She paused. "Perhaps it is for the best. Someone is bound to ask me what my connection is to one or both of you and—"

Ben and I started to speak, but she shushed us.

"My dears, I am proud of the services offered by Eligibility Escorts and the work you did for me, Ben, but villages such as this are like the Whispering Gallery at St. Paul's. And considering today's practical joke . . . My advice is don't let on how you really met. Say a fond aunt introduced you."

Rain began coming down in splotches. Mrs. Swabucher's chauffeur appeared with an umbrella.

"You both take care of yourselves," she said. "We don't want you catching colds. Speaking of health matters, you don't patronize that awful Dr. Bordeaux, do you? I didn't bring you darlings together to have anything happen to either of you. And now, take me away, James." She tucked an arm through that of her chauffeur and was gone.

What people remained in the churchyard started turning up collars and unfurling umbrellas, fast-trotting to the cars. I heard Uncle Maurice and Aunt Lulu urging Jill to accompany them in their vehicle. Oh, cripes! They must think her relationship with son Freddy was serious, thereby making her good for a loan of at least twenty pounds.

"We can't have Jonas getting wet," I said to Ben, but I needn't have worried. Dorcas, camera case slung around her neck, was buttoning Jonas up at the neck. Rowland was less lucky. In a voice that cut through the wind, Aunt Astrid assured him that she would see him at the reception.

"Won't we, Vannie?"

"I hope so, Mummy."

The wind heightened to a hard shrill whistle, echoed by the sea breaking against the cliffs below. The sky went suddenly quite dark.

"Home," urged Ben, but as we stepped onto the gravel path, three teenagers, lurking behind tombstones, came scampering up, laughing and pelting us with confetti. It was, I thought, rather like being inside a kaleidoscope.

"Better wed than dead!" yelled a burly girl in school uniform.

The dizzying swirl ebbed. A boy with stubble hair grabbed for my hand and, amazingly, kissed it. Rain made some of the brilliant patches stick to our faces. Another multi-coloured shower went up and when the air cleared, the kids went roistering off toward the church hall which abutted the vicarage. All except one. A girl, the smallest of the group, remained on the path. We stared at each other through a shimmer of rain.

"I must look like I've got some exotic form of measles," I said.

"You do realise this sort of thing is against the law." Ben was shaking out his jacket.

Perhaps she didn't realise we were joking. She didn't smile. She had sandy-coloured plaits, a small retroussé nose, a wedge-shaped face, and skin which seemed almost translucent under the sheen of rain. She kept staring at Ben and me. A bit spooky, considering the tombstone surroundings. This girl's eyes were very green in the wavering half-light, eyes at odds with the two youthful plaits. Those plaits touched me. I found myself remembering myself at fourteen—always the outsider. On an impulse, I tossed my bouquet to her.

"I love you, Ellie," whispered Ben.

The girl didn't say thank you. She stood under the quivering branches, my roses pressed against her face like a painted fan, their scent drifting between us. The wind bit through my gown and grazed my veil against my cheek. I drew closer to Ben. What more could I want from life than to be warm and dry and alone with him?

"What's your name?" I asked the girl.

"Jenny Spender."

"We're pleased to have met you," Ben said.

"Me, too." She looked at me.

"Well . . ." Ben squeezed my arm. "Darling, our carriage awaits, unless it has turned into a pumpkin."

He laughed and I joined in, but only to gain time. Unwelcome memory slid into place. There was no white-ribboned taxi to pick us up in state and deliver us at the portals of Merlin's Court. I had been so angry with the taxi driver who had failed to get me to the church at all, let alone on time, I had not only told him to get lost, I had informed him I would puncture his tyres the next time I saw his vehicle. I had planned to thumb a ride from one of our guests. And, I brightened, it might still be possible to leap onto a running board if we hurried.

"Ben, I don't know how to tell you this . . ." Evading Ben's frown, I smiled at the solemn girl with plaits, who was now sitting on the bottom church step, fingering the roses.

"Ellie darling"—Ben rubbed the rain from his brow and worked up a smile—"wouldn't a smallish tip have sufficiently made your point?"

He was right, and with a quiver of repentance, I realised that a certain heedlessness which may be thought appealing in a fiancée is unacceptable in a wife.

"Let's go, Mrs. Haskell," he said. At least it had stopped raining. And he'd called me Mrs. Haskell.

We were halfway down the path when Rowland stepped out from between trees into our path. The last of the cars vanished through the gateway.

"A charmingly eventful wedding." He smiled as we joined him.

"Thank you." Was that . . . ? Yes it was!

A vehicle approached. Rubbing my chilled arms, I saw Ben's face relax. A samaritan was coming back for us. A long dark car broke through the gloom, and immediately my optimism evaporated. No hope of this conveyance offering us a lift home. It was a hearse.

"I'm sorry about this unfortunate er . . . scheduling overlap," Rowland touched my arm, then moved to walk alongside the hearse with measured steps, silvered head bent, cassock fluttering in the wind. Poor Rowland, this wasn't his fault.

A procession of vehicles grimly slid through the gates.

"We'd better duck out of the way," said Ben. "We strike a disharmonious note."

"Won't we be more conspicuous fleeing between the graves?"

He looked unconvinced. The cars drew to a standstill. Doors

opened and closed. Were we to move a foot, we would be trapped in the surge of mourners and swept back into the church. Out from the lead car stepped a tall woman with silver blue hair, clad in a military-style mulberry coat. A handkerchief was clutched to her eyes. Soldiering up beside her were two tweedy, middle-aged women. The other mourners kept a respectful distance. As the woman in the mulberry coat and her companions neared the church steps, they suddenly halted. I realised why when a white scrap of cloth streamed toward me. The wind had grabbed her hanky. A few mourners futilely snatched at the air. The hanky blew right into my hand.

"I thought you couldn't catch," said Ben.

"Sorry." I hitched up my skirts and hastened across the gravel to the woman.

"Frightfully kind of you. I do hope . . ." Her voice broke. Pressing the hanky to her eyes, she turned away. "I do hope that this"—she blindly waved a hand toward the coffin being lifted up the steps—"has not cast a blight on your day."

"Oh, not at all!" I hastened to assure her, then realised I must sound callous. "Please do accept my condolences on the loss of . . . of . . ."

"My husband, my dear, wonderful, irreplaceable . . ." She couldn't go on. The words I did not remember saying, but must have said, only minutes ago seemed to rise between us. *Till Death Us Do Part*. I found myself looking away, focusing on the little bar brooch worn by one of her tweedy companions. That brooch had blackbirds enamelled on it. Pretty.

"Madge, we should be getting into church." Its owner prodded the new widow gently. With a feeling of escape, I hurried back to Ben. Several of the mourners stared.

"Are you all right, Ellie?" Ben asked.

"Yes." I was watching the widow mount the steps.

"We're going to miss the reception."

We made for the lich-gate and had just reached it when the wind swooped up my veil and swirled it around my face. Laughing, Ben spun me around to unwind it.

The mourners had entered the church and the pallbearers were coming around the side of the building. Slowly they made their way up the steps. A flash of sun broke through the clouds. The girl with sandy plaits stepped forward and gently placed my bouquet on the coffin lid.

It began to rain again.

. . . "The widow's handkerchief"—Hyacinth's lips curved into a smile and her eyes became hooded—"was it wringing wet with tears? Ah! I thought so—dry as a bone." . . .

The sky darkened and the rain changed from a drizzle to a downpour. I was doomed to enter the drawing room at Merlin's Court looking like a corpse fished from the briny deep. Ben and I would wile away our honeymoon sipping cough syrup instead of champagne. Never would I recline in my foamy pearl-pink nightgown upon the four-poster at the Royal Derbyshire Hotel, idly turning those last few pages of *Myths of the Bridal Bed: A Novice's Guide*. What idiot said, "Love is blind"? If Ben found me entrancing with a reddened nose and chapped lips, I would lose all respect for him.

"Nothing for it, Ellie, we have to take cover."

My bridegroom opened a random car door, and I made a token protest as we settled ourselves on the front seat.

Ben rolled his window one-third of the way down and the wind burst in upon us. It yanked at my veil and crawled icily inside my thin bodice.

"This is cosy," I said. A good wife understands all about male pride. Ben was extremely self-conscious about the claustrophobia which had plagued him since an early childhood trauma. He had been trapped inside a potato bin while playing hide-and-seek in his father's greengrocer's shop.

"If you aren't one hundred percent satisfied with this accommodation, I am sure I can find you something nicer further down the line." Ben nuzzled my neck.

"This is ch–charming."

"You mean it's musty and we're sitting on a hairbrush."

Rain does have that nasty habit of ripening fusty odours, and the car interior did smell rather pungently of spilt milk, cigarette butts, old newspapers, and dog hair. The hairbrush wasn't the only object making the seat less than comfortable, but I was not about to subject our port in a storm to the white-glove test. Any more than I would dwell on that moment when I had seen my bouquet reverently laid on a coffin lid.

All things considered, this was wickedly snug. And, after a life of deplorable virtue, it was thrilling to be in a stranger's car with Ben's lips on mine and the warmth of his body closing in. How should I comport myself if he suggested our climbing over to the back seat?

The car doors vibrated. The wind had deepened to an anguished lowing; the windows were awash with rain. But for all that, Ben and I were as blissful as Mr. and Mrs. Noah when the wicked drowned, the earth sank, and the ark went bobbing on its merry way.

What cared I if the Aunts Astrid and Lulu were enlivening the reception by throwing wedding cake at each other? Or if Uncle Maurice were assiduously attempting to seduce the most sexually repressed woman in the room? Ben and I needed these moments alone to gird ourselves for the fray.

Ben's hands moved under my veil. He was loosening my knot of hair. I felt the weight of it tumble heavily, wantonly, about my shoulders. I closed my eyes. My mother's idea of informing me of the facts of life had been to hand me a brandy and say dreamily, "People who make love at night in bed are past it." Ben's breathing became possessed of a wondrously ominous rasp. His jacket buttons were embedding themselves into my flesh, but I felt no pain. I was having trouble breathing, and my temperature kept going up and down like a department store lift. Perhaps I had already caught pneumonia. I was turning limp, utterly unable to resist as, his hand cradling the back of my head, I was borne backward by his body. I could see only his eyes, brilliant as emeralds—no, sapphires—their colour changing, blazing from one to the other until I had to close my own for fear of being scorched.

Time fell away, as the earth had done in Noah's day. Then it came, a strident, almost explosive rattling of the car doors. Who? What? Oh, my heavens! Blood pounded through my veins. Perhaps nighttime and bedtime and privacy were not totally to be despised. In one movement I was upright, ripping my tablecloth veil and hurling Ben backward across the seat.

"What happened? Weren't we enjoying ourselves?" His voice was peevish but his eyes were laughing.

The rattling had stopped. Perhaps only the wind . . . I bundled up my hair and stabbed it back to respectability.

"My darling," I said, "let us vow never to let this happen again until tonight. Is it fair, is it decent, to create the possibility of some bereaved person entering his or her car to be met by the appalling vista of entwined lovers in a state of lascivious disarray?"

"If you will excuse me a moment, my dear." Reaching for the handle, Ben battled the door open. He climbed out and seconds later climbed back in.

"A cold shower always helps," he said with a grin.

I refrained from saying he had given the inside of the car one too. A good wife never nags. Drying his face with my veil, I asked, "You don't think I am being frightfully spinsterish, do you?"

"Darling, I think you are being breathtakingly—right." Ben realigned my tiara. "My mother wouldn't want to live if word went up and down Crown Street that I had been had up for lewd conduct in a Vauxhall."

"Mm." Never having met Mrs. Haskell, I could be no judge of her feelings on any subject. Save one. Her belief that to set foot inside a Church of England was to be turned into a pillar of salt. But the loving wife keeps such thoughts to herself.

"What about you?" I said. "Haven't you had enough catastrophe for one day?"

Ben smiled. "I'm hardened. As boys, Sid and I got routinely marched down to the police station by the wicked landlord of Crown Street whenever he caught us watching stag films in whichever of his houses happened to be vacant at the time. Ellie, I think we should try and swim for it."

Aptly put. The rain was now battering the car and spurting through the partially open window, but we had to get home. Failure to do so would not endear us to the unknown neighbours who had responded so enthusiastically to the announcement in *The Daily Spokesman*.

"What are you doing?" Ben asked, as I rummaged about on the seat. "Checking for an umbrella to steal?"

"Good idea, but my object was to straighten and remove all signs of our illicit occupancy." A prickly stab and I triumphantly grasped the hairbrush which had wormed its way down the back of the seat. And what was this? Ah ha! A bulky cardigan with a woolly hat tucked up one sleeve. And here? A glove, a wad of newspapers, and a crushed box of tissues that would now fit through a letter box. Had the pretty pink and gold cardboard been this compact before our intrusion?

I attempted to plump it up. "Ben, dear, we should have climbed in the back."

He gave a pained sigh. "I do wish you would stop toying with me like this."

The tissue box came down on his head. "I meant that the owner of this car is a front seat dumper and we've squashed his—"

"Her. The owner of this car is a woman."

"Forgive me, male . . . person, but you cannot so assume on the basis of one pink cardigan."

"Ellie, an Englishman's car is his castle. Only a woman would drive around in this state of chaos." As if to prove his point, he picked up an earring and tossed it from hand to hand.

I took slow, deep breaths. Remember, Ellie, how far he has come in terms of eradicating chauvinistic leanings since first we met. "Darling, don't you think that remark is just a teensy bit sexist?"

"Absolutely. Women get housework up to the chin; they don't have anything left over to give to the car. Whereas we males"—he thumped his chest—"find fulfillment for our domestic urges in shining up leather and spitting on chrome in an area the size of the old tree house."

"Mm!" I was only slightly mollified. A name tag on the woolly hat read Beatrix Woolpack. "Would you please budge? You're sitting on more stuff."

"Ellie, leave everything. She's more likely to notice if—"

"Just look at this piece of paper! It's all crunched up, as well as being decidedly damp."

"Ellie, let's go. We didn't take a year's lease."

"One minute." I was smoothing out the scrap of paper. "What if this is something important and you've got the writing all smeared? One quick peek and . . . oh, splendid! Just a shopping list and still legible, I think." Tilting my body closer to the window I read out loud.

"Two tins cat food, twenty Players, one hair tint (Wistful Fawn), dog biscuits, one-quarter pound tea, steak and kidney pie, frozen peas, milk of magnesia—"

Ben's voice broke into my ear. "Ellie, this comes as a hideous shock."

In this light I doubted he could see that I was blushing. Even so, I held the paper in front of my face. "You're right! I should have told you before we married that other people's shopping lists hold this kinky fascination for me."

"Ellie, you can read the labels on people's underwear for all I care. What appalls me is my abysmal naiveté. I never realised that civilized people actually consume shop-bought meat pies." Ben tried to take the list away, but I held on to it.

"Therein," I said, "lies the fascination of shopping lists. They tell us all sorts of things. For example, the owner of this car is a middle-aged female (no one under fifty wants to be wistful); she smokes (cigarettes high on the list); she is a pet owner, does not like to cook, suffers from constipation, is disorganised—"

"You got that from the state of the car."

I tut-tutted. "The items aren't categorised. The pet foods should be together, ditto the chemist items."

Ben leaned against me and continued reading the list. "Instant caramel blancmange." His tone was one of extreme revulsion. "Whatever happened to good old-fashioned crême bruleé?"

"Dear, dear!" I skimmed to the bottom of the paper with one eye, while watching the window with the other.

Porridge oats, one lamb chop—obviously single; my guess was a widow—three wild mice.

My turn to shudder. Surely if the cat's owner could eat convenience foods, Puss could be persuaded to do likewise.

"What's wrong?" From the sound of him, Ben was still dwelling on the decadence of caramel blancmange.

I moved his finger up a notch to the offending item. His dark eyebrows drew together, but he shrugged. "Nothing wrong there. I happen to prefer white, because of the greater scope for play, but everyone to his own taste."

"Taste!" I twitched the list away, staring at that mouth which I had so recently kissed. "Sweetheart, you *are* joking?"

"Do I ever joke about food?" Ben drew the list back from my nerveless fingers and laid it on the seat. "I concede that wild rice has its place in the scheme of things, but the texture is so often flawed by impetuous boiling. It is at its best when simmered for thirty-two and one-half minutes and served with almond butter."

Light dawned—my mind had leapt to the macabre; it had been that sort of day. I saw again the widow going up the church steps, poor woman, so . . . so . . .

"Ellie, do let's get out of here. This discussion reminds me that our nuptial bash is at the mercy of that woman Dorcas hired to serve, and I keep getting these flashes that something terrible has happened to the lobster aspic." Ben had his door halfway open when we heard it—a roar, deeper, throatier than the wind and charged with a different kind of energy. We looked at each other.

We were outside the car, my dress and veil bundled up in my hands, when the motorbike leapt toward us through swirling rain, accompanied by a joyful *hoot hoot* loud enough and sacrilegious enough to waken all the dead in the churchyard. Bike and rider slithered between the lich-gate, dispersing gravel right, left, and center, and came to a lunging sideways stop millimeters from us.

"Freddy!" exclaimed Ben, with rather more pleasure than I thought necessary or appropriate.

"You two sure are my kind of people. Couldn't hold out till you got home, could you?" Freddy favoured us with his familiar leer. He was now dressed in everyday attire—a black leather jacket, a shirt collar, but no shirt; a weighty tangle of chains flattened the damp hairs on his chest.

"Sorry to disappoint you, old man, but we were merely seeking shelter from the deluge." Ben wound an arm round me.

"Got you!" Freddy lowered an eyelid in a man-to-man wink. "Can't wait to tell Jill. She was rather concerned, Ellie, that you might suffer from the flannel nightie and woolly bedsocks syndrome."

He moved before I could grab hold of his long, untidily plaited hair and wrap it around his throat. A dark huddle of figures was forming outside the church. I could hear the distant murmur of Rowland's voice, but Freddy wasn't looking in that direction. "By the way, where is Jill? Don't tell me the girl who worships the shadow I cast has nipped off to the wedding feast without me."

"What did you think she would do, you turnip, stand under a tree until you returned or she got struck by lightning? Don't worry, Jill is being looked after," I said benignly. "She accompanied your parents in their car back to Merlin's Court."

"Oh, God!" he groaned. "Mum will have pinched her purse en route, and we all know what Dad will have tried to pinch!"

Damn Freddy! I watched his eyes, the lids still dusted with neon purple. Should I be held accountable for his romance with Jill simply because they had met at Merlin's Court? Admittedly, Freddy considers being asked for the time by any female under ninety a romance. But I did suspect that Cupid's arrow had got him in the aorta this time. Despite all my claims to sanity, I was fond of Freddy, and it was hard not to feel some pity for the person the fates had assigned Aunt Lulu and Uncle Maurice as parents.

Faking a yawn, Freddy yanked at the chains around his neck. "Okay, love doves, the meter's running. Afraid I can only manage one passenger, so will it be you, Ellie?"

Motorbikes terrify me. However, the wedding guests were beginning to prey on my conscience and Ben refused to ride while I jogged home. I gazed into my husband's face, memorizing every line, as I warned him to keep to the middle of Cliff Road. He tends to daydream while out walking about such things as the ultimate marinade.

Freddy leaned on the hooter. "Come on! I realise this is the first time you two have been parted since your marriage, but I would like to get there before Mum has nicked half the family heirlooms."

One last lingering kiss and I hoisted aboard. The rain was now a gauzy mizzle; the elms were sketched in charcoal. Even though I knew it was unlucky I looked back over my shoulder.

The dark morass of humanity around the newly dug grave was separating into forlorn shadows. Something squeezed inside me. Tonight, the widow would go home to her empty house, empty bed . . . The bike vibrated and we were off. Flung vertical, we zoomed onto the narrow, bumpy road.

"By gum, this is the life," bawled Freddy over his shoulder.

Soaring like a seagull on airwaves of terror. Below us, the waves seethed against the jagged rocks. Think happy thoughts, Ellie! Do not focus on that Mr. Woolpack who had driven over the cliff edge one foggy night last spring. What would it take, a pebble in the wrong place at the wrong time, to send us in Mr. Woolpack's flight path? I fear I almost gouged out Freddy's appendix. Life was rather meaningful to me right now.

Through the wrought-iron gateway of Merlin's Court we blasted. The motorbike hit a blemish on the surface of the drive, leapt two feet in the air, and flew like Mary Poppins onto the narrow moat bridge and under the portcullis.

"Aint much, but it's home, right, El? The place has class—ivy-encrusted walls, turrets and battlements galore, whence the lovelorn can hurl themselves, and never forget the gargoyle doorbell. All mod cons, really! Except a comfy dungeon or two."

"No house has everything," I said stiffly. Ours was but a small-scale, nineteenth-century repro of a castle, but the dearth of dungeons with manacled skeletons crumbling to dust was rather a sore point with me.

"Ellie"—Freddy lurched to a stop—"how about spotting me a few quid so I can take Jill out tonight for a bang-up tofu dinner?"

"What's a few?" I was struggling to flounce out my dress.

"A hundred?"

"Freddy." Taking his arm, I moved us to the door. "Why don't you get a job? A proper job instead of pinging a triangle in that dismal band."

"Work?" He looked aghast. "The way I see it, cousin, if you have to be paid to do something, can't be much fun, can it?"

"Wrong. Some people love their jobs. I do, and Ben can't wait to begin another cookery book and open his restaurant in the village."

Freddy reached for the doorknob. "My heart bleeds! Inventing new ways to fry bacon. My! My! I'll wager that when Ben opens that restaurant, he won't lift his pinky to crack an egg. Eh, but it makes a chap glad to be born shiftless. About that two hundred nicker, Ellie?"

"After the wedding cake, I'll look and see what I've got stashed under the mattress."

Simultaneously, Freddy released the brass knob and I grasped it; the iron-studded door flung inward, almost sending me sprawling.

After these many months in residence, I still experienced a sense of embrace on entering Merlin's Court. "Thank you, Benefactress Ellie," the house would whisper, "for everything—these gorgeous Turkish carpets on the flagstone hall floor, the peacock and rose elegance of the drawing room, the Indian Tree china in the blackened oak dresser in the dining room. And, especially, thank you for loving me as passionately as Abigail Grantham once did." But on this most venerable day, I didn't get that sort of greeting.

A complete stranger stood beyond the threshold—a stocky man with a sallow-skinned pug face and an oversized mop of glossy black curls. He held a half-filled wineglass and his expression was one of extreme disappointment, like someone expecting the postman and finding a policeman on the step instead. The man started to close the door with his foot as Freddy and I stepped inside.

He tapped the wineglass to his forehead in a mea culpa of embarrassment. Wine slopped out. "A thousand pardons. For the minute I didn't recognise you, Mrs. Haskell."

Oh well, when a man used the two most beautiful words in the English language, I had to smile at him. "It's the veil," I said. "We brides all look alike."

The man with the black curls and eyes like ripe olives was graciously stepping aside, but as the door opened wide, my smile shrank; I found myself looking into a madhouse. Could this bellowing uproar be a cheering for my belated arrival? Afraid not. There was no escaping the raw truth. The mob milling in and out of doorways, crowding the stairs, jostling the two suits of armour, was, in the main, drunk.

6

. . . Hyacinth's earrings swayed so fast back and forth, I feared they would nick her throat. "I must say, Ellie, had I been you, I would have grabbed the nearest broom and swept the lot of them into the garden and turned on the gardening hose. But where was Bentley?"

"He arrived at that very moment. He had thumbed a ride from Rowland, who had come driving up with Miss Thorn, the organist."

"Pray tell me that Bentley swept you into his arms and carried you over the threshold." Primrose sighed ecstatically. "I cannot think of anything more splendid."

"It was, considering that one year earlier a crane could not have lifted me. . . ."

How could Dorcas and Jonas have let things get out of hand like this? The mayhem intensified as I gazed around from the blissful haven of my husband's arms. A blue-haired woman, sporting more chins than I had owned in my heyday, went squealing past us up the stairs, the skirt of her paisley silk dress clutched in both hands.

"I'm coming to get you, my sugar plum!" A paunchy gentleman transporting two champagne glasses broke through the crowd in hot and heavy pursuit of the Paisley Lady, who was now peeping coyly through the bannisters; he collided heavily with Ben.

"Beg pardon, children!" A glass of champagne was thrust at me. The gentleman proceeded to elbow his way onward and upward. He didn't get very far. Freddy reeled out a hand and hooked a finger under his collar.

"Daddy, don't be a tart," he drawled, "you're not cute with your brain sloshing around inside your skull."

"Unfilial brat!" Uncle Maurice held the wounded expression for a full second, and then made a dive for the stairs.

"The man needs to have his mouth and his fly sewn up." Whereupon, Freddy tipped my tiara over one eye, knocked his elbows sideways to clear a path, and went off to find Jill.

Ben having, I believe, enjoyed this vignette as much as I, now whispered, "Ellie, may I put you down?"

It seemed we said a kind of good-bye as he set me gently on my feet. My eyes clung to his, unwilling to disconnect, until I realised he was looking not at me, but at Miss Thorn. Had she been any other woman, I might have experienced a pang of jealousy. Instead, I fondled my wedding ring. Did this woman never tire of being always the organist, never the bride? Or was she resigned to her fate? She towered over Rowland, who was six feet; she made Ben look short. Many women turned height into an asset: Miss Thorn had succumbed to it. She wore horn-rimmed glasses, and her dreary brown coat drooped to her ankles. I was an ardent convert to thin, but Miss Thorn had carried a good thing too far. She caved in where she should have caved out. Her complexion was poor, her shoulders hunched, and her hair was lank and mouse-coloured, parted in the middle and clamped back from her forehead with two slides. Tucked into each of those slides was an artificial daisy. She collided with Ben and me and tipped her steamed-up spectacles down her nose to see who we were.

"Oh, do please excuse me. I kept seeing a lot of white, Mrs. Haskell, and thought you were a wall. I'm so glad of the opportunity to say how honoured I am at being included in these nuptial celebrations." Here she did a little dip at the knees, something between a curtsy and a nervous tic. Ben and I hastened to assure her of our pleasure that she could come.

She tittered. "As a rule, I am not much of a social butterfly—I stay busy with my music, my tatting, and adding to my collection of antique telephone directories. But I was very ready to be persuaded when the vicar insisted I would be welcomed today."

There came a lull in the general hubbub, broken by a meowing from the staircase. I looked up, expecting to see Tobias, but it was the Paisley Lady. Skirts clutched in her hands, she came frisking down the stairs with Uncle Maurice close on her heels.

A voice to my right chirped, "I never saw anything like it! Have to be his decadent London friends."

"Ellie, you were a lovely bride." Rowland recaptured my attention.

I felt myself blushing; I'm not used to compliments. Ben was helping Miss Thorn off with her coat.

"It goes without saying," Rowland continued, "that I wish both of you the best of everything. I think we have become friends and I value that."

"So do we, don't we, Ben?"

The noise level shot back up, and suddenly Rowland was hauled away by a female parishioner. Miss Thorn edged up close, her knobby hands clasped to her concave chest. "You may smile, Mrs. Haskell, but when I was a girl I used to lie awake at night and dream of being inside this house. So romantic a place! Exactly like those in Mr. Digby's thrillers." She peered round. "I don't suppose he is here among us?"

"We may never know for sure; but I doubt it. Isn't he known to be unsociable?" My voice was drowned out by the hubbub.

"Incredible as it may sound, I have never been here before. Unless we count the front steps. Years ago I came to ask if I might buy any old telephone directories"—Miss Thorn knotted her bony hands together—"but old Merlin Grantham threatened to drop the portcullis on me when I left. Such a colourful character, wasn't he, like Mr. Digby or Smuggler Jim?"

The spectacles had cleared and her eyes were nice. A warm doggy brown.

"And then you came! So thrilling! The young heiress returning to the ancestral home"—a maiden-lady glance at Ben—"accompanied by a dark, handsome man from the big city. The village concluded you were cousins of sorts."

"How charitable," said Ben. Then, like an echo of our conversation, a voice drifted up from a leopard-skin hat.

". . . *Quite like a fairy tale—in every sense of the word; the best man a hairdresser.*"

Miss Thorn was saying she would take her coat upstairs, pretty herself up a bit, and then (if we wished) be delighted to play for her supper. But she became another piece of human flotsam before I could tell her the harpsichord was stuck in the boxroom.

"Miss—Mrs. Haskell! Fancy meeting you again so soon! And Mr. Haskell!" The man with the oversized mop of black hair and jaundiced complexion, who had admitted us to the house, stalled in his tracks and affected a look of immense surprise and delight. He tucked two fingers into the pocket of his yellow waistcoat, then handed Ben a small white card.

"Vernon Daffy, estate agent. Five hundred houses sold in the past five years. My best wishes on this auspicious occasion. Should you wish to trade up, or down, remember we're the best in town! Feel at liberty to phone day or night. Sometime in the near future you must tour our office—we offer free coffee." All the while he was addressing my husband and me, Mr. Daffy was looking at Miss Thorn's head, bobbing up the stairs.

"Thought I just heard that female say something to you about a thrill of a lifetime" he said.

"Her first visit to this house," I explained.

A burst of laughter from our rear. Mr. Daffy rubbed ginger-haired hands together. "Couldn't for the life of me think what she could be talking about. Shouldn't think her life is fizzing with excitement—ugly duck, isn't she?" His eyes followed the sweep of the staircase. "A lot of charm these old places, wouldn't lie to you on that score. But they don't fetch what they did. Too much upkeep. Notice second bannister from bottom is loose. Now I concede that a certain amount of dilapidation may be complimentary to your antiques but . . ."

Mercifully, we were borne backward by the surging masses. Mr. Daffy's voice drifted away like a man gone overboard. "Better find the wife—name's Shirley, but I always call her Froggy."

"I wouldn't trust that man to sell me an egg timer," said Ben. "Ancient proverb, Ellie, never trust anyone, male or female, when the hair on their hands doesn't match the hair on their head."

"Imagine," I said, "a man calling his wife Froggy!"

I was talking to myself. Ben was gone. Attempting to follow, I was swept in the opposite direction.

Someone bumped into me. Dorcas! She was enveloped in one of Ben's aprons and was holding my cat Tobias, looking a bit overdressed by comparison in his white satin bow.

"Thank God, you're alive," she rasped into my ear. She handed me Tobias, but taking exception to my veil, he leapt, hissing, onto her shoulder. "Where's Ben?"

I explained.

"Never fear, Ellie, old chum, he'll turn up." Dorcas yanked at her apron straps. "Hell's bells. Best say it and be done. I've bad news for you."

I hate sentences that begin that way. Had a notice arrived from the Archbishop of Canterbury voiding my marriage until further notice? Or—I clutched an anonymous shoulder to steady myself—had Ben's parents been fatally injured while speeding down the motorway in a rush to be with us after all?

"The temporary household help," Dorcas continued, "has proved unsatisfactory."

"Surely not," I shouted, "the estimable bartender described by you as Lord Peter Wimsey come to life?"

Dorcas nodded bleakly. "His lordship sampled the gin. Found him in the pantry, face down in the lobster aspic. Sid Fowler put him to bed in one of the spare rooms."

This was bad. That aspic was the culmination of months of experimentation. Ben might be so anguished he would be unable to function for the rest of the day—or night.

"It won't be missed," I lied. "What about the woman who came in to serve and do the washing up? Is she, by the good Lord's grace, still on her feet?"

"Mrs. Malloy? She's walking around, but not in a straight line."

"From the general state of inebriation, I surmise our guests have been mixing their own poison."

Dorcas shook her head and Tobias clamped a paw on it. "Jonas took over drinks, while Mrs. M. and I began getting the food out. He fixed a punch. Equal quantities of scotch, gin, vodka, brandy, and champagne. Can't blame the old chap! Never drinks anything stronger than Ovaltine himself. But I agree mightily, Ellie, either we get some food into these people to sop up the booze or offer overnight hospitality."

My heart sank. Already I was counting the minutes until I could get Ben into our hotel room. I would don my pearl-pink nightdress and he'd insist I take it off again, at once. . . .

"Let's find Ben," I said, "he'll be putting the final touches to the buffet table."

"Can't take Tobias into the drawing room." Dorcas reached up a hand to haul him down but he leapt from her shoulder, ran along a roof of hats and was gone.

Dorcas snorted. "Already fetched him out of there twice. That antique dealer, Delacorte, is allergic to cats. Don't like the man. But don't want him ill."

I agreed. "People might think it was the food. "Better let me chase down Tobias while you put on some records."

"Hope you can find him in this mob."

"Foolish friend"—I patted her shoulder—"where food is, there too is Mr. T."

"*. . . The milkman told me she had done a marvellous job restoring the place.*" I smiled at the leopard-skin hat who made this kind remark and began making circles like someone trapped in a revolving door. I would also do a marvellous job decorating the restaurant.

"*And the butcher told me*"—it was the same voice—"*she inherited a bundle of money. Even so, she'll be wise to keep busy; it's my guess it won't be long before she finds herself scribbling a few lines to Dear Felicity Friend.*"

I was almost afraid to enter the drawing room. Unsuppressed sigh of relief. No overturned flower vases. No pictures knocked cockeyed on the walls. Lamplight illuminated the sheen of polished walnut and ivory brocade; and, as so often happened, Abigail's portrait above the mantel warmed me more than the ruby glow of the fire. The wedding cake rose in tiered, pristine splendour on its own table.

I averted my eyes. I once read a story about a woman who had lived a prior life as a cat and every time she came near a mouse, her lips started twitching. Having lived my former life as a pig, icing sugar had the same effect on me. I sidled past.

The dozen or so people in the room appeared to be comporting themselves in an orderly fashion. I even recognised a few faces. Lionel Wiseman, solicitor, stood by the buffet table conversing with two ladies.

One of them was a woman of fiftyish. A beige sort of person. Her complexion, birds-nest hair, tweedy suit—even her eyes—all came in variations of that shade. I knew she was Mr. Wiseman's secretary because she had been seated in his outer office, typing, on the day Ben and I went to discuss with him the legalities involved in purchasing the building we wished to convert into Abigail's. Mr. Wiseman had introduced her to us as Lady Theodora Peerless. Did he joke? Or did some riches-to-rags tale lurk behind that monochromatic exterior? The other woman with Mr. Wiseman was a Marilyn Monroe blonde.

His daughter? Her photograph had been featured on his desk. At the other end of the buffet table stood Charles and Ann Delacorte. Another handsome man, if you like Nordic types with fair, almost transparent, hair. He was poking his fingers through a plate of munchy morsels, searching, I heard him say, for something nonfishy. Ann was impeccably, if not fashionably, groomed. The shoulders of her emerald green dress were heavily padded which, coupled with the way her dark hair was puffed up in front and drawn sleekly back into a roll low on her neck, made her reminiscent of a model in a nineteen-forties catalogue. I wished I could discover where Tobias was hiding. (Was that a meow?) That way I could drape him in front of me and Ann might not see that the Victorian gown she'd helped me select from Delacorte's impressive array of old-world finery was no longer in mint condition. She turned, saw me, and smiled wanly.

"Your husband keeps bringing out more food and everything looks delicious," Ann said, as I stole toward the table. "Usually I eat like a bird but . . ."

"Very true, my dear," responded her spouse, "like a vulture."

Charles Delacorte had eyes like iceberg chips. "Not that you don't sing like a lark." He touched her hand with his finger tips and lifted a pale eyebrow at me. "Did you not hear my wife's voice leading the choir during your nuptials? Might you, perhaps, care to have her sing a ditty or two for the enlivenment of your guests? Something of a child prodigy, weren't you, darling? Sang with some wildly famous people, long since forgotten—the Far Horizons and Sylvania, that toast of the night clubs! A rose that bloomed too soon, that's my Ann."

Courageous Ann. Her smile never dipped, and my heart swelled with admiration and pain for her. I found myself babbling. "It would be lovely to have you sing, but with everything so noisy it wouldn't be fair to you. You know, I think I did see that Sylvania, or rather an old film clip of her, on television recently; she was all in sequins, seated on a piano, with a cigarette in one of those long holders, belting out a ballad in this wonderfully raspy voice about some man that done got away." A meow cut me short, reminding me of who else had done got away. Urging the Delacortes to keep having fun, I hitched up my skirts and moved on.

A squat, muggy-faced woman touched me on the arm. It was Froggy—I mean Shirley—Daffy.

"Such a lovely bride! I cried all the way through the service. I wonder, have you seen Squeaky?"

"Excuse me, who?" My eyes strayed to the twitching tablecloth. Froggy let out a ribbitting laugh. "Silly me! Pet name for my husband. The old dear has to catch the London train so I wanted to remind him we mustn't stay too late. He *will* leave everything to the last minute, and rushing is so very bad at his time of life. Not that the dear old sausage is old! But I can't learn not to fuss. He's all I have, apart from our cat. Couldn't be without my Tibs. Yours went that way."

"Thanks." A group by the bookcase alcove dispersed, and I spied Jonas administering punch from the eighteenth-century wassail bowl. He had upended his top hat on the white-clothed table, behind a placard imprinted with the words Thank You. Terrible man. I caught his eye and mouthed, "Meow?" He lifted a hand to cup his ear; unfortunately, it was the one with the ladle. I went back to prowling.

Mrs. Roxie Malloy, the hired help, was also prowling—straightening ashtrays and tucking empty glasses into her apron pocket. Her hair was blackest black, and her face was layered with enough paint to do a small semidetached all through. Emerging from behind the sofa, she looked me up and down.

"I trust I'm giving satisfaction, mum? Your husband took over in the kitchen. Titivating the chicken tarts he was when last I saw him. I've had more than my share of husbands, let me tell you, and never a word of complaint out of one of them, so I trust they'll be no trouble with me wages."

She stalked off, slightly on the tilt, trailing a whiff of clove balls, Uncle Maurice's antidote for boozy breath. Speaking of whom, there was his better half, Aunt Lulu, dozing in the Queen Anne chair by the fire. I was tiptoeing over when she moved. Or, shall we say, when her hand did. It reached out, picked up a Sevres sweet dish, chocs and all, and disappeared into the little tote bag by her side. Her snores didn't miss a beat. If Aunty didn't wake up soon, there wouldn't be a knickknack left in the room.

I wished Ben would get the buffet officially started. He was probably anguishing over some recalcitrant sprig of parsley. Rightly so, of course.

Over by the window, Freddy was with Jill. He was doing conjuring tricks with cheese balls. And must have dropped one earlier. A slither, a scurry, and there was Tobias pawdabbing a furry ball, which desperately sought escape in the direction of Mr. Charles Delacorte. No time to delay. Scooping up Tobias, I muffled his outraged meows by swathing him in my veil.

The grandfather clock said 4:35 P.M. as I reentered the hall. The crowd had thinned. A rumba pounded the air, and several couples were dancing. Heading out toward the centre of the floor was one of our twin suits of armor. This one was named Rufus. And would you believe it, the jolly dog was dancing—swirling and twirling, dipping and whirling in a brisk and spirited foxtrot. Old Rufus was not alone. He was clasped in the arms of Aunt Astrid. My kinswoman's normally alabaster complexion was afire, her black hat with the spotted veiling was tilted over one eye.

"Don't get your hopes up, she won't stay like this." Hands brushed my shoulders, and I whirled toward Ben, almost dislodging Tobias.

Having explained why I was with cat, I asked if the food was under control.

"Does night follow day? I tipped Sid out of his chair and set him to laying out doilies. And, Ellie"—Ben's voice changed—"promise not to count calories today."

"Of course, darling." And it wasn't a lie. I would count items instead. Losing weight is a misnomer; it always knows its way back.

"Shall we announce that the feasting may begin?" I asked.

"Jonas is going to come out and ring the gong. Meanwhile, you have to dispose of Tobias and something has to be done about Aunt Astrid before she compromises Rufus. Wonder where Vanessa is?"

Once upon a time, several months ago, those words from Ben's lips would have made my blood freeze solid in my veins. Even before he came along, my feelings for my gorgeous cousin had been ones of uncomplicated jealousy. Now I was able to say with the confidence of a married woman, "Speak of the devil."

Hands in the pockets of her fox jacket, the Titian-haired lovely was descending the last stair. Men parted like the Red Sea to let her through.

"Hello darlings."

Vanessa, despite her puerile existence, is one of those rare specimens who look even better close up than at a distance. My hands constricted over Tobias as she touched back a tendril of hair with a gleaming nail, unfurled her eyelashes, and tiptoed up to kiss Ben on the mouth. His return of the kiss nicely indicated his married status.

She moistened her glistening lips and touched his sleeve. "When will the cookery book be out, darling? I can't wait to buy it for my coffee table."

Super! She had her hoof in her mouth. Ben had heard nothing from Brambleweed Press, the publisher to whom he had submitted his manuscript, and he claimed to have blotted out all thoughts of its acceptance or rejection. I didn't believe him, judging from the way he chased after the postman like a hungry terrier each morning.

"My, my, Bentley! You are certainly haute cuisine!" Stepping back, Vanessa flicked her lashes sideways and downways at me. Tobias did nothing for my figure, there were snags in my veil and dirt rimmed the hem of my gown. Her laughter tinkled.

Ben started to speak, but I was ahead of him. "I know, Vanessa, I do look bedraggled. But then"—I reached out and stroked the collar of her fox jacket—"I'm not wearing the sort of apparel that meows a warning when it is time to come in out of the rain."

"Anyone for a saucer of milk?" Ben's voice was undisguisedly amused. Vanessa's sherry-coloured eyes sizzled.

Flushed with success, I beamed. "So pleased you could come, Van; it seems ages since we've seen you on the cover of *Vogue*."

Instinctively I stepped back. I had struck a nerve, but she did not slash out with her bright claws. After an intake of breath, her lips curved into a smile.

"Pax, Ellie. I truly am lost in admiration when I think of how you unloaded yourself of half-a-dozen chins—just kidding!" She tweaked my cheek. "And produced gorgeous Bentley out of a hat! Do you know, until today I always thought Chitterton Fells about as exciting as a bubble bath with no bubbles, but—" She broke off. Aunt Astrid and Rufus had just collided with Rowland.

Vanessa's colour rose. "I've got to get Mummy out of here."

This from the girl who would have cheerfully let her mother sink into the bog without stretching forth a finger for fear of breaking a manicured nail.

Something crashed in the drawing room. Voices were heard exclaiming. Freddy burst through the doorway snarling, "Sorry about the table but it was right in my path." Whatever Ben and I started to say was drowned out by the booming of the gong.

A trembling silence ensued. Jonas's voice cut through it like a hacksaw. "Ladies and gents. A buffet is served. We hope you all partake. And remember, next time most of you get privileged to enjoy Mr. Haskell's cooking you'll be paying restaurant prices." You could have heard an eyelash fall.

At long last my husband and I were the focus of attention. Ben drew me into the centre of the room, cleared his throat to rid it of amusement, and embarked on a formal greeting. I clung to his arm, punctuating his remarks with wifely smiles.

"Handsome devil, isn't he?" observed a female voice from under a flower-pot hat. *"But then, they so often are. Most unfair, I always think."*

Clearly she meant other people's husbands! How often I had thought the same! As the guests flooded toward the drawing room, Jill came out. Face tight as a fist, she headed up the stairs without looking back.

"Ben, I think I should go after Jill. If anyone asks where I am, tell them I have gone to hem up my dress."

"Don't be long, Ellie!" He sounded thrillingly like the heavy husband in *Love's Wild Embrace*. People were looking at us. "You have certain *wifely* responsibilities."

It was hard to tear myself away when his eyes turned that dark emerald and the muscles in his jaw tightened. But Jill and I had been friends for years.

I entered several bedrooms without finding Jill or Freddy. I did find Uncle Maurice and the Paisley Lady, but will not elaborate on that scene. The bathroom revealed a woman in purple silk, inspecting the medicine cabinet. She was saying to another female seated on the toilet lid, "I only came on the slim chance of brushing shoulders with one of our elusive celebrities. Oh, I knew it wouldn't be Edwin Digby, and I don't know anyone who has ever set eyes on Felicity Friend, but I did have hope for Dr. Bordeaux. He's quite handsome, in an anguished sort of way. Never mind, I'm not sorry you persuaded me to come; this has been interesting in its own way. Don't tell me it doesn't mean something, *his* parents not being here. . . ." A paralysing silence fell as their eyes met mine through the open doorway. Each lifted a hand to fiddle with the brooch on her lapel as I drew the door shut.

Jill was behind a third-floor bedroom door, standing on her head. The unnerving part was that her eyes were open. "Don't gawk," she snapped. "I'm meditating. Leave me alone."

I sat down on the bed and sighed. "I guess Freddy proposed and you refused. Seeing his parents in action must have been a shock." I petered out. If Jill really loved Freddy, Uncle Maurice's peccadilloes and Aunt Lulu's kleptomania shouldn't matter.

"Freddy didn't propose marriage. He wants us to live together. But Ellie, that's so conventional. Personally, I find his parents inspiring. If *they* can stay married for thirty years, the institution must have something going for it. Now get out of here. Your happiness offends me."

"Yes, Jill."

I would search out Freddy and threaten to break his neck.

He had to be hiding under a bed; I couldn't find him. I was about to go downstairs when I heard music. Mozart, being played on the harpsichord. I headed for the boxroom with quickened feet and a slight sense of shame; Freddy had been telling me for years that he was a musical genius; I had never taken him seriously. This . . . was impassioned, soaring, sublime. I, who cannot trill a note, wanted to burst into operatic ecstasy as I thrust open the door.

The person seated at the harpsichord was Miss Thorn. Her fingers rippled, stirring, teasing the keys. Her shoulders were hunched, the daisies gone from her hair, but—amazingly—she had attained a kind of beauty. Her face was flushed, her eyes dark, languorous. Now she saw me. The fingers stilled, and she reverted to plainness.

"Mrs. Haskell!" She jerked to her feet. Gripping her knobby hands, she did a dip at the knees and twitched a glance around the room—at the chair with the broken caning, the bed tumbled with old blankets. "Oh, my deepest apologies, Mrs. Haskell! I fully intended to return to the festivities after parking my coat, but you had mentioned this precious instrument"—she reached out to touch the wood—"and I could not control myself. I took a peek and was swept away."

"I'm glad you found the harpsichord. You play magnificently."

I meant every word; the reason my voice sounded peculiar was because I saw something moving under the blankets. I knew it wasn't Tobias because he had just wandered in and was pawing at my legs. I knew it wasn't Freddy because I could see the top of a bald head. Who? The answer came to me as Miss Thorn emitted a terrified screech and Tobias slid across the floor, grabbing at what seemed to be a black astrakhan hat.

Miss Thorn had me by the arm. "I'm sorry, Mrs. Haskell, but I am terrified of cats, m–may we leave?"

She didn't have to ask twice. It would only take the inebriated bartender to awake and sit bolt upright in bed to make her faint. And I really didn't have the time. I had to find Freddy, and assist Ben in cutting the wedding cake before I could race into my bedroom, throw on my going-away outfit, tuck my suitcase under my arm, and then at last, at long last, be off on the honeymoon of the century. I, Ellie Simons—sorry—Haskell, was about to live out my most beautiful fantasies—unlike the heroine in a romantic novel who gets slapped in the face with The End. My heart started a drum roll that drowned out Miss Thorn's voice as we went downstairs. It could not, however, obliterate the hubbub, musical and otherwise, in the hall.

Then I saw something that squeezed the breath back into my lungs—Ben was near the front door, talking to a uniformed policeman.

He glanced round and spotted me. "Ellie, it isn't surprising you couldn't reach Mum on the phone earlier. She's been missing for three days." He sounded quite—ordinary.

The constable, young, fresh-faced, and eager, rifled through his notebook. "I have here some pertinent details. A Mrs. Beatty Long of Eleven Crown Street, states she grew concerned when failing to see Mrs. Elijah Haskell leave the house for church services on Wednesday morning, as was the lady's custom."

"Mass," corrected Ben. "My mother is a Catholic."

"No offence intended, none taken I hope, sir." Constable

Beaker scratched with a diligent pencil and continued. "The aforementioned Mrs. Long also states that she had been uneasy for some time, having noticed the Haskells' curtains being closed at odd times of the day."

"Beatty Long always was a meddlesome old woman." Ben ran a hand across his brow.

Someone grasped my elbow. It was Mrs. Malloy.

"Not now, please," I said.

"As you like, mum," she huffed, "but it *is* a matter of life and death."

Constable Beaker stiffened with professional interest. I grabbed Ben's hand. "When did Mr. Haskell report his wife missing?"

"That's the thing Miss—Mrs., he didn't."

Mrs. Malloy folded her arms. "Believe you me, I'm not standing here wearing polish off the floor for me own amusement. Seems to me someone should be told there's a young bloke up in one of the turrets, threatening to jump out the window and—"

"What?" The constable made for the stairs.

My legs wouldn't move, Ben looked ready to laugh. The dancers had frozen. But the jolly strains of the music flowed on and on . . .

"And I'm telling you straight, mum." Mrs. Malloy's bosom heaved. "I don't do ceilings, I don't do drains, and I don't wash blood and guts off the pavements."

From the Files of
The Widows Club

Telephone conversation reported by member of Calling Committee, 1st December

"Good evening, Mrs. Thrush, so glad to find you at home. You don't know me, but . . ."

"Excuse me, perhaps you would telephone another time." (*Sound of hanky being used.*) "You've caught me at rather a bad time. My beloved husband was buried this very afternoon, and I really cannot think of buying anything or subscribing to a magazine."

"I understand. But do let me explain that I am from The Widows Club and have been assigned the role of your special confidante during these first difficult weeks. May I leave my name and phone number and urge you to get in touch with me, day or night, if you feel the need to have a good weep or just talk?"

(*Smothered choking sound.*) "What about laugh? Oh, my dear, I can't tell you how glad I am you rang. The hardest part of this whole business has been keeping a straight face. The only moment when I did feel a bit down was when we were going into the church and collided with a bridal party. That poor young woman—so elated at tying the knot—to the noose around her neck. Oh, chatting to you is going to be marvellous. But I am afraid I do have to go. I see my best friend Vera coming up the path. She does need consoling. They—she and my dear husband—were unofficially engaged!"

(*Responsive laughter.*) "Mrs. Thrush, I cannot wait to get to know you better. Are you interested in ceramics by any chance? Splendid. I am also on that committee. My name is Millicent Parsnip of Honeysuckle Cottage. My phone number is in the directory."

"Thank you so very much."

"My pleasure. And Mrs. Thrush, one teensy hint: spray a little ammonia on your hanky. Brings on red eyes and sniffles wonderfully."

. . . "And did Cousin Freddy leap from the turret?" Hyacinth inquired.

"Of course not," I scoffed. "He was on his way downstairs as Constable Beaker hurtled up them. Claimed the police car parked outside the house had killed the mood. He was let off with a warning against breaking the peace. What peace! All those gawkers in the hall! And Freddy ranting on about his broken heart, relishing every minute until Jill sent down a message, via Dorcas, that if she allowed herself to be blackmailed by a temper tantrum she would be at Freddy's beck and call all of their unmarried life."

"My dear, I couldn't agree more," chirped Primrose. "But what of Mrs. Elijah Haskell?"

"According to Constable Beaker's notes, Mr. Elijah Haskell stated that his wife told him she was going on a spiritual pilgrimage."

"Dear me," sighed Primrose. "Ever since reading *Canterbury Tales*, I have thought one tends to meet some very peculiar people on that sort of tour. . . ."

* * * *

The honeymoon, officially speaking, was off. Ben and I, now in pedestrian dress, were seated on the six-thirty-three train, due to depart for London in eight minutes. There were only a few other passengers in the long compartment, all at the far end from us, which was just as well because Ben had lowered our window. His claustrophobia was acting up.

Chitterton Station looked seedy in the white flare of its lights. A poster of a glamourous blonde with a black handlebar moustache drinking the right whiskey peeled off the concrete wall. I suppose it was my mood, but the thin man in the grubby raincoat lounging against the station-house door, dragging on a fag, looked positively menacing.

One question kept going around in my head. Had the prospect of gaining me as a daughter-in-law driven Mrs. Haskell to suicide? Ben claimed to be convinced that Constable Beaker had simply dredged up any excuse to see inside a house of local interest. And Constable Beaker had admitted that no inquiry of an official nature was underway.

By chance, so the constable said, he had that afternoon been chatting with a friend assigned to the Crown Street beat, and one thing leading to another, they had discovered that one Magdalene Haskell, aged seventy, had absented herself from home to the concern of the neighbors. And said woman had a son, name of Bentley T. Haskell, living in a mansion on the cliffs above Chitterton Fells. Put that way, it sounded plausible enough.

We had decided against driving to London because Ben's Heinz 57 (it was part Austin, part Rover, part Vauxhall, part bicycle) convertible was growing increasingly unreliable in its old age. Sid Fowler had driven us to the station. Our troubles seemed to restore Sid mightily. He had carried the luggage, and while Ben was buying the tickets, Sid had chatted cheerfully.

"Magdalene was—no, do think positive—*is* a wonderful woman, Ellie. Never felt dressed without her rosary and always dampened her ironing with holy water. Did Ben tell you she wanted him to marry a girl named Angelica Brady? As for Eli, don't take it personally if he dislikes you. Eli thinks women over five-foot-two take hormone tablets and despises all people who inherit money. Comes from his having worked his way up from being a barrow boy to owning Haskell's Greengrocery, lock, stock, and pavement." I wasn't sorry when Sid went off to play bingo.

Accepted as a daughter-in-law or not, I was going to have to enter the flat above the greengrocery shop. We were bound for London to see Ben's father. My husband stared out the window, brows furrowed. "Ellie, see that chap with the cigarette dangling out of his mouth? I feel I know him from somewhere, but the where eludes me."

"I hate that feeling," I said, and warmed to the stranger in his grubby raincoat with the upturned collar. He was a bridge back to ordinary conversation. With the advent of Constable Beaker, Ben's past life on Crown Street had closed around him, separating us in a way that nothing had since we first met.

"Look," I said, moving closer, "he's leaving. Seems a bit unsure whether he's doing the right thing, keeps turning back."

"Probably decided this train is never going to move." Ben smiled in my general direction, but his eyes didn't focus.

A good wife knows when her husband needs to be left alone with his thoughts. I polished my wedding ring. Whatever else changed, our love would endure. I also faced facts. If Mrs. Haskell's whereabouts were not satisfactorily verified this evening, our honeymoon would be off in every sense of the word. I couldn't expect Ben to respond to the pearl-pink nightie with his mother's fate in limbo. I couldn't respect him if he did. My hope was that the disappearance would prove to be a stunt. What better way to put the nix on a son's budding marriage to an undesirable party than this? Anger warmed me a little. It held back the fear that something ghastly had happened to my mother-in-law. How many bridges are there in the vicinity of London with dark, oily waters thrashing below? I abandoned my sensitive resolve not to intrude on Ben's need for solitude and grasped for his hand.

"I wish we could have reached your father on the phone to tell him we were coming."

Ben put an arm around me, and the gap between us closed a little. "He must have had the receiver off the hook all day."

"You do think he will stop this silly feud and talk to you in this crisis?"

"Ellie, you don't know my father."

True enough.

The train was making deeper rumblings. Doors at the far end of the compartment opened, channelling more cold, smoggy air our way. A white-haired woman dressed in black like an old-world nanny entered. She was followed by a man carrying a child—no, a woman. The woman's head lolled away from his shoulder and someone coming in behind them reached out and moved it back, so that the auburn hair spilled down the man's arm. The nanny was taking pillows out of a carrier bag and arranging them on the seat.

Ben tapped his watch, bringing my eyes back to his. One minute to go. We both looked out the window. A guard was passing at a trot, pushing a wheelchair down the platform—to the guard van, I supposed. My eyes slid back to the newcomers. The nanny and the invalid had taken the seats with their backs to us. The man was standing in the aisle. His was the face of a poet, the kind who writes about the pleasures of the grave. But he became of only incidental interest. The fourth member of the group now stood up. She was a small girl with sandy-coloured plaits—the girl to whom I had given my bouquet. Jenny Spender. She said something to the man and then caught my eye. I flushed, gave a small wave, and sank back into my seat.

"You know, Ellie"—Ben reached his arms above his head and stretched—"I am becoming increasingly confident that Mum is fine. What do you bet she's on a retreat at some convent, having a thumping good holiday?"

"I'm sure you're right, darling." Who were they—the invalid, the poet, the nanny? Where were they going? What was their relationship to Jenny?

The train began to vibrate. The guard was moving backward down the platform, a whistle pursed to his lips, when two women erupted through the barrier, coats flapping, arms stretched to Neanderthal length under the weight of their luggage.

One of them, an enormous person, cried: "Guard, hold that train!"

A door behind us banged open; the two women came blundering down the aisle and made ready to park opposite us. Both were talking full steam ahead and looked so hot and bothered I was hopeful they wouldn't notice our open window. The woman wearing the tartan coat and tam-o'-shanter looked vaguely familiar, but she glanced at Ben and me without saying anything. Presumably she was not one of our wedding guests. She was middle-aged with a pussycat sort of face, emphasised by uptilted glasses. Even her hair was tabby-coloured, and seen close up, she was a little whiskery. The guard slammed the door, the whistle shrilled, and we were off, rocking away into the misty night.

Ben inched the window up a notch and stretched again. "Yes, I am growing convinced that this is all a storm in a teacup. Beatty Long always had it in for Mum."

I eyed the two women and lowered my voice. "Why?"

Ben blew on his fingernails and rubbed them against the lapel of his jacket. "I was always a lot brighter than her kid, and—"

"Better looking too, no doubt."

"That goes without saying."

"But, Ben, it seems to me that the one being injured by this woman's wagging tongue is your father. Your mother isn't around to hear what is being said about her curtains."

"Mum's seventy years old. Why shouldn't she take a nap—a dozen naps, if she wishes?"

"Yes, of course she may, but a change in routine, Ben . . ." A wife senses when it is best to change the subject. "Was your mother friendly with Sid's mother when the Fowlers lived on Crown Street?"

"They were fairly matey until George Fowler ran off with another woman and Mum went to church twice a day for a week to pray for his return. Seems Mrs. F. didn't want him back."

An overnight bag rolled off the rack above the heads of the two women sitting opposite us. It might have hit one or both of them, but Ben lurched up and caught it.

"One of you ladies missing this?"

A warm glow flared inside me. He was so athletic, so suave, so mine. The large woman was rustling about in her bag; it was the tartan pussycat who spoke. "Thank you so much. I must not have put it up there properly. Rushing for a train always distresses me. As a rule, I try to allow plenty of time. But I had a funeral to attend this afternoon and one can't hurry away, can one?"

"Allow me." Ben replaced the overnight bag.

So that was why the woman looked familiar—she had been a mourner at the churchyard that morning. Her blackbird brooch looked familiar, too. Her friend was also wearing one on her coat. Either these brooches were the insignia of a bird-watching society or a hot item at the church bazaar. The woman in tartan took off her glasses and polished them. Her friend snapped her bag shut and leaned forward.

"The bride and groom, I presume. Giselle and Bentley Haskell, am I right? Splendid." She gave a great billowing laugh. She was altogether a billowing sort of woman. Her bloated face shook with chins and her bosom was an entire feather bed more than a bolster. I pressed a hand to my waist. Never again must I let the words clotted cream pass my lips.

"I am Amelia Bottomly and this is my friend Millie Parsnip."

"How do you do," Ben and I chorused politely.

Who did she put me in mind of, other than a hand mirror of what I might have become? Queen Anne, after she was stricken with dropsy! That was it! That towering pompadour of greying brown hair, the heavy garnet and amber rings biting into the puffy fingers, the suggestion of pomp and circumstance in her manner. Her face was presently lathered with smiles, but the set of her mouth gave her away. Let anyone displease Amelia Bottomly and she would cry, "Off with his head!"

I smiled at Millie Parsnip, crushed into folds against the window by her friend's bulk. "We crossed paths this afternoon in the churchyard."

"So we did! And I have been wanting to meet you. You see, I have this sofa I wish reupholstered, and I wonder, Mrs. Haskell, whether you think a gold brocade would go well with my oriental rugs?"

Amelia Bottomly boomed a laugh. "Don't be tiresome, Millie." She hefted round in her seat to face Ben and me. "I missed the funeral. I'm a widow myself, as is Millie here, both lost our husbands about three years ago, so naturally I'm sympathetic, but I had to visit a friend who's a patient at The Peerless Nursing Home. She's been having a bit of nerve trouble—the change, you know." She mouthed the last few words. "And it's not as though I am acquainted with Mrs. Thrush, the bereaved. So hard, isn't it, at times, to draw the line between concern and vulgar curiosity? Especially in a case, like this, of a fatal accident."

"Indeed," said Ben. He was doodling on his railway ticket.

"A motor accident?" Mine was vulgar curiosity; it helped take my mind off my missing mother-in-law.

"Why, Mrs. Haskell!" The chins shook with astonishment. "Didn't you read about poor Alvin Thrush in *The Daily Spokes-*

man? The story was right below 'Dear Felicity Friend.' The man was electrocuted in the bath. He was a do-it-yourself electrician and had wired, or miswired, a heated towel rail."

I had overheard one of the mourners say, "His death was a terrible shock." Edging closer to Ben, I silently vowed we would always hire professionals to replace light bulbs.

The train hurtled through Snaresby Station. Opening her large handbag, Amelia Bottomly pulled out a gold compact and began flouring her purplish nose. "How I *envy* you two young people that wonderful old house. You adore it, too, don't you, Millie?" In turning, she almost smothered the other woman.

A muffled, "Yes, indeed."

"Marvellous stories are told about the place and some of the characters who have lived there. Quite the equal of anything in Mr. Digby's books."

A familiar refrain. Ben was pretending to be asleep.

"I feel uncivic-minded admitting I've never read an Edwin Digby book," I said.

"You do know he writes under the name Mary Birdsong?" Amelia Bottomly dropped the compact back into her bag. "*The Vegetarian Vampire*. Marvellous! I won't give the whole thing away, but the premise is one can't get blood out of a turnip!" After a great burbling laugh, Mrs. Bottomly speared Ben with her eyes. "I understand we have another author in our midst! A cookery book, no less!"

Ben pretended to be deeply asleep.

Millicent Parsnip leaned forward as far as she was able, her soft, whiskery face eager. "Perhaps Mr. Haskell would enjoy doing a little cookery demonstration for the Hearthside Guild."

"Splendid idea! I am on that committee as well as a few others." Mrs. Bottomly straightened the blackbird brooch, then began ticking off on her fingers: "Secretary of Lighthouse Preservation, board member of Active Women Over Forty, chairperson of the Historical Society. Have I missed anything, Millie?"

"I thought you joined Bunty Wiseman's aerobics class."

"I did, but dropped out before I passed out." The chins compressed into a great ruff.

"Would you nice young people"—Mrs. Bottomly's eyes again shifted to Ben—"agree to the Historical Society doing a tour of your home? A *marvellous* fund-raiser, don't you agree, Millie? Viewing the dungeons would be worth the price of admission."

Ben opened his eyes as the train pummeled through another station to a blaze of white light. "Merlin's Court doesn't boast dungeons," he said.

"What do you mean?" No longer beaming, Mrs. Bottomly enunciated each word with surgical precision. "Surely Mad Merlin did not seal them up!"

"Amelia," bleated Mrs. Parsnip, "Mrs. Haskell was related to the late, lamented—"

"I'm not *blaming* her for that—"

We entered a tunnel, diving through its blackness with an anguished howl. I grabbed for Ben's hand and found it clammy with sweat. This was torture for him.

"I'm afraid of slugs," I confessed in a whisper.

All clear. The light was murky grey again, pinpricked by houselights and street lamps. Mrs. Bottomly heaved up from her seat.

"I fancy a couple of meat pies from the buffet. Coming, Millie? What about you, Mr. and Mrs. Haskell?"

"No, thank you," said Ben, which would make a yes from me sound piggish. And I was hoping to lose another half-pound before donning the pink nightie.

Millie Partridge smiled her nice smile, reminding me so much of Tobias. "Are you sure?"

Mrs. Bottomly interrupted, chins jostling each other in excitement. "Why, Millie, if that isn't Dr. Bordeaux! I would recognise that classic profile anywhere. At the far end of the carriage, yes, in the black cashmere coat. He's with the sandy-haired girl. She must be the daughter of the paralysed woman who lives in the Dower House on the nursing home grounds. Yes, I can see now—she's with them."

I kept my shoulders pressed against the back of my seat. I would not gawk . . . Dr. Bordeaux!

"People say such wicked things." Mrs. Bottomly swelled with intensity of feeling. "But the B.M.A. thought the charges ridiculous. Why shouldn't he specialise in rich people if that is his forte? What is so sinister about sick old women dying? And what, I ask you"—her baleful gaze forced me back into my seat—"is so suggestive about a mere half-dozen such women altering their wills in his favour, hours before their deaths? Devotion should be rewarded."

"And greedy friends and relations should get what is coming to them—nothing," supplied Millicent Parsnip.

She would be told about interrupting later. Mrs. Bottomly swept on.

"Oh, I have heard all the snide remarks—that he has saved more lives than he has taken. But The Peerless is thriving. The patients all get such *personalized* care! Only the one doctor—" She stopped suddenly. It was the train. Something was happening to the train. . . .

We had been hurtling toward Pebblewell Station, lights zooming toward us like Olympic torch bearers, when came this shuddering jolt. The walls gyrated; the carriage threatened to tear apart. Shrieks, moans from other passengers. My mind became a screen blazing with the words The End.

When I opened my eyes, everything had gone quiet. Ben's arms encircled me like a safety belt. Millicent Parsnip, tam-o'-shanter askew, lay across her seat tugging at her skirt to cover her splayed legs. Scared voices queried, "What happened?" Two middle-aged men in bowler hats clung to each other. Mrs. Bottomly was wedged in the aisle. Never was obesity more stalwart, more magnificent, more inspiring.

Ben said, "Ellie, are you all right?"

I nodded. There was a turmoil of people on the platform. The train wasn't moving. The passengers pressed toward the exits. A guard threw a door open, leaned in and yelled in a voice guaranteed to escalate alarm, "No need to panic! Everything under control!"

"What happened?"

"What's wrong?"

"Is it the I.R.A.?"

The guard leaped back onto the platform. "A man fell on the line but it's—"

His voice was cut off by one even more authoritative than Mrs. Bottomly's. "Let me out! I am a doctor!"

And as I watched, the man with the poet's face stepped down and swiftly followed the guard down the platform. I was glad the British Medical Association had been merciful. I hoped Dr. Bordeaux could do something for the poor man, whoever he was.

. . . "Let me guess!" Primrose pressed a finger to her pursed lips, and closed her eyes. "The nearly deceased man was Mr. Vernon Daffy, estate agent."

"Very impressive," I said, "although the story was plastered all over the front page of *The Daily Spokesman*—'Man Pitches Onto Railway Line,' 'Gallant Rescue by Unknown Woman as Train Hoves Into Sight.' "

Hyacinth's orange lips formed a smile. "Would it improve the credibility of Flowers Detection if I gave you the name of the unknown woman?"

"As I have no idea who she was—"

"Oh, but my dear, I think you have." Primrose stirred a spoonful of sugar into my coffee. "According to eyewitness reports, Mr. Daffy was standing close to the edge of the platform when he screamed, 'mouse,' and pitched forward. Everyone froze except the woman—middle-aged, woolly-haired, and plainly dressed—who had been standing nearest him. She performed the rescue and disappeared in the general hullabaloo. Her courage was applauded by the press and public—but what *we* know is that she had lost her nerve at the final moment."

"Mouse," I said slowly, "as in 'three wild mice?' "

"Correct, my dear Ellie." Primrose beamed. "Therefore, the woman in question is indubitably Mrs. Beatrix Woolpack, in whose car you and Ben took shelter on your wedding day. She was instructed to acquire the mice, and being a conscientious soul, she jotted them on her shopping list. 'Three' because one or two might go in the wrong direction and not scare Mr. Daffy, who was mouse phobic, out of his wits, and 'wild' because white laboratory mice might raise questions." She sighed disparagingly. "Such a wanton disregard for animal life."

Hyacinth's hooded black eyes gleamed in the rosy light. "Mrs. Woolpack must have received a raking over the coals by the president and her associates on the board . . . if nothing worse. The Founder had to be very displeased. An exquisitely coordinated plan wasted. Note that Mr. Daffy did not catch the train at Chitterton Station where both he and Mrs. Woolpack would more likely be recognised. No, someone persuaded him to catch the train at Pebblewell—one of the wedding guests perhaps who happened to be driving to Pebblewell that evening and would be happy to save Mrs. Daffy a trip."

I touched my wedding ring. "Mrs. Daffy was so warm and friendly. She liked cats. And she spoke fondly of her husband, who called her Froggy."

Primrose shook her head. "My dear, she called him Squeaky, which surely is every bit as vicious as his calling her Froggy. Mr. Daffy had been engaged in an illicit affair for weeks. We have it on good authority that he had asked for a divorce."

I forced my mind away from Mrs. Daffy's amiable visage . . . and custom-made murder. "What do you make of Dr. Bordeaux and his entourage being on the train and his rushing to offer assistance to the victim?"

"An aborted alibi turned to excellent account," declared Hyacinth.

"What I wonder," Primrose interrupted, "is whether Mr. Daffy's wig dislodged when he fell off the platform? How very embarrassing that would have been. It brings back memories of that terrible time the elastic in our Aunt Ada's unmentionables gave way and—"

"Wig?" I stared at both sisters.

"My dear Mrs. Haskell," said Hyacinth. "I was so certain you had guessed when you made mention of"—she resorted to the notebook—'his oversized mop of black curls.' But enough of the Daffys. Let us wend our way with you to North Tottenham and the meeting with Mr. Elijah Haskell." . . .

We gave up on the bell. Ben rapped on the door of Haskell's Fruit & Veg., at first tentatively, then loud enough to set the Closed sign rapping back. Nose pressed against the pane, I beheld a fuzziness similar to a telly on the blink. The contents of the room, counters, and vegetable bins, were visible in the glow from a low-wattage bulb. Ben shoved his fingers through his hair and rapped again.

"He must be asleep." Stepping around our luggage, I peered up at the narrow rectangle of window on the second floor. The curtains were drawn shut.

"Dad's a light sleeper." Ben stared up and down the street, reabsorbing the feel of the place. Again I felt excluded by his past. It wasn't exactly raining, but the night had a cold sweat about it. The houses on Crown Street were terraced and of sooty, buff-coloured brick. Their front doors opened directly onto the narrow pavement. Lights burned in many of the windows.

A bus skimmed down the road. A man, hands in his pockets, head down, walked past opposite us; a boy of about seven airplaned along behind him, making zoom-zoom noises.

Ben stopped rapping.

"Do you hear your father?"

He shook his head. "That bloke across the street—I went to school with him. Tom somebody. Doesn't look like life's treating him too well."

"What makes you say that? The little boy seems to be his and they're well-dressed."

"His walk." Ben squinted in concentration. "It's depressed. Haven't you ever noticed, Ellie, how people often reveal more about their state of mind by their walk than their faces?"

I hadn't thought about it, and I wasn't sure I agreed. The widow going up the church steps had looked jaunty from the rear. I made noncommittal noises. A good wife does not set herself against her husband on every occasion. I wondered whether we should break into Haskell's Fruit & Veg. or knock on a nearby door and ask to use the phone. I pushed our luggage closer to the wall with my foot, then heard a sound that inspired hope—clanking beer bottles. "Ben, does your father frequent the local pub?"

Ben peered into the deepening gloom. About a dozen houses down, a humanoid shadow was emerging from the shadows. "No, but I am an expert on more things than human locomotion. Approaching beer bottles are to me what fingerprints are to Scotland Yard." The bottle noises were now accompanied by the *tat tat* of high heels on pavement. "These tell me that Mrs. Merryfeather is upon us. Damn! She is the biggest gossip since speech was invented."

"I thought that was Mrs. Long, the woman who informed the police that your mother was missing?"

"It's a tie. Sorry, Ellie"—Ben grabbed hold of me—"I have to do this."

Snogging on a street corner was every bit the vulgar thrill Aunt Astrid had led me to expect. There was only one niggle on the periphery of my delight: Was Ben scared that Mrs. Merrywhoever might dredge up stories about his youthful love life?

The bottle medley slowed to a jingle, the heels stopped tapping, and a high-pitched shriek pierced the air.

"Don't tell me, 'cos I won't believe it! Little Benny Haskell all grown up! And what's this?" The voice dropped to gravelly coyness. "Got yourself a nice girl, have you?"

Ben and I fell apart. He straightened his tie. "Mrs. Merryfeather, this is my wife, Ellie."

"Married, never!" The twin bags, full of beer bottles, trembled. "My Stella will kill 'erself when she 'ears Benny 'Askell is taken."

Mrs. Merryfeather turned to me, a headscarf tied package-fashion around her head and a froth of blond curls bunched at her forehead. Her apron bib protruded through the V-neck of her coat. "Oops! Me an' my big mouth. Cracking jokes at a time like this! I said to Stell, somebody's nipper will be netting for tiddlers under a perishing bridge, and he'll fish out Mrs. 'Askell instead."

Fumes were coming out of Ben's nose. "My mother is not missing. She knows precisely where she is."

"Right you are, love! Keep on 'oping until the very last." Mrs. Merryfeather poked Ben with her elbow, the bags lurching against her hip with a heavy *thwam*. "And in future don't be such a stranger. The place in't the same since you and Cassanover Sid did a bunk. I used to say to Stell, 'Them lads can pick their women like fruit off a tree.' " She looked me up and down, deciding no doubt that I didn't come up to Stella. " 'Ow do you like Crown Street?"

"Very nice."

"Well, it's 'ome, in't it, Benny? Course my Fred an' me always wanted a place at Southend. And, six months gone, whole street thought it was gonna be out on its lug'ole. Up to the armpits we was in talk that old man Patterson"—she nodded the blond curls at me—"the landlord he is, was ready to sell out and this was all gonna be an arcade, with all sorts of fancy shops. But it didn't come to nothing. Never thought it would! Them what got up the petition said it done the trick, but I says to Stell, someone be'ind the scenes 'as put a cog in Mr. Patterson's wheel."

Ben was leaning up against the shop window, a look of boredom hovering around his lips.

Mrs. Merryfeather wriggled her shoulders, setting the beer bottles off again. "Serve 'im right. Always seems 'is sort flourishes like dust under the bed." She prissied up her lips. "We now 'ave to post the rent to some fancy address office. The dimwitted son don't come round collecting door-to-door no more. Remember 'im, Benny? Always pretending to be 'Umphrey Bogard or the like."

Ben moved away from the wall, his eyes bright in the lamplight. "I remember he stole an apple from the shop once and I gave him a nosebleed, but we mustn't keep you, Mrs. Merryfeather, your beer will go flat."

"Aren't you a caution! But I know you want to get inside and start cheering up your dad—not that he in't getting plenty of that already."

"What's that supposed to mean?" Ben's brows came down like iron bars, but Mrs. Merryfeather, with a coy giggle, was already clanking away.

Ben began idly punching the bell. "What was she implying?"

"I don't know." I nudged a suitcase with my foot. "But I do know you are wonderfully loyal to your father, who you say won't speak to you even if we do get to see him."

"He's a man of his word. I have to admire that."

Nothing in the Bible says a woman has to understand her

husband. A light flared with sudden and dazzling brilliance against the glass door of the shop. Someone was crossing the floor to open up. I was instantly very uneasy.

A key turned, bolts were thrust back, the shop door swung inward and a deep voice spoke graciously but remotely. "Who comes here at this time of night?"

This man looked nothing like the father-in-law of my imagination. I had pictured Mr. Haskell as short and stocky, certainly elderly, and prone to woolly dressing gowns. This man had to be at least six-foot-four, was broadly built, of similar age to Ben, and wore a flowing purple caftan. He was also indisputably black.

Had we come to the wrong address? Had Ben's parents sold Haskell's Fruit & Veg. and his mother not mentioned doing so in her letter?

Ben's eyes flashed with something I couldn't read. "Paris, what the hell are you doing here? I thought you were off treading the boards of some Shakespearian theatre."

"Ben—and your wife—how splendid!" The man stepped backward to let us enter. He was holding a book. "I work for your father. If you remember, it was my parents who dreamt that I would play Othello." He closed and locked the door. "I tell them that one day my name will be above a door, but not in lights. All I ever desired was to own a shop like this." His smile gave a glimpse of perfect teeth. "One day."

"Do your parents still live on the street?" Ben picked an orange out of a bin and tossed it in the air.

"They moved to Reading. I have the back bedroom here." The purple caftan swished. I had worn one once, but had not looked so magnificent.

"I hope you were not waiting long at the door. Eli and I were wearing earphones and listening to music. Mrs. Haskell has been a little edgy lately and the wireless bothered her."

The air was sweet and earthy. A hook of bananas moved above our heads. Paris tucked the book under his arm. "Forgive the inquiry, but is this a visit of reconciliation or have the rumours concerning your mother's disappearance reached you?"

Ben tossed his orange in the bin. He explained about Constable Beaker. "Is my father still listening to his earphones?"

"He was in the bathroom when I came down. He and I have both become rather fond of medieval love ballads. Shall we go up? Mrs. Haskell, I will make you some tea."

Such a voice—a sun-drenched sea of a voice, in which to drift forever. A gift, surely, from the gods. And those black eyes! In their depths I caught a glimpse of lost civilisations. The purple silk did not so much rustle as breathe softly. I adjusted the belt of my detestably dowdy coat and fingered a strand of loose hair. "Tea would be lovely, and please call me Ellie."

"Willingly." The perfectly chiseled lips lifted in a smile, highlighting his marvellous bone structure. A silken arm gestured toward the staircase in the corner. "Ben, please lead the way."

The stairs were sharply perpendicular, carpeted in a chrysanthemum yellow and burnt orange floral design. The treads were pinned down by gleaming brass rods.

A mezuzah was attached to the door jamb of the entrance facing us across a small, dark landing. My arm brushed a holy water font. Talk about hedging all bets! The room we entered was heated to intense stuffiness by a fake-log electric fire. While Paris went to find Mr. Haskell, Ben moved around, touching things. An enormous maroon sofa and chairs were positioned on a carpet of similar pattern to that on the stairs. The curtains at the wide window were mustard yellow with a green leaf design. Strung from the ceiling in front of them was a row of hollowed-out hen's eggs, each painted a primary colour and sprouting spikes of vegetation.

I dropped my coat on the sofa and studied the rainbow galaxy. "What interesting planters."

Ben lifted up my coat, hung it on a stand, and came back to plump up the cushion. "Dad's handiwork. The crocheting and tapestry work was all done by Mum. See those pictures over the fireplace? The one of the old rabbi won a blue ribbon at some church show."

"He looks like St. Francis of Assisi."

Mr. Haskell was clearly taking some persuading to see us. I sat down, then stood up, straightening the crocheted doily on the back of the chair. There were crocheted doilies on tables and cabinets, crocheted cushions on overstuffed chairs. I did covet one thing in the room—Ben's photo on the sideboard. He was about seven years old, in school cap and wrinkled socks, looking adorably cross.

"What do you think of the furniture, Ellie?"

"Very . . . solid."

"Dad made every piece, can you believe that? The man never took carpentry class."

"My word!" I looked admiringly at the sideboard, with its Victorian body and Queen Anne legs.

Ben was adjusting a bowl of plastic fruit when the door opened. My immediate impression of my father-in-law was that he was the spitting image of Father Christmas. He was stocky and wore a red cardigan. He had a beard and hair (minus bald spot) so white and downy it might have been made of brushed nylon. His dark eyes never moved from Ben as the door closed behind him.

"Hello, Dad," said my husband.

The silence became as stifling as the heat. I walked around the sofa, hand outstretched.

"Allow me to introduce myself. I am your new daughter-in-law, Ellie. Ben and I took the first train here after a policeman stopped by during our wedding reception to alert us to the fact that your wife—"

"Humph." Mr. Haskell stroked his white beard, then begrudgingly took my hand. "Better than I expected. You don't look rich."

I took my hand back. "And you don't look like a man who would quarrel with his only son and vow never to speak to him again, all because he wrote a . . . flagrante novel—which never got into print."

"It would have"—the dark eyes burned into Ben—"if he'd let me help him write the tricky parts. But he's stubborn—he was always that way. In the end I washed my hands of the book and him!"

Another silence. The two men assessed each other. I slumped down on the sofa. "What about charity and forgiveness?"

My father-in-law patted his bald spot. "What sort of a man would I be if I raised my son to be a man of his word and then broke mine to him?"

I must rethink having children. I had assumed that Ben's genes would water down any eccentricities I might pass along.

Ben leaned over the back of the sofa. "Ellie, ask Dad about Mum."

I felt like a ventriloquist's dummy. "What about Mum . . . um . . . Mrs. Has—"

"Call me Poppa."

Paris appeared with a loaded tray. Cups and saucers circulated, along with a platter of egg sandwiches. I took one and nibbled around the edges. Pretending to eat avoids a lot of outside pressure. Paris picked up his book and was about to leave again, but Mr. Haskell insisted he stay.

"You're one of the family." He turned to me. "Paris is very devout. We read the Torah together."

Ben put down his cup as though it contained poison.

Poppa leaned back in his chair and spread his hands expansively. "We're a devout family. When Maggie was three years old, she wanted to be a nun; when she married me, she still wanted to be a nun. When we would argue, which sometimes happened in forty years of marriage, I would tell her to make up for lost time and get thee to a nunnery."

I looked at Ben. If he ever spoke to me like that . . . but of course he never would.

"And this time"—Mr. Haskell emitted a sigh which sounded horrendously cheerful to me—"this time, for once in her life, the woman listens to her husband."

The only sound in the room was the whispering of the purple caftan until Ben pounced out of his chair. First he opened his mouth, then he closed it, then jerked round to me. "Ask my father what he means."

A more experienced wife might have taken the situation in stride. I stared, mute.

It was Paris who answered, imbuing his words with a grandeur worthy of the Old Vic.

"The sad truth, Ben, is that your parents have parted."

My husband staggered and I helped him to a chair. "You mean *separated*? At my age I find myself the child of a broken home?"

"Was it anything we did?" I stood twisting my hands like Miss Thorn. "Did the wedding feature somewhere in this catastrophe?"

Poppa chuckled. "You young people always have such a big sense of your own importance." He rose from his chair, smoothed out the bald spot, and spread his hands. "The reality is poor Maggie suspected me of having a romantic flutter with a Mrs. Jarrod, a nice widow lady who makes the best pickled herring in the world."

"Mum thought you were having an affair?" Ben visibly relaxed. "Why the devil didn't you tell her she was making something out of nothing; that at seventy years of age you are past making a fool of yourself, in some areas?"

His father stood in front of the fireplace looking like he had come down the chimney.

Paris bent to remove my cup as I said, "I'm sure the personal touch is very important in your business. Did Magdalene perhaps misinterpret? . . ." I left the question hanging open.

Poppa, brown eyes gleaming, closed it. "That, dear daughter-in-law, is *my* business."

From the Files of
The Widows Club

1st December, Commencing 7 P.M.

Vice President:

Kindly be seated, Mrs. Woolpack.

Beatrix Woolpack:

Oh, surely, must we be so formal? Please call me Beatrix!

Vice President:

Christian names are not permitted at emergency sessions, summoned only at moments of gravest crises. Our president being out of town, I, in accordance with Article Six, Section C, of the Bylaws, will preside. All board members are present, saving Mrs. Shrimpton, who is indisposed. Mrs. Howard, kindly pass Mrs. Woolpack that box of tissues so she may proceed to answer the charges that she willfully rescued a Subject To Be Retired. Tonight being the final episode of the BBC's serialization of *Pride and Prejudice,* I'm sure we all wish to facilitate matters.

B.W.:

(Gulping sobs.) I will try to get a grip on myself, but I am so utterly devastated! So ashamed! Please believe me, Mrs. Howard and all my dear, good friends, I meant to do everything perfectly. I purchased the mice, as instructed, from the source

in Bainsworth. I released them at precisely the right moment, using a magazine for camouflage. The train was coming. The S.T.B.R. was standing right at the edge of the platform—exactly as his personality profile suggested he would. . . . Excuse me, may I have a cigarette? Thank you so much. . . . When I released the mice, I felt productive, fulfilled. The S.T.B.R. screamed, clutched at his trouser legs, and pitched forward. (*More sobs*.)

Vice President:

As you say, Mrs. Woolpack, a job well done—until you forgot duty, loyalty, and sisterhood and snatched him off the line.

(Rumblings from the Board.)

B.W.:

I don't know what came over me! The noise from the train filled up my whole head, and those lights—charging! I was hypnotised. I couldn't think of anything, see anything . . . except the butcher's scraps I had fed my cat at breakfast, all bloody like Mr. Daffy would be . . .

(Fist pounding on the table.)

Vice President:

You were instructed never to put a name to the S.T.B.R.

B.W.:

I know, but—

Vice President:

Consider, if you will, Mrs. Woolpack, how you would have felt if the person charged with the office of dispatching your husband had been overcome with such sentimentality.

B.W.:

(Weeping.) I know, I know. What can I say, Mrs. Howard? I was abominably selfish.

(More rumblings.)

Vice President:

You volunteered for this assignment.

B.W.:

Indeed I did. But it was stressed to me during my briefing that murder is not an exact science. I was told there was only a fifty-fifty chance that I would succeed. Don't think I am excusing myself, but I do ask for a little understanding.

(Prolonged silence.)

Vice President:

Mrs. Woolpack, had the operation gone awry through no

fault of yours or had you unwittingly bungled, you would have met with profound sympathy. As it is, the Board and I will bear in mind the excellent job you did in Correspondence. However, I feel it my duty to advise you before we convene, Mrs. Woolpack, that to err is human, to rescue is unforgivable. All rise.

9

. . . Primrose's blue eyes misted. "Ben must have been seriously alarmed about his mother's state of mind."

"He was upset for her, but he didn't believe she would jump off a bridge, if that's what you are thinking. For one thing, her religion frowns on such behaviour. For another, Ben was certain she wouldn't want to make things easy for Mrs. Jarrod."

"Ben didn't think his father was showing off, in regard to Mrs. Jarrod?" Hyacinth's earrings hung motionless.

"Upon calming down, that's exactly what he did believe—a wink or two and an extra orange slipped into the woman's bag, that sort of thing. I didn't know what to think. Poppa looked so smug. Quite like Tobias when he knows we know he has been in the pantry. When we mentioned Constable Beaker, Poppa said he was glad the police had time on their hands. He told us that his wife had dragged her suitcase out from under the bed on the morning of the twenty-seventh November and announced she was leaving to take up a life of prayer and abstinence. I kept picturing her trudging some lonely road clad in sackcloth, but Paris relieved my mind on that score. He said my mother-in-law had telephoned the afternoon of her departure and told him she had found a safe harbour at the seaside. Ben spent the rest of our visit to the flat saying that a change of scene would do his mother the world of good and that he was certain she would soon come to her senses and return home, to the embarrassment of the gossips."

Primrose clasped her papery hands. "Paris! I do hope he was named for the Trojan. So romantic, that whole story! Aphrodite and the apple, the incomparable Helen: the face that launched a thousand ships. Foolish of me, but as a young girl I used to think I would be quite satisfied if I could launch a couple of rowing boats."

I know the feeling. I suppose every woman does on her honeymoon. . . .

The Hostelry was known the length and breadth of England for its home-away-from-home atmosphere. So said the liveried porter as he carried our luggage into the bridal suite. But looking around at the cream and gilt splendour, I could believe Ben and I were guests in someone's home—a someone who did not know we were here and would have been hopping mad if he knew we were treading down the pile of his champagne carpet, fingering his filigreed light switch plates and fogging his rococo mirrors. The marble fireplace reminded me of monuments in St. Anselm's churchyard. Drawing a silk handkerchief from his gold-braided pocket, the porter flicked a single speck of dust from a carved rose on the headboard of the exquisitely fragile Louis XIV bed.

"Slept in by the Empress Josephine."

"I trust the sheets have been changed since her visit." I had to say something, anything, to draw attention from the fact that Ben had rested a hand on the garlanded footrail while probing in his pocket for change.

The instant we were alone, I buffed away his fingerprints and examined the petit point rug in front of the fireplace. Ah ha! A footprint. Breathlessly, I ordered Ben to remove his shoes.

"And my socks and my . . ." My beloved's voice was hushed and raspy. This Versailles away from Versailles atmosphere was getting to him too. He kicked off his shoes without untying the laces (I would have to break him of that habit) and pulled me into his arms. When I could break away from his kiss, I had to repeat three times that we should unpack and go downstairs to the restaurant. Ben had to be starving.

"Ravenous." He was unbuttoning my jacket. "We'll have something sent up later. Maybe breakfast . . . tomorrow evening. We can unpack some other time." He was sliding my jacket off my shoulders, a look of intense concentration on his face. Was he thinking about his mother? Pondering Mrs. Jarrod's true role?

"My nightdress!" I closed my eyes; even as I responded to his renewed kisses I regretted not finishing that last chapter of *Everything Your Mother Did Not Tell You (Because She Did Not Know) About Married Bliss*. I had not planned on being nervous, but this had been an unsettling day, and I wasn't sure I could live up to this room.

"It's a gorgeous nightdress. Pearl pink, one of a kind. Made from the gossamer wings of one thousand and one Arabian fireflies." I trailed a finger under his chin. That sublimely masculine chin, betraying, as with dark, impassioned lovers everywhere, a hint of evening shadow. I could feel a pulse beating in his neck.

"I am sure it is the most beautiful nightdress in the world," breathed Ben. "But it might be a bit hot this time of year."

I backed away from him. "You must see it. And perhaps make a decision over a glass of champagne . . . a red wine would clash with the room." I was rummaging through my suitcase with increasing fervour. "I can't believe it! I must have forgotten to pack the wretched thing!"

"What a bitter blow!" Ben's arms came round me and he consoled me with kisses. My pulse quickened; I would have been transported on a tidal wave of ecstasy but for one thing. The bed. My experience as a decorator advised me that this one was purely for show, a place to display one's collection of drawn-threadwork pillows and china dolls. One wasn't supposed to sleep on such beds, let alone cohabit. But Ben was lifting me up, carrying me toward it, laying me down upon the silken counterpane.

Here it was at last—the golden moment. The drum roll I heard was my heart. The bedframe creaked, merely because I turned my head on the mignonette-scented pillow. But I could not entirely blame the bed for my Victorian flutters. I loved Ben. I had wanted him desperately for months, but had insisted we wait; I had not wanted our first encounter to be an afternoon tea party or a late night snack. Or had I been plain scared? Would Ben be disappointed? Would he find the dishabille me about as exciting as roast lamb without red currant jelly? I began taking the pins out of my hair. A pity I had had it cut recently; those extra inches would have provided extra coverage. Ben was peeling away my blouse and I focused on a new fear. Would he start humming? Our family M.D., Dr. McTweedy, had always hummed while checking me over.

"Ellie," he said gently.

"Yes?"

"This has been a long day. If you would rather . . ."

Anguished, I stared up into his blue-green eyes. He was having second thoughts. My heart slowed. Resolutely I wound my arms around his neck. Sometimes a wife has to fight for her marriage. My hands moved up into his thick black hair. I would make him forget his squabbling parents, his unsold cookery book, the responsibilities inherent in opening a five-star restaurant. I would be the strong one, the one who would transport us both to that transcendent star-studded sphere previously glimpsed only in the final pages of paperback romance.

My wedding night was delightful. But as I drew the counterpane over Ben's ears to keep him snug during the hours till morning, I was attacked by an infinitesimal doubt. Perhaps I hadn't done everything perfectly. Wasn't I supposed to have heard a symphony of scraping violins and experienced a sense of floating out of my body into a burst of golden light?

"Ben?" I touched his shoulder. "Were you carried away to another planet?"

"Wild horses couldn't have dragged me away from right here." He gathered up my hair, twined it round, laid it over my shoulder, and was asleep.

Light was beginning to creep through the window. If I didn't at least doze, I would be a walking corpse in the morning. An unfortunate turn of thought. Again I saw the widow on the church steps. Jenny was holding my bouquet, and then I was on the train. There was the infamous Dr. Bordeaux, Jenny again, and those two women—the nanny and the invalid. Who were they in relation to Jenny? My eyes . . . so heavy and Ben so warm and close . . . but somehow I was in the hall at Merlin's Court, and Mr. Daffy was trying to sell me my own house. His voice kept getting louder and I tried to shush him because my husband was sleeping.

Too late! Ben bolted up in bed and shouted, "Gladys!"

When I touched him, I found he was trembling. So was I. Gladys who?

"Ellie, I had the most ghastly dream about Miss Thorn—we were in this tunnel and I couldn't escape."

"*That* Gladys—"

"When we were talking to her, I thought she had funny eyes. The kind that peel your skin off." He sat up, trapping my hair under his hand.

"Ouch!" I clutched at the headboard. Ben rolled sideways and there it came—an ominous groaning. One brief second later, and the bed collapsed in a crash, sending the chandelier into a crystalline spin. Swearing and laughing, we struggled to crawl free from the tangle of sheets and blankets. He might have asked if I were injured, but happily only my eyes smarted—from the sunlight streaming through the open windows. And my pride. We must immediately don false moustaches and do a flit down the fire escape. Alas, immediately was not soon enough. The door was thrown open and the manager swooped into the room. Behind him stood a half-dozen smirking chambermaids.

Happy Ever After was off to a poor start, but I was still a believer!

Looking like an Indian without feathers, I faced Monsieur Manager and threatened suit. He countered with an offer of a complimentary breakfast.

"Sounds pretty decent, don't you think, Ellie?" said Ben.

I did not. The dining room would be standing room only, with people come to gawk at us. Had Ben ever been overweight, he would have been more sensitive to collapsing furniture.

"Darling," he whispered, "this is the bridal suite; the other guests will be green with envy."

Nine o'clock saw us prominently displayed between two Grecian pillars under the diamanté sparkle of the dining room chandelier. Hide as I might behind my napkin, I knew that everyone was staring at us. Far from keeping a low profile, Ben ordered in French off an English menu. The waiter, a man with black patent leather hair, vanished through the archway to fetch porridge for Ben and a boiled egg for me.

Leaning back in his chair, Ben tapped a spoon on the table.

"Ellie, sweetheart, did you have to make such a big deal about wanting a small egg? I thought you were going to ask the poor man to weigh it."

I came out from my napkin. "To me it is a big deal. A calorie saved—"

"Darling, are you becoming a little fanatical? You're forever poring over colour pages in magazines, planning what not to eat for lunch and dinner."

"That's a gross exaggeration." I smiled serenely for the benefit of the gawkers. "But I do have to keep one step ahead of the enemy."

"How? By getting down to zero calories a day?"

"Detachment. I don't look at what I am eating. I don't think about it. Aromas still give me some problems, but I am working on that area. Aren't you proud of me, darling?"

His smile looked a bit frayed. "Of course, but a man *does* hope his wife will share an interest in his work. Food is more than my work, it's my life"—he caught my eye—"my life's work. And Ellie, on the subject of Abigail's, with all the renovations required to the building, I don't believe we will be able to open before May. But that will be as well. It gives you plenty of time for the decorative end, selecting furniture, wall coverings, whatever. I'll arrange the building contracts and deal with the crews. You know how it is; men respond better to taking orders from a man."

I was about to ask if this meant he wasn't going to give Mandy & Mindy Plumbers a chance to bid, but remembered those wise words in chapter four of *Remaking Your Man*: "The male is like iron, hard to bend unless you have him properly hotted up." Ben went on talking about Abigail's opening, how we would have to have a bang-up celebration on the evening before the restaurant opened for its first meals. A premiere of sorts, starring some of Ben's most famous miniature morsels with a central fountain of champagne.

The waiter appeared at my side. Blast! This egg had to be at least five and a half inches around the fattest part of the circumference.

Ben studied the bowl placed before him. "This porridge looks unpleasantly damp."

"I believe, sir, that is a feature of porridge," the waiter replied.

Ben raised his spoon and sniffed the contents like a wine

cork. "Is it also a feature of porridge to be thickened with spray starch?"

"Perhaps, sir, you wish to accompany me to the kitchen where you may advise our chef, newly lured from Windsor Castle, on how to prepare *le porridge.*"

I sank in my chair. People were coiled around the marble pillars, hands cupped to their ears. Ben would laugh, of course; he would explain to the waiter that he had been joking. Wrong! Instead, he patted my hand, spouted off something about professional integrity, said he would only be a minute and followed the waiter through a pair of swinging doors. I was left twisting my napkin into a rope and smiling with false conviviality at my egg. Was this what the books meant about The Morning After?

I forgave him because wives do. I had believed that marriage was like baptism. Sin was shed during the ceremony. Ben the fiancé had been wonderful; Ben the husband would be a paragon. No more reading during meals, no more monologues on the quiche objective. No more laughing in the wrong place at my jokes. As I waited for him to come back to me, I readjusted my thinking. Some faults would remain, but I would begin to appreciate them. I hitched up my smile and stirred my coffee one time, two times . . . sixty-seven, sixty-eight times . . .

Because his parents' situation was still up in the air, when Ben rejoined me, we decided to return that day to Merlin's Court. And really I didn't mind. I felt the house was missing us, wanting us back. Dorcas and Jonas probably already had the kettle on. But first things first. We left our luggage in the Hostelry lobby and took a bus to Tottenham. As we jostled off the bus behind a girl in rickety high heels—a cigarette dangling from one hand, a pushchair and toddler from the other—some of yesterday's unease concerning my mother-in-law returned.

To be seventy years old and have one's marriage fall apart, what could be worse than that? Even widowhood might be preferable. This woman had brought Ben into the world. She had bathed him when he was little, hitched up his short trousers, and she most assuredly would never have smacked his thumb out of his mouth as the girl was doing while she jerked the pushchair out into the street. In twisting round to glare at her, I missed my footing and my shoe flew off. Ben caught it and, like Prince Charming, bent to put it on for me, but found the heel had twisted off. While he set to fixing it, I stood like a flamingo as men and women scuttled past us, their heads bent against the snappish wind, pinpricked by rain.

"Almost got it." Ben was tapping the heel down with its mate from the other shoe.

Stepping out of the way of oncoming pedestrians, I noticed a man leaning against the sooty brick wall of Haskell's Fruit & Veg. He was thirtyish, had no neck, long hair, and a pimply face. He wore an upturned raincoat and was picking his teeth with his little finger. The nasty part was that his eyes were drilling into me. Even nastier, I thought I recognised him. If he wasn't the man who had stood on the platform as we waited for the train to leave Chitterton Station yesterday, then he was his double. I was about to say something to Ben but as he handed me my shoe, a woman collided with us.

"Ever so sorry, loves." She was tall and had that sticky, rust-coloured hair which looks as though it hasn't been properly rinsed after a tint. She wore skintight jeans, a baby-pink sweater outlining twin pyramid bosoms, and she positively rattled with gold chains. The Pyrex dish she carried did not go with the rest of her, and she was staring at us with a blend of calculation and discomfort that seemed disproportionate to the collision.

"Why, Mrs. Jarrod!" Ben bared his white teeth and bit out the words. "Making sure Dad doesn't skip any meals, I see."

The Raincoat Man had disappeared.

10

. . . "A tall woman, you say." Hyacinth laid down the green notebook. "Brash but good-natured, I would imagine. The sort who offers to clean your windows along with hers and thrusts half an apple pie at you whether you want it or not."

"Very pushy," I agreed. "She shoved a handful of pounds sterling at me and said to buy something pretty as a wedding present—a china poodle for the front window. Ben was livid."

"Speaking of unattractive objects," said Hyacinth, "did you mention the man in the raincoat to Bentley or his father?"

"No. He looked so much a cross between a gangster and a seedy private eye I did wonder if he might be a plainclothes detective. But I talked myself out of that idea. It was too unsettling. I persuaded myself that the man at Chitterton Station and the one outside the shop could not be one and the same. . . .

We caught the early afternoon train home. Chugging along I sported a stiff upper lip, in conjunction with the stiff neck I was developing from the open window. As Ben slept, I contemplated the way the wind tousled his black hair. I thought about my missing mother-in-law and how brave Poppa had been that morning. I thought a little about Mr. Vernon Daffy and his narrow escape from certain death. But mostly I thought of home, waiting for my love and me—Merlin's Court—safe, sane, unchanging.

I sat at the scrubbed wood kitchen table, Tobias on my lap, a smile stapled to my cheeks. The wheat-sheaf patterned wall-paper with its border of wild flowers blurred. The quarry tile turned chill beneath my feet. For Dorcas and Jonas had greeted Ben and me with the news that they were leaving Merlin's Court. I was to be deserted. Had I been an old reprobate, I would have cut them both out of my will.

"Chicago, you say!"

"Knew you'd be pleased as punch." Dorcas clapped me on the back.

Jonas stuck his thumbs under his braces and released them with a snap. "You'll miss us. But t'is only temporary. Doesn't do to get into a rut at my time of life."

Absolutely! Especially when one hasn't left Chitterton Fells in fifty years!

It seemed that the morning's post had brought Dorcas a most gratifying invitation. Her participation was requested in the development of a field hockey institute in Chicago.

Jonas punctuated his pronouncement that he could not allow a frail woman to pioneer alone with gravelly snatches of ". . . My kind of town, Chicago is . . ." What a world this was. First Ben's mother and now Jonas wanting to fly the nest.

Tobias struggled off my lap without a backward glance to paw at Dorcas's argyle socks, hoping, doubtless, for future overseas parcels. Picking him up, she wrapped him around her shoulders like a fox fur and paced the room talking about our nasty experience on the train. "Frightful for you—and Mr. Daffy. Course to my mind, anyone who's afraid of a little mouse shouldn't wear long trousers. According to *The Daily Spokesman*, the woman who saved him should receive a medal—if they knew who she was."

I started rearranging the pots of herbs in the bay window. "Accidents can strike at any time. That man Thrush electrocuted himself. And what about the dentist, the one on Kipling Street, whose drill went berserk when he was giving himself a filling?" I moved the pots to the sink, turned on the tap, and squeezed in Fairy Liquid. "Both of you must promise to be very careful crossing streets and find a flat with a doorman."

"Apartment." Jonas was practicing lassoing with a piece of string.

"And do we have your promise you won't go to wild parties"—Ben folded his arms—"or drink the water?"

This was no time to be frivolous. We must make lists, air suitcases, buy traveller's cheques. "When do you leave?" I asked crisply.

"In a fortnight," replied the deserters.

"Before Christmas! The drawing room will look naked with only two stockings hanging from the mantel."

Dorcas was still wearing Tobias. She tossed his tail over her shoulder. "Mistletoe's wasted on the likes of us, right, Jonas?"

"Yup."

I saw Ben grin and noticed something else. Dorcas and Jonas had not once looked directly at each other during this entire conversation. Guilt, that was their burden.

Ben looked in the sink, draped an arm around my shoulder, and stage-whispered, "Alone at last!"

The clock ticked into silence. Then, amazingly, the hall door slammed open. "Alone? You aren't alone—you have *me*!"

My eyes did not deceive me. This ghastly, unkempt apparition standing before us was my cousin Freddy. Tobias leapt away from Dorcas and skirted the intruder, hissing. My sentiments exactly. "I knew we would come home to leftover food, but not to leftover guest."

Ben was shaking hands, all man to man with him. "Ellie, dear, I know you're joking, but old Freddy may take you seriously."

"I *am* serious, darling. The last time this creature came for a weekend, the weekend lasted three months."

Dorcas jabbed her hair behind her ears. "Think I'll start packing."

"Me, too." Jonas trudged after her.

"Good idea," I called after them. "Maybe it's contagious."

Freddy flopped into the rocking chair. "You were a saint, Giselle, taking me in that time when I had no place to go. There I was, appalled at the thought of being a burden to my parents, not working—"

"Oh, don't sell yourself short. We both know you did rather well as a salesman, hawking *my* groceries door to door."

"Ellie, why don't we hear what Freddy has to say." Ben's voice wasn't quite as devoted as I would have liked.

Freddy gave a dejected wave. "Forget it, mate. Ellie's the boss—that's how it should be. Sorry I've outstayed my welcome."

Ben shot me an ambiguous look. Freddy was shifting his shoulders up and down. "Sore muscles?" I inquired. "From bracing yourself to leap from the tower?"

"Snickering does not become you, cousin. I would have jumped could I have been assured of an injury that looked bad but didn't hurt. I wanted Jill on her knees with remorse."

Freddy stood up, flipped the chair over, and assumed a heroic pose. Reaching a hand inside his shirt, he brought out a folded piece of paper and held it out to Ben. "Behold! My application for employment in your pending restaurant. Jill is going to weep her eyes out."

Ben took hold of the paper, as I said, "Oh, what a shame. You were just saying this morning, weren't you, darling, that Abigail's won't open until spring."

Freddy clutched at his heart. "Cruel Ellie! I'm sorry now I put you down as a reference." His eyes moved to Ben. "Well, mate, what's it to be? Is she the boss at work as well as at home?"

I moved to my husband's side, slid my arm through his, and smiled.

"What exactly did you have in mind, Freddy?" Ben slapped the application in his hand.

It was stupid to feel betrayed. Ben was undoubtedly doing this for me. He believed that I really wanted to help Freddy but was afraid to show signs of nepotism so early in our marriage. I only removed my arm from Ben's because I was getting pins and needles in my elbow. Freddy shot me a V-for-Victory sign and a smile that said, No hard feelings—loser.

"To be straight with you, Ben—sir—I would prefer to start at the top and work my way down, if necessary. My grand plan is to achieve, then thumb my nose when Jill comes crawling on bleeding knees, begging for one more chance."

Looking from me to Freddy, Ben twisted the application into a plane and tossed it into the muddy waters of the sink.

"At the moment, all I've got to offer is a sort of Man Friday. You would help me get the building ready for occupancy, do some clerical work, and learn a few fundamentals of cooking."

Freddy held up his hand. "I've only one question: Does the job come with a car?"

"Afraid not," I said, "but we will throw in the chauffeur's cottage." I certainly wasn't having Freddy and his guitar installed here. Just look at him! He already had the refrigerator open and was hauling out trays of hors d'oeuvres.

"How about putting the kettle on, Ellie—unless you two would rather have champagne? I'm easy." My cousin grinned at me.

Had I felt any anger toward Ben it would have vanished when we turned off the lights and the pheasants on the wallpaper in our bedroom came to burnished life in the glow from the fire. I fell asleep curled up against him and dreamed about my mother-in-law. I couldn't see her face. But I could hear her. Someone was carrying her away into the mist. She was screaming, "Help! Help! Murder, murder!" It was like something from one of those forties films where all the women are young war widows being preyed upon by fortune hunters. Off in the distance people were weeping and wailing; slowly the screen filled up with something long and dark, moving closer—closer. It was a coffin and I knew who was inside. "Well, no wonder she couldn't come to the wedding," I thought.

I woke to find the wind hurling the maroon velvet curtains against the walls and rain dripping over the sill. We had to leave the window open a crack because of Ben's claustrophobia.

Poppa telephoned the next afternoon. Ben answered the phone. When no voice responded to his hello, he promptly handed me the receiver.

"That you, Ellie? Can't be long—have to unload a crate of bananas—but thought you would like to know that Paris received a postcard from Maggie this morning. Said she was still staying at that nice quiet place at the seaside."

"Which seaside?"

"It wasn't a picture card."

"What was the postmark?"

Ben was making it hard for me to hear. He was walking in circles, making deep breathing noises.

"It was smudged."

"Did your wife send any message for you?"

"She did. She told Paris to see I took my cod liver oil."

I made encouraging noises to Ben. "That sounds very positive."

Poppa snorted. "What do you know? I think she poisoned the bottle before she left." The receiver went dead in my hand.

"I expect I will get a card or letter from Mum tomorrow." Ben sounded cheerful, but looked defensive.

His mother didn't write. And still no word from Brambleweed Press.

Fortunately, Ben did not have much time to stand at the letter box. He and Freddy (now installed in the cottage at the gates) spent most days in the building which was to become Abigail's. Ben swore that Freddy might become a credit to us in time. And he did seem to be buckling down. Occasionally the pair of them even skipped dinner, grabbing a bite at The Dark Horse. I didn't mind—terribly.

I had a lot of work to do myself, and I was glad of time to devote to Dorcas and Jonas. Marriage to Ben was utter bliss, but living with a gourmet chef when one is chained to a diet is rather like a nonsmoker living with a smoker. I inhaled calories when Ben used words like flambé and fricassee.

The days passed swiftly. Most days I would putter into Abigail's with slide rule, paint chart, and fabric samples. And I did some shopping with Dorcas and bullied Jonas into being fitted for a new suit. His current Sunday best was older than I.

On the fifteenth of December, the eve of Departure Day, Ben prepared a fabulous dinner. The dining room gleamed with dark oak, silver, and the Indian Tree china. Freddy joined us, looking very spruce. Even his fingernails were clean.

"Quite the dandy, aren't you, boy?" harrumphed Jonas, who was wearing a plaid shirt and shoestring tie.

Dorcas moved around the table, arms swinging briskly. "A sight for sore eyes, each of you. We shall always treasure the memory of this final hour."

"Don't!" I whispered, and only just stopped myself from adding "don't go." And I, a grown-up, married woman. How could I spoil the voyagers' pleasure? How could I be so disloyal to Ben? He was bringing in the turkey, garlanded in holly, amid cheers from everyone but me. Jonas was tucking his serviette into his neck, Dorcas was moving her chair to allow Freddy more room.

Freddy tilted his chair on two legs and whispered, "You look beautiful, Ellie."

"Why, thank you."

Jonas and Dorcas laid their soup spoons down with echoing clanks.

"The fang marks in your neck are barely noticeable." Sorry"—Freddy swung the chair out of reach—"but sometimes I kinda miss the old Ellie. I feel sorry for her." He proclaimed mournfully, "Thinny rolled over and Fatty was dead."

What idiot Freddy didn't understand was that Fat Ellie's ghost still walked. I took the vegetable platter from Dorcas and smiled into Ben's eyes. "We don't miss her, do we, darling?"

"No."

"But we will miss our dear Dorcas and Jonas." I lifted my wineglass. "Come back soon, both of you." My vision was so blurred the jolly wanderers looked like they were teary-eyed, too.

Virtue is its own reward. As I lay between the silver-grey sheets that night, feeling the night air on my skin and Ben's hands slipping over the green silk of my nightgown, I was glad I had not succumbed to the buttered parsnips and sherried trifle. As it was, I would have to find a way to burn up the calories in the brussels sprouts. The pheasants on the wallpaper shifted as I felt the rasp of Ben's cheek on mine, his quickened breathing, and those wonderful hands—I smiled dreamily up from my pillow.

They were waiting for me in dreamland. Two humanoid hamburgers. One had the face of Mrs. Shirley Daffy, the other Mrs. Amelia Bottomly. They both kept screaming at me as they drew me inside a refrigerator and locked the door: "You'll lose him, you stupid girl. He'll run off to Chicago with someone meatier. Someone like me!" Their lips cracked into huge tomato sauce smiles. It was so dark, so cold. My heart tried to fight its way out of my body, and I knew, as I fought my way out from the refrigerator, this buried-alive feeling must be what Ben had feared ever since someone had locked him in the potato bin.

I was suddenly awake but the bedroom looked different, alien. Moonlight spattered the room. The dark oblong facing me looked too tall to be Ben's chest of drawers. I moved to sit up and realized that I was up. Standing up. Worse, I was clutching something. I fumbled for the light switch and in a blaze of blinding light, found myself in the kitchen. In my hand was a sandwich—a grotesque sandwich of lettuce, tongue, raw egg, and mandarin oranges slathered in tomato sauce. Shuddering, I dropped it into the sink, turned on the hot tap and punched the monstrous thing through the drain holes with the handle of a wooden spoon. No one, with an emphasis on Ben, must ever know.

No need to put on the hall light. There was plenty of moonlight breaking through the windows. I wouldn't stumble over Rufus or his compadre, but I did get a jolt when I saw the shadowy form of a man standing in front of the drawing room fireplace. I grabbed at the stone moulding of a niche in the wall; the Egyptian urn it contained almost toppled over. The figure moved sideways to the window. But as my breathing slowed, my brainwaves quickened. Jonas must have wanted one last undisturbed look at Abigail's portrait. For luck? For . . . love? Surely, he and Dorcas weren't having regrets about this trip to Chicago? Stealthily, I reached the stairs and stood on the second one up, twisting the loose top of the bannister in my hand. Perhaps I should go and ask him if he and Dorcas were leaving because of some misplaced idea of chivalry: "Let the young couple have a few months on their own."

My feet took me slowly upstairs.

The curtains billowed into the room as I slid into bed. Inching toward Ben, I felt like a parasite draining his warmth, but I didn't begrudge him the open window. Not after my sojourn in the refrigerator.

The next day, I did not flood Heathrow with tears. Dorcas, wearing a navy blazer with her old school badge on the pocket, was the one with last-minute flutters. She wasn't afraid of crashing; what scared her was eight hours of no sit-ups or chin-ups.

"What you need is a good book," I said.

"Now you mention it, wouldn't object to a little fictional excitement—perhaps something on Girl Guides."

"Right, ho!" Ben vanished into the crowd and returned with a paperback with red lettering spattered on a black cover —*Friendly Death*.

Ben's voice fought a loudspeaker announcement of a flight to Paris departing from Gate Eight. "Read the back; it does fulfill the Girl Guide criteria: 'Pretty dimpled Sarah Lynn Webster goes to camp for the first time and finds something nasty in her bunk.

If you've guessed frog, you're wrong. If you've guessed dead —you're right.' "

Jonas smacked his gum contemptuously.

"How positively ripping. And by Mary Birdsong." Dorcas clapped the book to her brow. "Quite forgot to mention. She —I mean, Mr. Edwin Digby—came to the house the day of the wedding, minutes after you left."

"Is this on a par with a visit from Garbo?" Ben was propping hand luggage against our legs.

"Fellow was drunk," grumphed Jonas. "I opened the front door to see him struggling to put his key in the lock."

"An understandable error," said Ben mildly. "Our houses are a scant half-mile apart."

"Had a goose with him that looked as though it could have done with a few gins. Asked them both in but they turned tail and went."

Dorcas winced. "Feel sorry for the man. Hear he hasn't published a book in years. Must make him feel a bit inadequate." Her eyes met Ben's and her face mottled. "I say, is that our flight? Whamo! Shoulders back, Jonas, no snivelling, anyone."

The men started gathering up the luggage, and Dorcas gave me the familiar clap on the back. "Sorry about the blooper. Know Ben will hear about the masterpiece soon." She raised her voice. "Don't worry, Ellie; I'll see Jonas gets forty winks plus on the plane."

"Doubt I'll close my eyes." Jonas adjusted his cowboy hat. "Slept like a top last night. Must have been the sherry in the trifle, Ben."

Dorcas's hopes regarding Ben's masterpiece were realised the very next day. Brambleweed Press wished to publish his cookery book. An editor named A.E. Brady wrote, "All at B.P. adored the recipes, the anecdotes, indeed the whole essence, and would consider it a privilege to include so important a work on our spring list."

Ben brought the letter up to the bedroom. I was still in my nightdress.

"What a charming, insightful man, this Mr. Brady." I reached for Ben, but he slipped through my fingers. Never had I seen him more ecstatic. After leaping on and off the bed a few times, pummelling the pillows and tossing them across the room, he whipped on some clothes, rummaged through his hair with his fingers and announced he must dash down to the cottage to share the news with Freddy.

"Don't you want to phone your father?"

"And listen to his enthusiastic silence? Freddy and I have talked about including some of the recipes from the book on the restaurant menu—"

I opened my mouth but he was gone. Had I brought this exclusion on myself? I lay down on the bed and pressed my hands against my stomach. I was sure I had gained five pounds in the night. Ben had been muttering in his sleep about floating island pudding with a *crème de Lyons* sauce, but were I a model wife, I would be up cooking him a celebration breakfast. Would he notice if I diluted the marmalade? I was half out of bed when I felt the crackle of the newspapers. I might find some intriguing low-cal recipes in the Food Section . . . stuffed ox heart? Not on an empty stomach, thank you.

I flipped to the Employment Wanted section. Ben had been urging me to find someone to help out with the housework. A personal secretary was on the lookout, as was an accountant and someone wishing to teach trapeze, but I didn't think any of them would be interested in domestic work. I would have to advertise. I turned the page; thinking about the day Dorcas had responded to our plea for hired help would start me crying. Better to read the Personals: "Lost—adorable Pekingese. Answers to Valentino. Reward." And this—"Man seeks attractive mature woman for dating and beyond. Must be nonsmoker, teetotaler, and bingo enthusiast."

How fortunate I was to have escaped the clutches of loneliness. The door inched open. Tobias entered, yawning with every outstretched paw. I patted the counterpane and he tumbled alongside me. "Want me to read Dear Felicity Friend?" Only cats and the happily married can fully enjoy advice to the lovelorn.

" 'Dear Felicity: I am desperately in love with a man who is married to another, a woman unworthy to untie his shoes. At night I lie awake, fantasizing about invading his place of work and ripping off my clothes. I have a superb figure and know him to be a connoisseur. I am prepared to do anything to get him. Signed, *Hot and Bothered*.' "

Tobias yawned mightily.

"Dear Felicity replies: 'Dear Hot: Invite him to your home

and rip off your clothes. That way you can butter the police up with crumpets and tea when they come to take you away.' "

I flopped back against the pillows and scanned a paragraph of moans from a woman with a mother-in-law who smothered her with attention. Some people and their problems! Now for the Confidential. "To Teary Eyes. Your problem will soon die a natural death."

What sort of problem? Pain? Fear? Perhaps guilt—the guilt of a woman who has everything she could possibly want.

Dear Felicity, I imagined myself writing. I am married to the most marvellous, gorgeous, exciting man but there is something lacking in me. My first clue was that I don't hear violins when we make love. And now I find myself missing, desperately, two friends who have gone away. Isn't a husband meant to fill every need, every empty space of the heart?

From the Files of
The Widows Club

15th December

President:

Mrs. Mary Elizabeth Hanover, we thank you for accepting the place on the Fairwell Committee recently vacated by Beatrix Woolpack. Do join myself and the board in a celebration glass of sherry.

Mary Elizabeth Hanover:

Oh; how kind, Madam President. Words do rather fail one. When one has so long wished to give back to the organisation some particle of the kindness and support one has received! Oh, my! Harvey's Bristol. Most salubrious. As one says to the customers at The Dark Horse, nothing like the best."

(Applause from the board.)

President:

I must advise you, Mary, that we may not have an assignment for you until sometime after Christmas; Daisy Smith has seniority. But we trust you will, in the interim, prepare yourself emotionally and physically for the Grand Summons. You understand there must be no repeat performance of the train travesty.

M.E.H.:

Appalling. I hear Mrs. Woolpack is close to a breakdown, which I suppose says something for her. Dear! Dear! At our meeting last Wednesday, I had to cover my eyes when she stepped onto the dais, handed in her board resignation, was stripped of all honours and asked to step down as Chairperson of Dried Flower Arranging. One learns from witnessing something like that, although in my humble opinion she was fortunate to escape a harsher penalty.

President:

Now, now, Mary! You know as well as I, that we in The Widows Club are safe from being an S.T.B.R. ourselves unless we commit the Unforgivable Offence. Cheers, everyone!

. . . "Our dear mother used to say," remarked Primrose as Butler set down a pot of fresh tea and crept from the room, "that the best way to stay happily married is to keep busy. . . ."

We were happy, but that was the problem. I couldn't quite adjust. Take the morning in point. Instead of bustling down to the kitchen in my housewifely dressing gown, I was still in bed pondering whether Dear Felicity shunned the limelight because she was afraid of being cornered at Sainsbury's cheese counter with questions on frigidity or because the elusive element improved readership. Edwin Digby, being a man of mystery in more ways than one, certainly added local colour. I would have to ask Rowland if he had ever asked either celebrity to open the church fete. That is, if I saw him before I had forgotten the question; Rowland didn't stop by as often as he once did. I missed seeing him, and I hate to admit it, but I missed thinking about him. Marriage did have its curtailments.

A knock on the bedroom door and in came Ben with eggs

Benedict and champagne. He really was wonderful. I was so ashamed.

To enhance the possibility that champagne did burn up calories, I did an exercise Jill had taught me: lifting and lowering my chin three times between bites. Ben eyed me askance a couple of times, but he was occupied balancing the tray on the bed and talking about *The Edwardian Lady's Cookery Book.* I stopped doing chins and felt a spurt of renewed interest in championing my husband's career.

"Ben, perhaps this editor of yours, Mr. Brady, might wish to attend Abigail's premiere and plug the book." So much to be accomplished in a short time—and with Christmas in between. Some of the vigour fizzled. I was back to no Dorcas and Jonas.

"Remember last year?" sneered the Ghost of Christmas Past. All too clearly. Oh, the anguish of searching my client listing for the name of a single man who, for the price of a new window treatment, might accompany me to the office party.

I would invite Miss Thorn and Rowland for Boxing Day dinner. Moving the tray aside, I slid my arm around Ben, who was sitting on the edge of the bed talking about glacé pheasant Viennese style.

"Sounds delicious," I said.

"So you said at breakfast." He turned sideways, met my lips in a kiss, stood up and placed my plate of eggs Benedict on the floor. "Here Tobias! Thousands of starving cats in China."

Those words hurt. They also made me mildly angry. My husband's ego was upstaging my physical well-being. "Ben . . ." I stopped. The mirror showed that yesterday's calories had settled on my hips. As I twisted this way and that, striving for a better angle, Ben caught me by the shoulders. His eyes shot blue-green sparks off the mirror.

"Ellie, no woman looks her best with her jaw out of kilter and a look of unspeakable horror in her eyes. You know what your problem is?"

"I fail the can't-pinch-an-inch test."

His voice softened. "You haven't gone browsing in the shops for a while. You're suffering withdrawal. Go into the village, squander money, have your hair done."

I began brushing my hair. "While I'm about it, I'll get a nose job and a tummy tuck." My spirits lifted. "I'll phone Sidney for an appointment; you and I can drive into the village together."

Ben moved my hair aside and kissed my neck. "Darling, I wish I could wait for you, but Freddy and I are due to meet Mrs. Hanover, owner of The Dark Horse, in twenty minutes. We have to discuss sharing some deliveries of wine. But you're free to take the car. We are going on the motorbike." A kiss on the other side of my neck. "How about joining us for lunch?"

"I don't think so, thank you."

"Is something wrong, Ellie?"

"Of course not." I plunged the brush into my hair, "A passionate embrace ere you make your getaway might have brightened my day, but . . ."

"I'm sorry, Ellie. Unlike the heroes in those da—romance novels you are forever glued to, I can't stand with my arm draped over the mantelpiece all day, looking delectable."

He did have this habit of reducing everything to culinary terms! He took a step toward me, then retreated to the door. "Drive carefully, dear."

Not "sweetheart," not "my beloved"! The brush flew through my hair. "Don't worry, Ben, I will rescue any car parts that fall off en route."

"We aren't quarrelling, are we?" He spun the door handle.

"Absolutely not," I said with a pang of nostalgia for the old days when quarrelling with a vengeance meant a sizzling relationship, not a marriage with problems.

And that's what comes of reading Felicity Friend.

This was my first visit to Sidney's salon. My initial impression was that I had made a mistake. This wasn't the sort of place that automatically made a girl feel pretty. The air was laden with hair spray and permy smells. The linoleum was maroon, speckled with grey; the lighting was harsh, and the washbasins lining one wall looked like urinals for extra tall men. The girl behind the desk had surely been employed as a warning against do-it-yourself glamour. Her hair was straw-coloured . . . straw.

"Hallo?" She beamed a gapped-tooth smile.

"Ellie Haskell. I have an appointment at—"

She looked me over. "Wouldn't bother if I was you—look lovely the way you are, but if you're sure . . ." She threw up her hands. "Sidney will be with you in a few minutes. Hang your coat on a peg and take one of them pink overalls. Quite like Vidal Sassoon, aren't we? Coffee's on the table."

It came out of the pot like treacle, but the assortment of teacups and saucers didn't come from Woolworth. Each piece was different; some were old, all were pretty. I studied the urinal wall. Two girls in trailing skirts and lumpy sweaters were shampooing. Sidney, stationed between them, looked in this environment more than ever like a caveman. Gloom radiated from him. The woman whose hair he was swirling into puffs and coils was talking away at a furious rate. Rings flashed as she gesticulated. Her face shook like a blancmange which wouldn't set.

I leaned sideways. It was Mrs. Amelia Bottomly. Better not to be seen by her. She would want to know if I had located any dungeons yet at Merlin's Court.

"Psst! Mrs. Haskell!" A hairdryer lid flipped up and a blond head emerged. "Thinking about that brand-new gorgeous husband, eh? Remember me? Bunty Wiseman?"

"Yes—hello." She was the young woman in the thigh-length, ostrich-feather coat at the reception, the one whose photograph had been on Lionel Wiseman's desk.

"Bunty's a nickname, but don't ask me what my real one is, it's too awful. Most times I let my hair dry natural, but I promised Li I wouldn't walk down Market Street with a wet head."

"Not the weather for it," I said.

She wiggled her shoulders and flapped a hand at me. "Doesn't fit the image of a respected solicitor's wife. Balls, is what I'd say to that, only I've my eye on this nifty diamond dangle at Pullets Jewelers, so have to keep the old darling's fur laying right."

Mr. Wiseman's wife? I had thought she was his daughter.

"Mrs. Haskell," the receptionist's voice cut in, "Sidney is ready for yooo."

"Hold on." Bunty had both hands on the dryer lid. "Teddy Peerless—she's Li's secretary—and I are lunching at The Dark Horse. Care to join us?"

"I . . ." Amelia Bottomly was coming our way, like a buoy bobbing on the ocean.

"See you. Twelve-forty-five." Bunty clasped the hairdryer on like a crash helmet.

Mrs. Bottomly's voice boomed, "Ellie Haskell!" The chins shook with apparent pleasure. "Tell me, dear, what do you think of Sidney's handiwork? Makes me look years younger, don't you agree? The man's an artist. Well, they so often are. The sweet things give us women the coiffures they would like themselves." She lifted a mirror off a wall shelf, twitched a side curl, pursed her lips, and patted the chins into shape with the back of her hand. "You get my meaning, don't you, dear? You *are* a married woman."

"One who's keeping her hairdresser waiting," I said.

"And that certainly won't do. Believe you me, a visit to Sidney is a health cure! I tell him everything from the pills I take for constipation to what I enjoy most in opera. Take my advice, dear, put yourself *totally* in his hands. If Sidney says cut"—she patted down a loop atop the mound—"then so be it. And, dear"—she jerked me back by the shoulder—"I will be phoning you about the Historical Society doing a home tour, and the Hearthside Guild is interested in having your husband put on a cookery demonstration. Nothing too Frenchified—a stew perhaps. I did try to catch Mr. Haskell a half-hour or so ago as he was going into The Dark Horse but he was lost in conversation with that cousin of yours who created such an uproar . . . ious diversion at your wedding. And now he's moved in with you, I hear."

Somehow she managed to make the situation sound unseemly. My natural defensiveness was aroused. But before I could explain that Freddy's life had derailed and I was the depot, a hand touched my elbow.

"Excuse me, Mrs. Bottomly," interposed Sidney. And before she could get going on an apology, he led me to a chair and spun me to face a washbasin and mirror.

Taking the pins from my hair he tossed it dispiritedly into the air. "What's it to be, Ellie luv? Oh, don't you look awful! Hollow eyes, white lips. Either the honeymoon didn't agree with you or you've just lost your best friend."

My eyes met his gloomy ones in the mirror. Problems were what this man did best. At last someone who understood that happiness is sometimes burdensome.

"The honeymoon was fine, but you're right about the best friend—doubled."

My hair floated into the washbasin as I explained how the

U.S.A. had enticed Dorcas and Jonas to defect. Warm water soothed; its gentle rushing softened my lament.

"Terrible, Ellie! How you must have suffered. I feel your pain—right here." Sidney's hands sudsed and massaged so it was impossible to tell with which part of his anatomy he empathized, but his sigh, gusting down my neck, warmed the cockles of my heart.

"And to top it all, Sidney, there has been this worry over Ben's mother. You understand, we are not broadcasting the facts over the BBC, but since you've known the family for years, it won't matter telling you, Sidney, that her disappearance is connected to rumours that my father-in-law is involved with another woman. Not to mince matters—Ben's parents have separated."

"Never! Won't my mum be shocked! This other woman, would she be a Mrs. Jarrod? Redhead? Given to tight-fitting jumpers?"

I got water all down my back. "None other."

"Good God, I can't believe it! The woman's not his type at all. Why, she's yards taller than him—he'd have to hop like a rabbit just to kiss her good night. And I told you what Mr. Haskell thinks of tall women. I hate to make you feel worse than you already do, Ellie, but has to be the man's in love and his brains have dropped below the belt. Believe me, it happens!" Sidney draped a dry towel around my neck and gusted another sigh. "Poor sainted Mrs. Haskell. Ben must be out of his mind with worry."

I shook my head and apologised to the woman at the next basin for spraying her. "He speaks with surprising calm of his mother going off on an extended holiday. Whenever I bring up the subject, he brushes me off."

"You feel shut out. Who wouldn't?" Sidney deftly parted the front of my hair into sections.

"Sidney, if I didn't know Ben to be a very deep-feeling person, I might be concerned at his apparent callousness. I might wonder just how bothered he would be if anything happened to me."

Sidney produced scissors and began snipping. "Ellie, you mustn't let yourself get worn down. Are you sleeping well?"

"I hate to complain, Sidney, but since you ask—no. I keep having these dreadful nightmares."

"Ask your doctor to prescribe something."

"I don't know. I keep hoping the nightmares will stop. Mrs. Haskell is always in them—and so is food. One night I was pursued by chickens—cooked ones. And there was the one about the hamburgers with their tomato sauce smiles. Ben thinks I am becoming obsessive about my diet."

Sidney plugged in the hand dryer. "Obsession," he said with relishing gloom, "is part of our culture. You're not normal if you aren't a little cracked. Even dear Ben has his claustrophobia." The broad shoulders lifted and fell. "I don't think he ever believed it was that idiot Patterson kid, not me, who shut him in the potato bin. And your goblin is . . ."

"Yes?"

"Trying to please that savage little tyrant—you."

"Really? What about you, Sidney?"

"Duck-waddle Sid?" He turned the hairdryer down to a hum and blew a welter of hair over my forehead. "Old-fashioned bloody greed. I tell you, Ellie, it can be a pain. I can never buy two matching pillow slips. I can't be satisfied with stripes, I want flowers—until I see polka dots."

"I noticed the teacups. All different and beautiful."

He turned off the dryer and rippled his fingers through my hair. "Mum thinks I'm this way because Dad left us. Course, she thinks Maggie Thatcher's Prime Minister because Dad bunked." Sid's eyes met mine in the mirror and he gave me a clown's sad smile. "Is this satisfactory? We didn't want anything too drastic, did we?"

I reached up a tentative hand. "Perfect, Sidney."

"Nice seeing you, Ellie. Best to Ben. That will be five pounds fifty, please. Pay Sally at the desk."

Another customer approached. Time for me to decide whether Sidney would consider a tip an insult. Something about the way his right hand dangled, palm outward, indicated he would not. Sidney must rake in a lot of pennies to keep himself in pillow slips and Minton teacups. I walked outside into a grey drizzle and wondered what the devil had come over me in there.

According to the tower clock it was only five to twelve. Would Ben still be at The Dark Horse? My feet hesitated under the creaking pub sign. But, after downing a few pints of malt-liquor air, I crossed the square. The secure, confident wife does not tread on her husband's shadow.

High noon. Before meeting Bunty, I had time for a little

window shopping. I idled past The Muffin Pan Bakery and drooled past The Chocolate Box. Damn this diet! I would break out at lunch and eat . . . the leaves on my celery. To sublimate my base urges I would look in at Abigail's and measure the staircase window. I had found a marvellous ruby-and-gold damask which would be ideal for a valance. And if Ben had finished at The Dark Horse and happened to be there, I could lure him into the buttery to . . . to take its measurements.

I went up the red brick steps of Abigail's and stepped under the dark green awning to the pounding of invisible workmen. A building inspector had denounced sections of the attic floor as dangerous, so I imagined that most of the carpenters were up there. Not so the painters. A little man, so wizened even his bald head was wrinkly, a paintpot dangling over his arm, careened into me as I came through the door. Before I could say hello, he was off down the hall, muttering.

"I know, I know, your husband told you to come spying. But I'll have you know this is the lunch hour, so don't give me any gaff. Get enough of that from the gov'ner."

Really! Naturally not everyone could love Ben as I did. But such hostility!

Then I forgot the painter. A wave of warmth flowed over me as I looked around the square hall with its heavy, timbered door frames and uneven floor. This building had originated as a small inn in 1703, and the ghosts of caped and bewigged travellers passed to and fro as I went from room to room. No sign of Ben. However, he was present in spirit. Taped to the walls I found numerous notes to workmen. Some kind, some restrained, many caustic, all ending with a scrawl of initials.

A firm hand, yes—I could see that might be needed (as I stepped around two purple-haired youths doing lasso tricks with electrical cord), but I would probably have inserted it in a velvet glove. I went into the kitchen which was stripped pathetically naked, imagining how it would be when all shiny white and stainless-steel bright, with Jonas's geraniums flourishing on the wide quarry-tiled window sills. I knew equally well how the reception room to the left of the front door would look. That bluebell wallpaper I had discovered would be perfect. Trailing up the stairs, my fingers savoured the satin feel of the bannister. I took the measurements of the landing window and went on to the second floor. This long room with its linen scroll paneling, elaborate ceiling molding, and tall latticed windows would be ideal for our opening bash. There would be candles in sconces and white roses in silver bowls on refectory tables flanking each side of the room.

I unflipped my tape measure and went into the room two doors down, already being used as Ben's office. Its neatness brought a tender smile to my lips. Even the paper clips were stacked in rows, and the notes he had made to himself were all lined up. I stopped smiling. One of the notes was to me. It said: *Ellie, don't care for the paint you chose for the kitchen. Would prefer oyster shell to oyster pearl, and darling* (this word was an afterthought, a little arrow pointing to it), *don't leave your wallpaper books laying around. It undercuts morale.* It was signed with the initials *B.T.H.*

I almost forgot myself to the point of crossing out the 'a' in laying and initialing above the correction, but a passage from *Deadlock in Wedlock* swam before my eyes. I unclenched my fist, smoothed out the paper and wrote, *Will make requested changes,* then signed it *E.S.H.*

My watch told me I had time to nip down to Delacorte's Antiques to see if they still had those picture frames. Even should they be gone, there was bound to be something to tempt me.

Delacorte's bow window was lush with treats. There was a late nineteenth-century copper kettle and matching trivet, an embroidered shawl draped over an easel. Cold and repellent Mr. Charles Delacorte might be, but he did know his business.

I entered to a tinkling rendition of the *William Tell* Overture. Should I stick an apple on my head and stand to attention? Better not. The crossbow hanging on the wall behind the brass till looked in good working order, and above, a quiver sprouted bolts like a porcupine. Oh, good! There were my picture frames. Now all I needed was someone to sell them to me quickly before I began filling my arms with things I couldn't live without. I coveted so much here except—the feeling crept over me slowly—the ambience. This was odd because usually I love the reek of age. I moved between tables, fingering an enamelled snuff box and a pair of silver grape scissors. Was it that everything here was almost too indicative of a stage antique shop? Those amber velvet curtains screening the nether regions should part right now and a body plummet to the floor. As I watched, they did inch apart and Charles Delacorte entered.

"Good afternoon, Mrs. Haskell." Inclining his head of fair

hair and consulting his watch, he stationed himself behind the counter. As I went up to him, the curtain spread again and Ann came in. Today she was wearing an olive green brocade suit, the skirt narrow, the jacket pinched at the waist and fanned out over her hips. Her dark hair was puffed into a roll in front, the back falling in a smooth pageboy behind. Very elegant and undoubtedly the height of fashion forty years ago.

"Ellie, how charming to see you." Her cool hands touched mine. "I have been wanting to tell you again how radiant you were as a bride."

"Thank you."

"And the wedding dress was a good fit? When you bought it, I was somewhat concerned about the waist."

"Oh?" I clutched my side.

"I thought it might be too big."

"How kind . . . of you to worry."

"My dear wife lives and breathes worry." Charles Delacorte's voice chilled the room. "What is one more sleepless night in a good cause?" Horrible man. Other than sharing his interest in antiques, what could have possessed Ann to marry him? That she could ever have loved him was frightening.

"I did appreciate your help in selecting the dress," I told her.

"You are certainly intrepid, Mrs. Haskell," commented the man with acid flowing through his veins. "My wife might have sent you down the aisle dressed as the ghost of Joan Crawford." He picked up a silver-backed mirror and buffed it. "Not that your wedding lacked excitement."

Ann touched my arm and gave a low laugh. "Charles likes to tease about my taste in dress."

"I have never found the forties interesting." He jiggled a finger on one of the keys of the till.

Ann, who would never see thirty-nine again, pressed a hand to her throat and laughed. "I suppose I am time warped, but I admire everything about that era. Those were the days when I was happy, perhaps not a child prodigy, but a child success. I could sing, and I had parents who wanted me to shine. They entered me in talent contests and for several years I toured the country." Her eyes took on a far-away look; she leaned against the counter, one hand rippling along its surface as if it were a piano keyboard.

And suddenly, incredibly, she began to sing, "Where did

you go, man of my tears, leaving nothing on my horizon, but lonely, lonely years . . ."

I was excruciatingly embarrassed. Charles Delacorte was smiling as if his wife had finally made his day. Her voice (which wasn't great) petered out. She gave a choked laugh.

"As well I retired at age ten, isn't it? I never had the magic of the greats like Sylvania. Hers was a voice like Irish whiskey, all fire and passion. I did a show with her once." The far-away look was back in Ann's eyes. "She must have been about eighteen at the time, and she lit up the place with her sequins and her flaming hair. She sang 'Goodbye, Again.' I wanted to grow up to be exactly like her." Ann lifted a hand to her face. "I don't need you, Charles, to tell me that she was a great beauty and I never was. But I think my figure is comparable; I'm still thirty-eight, twenty-three, thirty-seven. One of the benefits of never having had children."

Charles fixed his arctic gaze on me, increasing my discomfort. A clock chimed the quarter hour and I slid the picture frames across the counter and opened my bag. I had yet to overcome my feeling that measurements were a private matter, never to be casually discussed, especially in mixed company.

"I'm not really familiar with this Sylvania." I glanced at the bill Charles handed me and started writing out a cheque.

Ann moved around the counter. "She shunned publicity. Her private life was always exactly that. There were rumours that she was secretly married, first to this man and that and even that she had children. But then her music went out of style, like this dress. For ages nothing was written about her, except for the occasional piece in the gossip papers pondering her fade-out and hinting that some tragedy had befallen her."

Poor lonely Ann. Forty-some years old and a crush on a dead singer. I was tucking my parcel under my arm when the *William Tell* Overture sounded again. Gladys Thorn entered the shop.

Surprisingly, Charles Delacorte warmed to tepid enthusiasm. He smoothed his transparent hair and adjusted the knot of his tie.

"Good afternoon, Miss Thorn. Have you come to look at that sheet music which Dr. Simon Bordeaux discovered in an old trunk at The Peerless Nursing Home?"

"Oh, how well you read me, Mr. Delacorte!" The organist's skin soaked up an unbecoming blush and she adjusted her spectacles to a more lopsided angle. "I have long been aching to do something special for Lady Theodora. She has been so good, assisting with the children's choir. And always so jolly—saying she is the ideal person because she is tone deaf. Do you agree, Mr. Delacorte, that she would like the music as a souvenir of the childhood home whence she was so cruelly evicted by her male relations?"

"Why not? I almost wish I could make a present of the music to you."

Ann, who had come to stand beside me, looked at him as though she couldn't believe her ears.

Miss Thorn twisted her hands. "Oh no, I couldn't permit that. I do have my little private income, you know. Of course, I'm not an heiress like—" Miss Thorn gave a start and squinted at me through the thick lenses which magnified her eyes to mushrooms.

"Mrs. Haskell! How rude of me! But truly I didn't see you, or rather"—another grievous adjustment to the spectacles—"see that you were you."

"Nice to see you."

"How incredibly kind—oh, Mrs. Haskell, I do wish to mention that I find your cousin so convivial. As does the vicar. Twice at services, on consecutive weekends. And to come such a distance!"

"Freddy?" He who eschewed habitual churchgoing on the grounds that familiarity breeds contempt? Well, it must be all of two minutes on the bike. . . .

Ann murmured that she was slipping into the back to fetch her coat.

"The person who interrupted our—*your*—beautiful wedding?" exclaimed Miss Thorn. "Oh no, I haven't seen *him* at church but I suppose he is very busy with your husband—and business." I wished people would stop talking of Ben and Freddy as if they were inseparable schoolboys. Miss Thorn peeled back the collar of her coat, revealing a crimson blouse. "Your cousin's so friendly and . . . flattering. She suggested I wear red more often to heighten my natural vivacity."

That blouse made Miss Thorn look as though all her blood had drained from her to it. Vanessa! How dare she go to church—*my* church! This was my punishment for not attending the last two Sundays. What was she up to? A thought slid into mind but I swiftly dismissed it. Rowland was too strong to be taken in by empty beauty and rampant sex appeal. No, cousin Vanessa wanted to nose out any gossip about Ben and me. But she wouldn't luck out.

"Excuse us, if you please." Charles Delacorte raised a gilded eyebrow at me and beckoned Miss Thorn with a frostbitten smile.

"Good-bye, Mrs. Haskell." Handbag clasped to her concave bosom, she moved along the counter. "Do please remember me kindly to Miss Fitzsimons next time she comes down to visit you."

"I will." To admit that Vanessa hadn't been near Merlin's Court since the wedding would make me look the mean sort who wouldn't offer my own cousin a cup of tea.

Miss Thorn, with an expectant smile, followed Charles into the back room. I put down the lamp shade I had been pleating into a fan as Ann came through the curtains wearing a beaver coat and a wide-brimmed black hat dipped at the front. She pulled on a pair of leather gloves.

"Miss Thorn will enjoy talking to Charles alone—you know how these spinsters are—and I felt like going out to lunch today." She hesitated. "Would you like to join me?"

I explained about meeting Bunty and her husband's secretary and suggested that Ann join us. She seemed hesitant. "Oh, do come." I propelled her across The Square. "We may bump into my husband and Freddy and get treated to drinks."

I pushed open the heavy oak and glass door of the pub.

"They're quite close, aren't they?" said Ann, following.

Same old song. "Mmmm." I gave a secure married laugh. "Isn't that Bunty Wiseman over there in the corner, next to the man in the raincoat?" It wasn't. And I couldn't see Ben and Freddy among the beer swillers at the bar or among the diners seated at the benches against the walls. The stout woman presiding at the bar, pulling on the brass tap handles and handing over foaming tankards, had pale gold hair and wore rhinestone-studded glasses. Mrs. Hanover (as I heard her addressed) spoke with meticulous poshness. A kind but crisp smile was affixed to her lips.

"That's the last one for you, Mr. Daffy."

Quite right, Mrs. Hanover. Having escaped death by inches, it behooved the real estate agent not to walk blithely under a bus. But when Mr. Vernon Daffy turned his curly black head and his ripe olive eyes in my general direction, my smile faded.

I had no desire to buy a piece of residential property just to get rid of him. Spying a corner staircase, I suggested to Ann that we avail ourselves of it and look for our luncheon associates on the second floor. She nodded, and we circumvented a group of plaid-suited young men who were attempting to gulp down pints of bitter without dislodging the cardboard coasters balanced on their heads.

Snatches of song followed us up the poorly lit, steeply pitched stairs. At the top was a door. I had opened it a wedge when Ann said from the rear, "Ellie, I think that room is reserved for private parties."

Too late I saw the little brass plate that said Reserved. The scent of cut flowers wafted toward me and inside I saw rows of women seated at white-clothed tables, sipping from sherry glasses. Chairs scuffed back; all persons were now standing. A voice commandeered the floor, but the speaker was out of my sight.

Ann tugged at my arm, but somehow (it was becoming a habit) I had lost a shoe. I fumbled around for it with my foot, keeping my mutterings low and my ear to the door. Terrible, isn't it, but remember I am the sort who reads other people's shopping lists while making myself at home in their cars.

"Ladies, dear friends, our monthly meeting having been called to order, I wish to address a subject of concern. Yes, Mrs. Beatrix Woolpack has suffered a major nervous breakdown. She collapsed last evening while attending the Amateur Symphony. She has been admitted to The Peerless Nursing Home, where I understand she has placed herself unreservedly in the good Dr. Bordeaux's hands. In view of Mrs. Woolpack's current standing in the club, Correspondence will confine itself to sending a card with printed good wishes. No visitors are permitted."

A buzzing from the assemblage.

Ann handed me my shoe and I followed her downstairs, not wanting to linger any longer. Poor Mrs. Woolpack. I felt I knew her through her car. Stumbling down the last step, I took a couple of seconds to realise that the voice hailing me above the babble was Mrs. Lionel Wiseman's.

Sidney had whipped Bunty's hair into a blond cloud, the kind which must present doorway difficulties. "Sorry we're late! Ellie, you remember Teddy?" Bunty tapped her tweedy middle-aged companion on the head. "And I see you've brought Ann."

Perhaps she didn't mean to sound the way she did. Her eyes slid over Ann, who gave an almost imperceptible shrug. "Let's bag a table over by the window, as far as possible from that creep in the raincoat. Yes, over there—doesn't he give you the willies?"

The man was standing in front of the Gents. He had a beer glass tilted up to his face. My heart skipped some beats, then put them back in the wrong place. Could he be the man I had seen before? No, Ellie, don't be paranoid. England is a country of raincoats.

"Is this hunky-dory?" Bunty patted the floral cushion in the window nook overlooking The Square.

"Very nice," said Ann. There was a slight draft, but not from the window.

The Raincoat Man opened a box of matches, tumbled the contents into his palm and began snapping them in half, a stick at a time, dropping them on the floor.

Teddy removed her gloves and adjusted one of the combs poked at random through her bundled-up hair. She looked a safe sort of secretary for a married man. When she spoke, her voice was as beige as the rest of her. But to be fair, Bunty's vivacity probably did that to all of us. Certainly Ann looked more wan than usual.

"This is nice, Mrs. Haskell," Teddy's projecting teeth gave a slight catch to her speech. "I enjoyed your wedding. Please tell your husband I liked the little chicken tarts."

"He'll be delighted." This sort of chitchat was the real world. I stopped eyeing the Raincoat Man.

"Teddy," I said. "Is that short for Theodora?"

"That's right."

"Are you Lady Theodora Peerless?" The mysterious Theodora who had grown up in the mansion that was now a nursing home? The Theodora on whom Miss Gladys Thorn was to bestow the music found in an old trunk?

She was easing out of the tweedy coat, revealing a hand-knitted oatmeal cardigan and twin strands of pearls. Pink plastic ones.

"Mrs. Haskell—"

"Ellie, please."

"All right, Ellie, I'm Teddy to my friends. I gave up the title years ago, along with other unimportant things."

"To make it short and sweet," Bunty interrupted cheerfully, "Teddy said balls to the ancestral home when Daddy, the earl, left all the lolly to unlovely brother Walter, who offered in turn to give her two quid a week pocket money."

"You exaggerate, Bunty," scolded Teddy gently.

"Okay. So it was twelve pounds a week. Walter is as miserly a worm as my first hubby, but things turn out for the best." Bunty grinned at me. "Teddy is devoted to Li. Although I have to admit (don't I, Teddy?), the reason I first decided to be chums with the other woman in my sugar's life was to make damn sure that when they worked late at the office, they kept the lights on. I may not look too smart but, believe me, I learned my sums from hubby number one."

Ann clearly didn't like this baring of the soul. She touched her dark hair and said, "Mr. Wiseman's professional reputation has always been above reproach."

The Raincoat Man was going into the Gents.

Bunty crossed shapely legs. "Listen, pals, when the likes of me has angled long and hard to reel in a rich and able-bodied husband, he has to be kept safe from those who might also want to stick a hook in his neck. And Teddy here is a very fascinating woman."

"I do have a way with writs." Teddy smiled. It gave her face an elusive charm.

Reaching across the table, Bunty flipped at a strand of my hair. "You look the romantic sort, Ellie, a bit like Lady Godiva with clothes. Don't you think Teddy has *lived*?"

Ann looked at me, I looked at Teddy, who was her monochromatic self again. But Bunty was off and running.

"So what does brother Walter do after he gets to be earl? He sells the estate to Dr. Bordeaux (who rents it out for a while, then turns it into a rest home) and whips off to the south of France with his ugly wife, Wanda—the woman who asked Teddy if it wasn't nifty never again having to worry about being married for money."

A leaden pause. The three of them might not be deliberately avoiding my eyes, they might not be wondering if Ben had married me for my money, they might . . . simply be looking around, thinking what a pleasant room this was.

"Are we ladies ready?" Mrs. Hanover spoke from beside us.

I ordered a Gorgonzola sandwich.

"Ughh!" said Bunty.

Exactly. I wouldn't be tempted to eat it. While the others decided, I studied the horse brasses on the walls.

"And so," Bunty continued, "Teddy was thrust out in the world with her suitcase and typing diploma and if that isn't 'orrible enough"—she stopped and drummed her fingers on the table—"she was the victim of blighted love."

"It wasn't as exciting as that." Teddy's voice was flatter than usual. "Let's hear about a romance with a happy ending. Ellie, how did you and your husband meet?"

They were all looking at me expectantly. "We were introduced by a friend."

"Oh," Bunty shrugged. "I thought it was something more dramatic than that. Teddy, you knew your bloke from the cradle, didn't you?"

Silence. Again, that touch of a smile on Teddy's face.

"A son of friends of the family, that's who he was," Bunty said, answering her own question. "Interestingly older . . ." Mrs. Hanover returned and began sliding plates onto the table. "All those long summer days ogling young Galahad in his cricket pads and romping through the buttercups, and what does he do but grow up and marry another."

Bunty slipped an arm around Teddy's shoulders. "Final scene is a real tearjerker. They met again—in another city—years later, shortly before she came to work for Li. Love flared anew, but in the way of this wicked world he was still married, and they were forced to crush their passion underfoot, knowing they were doomed never be together on this earth."

A hush. Ann's lips parted and I had this terrible fear that she would start singing again. "How terribly sad."

"Isn't it," enthused Bunty. "Just like something out of one of Edwin Digby's books."

This time the hush went pit deep. I couldn't look at Teddy. What woman wants her grand passion likened to the works of anyone less than Shakespeare? Surprisingly, the atmosphere at our table seemed to be affecting the rest of the room. People stopped talking and stared toward the window.

Bunty giggled. "Don't all be surprised that I'm literary minded. Ex-chorus girls do read, you know. I even like poetry that doesn't rhyme."

Out of the corner of my eye I saw a man lean forward in his chair and twitch back the curtain. We weren't the cause of interest after all. Something was happening in The Square.

As I started to turn, Bunty tootled her fingers down the back of my hand. "Li spotted me from the balcony when I was in *Music Maestro, Please*." She fanned her face. "He steamed up the thee-ater so much the radiators had to be turned off. All things considered, I don't think I could have done better. He's good to look at, I have a lovely house, spiffy clothes, and jewels." She tucked two fingers under her neckline and pulled out a bauble. "Li grumbles sometimes that I'm going to ruin him, but he always manages to pull something out of his pocket. Besides, like Teddy here, I have a job. A pretty classy job."

No one answered.

Mrs. Hanover had come out from behind the bar, and other patrons were converging toward the windows. There were exclamations of "What in the world?" And from outside came shouts, feet pounding.

Bunty peered around and shrugged. "I'm a teacher. Aerobics. Every Thursday afternoon at the church hall, St. Anselm's, which is superconvenient for you, Ellie. Didn't you just lose a lot of weight?"

I hate that expression. I hadn't misplaced part of me. I'd starved it to death an ounce at a time.

Now the patrons of The Dark Horse were piling toward the glass doors. All except the Raincoat Man; he was standing at the bar, his back to me . . . and he was so familiar in that stance that I couldn't move, even when I heard someone ask whether Lloyd's Bank had been burgled. I shut my eyes and saw myself looking into our drawing room in the middle of the night and seeing a man in front of the fireplace.

The pub door crashed open; a voice broke over the gabbling. "Terrible accident . . . building under reconstruction . . . half the bloody floor caved in . . . poor devil fell forty feet! Someone said his wife was here in town . . . anyone seen her?"

I forgot the Raincoat Man. My legs felt like they were dissolving. The carpenters had warned Ben that the attic floor of Abigail's was unsafe.

* * * *

From the Files of
The Widows Club

WRITTEN REPORT FROM MRS. M. SMITH RE:
MRS. SHIRLEY DAFFY, 15th December

I trust the Board and our venerable President will appreciate I imply no criticism when reporting that Mrs. Daffy is upset over the failure of The Widows Club to admit her to its ranks. As her contact, I have explained that some men cling to life after everything humanly possible has been done to remove it from their grasp.

I have attempted to boost her spirits with the old adage, third time lucky. But I feel that Mrs. Daffy is in need of special moral support. I, therefore, request that we make an exception and allow her to participate in club functions even though she has not been initiated or received her badge. Inclusion in the bus trip to Skegness might do her the world of good.

Respectfully submitted,
Mabel Smith

Notation by Millicent Parsnip, Recording Secretary:
Suggestion vetoed by the Board, but a basket of fruit sent to Mrs. Daffy.

12

. . . "The accident victim, was, of course, neither Ben nor cousin Fredrick," supplied Hyacinth. "It was that cat-o'-nine-lives, Mr. Vernon Daffy. He had gone to look at a house scheduled to be condemned and suffered only a few fractured ribs in the fall, I understand."

"According to his receptionist, as reported in *The Daily Spokesman,* someone had telephoned to say the town council might change its mind about demolition. Mr. Daffy could get lucky, if he put in a quick bid on the building."

"His wife was where?" Hyacinth separated a couple of pages in the notebook which had stuck together.

"Having her hair done at Sidney's, but apparently she quite frequently stopped at The Dark Horse. She and Mrs. Hanover are chummy."

"The man in the raincoat interests me." Primrose adjusted the shawl around her narrow shoulders and fingered her Mickey Mouse watch. "Foolish creature to be so conspicuous but men don't have our flair for disguise. . . ."

* * * *

We were in the drawing room sipping our predinner sherry. Freddy had joined us for dinner, yet again, that evening. After discussing Mr. Daffy's close call, I mentioned Miss Thorn's news concerning Vanessa's recent trips to Chitterton Fells, notably St. Anselm's. Freddy scratched at his chef's hat (which he wore everywhere these days, even on the motorbike) and said, "Guess this means we'll have to invite dear old Vinegar for Christmas; can't have the neighbors chinwagging about our neglect." He licked the inside of his glass. "Ah, well, shouldn't be too bad if we include the worthy Reverend Rowland and the gruesome church organist. It might even be fun watching Vin hone her wit on their deadly dull lives."

Getting up from the Queen Anne chair, I set my glass on the mantel. "Nice of you to take on the burden of planning Christmas, Freddy." I ignored Ben's look. "Will Jill be joining us, too?"

"No." Freddy punched down his hat. "We agreed when we parted on total noncommunication, except of a telepathic nature, until the eighteenth of May. My birthday."

"Shrewd move." Ben gathered the glasses onto the silver salver. "Ellie, perhaps you should get in touch with Vanessa. If she's been coming down here, she must be very much at loose ends. And it does look bad, our not having her over even for tea."

"All right . . . darling." Anything else would have sounded insecure. I read his eyes; he was already orchestrating that tea, succulent shrimp toasts, gooseberry tarts. Vanessa would rave while I said the radishes tasted fresh. Damn. It would have been so much easier if Ben had been a banker or an undertaker.

"Freddy, want to give me a hand with dinner?" Ben picked up the salver. "Ellie, sweetheart, put your feet up and relax."

Nothing is more tension-inducing than striving to relax. I stared at the closed door. Phoning Vanessa might be an improvement. First, I would ask Ben how many minutes we should invite her to stay.

The kitchen door was ajar and I heard him say, "Darn it, Freddy, of course I'm worried about my mother, but I don't want Ellie to think—" The electric mixer blared on. "You know how she's been lately."

Tobias came meowing down the hall. He'd get me caught eavesdropping on my own husband. "You know how she's been lately;" that had to mean since the wedding. I scooped up Tobias. Was it possible Ben, too, had noted the absence of violins? But supposing he had. Surely he wouldn't discuss anything of so intimate a nature with Freddy, of all people. Wait —hadn't I read that men did that sort of thing? Engaging in male-bonding conversations such as, "I say, old chap, been having a spot of bother with the wife. Isn't twanging as she should."

Everything I had read in *Marriage Takes Two* stressed the importance of confronting issues head-on, before insecurities grew like weeds and took over the marital flower garden.

I scratched Tobias's ears and told both of us that Ben had only meant I was depressed about Dorcas and Jonas leaving. A secure wife wouldn't resent his talking to Freddy about me—or his mother.

I went to the phone and dialed. She answered at the exact moment I felt justification in hanging up.

"Hello, Vanessa."

"Oh, it's you. Imagine you've heard I've seen the light. It happened when I saw my first miracle, your wedding. Ellie, don't screw up your face like that; it makes your cheeks bag."

"I am not." Now I would spend the rest of this bloody conversation kneading my cheeks.

"You will remember, Ellie, that Mummy was being particularly obnoxious that day, trying to seduce that suit of armour. I don't know how I could have borne the anguish"—Vanessa yawned into the phone—"if Reverend Foxworth hadn't been so divinely kind. He made me finally see what I have been missing all my life—spiritually speaking."

Naturally he had been kind to her. She was my cousin. I gritted my teeth. "Vanessa, you are welcome to stay at Merlin's Court whenever you are in Chitterton Fells."

"Have you left it to me in your will?"

"Of course not."

"Then I don't think so, thank you. As I said to someone—I think it was Reverend Foxworth—Ben and Ellie only have a couple of dozen bedrooms; I would feel I was intruding."

Stuffing the telephone cord into my mouth, I clawed at the air. Calm again, I said, "So you couldn't manage Christmas?"

"Let me check my calendar." A pause. "No, darling, I have other plans."

Good. I would invite Rowland and Miss Thorn.

Both declined with regret. Previous engagements. Ben's father didn't, of course, celebrate the twenty-fifth of December and explained over the phone to me that this was a very busy time for him, selling Christmas trees.

"On Christmas Day?"

"A lot of last-minute shoppers."

"Any word from Mrs. . . . Mum?"

"Paris got another card a couple of days ago."

She had been absent almost a month and still no word for Ben. It really was awful, but when I tried to console him he got snappish, saying it was clear his mother did not wish to put him in the middle. How could a postcard put him in the middle?

Speaking of the mail, I had heard from my Chicago correspondent, Dorcas.

Dear Ellie old sock,
Best way to describe this place is tall and cold. Breath freezes to your face. But natives are charming. Get bombarded with such questions as, do we Brits have hot and cold running water? Inside loos? Can't count the times I've been told I speak English frightfully well for a foreigner. Our monetary system also fascinates them. Want to know what's a sixpence, a shilling and a farthing. Get frightfully disappointed when I say the old coinage has gone the way of the bustle. Now Ellie, no need to worry about Jonas, unless you are averse to baseball caps and TV dinners—only food the man eats anymore. You have my word—won't let him out of the apartment until weather breaks. Enjoyed all news in your last letter. How is the household help situation?

Ah, yes. During the latter days of December we had received several applications in response to our 'Help Wanted' advertisement in *The Daily Spokesman*. The first woman, a Mrs. Philips, was aged. How would I ever be able to leave her alone in the house, let alone see her wheezing into her bucket? For her interview I sat her in the rocking chair, fed her lunch, and heard how she was working to buy a knitting machine, something she had always craved.

The next day I had one sent to her anonymously and proceeded to interview Mrs. Hodgkins, who was young and stalwart, but wanted to bring her boxer dog, Alfred. Personally, I didn't object, but Tobias is rather given to these silly prejudices.

The upshot of these negative experiences was that when Mrs. Roxie Malloy presented herself on the back doorstep, on the twenty-seventh of January (Christmas had been pleasant but nothing to write about), I didn't say the position had been filled.

"Well, what's it to be, Mrs. H., am I to be left standing on the step like a milk bottle?"

Time is a great mellower. The memory of how she had taken an uppish attitude when Freddy threatened to jump from the tower on my wedding day had scabbed over.

Which doesn't mean I clasped Mrs. M. to my bosom and begged her not to leave us till retirement. She entered the kitchen carrying an enormous bag containing "me supplies, Mum." Off came her coat, revealing her tree trunk figure compressed into a bronze-and-black taffeta cocktail suit, its hem three inches lower at the rear. She wore stacked black suede shoes, and so many rings I doubted she could bend her fingers. While I put her coat on a chair, she toted the bag over to the table, stepped out of her shoes, and disparagingly assessed the navy Aga cooker, the wallpaper with its wheatsheaf pattern, and Ben's beloved copper pans.

"Husband not home?"

"He's at work."

"Quite a superior establishment, this"—a hiccup punctuated this observation and confirmed my suspicion that she had diluted her morning orange juice with gin—"and in a fairly salubrious neighborhood, but we both know that anyone deciding to work here would have their work cut out for them." Exhausted by the prospect, Mrs. Malloy sagged into a chair and lit up a fag.

"Work cut out for you?" The place gleamed. I had spent hours keeping everything shipshape for the stream of candidates.

"Got a lot of dust traps." Mrs. Malloy waved a ring-encrusted hand past the greenery curtaining the window, to the shelf containing Ben's collection of Victorian mixing bowls. "But should Roxie Malloy decide to take you on, you won't have reason to complain."

Picking up a wooden spoon, I struck out at an imaginary

insect. "Mrs. Malloy, I am happy to discuss the position with you, but I do anticipate other applicants."

"Don't see them knee-deep at the door, do we? But suit yourself, Mrs. H." She heaved to her feet and stubbed out the cigarette in a plant pot. "You won't find many with my credentials. Two mornings a week I do the executive toilets at *The Daily Spokesman*."

"*The Daily Spokesman*? You wouldn't happen to know *the* Felicity Friend?"

Mrs. Malloy smacked her raspberry lips. "We have met in the course of my work; to say more would be a violation of me code of ethics. Three evenings I do the offices of Bragg, Wiseman & Smith, which tells you I can keep me eyes and hands to meself, all those documents sitting around; though who could make top nor tail of them I don't know. That poor Lady Peerless. But I suppose these modern typewriters do Latin and such. And an old maid like her, she'll have the hot chills for him."

"Who's 'him'?" I asked, feeling horribly low.

"Mr. Greek God, Lionel Wiseman, but I doubt she's got lucky. Not with him being married to the blond chorus girl—if they *are* married, which some in these here parts doubt." Mrs. Malloy heaved a sigh. "On the subject of men—your husband isn't the sort who makes a nuisance of himself, I trust?"

Here was my out. I heaved an echoing sigh.

"Unfortunately, Mrs. Malloy, you have touched upon the one drawback to this job. He will be home sometimes during the day. Cooking." I made the last word sound as sinister as I could.

"Mrs. H., you don't grasp my meaning." Roxie Malloy adjusted the diamanté clasp on her rope of pearls. "I don't care a farthing what sort of floury muddle the man makes, so long as he cleans up after himself. Now was I married to the man"—she picked up a Victorian mixing bowl and inspected it—"I might feel all me femininity being sapped away, never getting to open a tin of peas. But what interests me is whether or not Mr. H. is given to lecherous advances. Having buried three husbands, I'm giving up men. Undependable lot." She pinned me to the wall with her gaze. "So, give it to me straight, Mrs. H. Can you vouch for your man?"

"My husband is completely harmless." The words came out like bullets.

"I'd guessed as much. Women aren't his type . . . of vice."

Her eyelids fluttered. "But then—I've been known to bring out the beast in men a bishop would swear to. Still, I've put me cards smack on the table. And I'm giving you a month's trial. Can't say fairer than that, can I?"

"Well—"

"Only reason I've got any spare days is that one of my ladies, Mrs. Woolpack, has gone batty and is in hospital."

And so she joined our happy home.

Of course, even with Roxie coming in two mornings a week, there was plenty to do in the house.

Every Thursday afternoon was aerobics class. Bunty had phoned me immediately after our curtailed lunch at The Dark Horse to solicit me as a pupil. When I had said that the Historical Society was more my speed, she had responded, "That lot! They weren't born, they were *exhumed*; and their leader is Mrs. Bottomly!" The magic words.

Three years previously, a foray into the world of organized exercise had resulted in a week off work and a plea for forgiveness to my body. But as this new year got underway, I was determined to make good. If I could once learn to hop and bob in time with the rest of the group and stop smacking the woman next to me in the face with my foot each time I did a leg lift, I would be a marginal student. Bunty was an exuberant teacher. The rest of the class found her instructions easy to follow. I found the sight of her legs kicking to the ceiling demoralizing. All I wanted was to pull in, firm out, and be able to eat a little more, so Ben wouldn't look so wounded when I tried to hide the potatoes under the parsley sprigs.

All of Bunty's students were to be in the burlesque routine she was planning for the middle of May, benefits going to the St. Anselm's youth group. And I was assigned a starring role, one which had the advantage of keeping me offstage much of the time. I was to leap out of a cake and cry, "Ta-Ta!" in the scene entitled Bachelor Party. The cake would supposedly have been baked by Ben. A little free advertising, which a good wife could not refuse.

Another plus was that I got to know Ann Delacorte better; she did wardrobe and sets for all the St. Anselm's productions. She loved theatre, which helped in this case because for some reason she did not love Bunty Wiseman.

Ann appeared to have only one friend, Millicent Parsnip,

the tabby woman who had been with Amelia Bottomly on the train. And although no one could replace Dorcas as a confidante, I needed a woman to talk to. The marriage manuals, I was discovering, often focused on the obvious, and I already possessed the sophistication not to wear rollers, a face mask, and flannel pyjamas to bed or devour onions by the plateful—even though they are low in calories and make a pleasing change from naked lettuce. Where I needed instruction was in how to deal with the revelation that after only a few months of marriage Ben did not think of me exclusively twenty-four hours a day. Equally saddening was my own growing indifference. I found I no longer begrudged him the occasional drink with Freddy at The Dark Horse. And on those evenings when he retreated to the study with his recipe collection, I could quite happily occupy myself with a book or sketch pad until it was time to go upstairs and fill my bath with Essence of Orchid. Was it possible that after four months our marriage was developing middle-aged spread?

I didn't verbalize all this to Ann or confide in her my concerns about my missing mother-in-law or remark that Ben put the shutters down when I brought up the subject of his parents' separation. Rather, Ann confided in me, taking my mind off myself, giving me a sense of perspective. On Thursdays, after aerobics class, she would accompany me on expeditions for Abigail's accoutrements. Usually we took her cute bottle-green Morris Minor, because I had still not persuaded Ben to bury Heinz and get a new vehicle. But on an afternoon in mid-April, I drove because Ann's car was in the garage.

"If we can make it to the village," I assured her as we lurched through the church gates, "we should be all right. Usually when the sweet old thing conks out, he does so during the first five hundred yards."

"Nice, though—having a convertible." Ann put on a pair of dark glasses and hugged up the collar of her beaver coat.

Gracious, as usual; Ann knew this car did not convert. Its roof was permanently compressed into accordion folds. Ideal for Ben with his claustrophobia.

"Ellie, do you have to stop in at Abigail's and get that sample of tile for the ladies' room from Ben?"

"Actually, no." I downshifted. "Ben vetoed . . . I mean, we mutually agreed last night that I should look for something more restful in colour." Biting my lip, I stared through the windscreen. All euphemisms aside, Ben and I had verged on a quarrel the previous evening. I hadn't been able to get through to him that we didn't want the customers taking forty winks while freshening up. At one point I had come close to raising my voice, above the level of what it was already raised; but then, bathrooms had become something of unhallowed ground for us. Twice that week I had caught Ben removing my still damp hose from the towel rail in the bathroom, and once I'd nabbed him in the act of stuffing them in a drawer. The wrong drawer!

"I was just trying to be helpful, darling," he'd said with that innocent look on his face.

"It would have been helpful if you had left them where they were . . . darling."

A kiss on the back of my head—where I couldn't feel it, let alone see it. "Ellie, you know I can't stand clutter. I was brought up to be orderly."

"And I was brought up to dislike mildewed drawers."

The Heinz did a swerving figure eight. Relaxing my hold on the steering wheel, I turned to Ann. "Speaking of Ben reminds me—mind if I stop in at Mr. Wiseman's office? Ben wants him to check some point on the lease." We were vibrating down Cliff Road. The sea below was dark as malt liquor, its white head foaming into great spills.

"Of course not, Ellie!"

Something in her voice made me glance sideways, but I couldn't read her face because of the glasses.

"I can as well go tomorrow."

"I wouldn't think of it; I know you and Ben are down to the wire where the restaurant is concerned."

Teddy Peerless was pegging away at a fantastic clip upon a medieval typewriter, her projecting teeth clamped on her lower lip in concentration, as we entered the outer office of Bragg, Wiseman & Smith. In a corner of the book-lined room near the window a green and crimson parrot strutted and squawked in its cage.

"Greetings from your king, pretty damsels!" That was the parrot.

Teddy stopped typing. She rose, tugging the ends of her beige cardigan, and jabbed a comb more securely into her birds-nest hair. She was introducing us to Flinders, the parrot, when

Lionel Wiseman came through the door. Some men have the knack of making an entrance—even I, a comfortably married woman, acknowledged that. Pressing my fingers, he thanked me for coming in about the lease. I found myself a little captivated by his deskside manner, the deep timbre of his voice, his impressive height and broad shoulders, his crisp, silvery hair glinting in the light from Teddy's lamp, but, needless to say, only in the way I would have been captivated by a handsome piece of furniture. I pictured Lionel Wiseman's first meeting with Bunty, imagining him leaning over the theatre balcony rail, deciding he wanted the second girl from the left in the chorus line, the blonde with the legs that went from here to eternity.

Releasing me from his intent dark gaze, he gave me back my hand and said he would sort out the lease quibble. I was sure he would. Teddy was at the file cabinet plucking out a yellow folder. She was saying something about the weather to Ann, who was sinking slowly into a chair, her face the colour of moonlight against her dark glasses. Teddy dropped the folder and pressed Ann's head down toward her knees. Lionel strode over to them; concern made him even more handsome.

"Mrs. Delacorte, let me fetch you a brandy, or ring for a doctor."

"I'm perfectly all right." Ann grew, if possible, paler.

A question mark took shape in my mind. Was there more here than met the eye? I had sensed an antagonism between Ann and Bunty at The Dark Horse. Had Lionel botched some legal matter for the Delacortes or (I studied his Saville Row suit) sent them an exhorbitant fee for services rendered?

Ann, truthfully or otherwise, blamed her dizzy spell upon Flinders, saying in a faint voice, "Silly of me, but I thought he was going to peck me through the bars."

I offered to take her directly home, but she insisted the zesty sea air was what she needed. So we said our good-byes and drove along Coast Road through Pebblewell to Snaresby. There we got out and walked, coming almost immediately upon a little tucked-away shop which sold china doorknobs. I found one with enamelled bluebells. Perfect for the ground floor reception room at Abigail's. Afterward I pressed Ann to stop at the cafe next door for tea. As we sat sipping away, I strayed the conversation back to her fainting attack.

"It was nothing to do with Mr. Wiseman." She was quite

definite. Too definite? She twisted her cup around in her saucer. "Ellie, do you recall my telling you that several people have hinted that Charles is having an affair?"

"You told me you didn't believe it," I replied.

"I didn't, but this morning I received a letter signed A Friend, informing me that I am a wronged wife."

"Did it look like a form letter?"

Ann smiled. "Do you think it could be that sort of thing, Ellie?"

"Absolutely." As it happened, I was speaking the truth. I could not imagine Charles Delacorte thawing out long enough to start an affair.

Ann spread her fingers and looked down at them. "Charles and I . . . He never was very keen, you know; he always said"—she twirled the necklace at her throat—"that sex was . . . untidy."

"I see." I blushed.

"It could have been worse, I suppose." Ann tried to smile. "The note could have said, 'Your husband is carrying on with another man.' " Now it was her turn for her eyes to avoid mine. Was I missing something? My eyes fixed on a man with an abundance of glossy black curls seated at the corner table. Mr. Daffy? Yes, but a drastically changed Mr. Daffy. Pale, hollow-cheeked, thin. Or was it that all the stuffing seemed to have gone out of him? He saw me looking at him, but instead of bouncing out of the chair and foisting his relentless sales technique on me, he actually shrank back in his chair, his ripe olive eyes growing dull. So this is what I got for refusing to sell Merlin's Court! After a minute, he walked slowly over to the table.

"Well, well, ladies. Fancy seeing you here! You weren't looking for me by any chance, were you?" He was inching backward as he spoke.

"No, I'm afraid not." I felt guilty about it.

"Good, good." His face broke into a trembling smile. "I've been having these odd notions recently that I'm being followed, that . . . the bloodhounds are after me, closing in." He wiped a hand across his sticky brow. "All nonsense, of course. But I think I'll see my doctor, get a tonic. Here, let me give you another of my cards." He dropped one in my hand, as if it were hot, and virtually fled out the door.

* * * *

We were on the outskirts of Pebblewell when I noticed the first beading of moisture on the windscreen. In seconds water sheeted down, puddling in our laps. And, to make matters worse, the road kept getting narrower until it looked like a smoker's breath. A glance over the stupidly low wall to my left showed waves far below, whipped by the wind into a spiteful froth, encouraging me to drive as straight a course as possible. Minutes later, seeing became the number one problem. Heinz scraped against the wall, which now seemed to be on my right. Add to that our feet being underwater and I had to agree with Ann that it might be wise to pull over and wait out the deluge. But pull over which way? Right meant running up the side of the cliff; left meant going over the sea wall. Time out for a moment of prayer.

Miraculously, the gusting wind lifted my hair away from my eyes and through the downpour I espied two towering pillars. Affixed to one was an unreadable sign board. The essential point was that between them ran a steepish track, pathway, lane, whatever.

"Mind if we pull in here?" I asked.

Ann removed her hat, shook it free of water and replaced it. "I'd mind if you didn't."

Not trusting Heinz to stay parked on an incline, I drove up the short rise. We were in an avenue, darkened to heavy shadow by the thick overhead branches. Rain drummed against the windscreen. Turning off the engine, I wiped my face on my soggy coat sleeve and apologised to Ann for bringing her to this pass.

"Ellie, really—this makes an interesting interlude in my uneventful life." Her lips smiled serenely but her eyes were hidden by rain-spattered glasses.

"I wonder where we are?"

Ann lifted the glasses to her forehead then lowered them, without looking round. "Sorry, Ellie, I'm quite useless when it comes to getting my bearings."

I glanced around. This avenue was undoubtedly pleasant at times, but now the sea was muffled to a soft, ominous stomping.

Never mind, we were about to get out of here! To my joy, I could count the raindrops landing on my upturned palm. A cheery word to Ann, a flick of the ignition key, a trounce on the accelerator, and . . . Nothing.

This is all Ben's fault, was my unwifely thought.

"Do you think . . . ?" suggested Ann.

"No."

We sat and listened to the trees drip.

Ann buffed the face of her watch, then pulled up the collar of her beaver coat. "We'll be all right, Ellie."

Easy for her to talk. Beavers dress for this weather.

Being females of passably quick brains, it occurred to us that there might be light at the end of this tunnel—er—avenue. We climbed out of the car and trudged forward until we emerged from groping shadow to a bleariness wherein drenched sky and earth merged. We stood at the edge of a semicircular sweep of lawn, ornamented by mossy statues and bordered by box hedges, glossy and olive-black with rain. Beyond the lawn rose a huge, granite slab of a house. Its windows were so heavily mullioned they looked barred; its double doors led out onto a pillared terrace.

Ann's arm brushed mine. "Ellie, this has to be The Peerless Nursing Home."

"A bit grim, isn't it? I see why Lady Theodora didn't repine—"

At that moment the huge doors cracked open to reveal a woman dressed as a nurse. Two dogs, one white, one black (quite small but with such oversized heads they had to be transplants), bombarded out from behind her, barking furiously.

Ann's elbow jabbed me. She stumbled over my foot. "I don't like dogs."

I didn't like the nurse. She had stepped swiftly back inside and closed the door. Gripping Ann's arm, I warned her to keep her voice down. The animals ceased plunging up and down the terrace. They froze. Necks arched, muzzles pointing to the silvery haze above, they sniffed the air. The gloom of the place, as well as the chill damp, seeped into my pores. Particularly menacing was the fact that the dogs' eyes never once swivelled our way.

Until, that is, Ann blundered up against a tree. Hands moving in slow motion to her throat, she let out a moan and, before I could grab her, flung around and was gone, stumbling across the lawn.

The dogs came down the terrace steps like bullets.

"Ann, don't! You're encouraging them to play. If you will

only . . ." I caught up with my elegant friend as she scrambled to climb the hedge. Her wits had completely gone. A forty-foot tree would have made better sense.

She threw off my hand. "Ellie, leave me alone!"

The air bristled with fur and canine breath.

"Heel, Virtue! Heel, Sin!"

The words were spoken calmly and conversationally, by a male standing several yards away. His face swam before my eyes. The danger was past. Tails whirring, sniffling with puppyish pleasure, the dogs now gamboled about the black-trousered legs.

"Home!"

Ann had grabbed me around the waist and was holding me in front of her like a shield. I didn't blame her. My legs had gone peculiar. I wanted Ben. I wanted to sit by the fire, sipping Ovaltine, writing to Dorcas and Jonas.

All of a sudden Ben was no longer the husband who hadn't quite measured up to his potential; he was the lover who had awakened me.

Slowly, Ann detached herself from me. The dark glasses cast semicircles of shadow and her face gleamed as though with rain, but she was steady on her feet.

"How can I be of help to you, ladies?"

There could be no mistaking those melancholy eyes, the black hair swept back from the high forehead. At close quarters Dr. Bordeaux looked more than ever like a poet suffering for his art. I could visualize those bone-white fingers clenching the quill—

I extended my hand, and he brushed it with his fingertips before letting it fall as though amputated. I blundered into explanations about the car. There was a clammy sort of fascination about this man. How many of the stories whispered about him were true? Perhaps a doctor's license to practice was revoked only if the murder victims complained personally.

Dr. Bordeaux held Ann's hand longer than he did mine. Was he taking her pulse?

"Do you have any idea what is wrong with your auto, Mrs. Haskell?"

"It won't start."

His eyes were black, not brown. I had never seen black eyes before. Yes, I could picture him tucking a little old lady into bed and murmuring, "Sleep, Mrs. Jones, a sleep unbroken by dreams or waking." The spooky atmosphere of The Peerless Nursing Home grounds was clearly not conducive to my mental health.

"I will take a look at the car and see if I cannot have you both speedily upon your way. I wish I could invite you to wait in our reception rooms, but we are in the process"—he smoothed back his hair—"of varnishing the floors."

With the dogs running in and out? I wondered. Ann said hastily that she would prefer to stay outside on their account.

Dr. Bordeaux glanced toward the massive house. "We are rather isolated here. And Virtue and Sin do make us all feel more secure. They are devoted to the patients; so much so that sometimes they don't want them to go home."

The wind knifed through my damp coat. I did hope that Mrs. Woolpack's stay here would not be prolonged by severity of her illness or the dogs.

Dr. Bordeaux began walking toward the avenue. "Shall we set to work on your car, Mrs. Haskell?"

"This is very good of you." I linked arms with Ann, to help her feel warmer, safer.

"Not at all." He flexed his white fingers. "I quite enjoy fixing things. It relieves tension."

What sort of tension? Professional or personal? In the gathering dusk, the statues on the lawn seemed to move. I imagined they became people on a train—a man with an invalid in his arms, an old white-haired woman hovering. A small girl with sandy plaits proffering pillows. Jenny.

"Hello," said her voice.

She was moving between the statues. The wind tousled her plaits. Her eyes, those too grown-up eyes, looked into mine, as they had done when I handed her my wedding bouquet.

"What are you doing here?" Her arms were wrapped around her thin chest; her blue-and-white check dress whipped around her legs. She never looked at Ann.

I explained about the car, all the while sensing Dr. Bordeaux's contained impatience and . . . something else. He was displeased by this encounter.

"And what about you, Jenny?"

"I live here."

"Oh!" My surprise was reflected in Ann's face.

Jenny laughed. It was, I realised, the first time I had heard her laugh. "Not in the hospital." She hugged her arms tighter. "I live at the Dower House. With Mumma and Nonna. Mumma was a friend of Uncle Simon's"—her eyes flickered to Dr. Bordeaux—"before she got sick. And a few months ago when we had no other place to go, he brought us here. Would you like to come and meet Mumma and Nonna?"

"I would love to."

"Ellie." Ann tightened her hand on my arm. "I would appreciate the opportunity to sit and rest for a few minutes."

"Jenny," said the doctor sternly, "your mother will be resting." The smile he tacked onto this statement only made it colder.

"Then, I'll wake her." Jenny lifted her pointed chin and flicked one of the plaits over her shoulder. "She needs company. And so do I. Apart from school, the only time I ever see people is when I go to the youth group or out on my bike."

"Which school?" I asked.

"The Miriam Academy. It's on the other side of Snaresby."

"I know," I said. "A friend of mine named Dorcas used to work there." If Dr. Bordeaux let Jenny go to school and the St. Anselm's youth group, her plight could not, I supposed, be too dire.

"Where's your friend now?"

"In America."

"Oh; I'd much rather stay at home and have Nonna teach me. She used to be Mumma's governess. Then later . . ." Jenny dropped her arms. "Are you coming? The Dower House is quite beautiful. The Peerless family used to send the old grannies and such to live there." She was pointing to a gap in the trees beyond the hedge to the left.

Dr. Bordeaux had turned as inclement-looking as the weather. What sort of lives did Jenny and her family endure, under the domination of this man?

13

. . . "Ellie, I sense something momentous happened at The Dower House?" Primrose quivered and gripped her shawl.

"No." I fiddled with my spoon. "The sitting room to which Jenny took Ann and me was brim full of charming simplicity—the floors were natural pine, the chairs were cane-seated and ladder-backed, the curtains at the window nooks were yellowed lace. There were several rather nice prints, a seascape and portraits of Sarah Siddons and David Garrick."

"Any mirrors?" The pages of Hyacinth's green notebook fluttered shut.

"No."

"Are you saying, Ellie," Primrose touched my hand, "that there was something rather *unsimple* about the mood of that room? The feel? . . ."

When I replay that visit in my mind, I don't see movement. We're all frozen in place. Jenny pouring tea, the old woman—so like an old-world nanny she only needed a frilled cap on her white hair, stooping to adjust the rug covering the invalid who lay on the sofa before the blazing fireplace. The nanny's gnarled hands are fixed in the act of holding back a corner of the quilt so Ann and I can glimpse the pallid face on the pillow, a face that must have been very beautiful once. It is impossible to tell her age. She might be in her forties or sixties. There are lines on her face but they may have been put there by pain. The auburn of her hair could be artificial, but the most striking thing about her is her eyes. They are empty. I can't tell their colour. A record is going around and around on one of those marvellous old gramophones with the horns. A pain-drenched voice sings, "You are my rainy days, my rainy days, my rainy days . . ." over and over until Jenny lifts the mechanical arm and turns the machine off.

Jenny said her mother had been ill about ten years. The nanny's face seemed to disintegrate. "My darling wasn't struck down by the Lord." Her voice filled the room. "It was him—him. But he didn't kill her. She's in there safe and sound. It's all right, Vania, my dove. Nonna's got you." She was crooning into the unseeing eyes.

Jenny sat without moving. So did Ann. Upon entering the room, she had felt rather faint again. Dr. Bordeaux, when he came to tell us the car was functioning, said she must have suffered a delayed reaction to her fright over the dogs. He was patently anxious for us to leave, a feeling I heartily reciprocated.

When I looked back at the house from the end of the driveway, Jenny stood motionless at the window, watching us. I had the feeling that she would have liked to call me back. Poor kid.

And poor me. I know science has decreed in its infinite wisdom that we don't catch colds from getting chilled, but it seems a bit coincidental that I woke one morning a fortnight later feeling as though there was standing room only on my chest.

The Friday (24th April) I was stricken, Ben was due to go to London to meet his editor, A.E. Brady. Instead, he received a letter respectfully requesting that their appointment be changed to the following Monday. In my weakened condition, it seemed to me my spouse reacted with an undue petulance to this deferment. But I refrained from saying so because a) Ben's reaction to my visit to the Peerless Nursing Home and my description of Dr. Bordeaux and his doggies had provided our marriage with enough zip for a while (he thought my "riotous imagination" was "endearing"); b) I had chosen to work that week on my unbecoming tendency to be critical (suppressing the conviction that damp hose had contributed to my illness); c) it hurt to talk.

I must not give the impression that Ben was unsympathetic to me or my snuffly nose. Before leaving for Abigail's that morning he hovered by my bed offering—eagerly—to rub my chest with Vicks.

"How do you feel, sweetheart?"

"My nobse hab grown and my legs are melting like candles."

"Poor precious. You do look pretty foul."

"Kimb ob you to say so."

His voice was muffled too. "Ellie, you do understand why I am wearing this surgical mask? My God, can you imagine anything worse than my being struck down nigh on the eve of Abigail's premiere? Sure, Freddy could handle the simple stuff. His latest lamb chops Strasbourg are a credit to me, but he could never cope on his own. He'd only do a marginally better job than you, El." He kissed the back of my head. One of my least favourite places for being kissed but—cough, cough—in my unappealing state I settled for crumbs.

"And, darling"—he smoothed out the silvery grey sheet—"you will promise to eat the meals I have left prepared for you?" The mask made his voice sound like it was being pressed through a sieve.

I slid down in the bed and folded my hands piously over my breast. "Ob course, darling." No need to tell him that I had already figured that my illness should be good for a three-pound loss.

"Good, because I've noticed your clothes are beginning to hang on you."

A lifelong ambition fulfilled!

"They'b stretched in the wash."

He touched my hair. "Want a hot water bottle or would you rather I tucked Tobias in at your feet?"

"I don't want him in here in cabse he catches it."

"A mouse?"

"Silly—my colb." Since Mr. Daffy and the train, I hadn't enjoyed mouse jokes.

Ben glanced at his watch and moved my water jug a little closer. "Good thing this is one of Mrs. Malloy's days. She can minister to your needs."

His footsteps died away; the house settled into silence. Throwing off the blankets, I lurched over to the window, closed it, and pulled the curtains tight. Had Ben locked the garden door? I had been nagging at him about that lately. Was that pounding coming from inside my head or downstairs? I got back in bed and pulled the covers up to my poor nose. A fire would have been cosy. Nine o'clock said the bedside clock; time for Roxie to arrive and always time for Tobias to be on the scavenge.

At the end of our month's trial period, Roxie had summoned me to the kitchen for her decision. Would she say the working conditions at Merlin's Court weren't up to snuff? After pouring us each a glass of gin from the supplies bag (wonderful stuff for buffing chrome and giving glass a sparkle), she had made her portentous pronouncement. The gossips could stop cackling and start laying eggs. She had observed Mr. H. was a decent gentlemen, as men went, except when one of his cooking experiments failed.

The buzzing in my ears became the revving of the Hoover outside my bedroom. The door pushed open and Roxie poked in her black and white head, bellowing over the motor.

"Hangover, Mrs. H.?"

Easing up on my elbows, I fetched forth a wan smile. "I gob a bit ob a colb."

"So've I, but some of us have to stay on our feet. Anything I can get you? A scudsy book? Guinness and milk?"

"I dob't—" Throwing a tissue over my face, I surrendered to a sneeze that rocked the bed.

"Don't do to just lie down and die, you know. I had me appendix out, and I—" An explosion of annoyance. Her red butterfly mouth stretched into a shout and her brows rose into inverted commas above the very violet lids. "There goes the Hoover! Making off down the landing like a bleeding robot! Best catch it before it makes a break for the stairs." Her muffled voice came back to me. "On the subject of stairs, Mrs. H., three times I have sprained me wrist polishing that loose bannister and I don't have to tell you it's against union regulations for me to work under such conditions."

To my knowledge the only union of which Roxie was a member was the Mother's Union. She had a few words to say on the subject of its sister organization when she returned at 11:00 A.M. to plump up my pillows and spill water between my parched lips.

"Her Graciousness, Mrs. Amelia Bottomly, rang. Wants to fix a date for Mr. H. to do the cookery lesson for The Hearthside Guild."

"I dob't knowb when Ben could do it."

"Don't worry your woolly head. I swung me pencil over the calendar by the phone, and when it stopped moving, I marked the spot. Third Saturday in May. Twelve noon in the church hall. A word from the wise, Mrs. H. When you've been married as often as me, you'll know we don't ask men if they can spare the time. We tell 'em. Put on your trousers. Be there."

That was all very well! My darling could be run off his feet, whipping up eggs here, pounding pastry there. The date in question was only three weeks away and Abigail's premiere a week today; our calendar would begin to look used. It had begun to dawn on me recently that Ben and I had not become swept up in the social whirl as a couple. We were either together at home or he was out with Freddy.

"How about something to read?" Roxie reached into the pocket of her plum synthetic dress with the sequined neckline and brought out a paperback book. "Hoped I'd get to put me feet up and have a little wallow with me elevenses. But, no rest for the wicked." From the reek of Eau de Lily of the Valley on Roxie's breath I suspected she had already had elevenses. "Nothing like a corpse, I always say, to lift the spirits."

"Ib's a thriller, then?" A sneeze prevented my taking the book.

"I wouldn't be talking about the corpse de bally, would I?" Roxie plopped down on the bed, making my lungs rattle, and lit up a fag. "I won't spoil it for you, Mrs. H., but there's this Victorian kitchen maid named Ethel who chops up the young master of the house on account of him making advances and turns him into chutney. Pots and pots of him. You'd think the old Earl and his Mrs. would be worried about sonny-boy, wouldn't you? Not on your life—they think he's gone foxhunting or wenching—and been delayed, but they're delighted with Ethel, what with her working overtime." Roxie dropped ash on the carpet and rubbed it in with her foot.

"What utter rubbish!" Contemptuously, I blew my nose.

"I didn't say it was Shakespeare, Mrs. H." Mrs. Malloy ruffled up like a chicken. "But who reads Shakespeare unless they're made to? Don't see chaps strap-hanging with their eyes glued to his stuff on the train, do you?" Roxie stomped across the room, tossed the cigarette in the grate, flung open the maroon velvet curtains, did a half turn, then with deliberation pulled wide her apron pocket to plop in the book.

"Thought you might be interested because it's written by Mary Birdsong—otherwise known as Edwin Digby—your neighbor and a person with which I do have a nodding acquaintance through seeing him"—she heaved a breath—"at The Dark Horse of an evening."

I took the book. One does have a moral obligation to support local talent.

Roxie was right. *In a Devil of a Pickle* was not Shakespeare. It was literary lunacy, but (quite against my better literary judgment) I became so absorbed in discovering whether Bingham, the butler, would discover the secret exit from the subterranean stillroom into the smuggler's tunnel before Villainess Ethel returned with the silver platter for his head, that I had to keep shoving my nose out of the way in order to race to the next page until a knock at the bedroom door heralded Dr. Melrose, little black bag in hand.

"Hello, Ellie." His was the tentative smile of the door-to-door salesman. Social or professional visit, I wasn't pleased. No time to change from my flannel nightgown into something with rosebuds.

When ill at ease, attack. "Hello, doctor. I must be sicker than I realised—I don't remember sending for you."

"Your husband"—the doctor fussed around in the bag—"felt I should check you over. Ah, yes, here comes Mrs. Malloy. Would you like her to remain?"

I wasn't going to like *anything* about this. Ben had no right to foist medical attention on me. All I had was a colb.

"Could be worse, Mrs. H." Roxie shuffled the mop around the bed. "Master could have sent for Dr. Bordeaux."

"Open wide. Say, 'Ah'!"

I hate surprises unless they have bows on them.

"Take a deep breath, please."

The last straw would be if I lost my voice before Ben got home.

Refolding his stethoscope, Dr. Melrose stood flapping it around in his hands.

Roxie said with great relish, "Give it to us straight, Doc. Will this prove fatal? Because if so, I'll think about finding meself another job."

Dr. Melrose shook his head and paced. "No need for alarm, I assure you."

Roxie struggled to conceal her disappointment.

"Ellie, I'll prescribe something for the cold, but more important, I want you on a strict diet."

His words came pretty close to proving fatal for him as well as me. Was nothing I had done in the service of starvation enough?

"You are to eat three well-balanced, man-sized meals a day, take two milky drinks and . . ."

That buzzing in my ears wasn't just the colb, it was the giddiness of relief and shock. I liked Dr. Melrose (as much as I could like any man who knew as much as he about my inner workings), but I had never suspected he had a grain of humour. Something else struck me about him; he had grown a little pudgy. And had probably 'doctored' the numbers on his Ideal Weight Chart accordingly.

Now if he would only get out of here so I could get back to Chapter 7 of *In a Devil of a Pickle*. Was it possible that Villainess Ethel had an accomplice in, that nice Mr. Snodgrass who did the exquisite petit point?

When Roxie put in a final appearance at five o'clock, I was on the brink of discovering who was going to be bottled next.

"Lovely little story, isn't it? Keep it overnight, Mrs. H." Roxie was magnificent as well as magnanimous in a fuchsia satin toque. Her fur coat bore signs of having been washed in hot water instead of cold.

"By the by, Mrs. H., Her Graciousness Bottomly phoned back. Seems the ladies of the Historical Society want to tour here next Thursday afternoon if convenient. I said it was, seeing Thursday is not one of my days. And now, if it's all the same to you, I'll be pushing off. Friday's bingo night for me. Wouldn't miss it for the world nor would Hairdresser Sid. Him and me always sit together and have a chum. People can say what they like, but the worst I have to say against him is that he's teetotal." She moved to the bed and gave the covers a twitch. "Locked and barred all the doors and windows, I have, Mrs. H. Put me into overtime, it did. But I'm sure you won't mind the extra under the circumstances."

I struggled to sit up. "What circumstances?"

Roxie sank down on the bed and tapped a slow dum-de-dum-dum on the footrail. "Now, understand, Mrs. H., I wouldn't frighten you, not for the world, but a couple of times when proceeding home from here, I have seen this nasty customer loitering near the gates."

My fingers gripped the sheet. "What sort of nasty customer?"

Roxie looked impatient. "The usual, like in the films or on the telly. Raincoat with the collar turned up, hat with the brim pulled down, scarf at the neck, chewed-up fag in the mouth."

"A mouthful of dingy teeth?" The stifled feeling was not due to my cold.

"You've got it."

"Eyes like jagged slits?" I had just read that description in Chapter 8.

"Hard enough to cut glass."

Roxie heaved a sigh, which chilled me right through my flannel nightgown, and stood up. "But you've not a thing to worry about, Mrs. H., all's locked up like a safe. Don't want to wake up and find the house stripped down to its vest and pants, do we?"

Time to face facts, Ellie. The Raincoat Man is not a figment of your imagination. Make what you will of the fact—he first put in an appearance when your mother-in-law disappeared.

I shrank back against the pillow, picking at Edwin Digby's book. The desire to read had vanished. The Raincoat Man had to be a detective of some kind. Watching to see if Ben or I made contact with Mrs. Haskell. Perhaps the nosy neighbors of Crown Street had hired him. I was certain now it was he, not Jonas, I had seen in our drawing room in the middle of the night. I cast a fearful glance toward the window. Ben's claustrophobia provided an open invitation. My mind was writing its own peep-show horror. Mr. Elijah Haskell swam in and out of focus in the starring role of villain. What if he wanted to marry Mrs.

Jarrod before either got too ancient? His wife's Catholic beliefs forbade divorce. My mind twisted down another dark alley—the Raincoat Man metamorphosed from sleazy detective to sleazy hatchet man. No, that didn't make sense; if he had done the foul deed and murdered Ben's mother in return for a lifetime of free vegetables, he wouldn't be hanging around for close on five months, sizing up the reaction of the family.

My nose tingled. I was about to be overtaken by a gigantic sneeze. My hand flapped feebly at the tissue box. There was a positive side to all this—during the past weeks I had stopped picturing my mother-in-law with prayer sores on her knees. Indeed, she had acquired a cherished place in my heart. This was the woman who had brought Ben into the world. So she hadn't jumped for joy when he married me! Who could blame her! It wasn't anybody's fault that Ben had found that girl Angelica Evangeline from Crown Street somewhat sexually repellent.

Speaking of things repellent, my bedroom door handle was turning—slowly. A sneeze stalled. In anguished immobility, I watched another quarter revolution.

"Whob there?"

A muffled, almost animal grunt; a metallic click, like a safe being cracked.

"I hab a gun amb a red-hot poker."

The door opened an inch. My lungs squeezed shut and my mouth opened in a soundless scream. Then luckily I came to my senses. The trick in this sort of situation is to stay calm. My options were numerous. I could play dead. I could make a break for the window and dangle from all that lovely ivy outside . . . No, no! First place the intruder would look. Ditto under the bed. But if I could wedge myself between the mattress and box spring . . . Too late, too late! I was floundering off-side when the door opened wide. A man with a blackened sack hoisted on his shoulder staggered drunkenly toward the bed. A handkerchief mask flattened his features. I opened my mouth to scream.

"For God's sake, Ellie!" The sack tumbled onto the hearth and Ben ripped off the mask. His next words were lovely and concerned. "My poor darling—you look even worse than this morning."

Actually I felt pretty good. Mary Birdsong was the real culprit. I had let my imagination run away with me. Propped up on one elbow, I pointed to the sack. "Have you come selling turnips?"

I couldn't tell whether he was amused. His black head was bent, and he was rubbing a finger. "Coal, actually. I thought you might enjoy the cheer of a fire. My difficulty with the door was that I didn't want to set the sack down and get coal dust on the carpet and I have never been very adept with my elbows."

"What's wrong with your finger?"

He stopped bending it and held it up to the light. "Tobias scratched me just now when I told him he still couldn't come in here."

"Poor pet."

"I'll live."

I had meant Tobias. But I did so love the way Ben's eyes darkened when he was being noble. Even more wonderful was that he showed no signs of being repulsed by my bloated visage. True, only the reading lamp was lit, but I was so gratified I decided not to utter a word of complaint about his sending for Dr. Melrose.

Such a loving evening. Firelight bathed the walls with a roseate glow and set red-gold angels to dance upon the ceiling. Dinner on a tray and Ben didn't expect me to eat a lot. Beatles records on the stereo. The two of us talking, laughing. I didn't miss my friends in America. I even loved Freddy. I hoped Jill would give him a reprieve and swoop him off to a guru who did weddings, but not immediately—Ben was anticipating between four and five hundred people at Abigail's premiere.

When Ben touched me, looked at me, his eyes glowing hotter than the fire, my blood started flowing backward in my veins and I turned all floaty, light as tinsel. It wouldn't have surprised me a bit if I had levitated off the bed. Tonight would definitely have been the night for violins. A pity about my nasty colb.

"Goodnight, Ellie."

"Goodnight, Ben."

Did ever a man look more heart-stoppingly debonair as he adjusted his surgical mask and turned out the light?

My dreams should have been all humming bees and sundrenched meadows. Instead, Mrs. Amelia Bottomly filled up my mental screen. A dozen identical men in raincoats took to stalking me, round and round for hours. I would be exhausted in the morning. A ghost with Ben's features wearing a black lace mantilla and a rosary strung over her arm was beckoning me to follow her into the mist, which turned thick and hot. Toss and turn as I might, I could not escape being sucked into it.

When I unglued my eyes the next morning I found that the brass candlestick, which usually stood upon the mantelshelf, had levitated to the window sill. Even more eerie was the fact that the candle was alight. For a ghastly moment I suspected a nocturnal visit from The Raincoat Man, until I saw the candle wax on my hand.

Sunday afternoon found me sufficiently recovered in body and soul to begin convalescence on the drawing room sofa. Ben came and stood in my light as I was deep in the pages of another Edwin Digby/Mary Birdsong book.

"My finger still hurts."

"What finger?"

"The one your damn cat scratched."

"Oh!" Prying my eyes off the page, I saw he was holding the affected digit to the light.

"How positively heinous!" The inane caretaker had kidnapped Lady Lucinda.

"Ellie, I don't think you give a damn about my finger."

I closed the book. My mother used to complain she never got any enjoyment out of an illness because my father always stole the limelight with his near-death experience.

At three o'clock, Freddy rapped on the open window, pushed the curtains aside, and entered bearing gifts: a plate of eccles cakes. Mark you, they weren't the greatest (the ratio of currants to dough was a little low), but feelings, which I had thought dead, stirred. There were six on the plate; one for each of us now, leaving three for later. One for Ben, one for me, and a spare.

"Not bad, Freddy." Ben tossed a sample in his hand. "Keep this up and in a year, possibly six months, you will be able to hold your own against the competition."

"Thanks, boss." Standing on the hearth, Freddy flung his arms along the mantel, causing candlesticks and clock to jump. "Ellie, that nose does nothing for you."

I smiled. "Come over here and let me kiss you."

He smirked through his beard. "I never get colds. Mind

over mucus." He kicked the fire tongs. "Anyone want to hear what Jill has to say in her letter?"

"Can't think of anything I would enjoy more." Ben settled in a chair and studied his finger. I held my book negligently in front of my face.

Freddy let out a sigh, directed at my heartstrings, then read aloud, " 'To whom it may concern: Answer remains the same —marriage with strings attached.' "

Good for Jill. But unfortunately Freddy was about to give us his interpretation of reading between the lines.

"Hark!" I cried. "Is that the doorbell?" And merciful heavens, it was! Ben went out into the hall and returned ushering two people into the room. For a moment I thought I was having a setback. It couldn't be . . . but, as with nightmares, it was. The Reverend Rowland Foxworth and Vanessa.

"Ellie, isn't this a pleasant surprise?" Ben wiggled his eyebrows into question marks. I lay on my couch, fanned myself with my book, and said everything that was trite and insincere.

"Good God, Vanessa, what brings you here?" Freddy inquired. "Didn't you see the cross on the door? We've all got the plague."

"Freddy, you *are* the plague." Vanessa sank into a chair. "But perhaps you could wait to expire until we've all had a cup of tea." She smiled exquisitely up at Rowland, who was fidgeting for his pipe.

"I do hope this is not an intrusion." Rowland looked at me, and I tried to arrange the book artfully in front of my face. "When I didn't see you or Ben at church"—he hesitated—"Vanessa and I wondered if something might be wrong."

"Thank you, but it's just an average, unexciting cold." Strange, I did not find Rowland, with his silvering fair hair and quiet face, as appealing as usual. The man was a dupe, a dope. For a long minute, the only sound was the wind whooshing around in the chimney.

"What brings you down here, Vanessa?" Ben finally asked.

"Oh, a little bit of this, a little of that." She slid her coat off her shoulders, and Ben and Rowland collided trying to catch it before it fell to the floor. Naturally a wife wants her husband to be a gentleman, but not to the point of silliness.

Vanessa's topaz eyes shimmered in the firelight. "As you know, Ellie, I wasn't envious when Uncle Merlin bequeathed you this house and all the loot. So what if Mummy and I have been forced to sell off a couple of fur coats! You deserved some little remembrance in return for sending Uncle those hand-knitted pen wipers at Christmas. And, until recently, the seaside bored me. She moistened her lips for Rowland's benefit. "Now, I find the bucolic atmosphere of these parts utterly restorative after the daily grind in London. And, cousin dear, I have always had this absorbing interest in tombstones."

There she didn't lie. I had always known she would like to have one engraved with my name.

"I think I'll don my pinny and cap and go out and make some tea," cooed Freddy. I wished I could escape so easily.

Rowland tamped down his pipe. His voice came out a little too eager. "Ben and Ellie, I appreciate the invitation to your party Friday night at the new restaurant and I'm delighted to accept."

"Glad to hear it." Ben handed round the plate of eccles cakes. Should I tell Vanessa her invitation had been lost in the post? Luckily, she was examining her nails, an all-consuming occupation.

Rowland smiled. "Several of my parishioners have asked me to suggest you make lots of those little chicken tarts, the ones you served at the wedding."

"Oh those!" Ben paced around the back of the sofa, wagging his injured finger and holding it up to the watery sunlight from the window. "Nothing challenging about them. I might have Ellie run off a couple of batches"—he looked down at me (in more ways than one, it seemed)—"if she feels up to it."

This from my husband? The father of my unborn children! A slow flame of anger sparked within me.

After our guests finally took the hint and left, I went into an orgy of straightening cushions and swooping up tea plates. Two eccles cakes remained. I would eat them both for breakfast. That would show Ben—something or other.

"What's all this busy bee stuff? We aren't expecting anyone else, are we?" He spoke as though he had truly no idea he had upset me, putting me in the invidious position of having to spell it out, or let my wrath stew—pardon me, braise!

"I'm just straightening up, dear, so we can leave the place spotless tomorrow, the way you like it."

"We aren't moving out, are we? You haven't sold the house behind my back to Vernon Daffy?" He ruffled my hair in passing, then dropped down on the sofa which I had just smoothed out.

"Why, no," I said in the glacial accents of Charles Delacorte. "Tomorrow we are up to London for the day. You to see Mr. A.E. Brady, editor. I to squander some of my—*our* wicked inheritance."

"Ellie, I really don't think so."

"Don't?" I picked up *Your First Fight—Spice or Spite* and slapped a duster over it. "Don't think I should spend money, *my* money—"

"Don't think you should come to London." He had a hand in a dish of cashews and was unconcernedly nibbling. I fought the urge to hurl the book at him.

"Why can't I go, darling? We talked about it the other day; you invited me."

"I didn't say *can't*, Ellie." He had his eyes closed, his head resting on a cushion as if this was all a bit too much for him. "And, yes, we agreed that you should come. But, upon reflection, I do think it would be advisable for you to be within call in case any problem should arise at Abigail's. As of this minute"—he opened one eye and looked at the clock—"we are proceeding according to schedule, but we can't afford any more botches." A smile. "Ellie, you can see the logic of that, can't you?"

"Perhaps you should run it by me again, in words of no more than one syllable." My withering gaze was wasted on him. Ben was taking his injured finger's pulse. Turning my back, I gave *Spite or Spit*—I mean *Spice or Spite* another wipe and my eyes one, too.

A hand touched my shoulder. "How about dinner in here tonight, Ellie? Wouldn't that be cosy?" Someone was now unpinning my hair.

"Yes, it would, thank you." Taking a deep breath, I reminded myself how lucky I was in having a husband who cooked for me, didn't forbid my family the house, and had the magic touch. But my mother's voice nudged at my ear: "Ellie, oh Ellie! Don't you know you are in trouble when you start toting up his good points?"

That night I awoke several times to the feeling that the

house was enveloped in a muffling stillness. And when I got out of bed at seven o'clock, the window was white with snow. Impossible on this the twenty-seventh of April! But true.

I trailed downstairs after Ben, wearing his plaid dressing gown, coughing into my hanky. It was mostly a sympathy cough as my cold was close to cured. My resentment at being left at home wasn't.

"Ellie, if you desperately want to come . . ." He opened the fridge.

A magnanimous offer, considering that the taxi he had arranged to take him to the station was due any second. (It wouldn't do for the Heinz to break down, causing him to miss his meeting with Mr. A. E. Brady and assorted bigwigs of Brambleweed Press). I was tempted—

Ben sloshed milk into a glass. "Still, considering that ghastly cough, you are better off here."

The fact that I had handed him that ace increased my annoyance. He proceeded to make my blood boil. In each hand he had an eccles cake and was rhythmically taking bites out of each.

"You do realise that at least one of those is mine!"

"Sorry." The taxi tooted. "Here, sweetheart, two halves make a whole." He stuffed the remains in my hands, kissed my cheek, and grabbed for his umbrella. "See you about seven."

The garden door closed—possibly slammed. How dare he! I tugged the dressing gown belt tight, charged to the alcove where we kept an assortment of outdoor gear and yanked on Jonas's gardening boots. A dutiful wife was one thing, a servile cretin quite another.

Two seconds later and I was out the door. A slam (my turn) sent me clobbering out into the morn, down the driveway, all fluffy white with snow, in pursuit of the taxi.

It was hopeless. The vehicle was moving away. Ben was a blurred blob against the back window, but I was stricken by a kind of madness. I stood with my hands cupped around my mouth shrieking, "You monster! Do you have any idea what it has been like for me all these months? The constant denial, the suppressed longing, then, when I can almost taste—"

"Sorry, lady." An apologetic male voice interrupted my soliloquy. "I try to provide prompt, reliable service." Coming around the hedge was the milkman.

I didn't stop to chat. It was after all, cold. I grabbed my

two pints and the milkman headed back to his little van at a run. Did I feel better for having behaved like a vulgar shrew? Upon reflection, yes. Ben's sins had been squashed down to size. A long day lay ahead. First a scalding hot bath, a morning's work at Abigail's, and then a lazy afternoon in which to nurse my cold through its final stages, and perhaps by seven o'clock I would love my husband completely and unreservedly again.

The kitchen door would not open. Either it had locked behind me or, having conditioned myself never to leave a door unlatched, I had automatically pressed the catch.

Hope springs eternal. I checked the front door and all the French windows, all the while keeping my final ace at my fingertips—at least our bedroom window was open. I could see the maroon curtains billowing in the wind.

Also billowing in the wind was a fresh supply of snow. The first cold flakes fell on my head as, dressing gown hitched up, I headed for the stables to get a ladder. The stable was locked. My fault: I had insisted it be kept so since Roxie had planted those notions about the Raincoat Man.

Okay, so I must risk Freddy's mockery and present myself at the cottage door. Brushing back my hair, which had to resemble the tails of dead animals, I slogged down the driveway. At the cottage, the final blow fell. No answer and another locked door. Who would have envisioned I would curse the day Freddy was corrupted by the work ethic?

Think positive. Roxie had a key to the house. All I had to do was find a phone and summon her to my aid. Clinging to the wrought iron gates, snow falling on my cheeks, I studied my choices. To my right stood the vicarage, inhabited by Rowland. Friend. To my left, perhaps ten minutes further from Merlin's Court, stood the house of Mr. Edwin Digby. Stranger.

I knotted my hair about my neck and started walking. There was, of course, no need for laboured deliberation. Rowland was young and handsome. Mr. Digby was a middle-aged tippler who delighted in the gruesome.

From the Files of
<u>The Widows Club</u>

Monday, 27th April, 7:00 A.M.

President:

Good morning, Mrs. Hanover. Did I wake you? . . . Yes, I'm sure, in the public house business one would rise early. And to good news this morning! . . . That's it—your voluntary services are needed at a Retirement Party this coming Friday, the first of May. Mrs. Hanover . . . Mrs. Hanover. Are you there?

Mrs. Hanover:

Forgive me . . . I . . . (*Sounds of weeping.*)

President:

Mrs. Hanover, I do trust you are not having second thoughts after all the time and energy expended in training you for—

Mrs. H.:

Heavens, no! Not for the world. One is so thrilled, for the minute one couldn't speak.

President:

Then I will report your concurrence to the board and ring you again this evening with the details.

Mrs. H.:

Such an honour! Words . . . words quite fail one.

. . . Primrose gasped. "A young woman, partially clothed, entering the premises of a single gentleman of unsteady reputation! May we hope, dear Ellie, that Mr. Digby did nothing to make you blush!" . . .

"The last time I admitted an unknown woman reeking pathos to this house, she pocketed a silver table lighter."

The great Edwin Digby might have walked straight from the pages of his own genre: goatee beard, natty daffodil-hued waistcoat, grey hair crinkling back from a lofty forehead, rheumy eyes under brows which twirled at the ends to tilt sinisterly upward. We were seated in his study, a red velour room crammed with Victoriana and dominated by a massive desk on which sat a cast-iron typewriter and a turbulence of papers, a hint that Mary Birdsong also dwelt here.

"I do not smoke." I spoke with credible aplomb, considering I was dressed like a film extra from *Gandhi*. Mr. Digby's eyes travelled from my towel turban to the three-piece suit I had taken (per his instructions) from the wardrobe in his bedroom.

I looked down at my boots, wishing they weren't six sizes too big. Fleeing through the snow in these would be no joke. "Thank you for the loan of dry clothes, I—"

My host sank deeper into his leather chair. "Mrs. Haskell, pray do not use the borrowed apparel as an excuse to pursue an acquaintance which we would both find tedious. Should your husband not wish to add the suit to his wardrobe, your woman will know of some indigent worthy." The lizard lids narrowed. "I trust you reached this Mrs. Malloy on the telephone?"

I inclined my top-heavy head an inch. Detestable Mr. Digby. He stroked the goatee with a bony finger. "And she will not tarry in bringing your key?"

I pushed up my sleeves, then yanked them back down. He hadn't so much as offered me a cup of tea. "She swore on the telephone directory, Mr. Digby, that she would haste herself to the bus stop and commit hijacking if necessary to get here."

The fingers stopped moving.

"You are fortunate, Mrs. Haskell, in having so devoted a servant."

"No." I looked him smack in the eye. "Mary Birdsong is fortunate in having so devoted a fan."

Mr. Digby grimaced, which did nothing to make him more appealing. "You err in your attempted flattery, madam. Nothing could be more abhorrent to me than some female churl, autograph album clutched to her overripe bosom, bleating a path to my door. Be warned—the instant she arrives, out you both go into the snow." He withdrew his gaze to the frosted window.

"I understand, sir, you have not written a book in years. Aren't you glad that some of your fans are still alive?"

The eyebrows vee'd sharply upward; Mr. Digby crossed his legs at the ankle, showing yellow socks to match the waistcoat. "Mrs. Haskell, I have been misled by the yokels at The Dark Horse, that home away from home wherein I quaff away the nights." Easing out of his chair, he paced, somewhat unsteadily, to a cluttered buffet and unstoppered a decanter. "Will you join me in a glass of Madeira?"

"Tea would be rather welcome, if it isn't too much trouble."

"Far too much trouble."

I punched down my turban. "How were you misled, Mr. Digby, about me?"

He replaced the stopper in the decanter. "Into supposing

that in comparison to your rent-a-date spouse you are a creature of dolorous decorum."

So! Word was out that Ben and I had met through Eligibility Escorts. Any one of my relations could have ferreted out the truth and spread their X-rated version. Or had Ben spilled the beans to Freddy? Never mind. Our love story may have started out as a commercial venture, but it had matured into passion, tenderness, and truth, if you delete a few moments here and there.

"Bentley was employed by a highly respectable service. I am not ashamed of how we met."

Mr. Digby's eyebrows twitched. "Assuredly your meeting was worth every penny it cost you." He downed the Madeira while I delved deep for something vicious to say in response, but he was quicker off the mark.

"I hear the transvestite who threw himself upon your bridal altar has, in essence, moved in with you."

Would Roxie never get here with that key! "My cousin Frederick is an estimable young man with an exuberant sense of humour, which I adore. He is of invaluable assistance to my husband."

"Relieving you of certain duties, no doubt." Mr. Digby swigged his second Madeira and poured another. "Does rumour lie or is your husband about to foist a new restaurant upon this community? One which specialises in unpronounceable food at unaffordable prices." He watched me nastily over the rim of his glass.

He circled the buffet, twirling the glass slowly between the fingers of both hands. "Your husband, in addition to his other peccadilloes, appears to be a man of industry. I hear he has recently authored a cookery book, laced with herbal nostalgia. One would have thought the world already harbors sufficient recipes for tomato soup, but I surmise that you, in your blind, wifely devotion, believe Mr. Haskell is now in my league?"

"Not at all." Flexing my lips into a smile, I stood. "Ben makes no claim to be a literary genius, and he is certainly not in competition with you. His professional reputation depends on nobody dying."

Again the eyebrows twitched. "You did assure me, Mrs. Haskell, when I admitted you over my threshold, that unlike your Mrs. Malloy, you are not a besotted fan."

What a childish manoeuvring for praise! Unwrapping the turban, I rumpled my soggy hair down about my shoulders, sat down, and plumped my cushion. A dazzle of sunlight broke through the curtained windows. The decanters on the buffet glowed red, gold, and bronze. "I know you don't care one way or the other, Mr. Digby, but I have read two of your books."

He thumbed the wineglass. "Which ones?"

"At the risk of offending you, Mr. Digby, I have to say that I found both extremely . . ."

The glass came to a standstill.

". . . extremely enjoyable."

"Trite of you, Mrs. Haskell."

"Thank you. That last scene in *The Butler Didn't Do It* almost did me in. I came out in goosebumps the size of gnat bites. Do you know that right up until Hubert Humbledee swung down from that chandelier, I was certain the bishop's niece was the one embalming the bodies in the attic?"

Mr. Digby set his glass down on the nest of tables beside his chair and closed his eyes. "*The Butler* was one of my better efforts, not up to the standard of"—he paused—"some of the others, but I was fairly well pleased."

I felt a pang of pity for him, goodness knows why. "My husband and I are staging a premiere performance on Friday in honour of the opening of Abigail's. Would you come?"

Mr. Digby opened his eyes. "I have told you, madam, I go nowhere except The Dark Horse." He intercepted my glance at the decanter. "You wonder, Mrs. Haskell, why, being such an assiduous hermit, I do not drink here in privacy of an evening. The answer is regrettably prosaic. I am a man haunted by demons. And at night this house spills forth an ambience of gaslight horror."

I could believe it. There was a desolation to this room, buried under the red plush, which could not entirely be blamed on my damp clothes.

"Perhaps if you were to redecorate?" I suggested brightly. "Danish modern tends to have a dispiriting effect on ghosts."

His smile was bleak. "Mine are made of sterner stuff."

I persisted. "The ghosts who prowl the night, are they of any great local interest?"

Mr. Digby brushed a slightly tremulous hand down his yellow waistcoat front and headed back to the decanter. "Of possible interest to you, Mrs. Haskell."

I had the feeling the subject had been subtly changed. He handed me a glass. "Rumour, borne upon the fumes of slopped bitters at The Dark Horse, Mrs. Haskell, credits the gentleman who built your house with misconducting himself, while in his late seventies, with the two elderly spinsters who inhabited this very house in the latter part of the nineteenth century."

"Good heavens!" I slopped my Madeira. "That would be my forebear, Wilfred Grantham. His building a house like Merlin's Court does rather suggest that he dwelt within the enchanted forest of the mind." I held my glass steady with both hands. "Did you say he was having a fling with *both* these women?"

The beard creased into a mocking smile. "Spare your blushes, Mrs. Haskell. Unless legend lies, your antecedent did not indulge in orgies. On Monday nights Miss Lavinia was favoured. On Thursdays Miss Lucretia got her turn. And neither sister ever knew about the other."

"Remarkable." I rolled up my trouser legs, walked over to the buffet, and refilled my glass. "How—even under the cloak of night—did great-grandfather Grantham enter this house and the allotted bedroom undetected?"

"Ah, Mrs. Haskell"—my host reached behind him and tapped upon the panelled wall, his face reflective—"that *is* a mystery."

"Did the sisters ever find him out?"

I thought that he would never answer, but finally he spoke. "You will be pleased to learn, Mrs. Haskell, that I have talked myself out of any growing enthusiasm for you."

I pushed back some typing paper hanging over the edge of the overloaded desk. "Does this mean you won't be coming to the party on Friday?"

To my surprise he countered with a question. "Who attends this free-food binge? The ex-chorus girl and the silver-haired, silver-tongued lawyer. The arctic antique dealer and the wife who dreams of being a nightclub singer. And what of the estate agent who refuses to die and his froggy-faced wife? And, yes, the Reverend Mr. Foxglove!"

"Foxworth."

The liverish lips curled. "I understand, Mrs. Haskell, that a sigh of disappointment swept the county when it was learned you were to wed another." I could feel him savouring my intake of breath. "But I imagine the church organist didn't make herself ill crying."

"Miss Thorn is a *very* nice woman."

"Ah! *Nice*: the ultimate disparagement from one female to another." Mr. Digby fingered the red velvet curtain. "Speaking of spinsters, will Lady Theodora Peerless adorn your little gathering?"

"I hope so."

"It seems you will be extremely crowded." He let the curtain fall. "Hence, I am not interested."

I looked through the window. The snow edging the glass was like ermine against the red velvet. Five bird feeders dotted the swath of white lawn. "The Aviary is the right name for this house."

"Originally it was called Rocky Meade. Sort of name Lavinia or Lucretia would pick."

"Have you lived here long?"

Mr. Digby was back at the buffet. "Five years."

"Why did you come here?"

"A foolish nostalgia. As a boy I was fond of the place; my family spent several summers here."

He was driving me into nosiness. "Do you have any family now, Mr. Digby?"

"A daughter . . . Wren, aged twenty-seven." Was the tremor of his hands more pronounced? "And to alleviate the necessity of your having to ask where she is, I will tell you—off living with some man who has nothing to recommend him. The old story of the new generation."

I restrained myself from scanning the room for photographs. To ask what had become of Mrs. Digby struck even me as unconscionably rude.

A sound somewhere outside the room made me forget all else save the hope that Roxie was at the front door. Mr. Digby half-turned.

"That must have been my . . . my gardener, Mrs. Haskell, come in to make himself a cup of tea. He's nothing to rave about, but whatever my other sins, I am not a putterer." He was puttering now, toward the door. "I understand your own gardener has deserted, Mrs. Haskell."

"Only temporarily. Ben and I have raked the leaves around a bit, but we are going to need someone to bridge the gap. Is this man who works for you fully booked?"

"I doubt it. Whatsit is new in the area and you well know, Mrs. Haskell, how long the natives take to accept anyone whose antecedents don't date back at least to the days of smugglers in the bay. As for his capabilities, I can attest that he is reliable. He turns up even on days such as this when all he can do is pick up his wages. Your Mrs. Malloy could learn a thing or two from him, but since you continue to be here, perhaps you would like to meet Mother?"

"I would be delighted."

As the door closed on him, a weighty hush settled on the room. Then I heard voices. Distance made Mr. Digby sound unduly caustic, and the gardener effeminate. My eyes nipped from the desk to the door and back again. A piece of thin yellow paper protruded from the typewriter. Straightening the towel around my shoulders, I rehitched my trousers and tiptoed forward. Just one quick peek to see what Mary Birdsong had in store for her patient readers. Technically it wouldn't be snooping if I kept my hands behind my back. *Chin up, my dear. You did nothing wrong in borrowing your best friend's earrings. Losing the pawn ticket was the only naughty part.*

Leaning forward to find the preceding page among the flotsam, the towel slid off my neck, sending an avalanche of paper swishing out in all directions. My aerobic conditioning came in handy. I was two feet in the air, hands grabbing, when Mr. Digby reentered. And strange as it may seem, even in that moment of awkwardness I noticed he did not look as well as when he had left me. The beard could not hide his purple-veined pallor.

"Yes, Mother"—he bent his head—"I know you are not overly excited at the prospect, but she . . ." He espied the spill of manuscript on the floor; I dropped to my knees, scooping as I crawled.

"Sorry, you startled me when you came in and . . . I collided with the desk. Nice goosey!" Stuffing paper back on the desk, I struggled to rise and back up all in one unfluid movement.

While Mr. Digby appeared to accept my frail excuse, clever Mother kept her beady eyes upon me.

Mr. Digby's face cracked into a smile. "Mrs. Haskell, I do believe Mother has taken to you. Perceive—she is heading toward you."

"Mmm!" Mother, the Persil-white goose, had indeed fanned

out her wings and was ominously waddling toward me, guttural squawks rising above the whir of feathers.

I dodged behind the curtain. Hopefully the colour red did not have the effect on geese that it did on bulls. Craving contact with something nonthreatening, I reached out toward a nearby shelf and heard a dull thud as something—a book—toppled to the ground. Mother swung her beak in an arc, snapped at the air and responded reluctantly to Mr. Digby's command. "Heel!"

"Mrs. Malloy did understand that you needed your key today?" Mr. Digby was back at the decanters. Mother gazed hopefully at him. What did she crave—a drink or the pleasure of booting me out of the house?

"How did you and Mother team up?" I asked; the silence would have buried all of us.

"She was a Christmas present. Came decorated with a red bow, cooking instructions attached. Needless to say, she is emotionally scarred for life. Hates Christmas and has absolutely no sense of humour."

Probably fiction, but my heart was touched. "Poor person!" I looked down at Mother, and surprisingly, she toddled toward me like an open-armed child. She skipped over the book I'd dropped and I picked it up. Stroking her with one hand, I noticed the title, *The Merry Widows* by Mary Birdsong. Intriguing, but I had to put it down because Mother was pestering for attention.

"Her feathers are—like clouds." I chucked Mother under the chin the way I did Tobias, and it seemed to me that the sound vibrating up from her throat was very like a purr. Of course, I know almost nothing about birds, which reminded me that Mr. Digby did. "As an ornithological enthusiast, can you tell me the significance of a line of blackbirds? Since coming to Chitterton Fells I have seen several women wearing brooches with—"

Something slammed; it was the decanter. My host's voice came out in angry jerks. "Blackbirds in a line are blackbirds in a line. The women you mention are indubitably members of some egg-stealing club. Soulless individuals who go clumping up the cliff faces, brandishing binoculars. Let them but trespass on my turf and I will throw rocks at them!"

He was enraged. Wishing I had not set him off, I apologised. "Sorry about knocking stuff off your desk."

"It makes no difference. None of it has either end or beginning." He didn't pretend to look at me. Silence smothered the room. I buzzed around in my mind for something to say and came up with:

"That's what happens when you do your own typing. You should have a secretary."

"I did indulge in that luxury once. The result was disaster." His words were chilly. "Speaking of hired help, I saw Whatsit when I fetched Mother. Have a word with him as you leave. *If* you ever leave."

That last word was severed by the chiming of the doorbell. The air positively hummed with joy. My host sucked in his lips, flung open the library door and with Mother gusting ahead we went out into the chilly hall.

"One moment, if you please, Mrs. Haskell. I must put Mother in the cupboard under the stairs. She can be most unwelcoming, and we would not wish your Mrs. Malloy to leave without you."

Mrs. Malloy crossed the threshold of The Aviary on waves of arctic cold and Attar of Roses. At a glance I saw why I had been kept waiting. Enormous pains had been taken to do justice to this impromptu meeting with Chitterton Fells's most famous. Roxie wore a three-quarter-length black astrakhan coat, below which extended several yards of emerald taffeta skirt. Her hair was capped by a velvet bandeau, sprouting veiling down to her painted-on eyebrows. Even her makeup was unusually lavish; a couple of charcoal beauty spots had been added.

"This, sir, is an honour I never expected were I to live to be a thousand." Roxie clutched a sequined handbag in her work-roughened hands. Affection for her welled up in me. I ignored Mr. Digby's hand at the ready on the doorknob.

"This is very kind, Roxie, considering my stupidity in getting myself locked out."

"I'm never one to cast stones, Mrs. H." Roxie's face was tilted rapturously sideways. "And I've made up me mind only to charge you the usual hourly rate, unless you absolutely insist on time-and-a-half, along with the bus fare, of course." The rainbow lids fluttered. "The privilege of being here in this house, breathing in that . . . smell." She gazed worshipfully toward Mr. Digby.

"I would have you know, madam"—he had his eyes closed—"that when Mother heeds that particular call to nature, she does so in the rookery."

Roxie wrung the sequined bag between her hands.

"I meant the smell of genius. I wonder, sir, would you do me the immense honour of signing me autograph album? I can't count the times I have wanted to speak when I saw you coming out of the Gentlemen's at the—" She stopped and gave a fluting laugh. "Oh, I am sorry. I shouldn't have mentioned—"

Mr. Digby dismissed her splutterings with a wave of his hand. "I will sign your book upon the condition you swear on the name of Booth's Dry Gin that you will not presume upon my good nature the next time you perceive me at The Dark Horse."

Roxie hovered like a star-struck teenager as Mr. Digby plunged a pen across her album page.

"I've read every word you've ever written, Mr. D.! My favourites are the ones you did early on and can't buy for love nor money anymore, but, believe you me, you don't owe no apologies for none of them."

He shoved the album at her. "My good woman, do not verbally cavort as though my tired little penny dreadfuls are works of great literature." He screwed the cap on his pen and stomped up the stairs.

"Let's take the hint," I urged, "and scoot."

Roxie ignored me. She blotted the signature with her hanky (that way she had two souvenirs), then called after Mr. Digby's vanishing figure. "Great literature, Mr. D., is those books that regular people like me and Mrs. H. can enjoy without needing a dictionary every second word. That includes your stuff"—she gave the album a pat and dropped it into her bag—"and even cookery books."

Mr. Digby's voice came floating down. "Do not think of me and Mr. Haskell in the same breath. His objective is to take the mystery out of the sauce; mine is to put sauce in the mystery."

"A very strange man," I said as Roxie and I plodded down the sloping walkway toward Cliff Road. Snow stung our faces. My companion didn't answer. Mrs. Roxie Malloy was a woman touched by greatness. Henceforth she would sit at her beer-spattered table at The Dark Horse, holding the other regulars spellbound with the story of how Mr. Digby had spoken to her with magnificent contempt and signed her autograph book.

Needing to move my lips to keep warm, I tried again. "A man carved out of tragedy."

"Did he speak to you of *it*, Mrs. H.? All about how his wife took the notion he was carrying on with someone else . . ."

Roxie paused, either for effect or because the wind had blasted her breath back into her lungs. What woman would want to make love to Mr. Digby, I thought, unless compelled by a sense of wifely duty? I recalled those purplish fingers with distaste. "Was this other woman his secretary?"

"Couldn't say, Mrs. H. All I know is the wife stuck her head in the gas oven."

Was that when he stopped writing books? Was he punishing himself? I should have felt sorry for Mrs. Digby. Loyalty to fellow wives. I told myself that should Ben ever betray me, I wouldn't stick my head in the oven. I'd put *him* in the oven and insert a thermometer. "Well, at least he gets some company at The Dark Horse," I said. "A chance to despise other people's chatter and listen to a singsong."

Roxie looked at me as if to say, What do you know? "He hates singing! Leaves the minute Mrs. Hanover starts sashaying her skirts and belting out 'Charmaine.' "

"Come into the house for a hot drink," I urged Roxie. But she refused, and when we reached the gates of Merlin's Court, she handed me the key. "Then I'll walk with you to the bus stop."

"I'd much rather you didn't." She slid the handle of her bag up her arm. "I want to be alone with me thoughts."

I should have insisted. Instead I hovered near the gates, arms wrapped around Mr. Digby's three-piece suit, until the last splotch of astrakhan coat disappeared around the curve. A gull screeched overhead. Steady—if I fell down I might go into a skid. Another screech found me clutching at the gate post. But did the sound come from the gull overhead? Gripping the post with my feet, I peered back in the direction of The Aviary. The man was trotting, sending up billows of snow. Mr. Digby! He must be desperate not to see me again if he'd come after me with my dressing gown. Cupping my hands around my mouth, I yelled an apology. It blew away in a frozen whisper. No matter . . . a pulse beat in my neck and I lifted a finger in slow motion to make it stop. The man wasn't Mr. Digby. Oh, that it might have been! Whatever his physical failings, Mr. D.

didn't have greasy black hair and rotten spiky teeth.

"Hey, you—Mrs! You wanting a gardener?"

I stood there perched on the top of that cliff, like a bride on a cake, within easy shoving distance of certain death. Alone with the elements and the Raincoat Man.

"I'm . . . not sure." As he drew closer, I could count the pores in his skin. But it was his black-currant eyes that goaded me to action. Diving down, I grabbed an armload of snow, clamped it into a ball, and flung it. Then I stepped out of my boots and was off at a skidding run, through the gates and past the cottage. The thought did traverse my mind that should he go over the cliff edge, I might be guilty of something—murder, manslaughter, or at the very least, killing a man in self-defense. One doesn't want that sort of thing on one's resumé, but neither did I want the Raincoat Man so quickly recovered he could crawl at a fast pace after me. Thank God for the wind. It pushed from behind, forcing my legs along at unnatural speed. The snow was coming down half-heartedly as I passed the stables and barrelled into the courtyard.

But I wasn't home free yet. I heard a noise. Something, someone came moving behind me. A scream began percolating in my throat. And then, in a snap, I realized I was a fool. The Raincoat Man couldn't have leapt over our high fence and sprinted here ahead of me. Either Freddy had returned from Abigail's and hoped to cadge lunch or Tobias had something similar in mind. Ah yes—here he was, creeping out from behind the rainbarrel, snow glistening on his fur.

"There, there," I crooned, as Tobias landed, hissing, spraying snowflakes, in my arms. "Poor baby, you got locked out, too. How about some nice Ovaltine?" My panic was gone. Stuffing him inside my coat, I rubbed my frozen feet against each other, took a step forward and saw the figure standing by the back door.

Not the Raincoat Man. This was an elderly female person in a grey flannel coat and a damson knitted beret dragged down over her ears. She was small and the black holdall she grasped with both hands, the way Roxie did, was pathetically big.

"Mrs. Bentley Thomas Haskell?" Her feet, laced up in brogues, were pressed tightly together; wisps of dust-colored hair escaped from the beret. Who was she, an elderly orphan? A terrible thought occurred.

"Yes, I am Mrs. Haskell. Do please come in and have a hot drink. I feel awful—your coming all this way in the cold and snow. You have every right to be furious, but what with one thing and another, I quite forgot to take the advert for household help out of the paper and we have already hired someone." Tobias slithered down to my waist and jumped to the ground, as I stabbed the key into the lock. The woman in the beret hadn't opened her mouth. Perhaps it was frozen shut. "I do hope you haven't been standing here too long." I pushed open the door. "As soon as I have heated you some soup and fixed you a sandwich, I will make some phone calls on your behalf." I stepped aside to let her enter. "Or better still, I will talk to my cousin Freddy (my husband is in London) and see if there are any vacancies in the kitchen of our new restaurant; the work wouldn't be too arduous." I stopped and, when she didn't budge, added desperately, "This way, please."

"Did you say *our* restaurant?" the woman asked in a tight little voice.

"Yes, I—"

"Do you work there?"

"Well, if by that you mean—"

"I see. In other words, the decision doesn't rest with you, and naturally I won't wish to be a burden."

Frostbite of the brain, and we knew who to blame. Me.

"Do please come into the kitchen and I will get the kettle going."

Still she hesitated. Tobias was lending his howls to the wind. Snow blew around the woman in silver eddies. She clutched the holdall tighter.

"I'm sorry, but I cannot set a foot over your threshold until I'm given the assurance I am welcome." She looked down at her hands. "Certainly I'm used to hard work and it's always been in my nature to keep the peace, but as we both know, there are a lot of very nasty jokes about mothers-in-law and it's not as though you and I are likely to have anything in common, saving my dear boy, and from what you say"—she tugged open the bag and dragged out a hanky—"he's off in London, not here to greet his mum."

. . . "May we assume, Ellie, that you gave Mr. Edwin Digby and this Raincoat Man scarcely a thought during the course of the next few hours?" Hyacinth flipped a page of the green notebook. . . .

Having my mother-in-law materialise on my doorstep brought home to me the realisation that for weeks I had been harbouring the nasty suspicion that she was dead. Murdered (by the predatory Mrs. Jarrod—I did not want my children to inherit a tendency to homicide from their paternal grandpa) and buried somewhere dark and slimy, waiting to be dug up by carefree little children with buckets and spades. I should have been overjoyed at seeing her. Instead, I was a little disappointed that I wasn't fortified for the interview by impeccable grooming, say an ascot, hat, lipstick, and fake fingernails. I had pictured this scene so often in my mind. My teary smile and outstretched arms had totally disarmed the imaginary Mrs. Haskell: "My son loves you, Ellie, so I love you, too." The message I read in the eyes of the real woman was, What sins have I committed that my only son marries a barefoot woman in a three-piece man's suit with hair like seaweed who mistakes me for a charwoman?

As we stood by the Aga cooker in the kitchen, I pecked at her cheek and, to her credit, she flinched only a little. Now what? I took her bag and set it on the counter.

"Ben's in London on business to do with his cookery book. He'll be back this evening." I squared the bag so it wouldn't fall over the edge of the counter.

"That's good." Her arms hung lank at her sides.

I picked up the kettle. "Ben has been so concerned about you, as have I." I sounded pitifully like an amateur actress who's been told to project. "He was relieved to hear that you had written to Paris, but I know he kept hoping for a letter." Should I modify that statement to delete any hint of criticism?

"Naturally I wanted to write to my only son. But he would have had to show the letters to you and it didn't seem fair to drag you into our family problems." She looked the room up and down. "This is a nice place you've got here, Eleanor. Some holy pictures on the walls and you could make it a lot more homey." She sized up the copper pans and hanging plants.

"Thank you." I reached into a cupboard, took a rubber band from a jar and dragged my hair back. Panic struck. What did I call her? Mother? Magdalene? "Do, please, sit down." Relax, Ellie! And will you stop talking to her as though you still think she is a down-on-her-luck applicant for a job! I shoved the kettle under the tap. Water splattered all over my waistcoat. Why couldn't I be warm and easy like Bunty? Or serenely gracious like Ann Delacorte? If Dorcas had been here, my inadequacies would have been less apparent. She would have slipped off my mother-in-law's coat, chafed her small hands, popped her teeny feet onto a stool, talking all the while—"I say, Mum, frightfully ripping this! By the time our man Bentley gets home tonight, you and I will be thick as soup!"

Mrs. Haskell had taken off her coat and was neatly folding it over a chair. I tried to flex my face into the type women want their sons to marry. It was hopeless. Some basic ingredient is missing from my personality. I cannot ease gracefully into new relationships. And to make excuses for myself, this situation was hampered by my being exactly what Mrs. Haskell had expected, and she being nothing like the made-to-order mum I had conjured up. Death had endeared her to me, and I was going to have some trouble adjusting.

She pulled a chair away from the big scrubbed table, peered down at it, brushed it off with a glove, and sat. "Don't let me keep you from what you normally do at this time of day, Eleanor."

"You're not keeping me from a thing. By the way, although it really doesn't matter a scrap, my name—full name—is Giselle. However, if you prefer Eleanor, by all means—"

"I don't like one better than the other." She folded her hands and pressed her feet together. "But I don't feel I can take the liberty of calling you Ellie."

"Oh, please do!" I plopped the kettle on the stove, soaking it and me.

She watched me sopping up with a teacloth. "I won't, if you don't mind—it's a bit too much like Eli, and—"

"Yes?" Now we're coming to it, I thought.

"Ellie's a frilly sort of name and you don't look that sort."

I restrained myself. This was not a propitious moment to reveal that I had locked myself out of the house as a direct result of a marital spat or that I had changed out of my wet clothes in the home of a strange man.

She rubbed her hands together and pulled down her beret, making her ears stick out. "Well then, Giselle, you won't want to call me Mother, so better make it Magdalene." Before I could answer, she observed, "I hadn't realised this house was so secluded."

I was about to stutter an apology for the location of Merlin's Court when she added:

"Nice."

At last—after all those minutes—my mother-in-law had paid me a compliment. My heart sang. The kettle gave a shrill echo, its metal cap going into a bobbling dance as steam clouded the air. I dropped a couple of tea bags into the earthenware pot (the silver one wouldn't be nearly as friendly) and sloshed on the scalding water.

"Don't think me interfering, Giselle, but did you forget to warm the pot?"

I counted to ten. The temptation to spit on the tea bags, floating like the bloated bodies of string-tailed rats, was strong. "I'll pitch this and start again."

"You don't find loose tea more economical?"

"I'll get some in."

"I hope you understand, Giselle, I am not criticising. My landing on you like this has you at sixes and sevens. Giselle, the tea cloth, is it about to singe?"

"Oh!" I fought to look casual. "I was just letting it dry." The smoldering cloth flew from my hand into the sink.

Magdalene moved her chair. "Ben will have told you I always vowed that even should something happen to Eli I'd never land myself on him. The thought of being a burden . . . but of course it's always easy to talk. After forty years of marriage and always doing my wifely duty, I never guessed that Mrs. Jarrod would happen to Eli." Her voice faded.

"No, of course not." Put the pot down, Ellie, an inner voice insisted; go over and put your arms around her.

"You mustn't feel that way," I said, feet still cemented down. "Ben and I will love having you here; although my guess is that when your husband knows you are here, he will be down immediately on the milk train."

"I don't think so." She took the cup of tea I held out to her. "I imagine, Giselle, that you and Ben do rattle around in this big house, but there won't always be just the two of you." Over the rim of her cup she pointedly appraised my middle.

"Ben and I want children at the appropriate time." My intent was to sound cheerfully optimistic, but due to my sucked-in breath, the words pinged out hard as tiddlywinks.

Magdalene's lips drew together. "That's your Protestant thinking. *I* left motherhood in higher hands."

My hands shook as I poured soup into a saucepan. My mother-in-law unbuttoned her cardigan and wrapped it around herself. I'd have to turn up the heat. If the soup would only boil . . . if Freddy would only come knocking at the door. What I needed was five minutes alone to pace up and down and sink my psyche into the role of good daughter-in-law. If I could only get her to tell me where she had been these last five months.

"I expect, Giselle, that Ben has told you I had him late in life and nearly died three times when he was born. Father Padinsky was a new priest then, and I'll never forget him getting in such a fluster, checking with the bishop on how many times he could administer the Last Sacrament."

Warmth crept through me. This woman had suffered to bring the man I loved into the world.

"Giselle, the soup is boiling over, but don't worry. I don't like tomato, or rather it doesn't like me." She shifted in her chair and I opened up the fridge to cool off and get out stuff for ham sandwiches.

"I don't suppose you read old medical journals, but I was written up in every one of them for months, years. I'll have to show you the scrapbook I've been keeping for the grandchildren, when—if—I return to Tottenham." She tweaked at her cardigan sleeves. "Did you say Ben went to London to see Eli?"

"No, to see his publisher."

"Ben's father not talking to him does complicate things, no getting around that." Now surely she would tell me where she had been all this time. I slid the sandwiches and teapot onto the table and sat down. I had forgotten the cosy, but perhaps Magdalene wouldn't notice.

"And when will my boy be home?"

"About seven."

"Hours to go." She said it; I thought it.

"Giselle, did you mean to leave off the cosy? It's a bit worn, isn't it? I'll have to crochet you a new one. After all, I have to do something to make up for landing on your doorstep, asking to be taken in like a stray cat."

"You mustn't think like that." My eyes crept to the clock.

"That cat—the one that followed you in here, it *is* yours, I suppose?"

I'd read in *Inlaws and Outlaws* that the ideal length of a maternal visit was a fortnight. Plenty of time to do all sorts of fun things like climb the walls a fingernail at a time.

"Tobias? I promise, he won't bother you."

Magdalene opened up the sandwich on her plate and rearranged the sliced ham. "I'm the visitor, making me the one not to bother anyone. Cats *do* affect my breathing, but I wouldn't want you to get rid of him on my account. You'll have to do so soon enough, won't you, when that first baby finally puts in an appearance."

"I—"

"There I go, interfering when I swore I wouldn't. What I have to remember is you're a different generation. Ben was *my* life's work, not a hobby."

I counted to thirty. Ben must not come home, weary from a hard day of lunching with Mr. A. E. Brady, to discover I had wasted no time in having words with his mother. Shoulders hunched as she sipped her tea, she looked like a victim of daughter-in-law abuse. And so she was. I got up from the table, went into the pantry, came out with a hot water bottle, filled it from the still steaming kettle, tightened the stopper, and wrapped it in a wad of tea towels.

"What are you doing, Giselle?"

"Seeing that you don't catch pneumonia." I plucked a cardigan off the hook in the alcove by the back door. Drat! It had a hole in one elbow. "We have a party planned for Friday to celebrate the opening of Ben's restaurant, and you must be in top form as guest of honour. Off with those shoes! We won't bother about your stockings. They can steam dry. There!" I planted her dinky feet on the tea towel hummock. "How's that?"

"A bit too hot, but—"

"No buts; pop on Ben's cardigan over your own."

"You knitted it for him, I suppose. Never mind, I'll give you some lessons on ribbing." Her back was curved and her arms were thin as drumsticks.

"Drink your tea, Magdalene, eat a biscuit, and then I want to know where you have been hiding yourself since the twenty-seventh of November."

"Well, perhaps a small one, if Ben made them. I can see you are the sort of strong-minded young woman in vogue nowadays. Of course that was clear from the start. Ben couldn't have wanted to be married in the Church of England. It wasn't as though his father and I hadn't given him enough faiths to choose from. It may come as a surprise to you, but religion was never a difficulty for Eli and me. There's a lot to be said for the convenience, when husband and wife each have a different day of rest. Nothing was a major problem until . . ."

"Until Mrs. Jarrod?" I poured more tea.

"A bit before her, I suppose." My mother-in-law tucked the beret down over her ears. "I blamed it on the rift with Ben. I don't know, but I came over very nervy last summer. I kept getting this nasty feeling that I was being watched." Magdalene looked through me with her sparrow eyes. "I wasn't safe anywhere, even in the house, with the curtains pulled. Least that's what I thought. Dr. Padinsky (brother of my parish priest) even had to give me tablets to help me sleep."

"Did they help?"

"Yes . . . and no." Her cheeks went pink. "I'm not like you young people; I don't like discussing intimate matters, but to wrap it up as cleanly as possible—a wife falling asleep the minute she gets into bed and staying that way all night long doesn't help keep the night fires burning."

"Quite." I crossed my legs, decided doing so emphasised the masculinity of the pin-striped suit, uncrossed them and crossed my arms.

"So I don't entirely blame Eli for succumbing when *that woman* came flaunting her pickled herring at him. What nearly killed me was him telling me there was nothing going on. All the while standing there"—her lips drew in so tight I thought they would pop—"with that *smile* spread all over his face."

"I would have spread him out the nearest window! Aren't we talking about the man who cannot break his vow never to speak to his son again because truth is all?"

Magdalene seemed to forget whose side she was on—hers or his. There was pride in her voice as she said crisply, "Never one lie from Eli in all those married years. If a customer asked were the oranges soft, he'd say, 'Yes! You want tough oranges? Go to the supermarket.' You won't understand, Giselle, but the carrying on I could have forgiven, if he'd only been a man about it. I'd have fetched Father Padinsky round to give Eli a dressing down and have moved into the boxroom until he came to his senses."

"Where *did* you go?"

Her skin turned dusty grey. Thrusting her chair back, she stood. "The Convent of St. Agnes, very pretty and secluded, near Little Hampton." She was scooping up plates, piling one on top of the other.

I got up and tried to take the china from her. "Ben and his father surmised you had gone on a religious retreat."

She was bundling the china and cutlery into the sink. "They were wrong. I wasn't on retreat. I did housework in return for sanctuary. Yes, Giselle, you were right in thinking me reduced to a charwoman. I picked the convent in Little Hampton because I'd never visited there and I was afraid Eli could track me down if I went to one of my favourites."

"You should have come immediately to us."

She looked at me as if to say, C. of E. and not very bright. "And this the first place he'd look?"

Thank God Ben had inherited none of his father's sneakiness.

"Magdalene, did you like the Convent of St. Agnes?"

"It wasn't like Maryville or Abbey Wood, but . . . I . . . can't deny that I did." She pressed a hand on the table, then began piling the sugar bowl on top of the butter dish. "The grounds of the convent are lovely. A nice view of the sea, and—like here—secluded. I grew so secure; I even began to think of petitioning the Holy Father for a special dispensation so I could enter. I can read your face Giselle, you think I'm a bit old to be a novice. But it's women your age who keep saying it's never too late to start a career."

"Oh, absolutely! But wouldn't it be rather hard on Ben, having to call you Sister?"

Magdalene either didn't hear me or pretended she didn't. She was clattering the dishes into the sink, butter, sugar, and all, while I stood by looking helpless.

What had happened within the walls of St. Agnes to send my mother-in-law fleeing back to the outside world? Those earlier words of hers—"landing on your doorstep like a stray cat"—somehow did not have the ring of a woman who had awakened one morning and thought, Today I will pay my son and his new wife a visit.

"Did someone recommend that particular convent?"

"I'd recently overheard someone talking about it and thought it sounded nice. When the coach let me off at the gates, I got such a warm, peaceful feeling and I was welcomed so kindly. I never for the minute suspected . . ." Her small frame trembled. "It wasn't until last evening that I made my dreadful discovery."

"Which was?" I was drying off the (still full) butter dish.

"Eli always accuses me of hearing only what I wanted to hear . . ."

My mind whirled with blood-spattered possibilities. I had once seen a film where the nuns at a convent on the Cornish coast had been in reality devil worshippers. They'd also been men. I took a step closer to my mother-in-law, instinctively hoping to shield her from her memories. That film—with the Reverend Mother whipping off her wimple and mask to reveal a goat's head and rocking back and forth in uproarious glee, had sent me crawling under the cinema seats. Those being my fat days, I had become wedged.

"You can't mean that they—the nuns of St. Agnes—were from the other side?"

"Oh, but I do," she replied fervently. "They were Protestants."

16

. . . "Ellie, how did you and your mother-in-law fill the hours until Ben's return?" Hyacinth inquired.

"I took her on a tour of the house. It may seem as though my emotions were on a pendulum, but by the time she'd done the white-glove test to every piece of furniture in her path, I was ready to get *me* to a convent."

"Were you able to find a bedroom to suit?" Primrose patted my hand.

"Magdalene insisted on one of the turret rooms, in fact, the one from which Freddy had threatened to leap. She commented several times on the thickness of the door, the sturdiness of the iron bolt, and the view from the window. She even got a pair of binoculars out of her bag for a better look at the cliffs and lighthouse."

"Certainly the room sounds ideal." Hyacinth reached in her bag for another pen.

"In every way! Within easy hearing distance—immediately over Ben's and my room. I was determined to make the best of everything, and I am sure Magdalene was equally determined on making a valiant effort to like me. . . ."

* * * *

Magdalene told me my rust skirt and blouse suited me better than the pin-striped suit; she would take up the skirt hem. Had I ever thought of having my hair cut short and permed?

On his return from London, Ben entered the kitchen with a smile on his face and a bunch of daffodils in his hand. Magdalene spilled her cup of tea at the sight of him; her pinched face tightened, her eyes brimmed with tears. Ben stood absolutely still, coat hanging open, briefcase dangling from one hand, the daffs from the other, until she crossed the floor to him, arms extended.

I took the briefcase and the flowers and nobody noticed. Ben picked up his mother so her feet hung inches above the floor and smiled down into her face.

"Where the hell have you been, Mum? I've been worried to death about you. This afternoon I staged a sit-in at Scotland Yard, until I finally got someone to listen to my story about your disappearance. Now I'll have to get in touch and tell them they can get back to their filing."

He'd never said a word to me about going to Scotland Yard, which was exceptionally dear of him. He hadn't wanted me to get panicky. For weeks he'd been telling me he had no doubts at all that his mother was safe and well.

"I couldn't write to you, son. You would have read between the lines. It was easier with Paris; I didn't get teary and smudge the postcards. One of the nuns posted them for me when she went to different towns on business." Magdalene broke off as Ben set her down. "That's right, let me look at you, son. Oh my, you don't look well. Are you sure you've been getting enough sleep?"

"Plenty." He eased out of his coat. Feeling like a coatrack, I took hold of it, shifting the flowers and the briefcase to my other hand. "But you could be right, Mum, about the way I look; I have been overdoing it a bit. These last few days I've had this damn sore finger, and all the way home on the train it's been throbbing to beat the band."

He held out his hand to her, and I could see the finger was very inflamed. I started to speak Dr. Melrose's name, but was drowned out by Magdalene pulling a chair away from the kitchen table and ordering Ben to sit down. It was decidedly touching the way he smiled up at her.

"You shouldn't have gone to London, son; all that way in

a bumpy train and then breathing in that sooty station air." Magdalene smoothed back Ben's curls from his forehead and cradled his hand in hers.

"I believe soot—or rather, a speck of coal—may have been the cause of the infection." Ben patted a chair for me to join them. "Remember the other day when I was bringing up coal for your bedroom fire, Ellie?"

It was evening, not day, and couldn't he have said I was confined to bed with a cold, so as not to make it sound like I had lolled in bed with chocs and a book while he rushed up and down the stairs with coal buckets?

"A little bit of coal dust shouldn't have done this, son."

"Not of itself, Mum." Ben took his finger back. "But Ellie's cat had just scratched me."

What a rotten sneak! I dropped the daffs, the briefcase, and Ben's coat on the table in that order.

"And the animal is still running loose about the place?" Magdalene's sparrow eyes lit on me. Ben gave his finger back to her and gravely watched her turn it. Not, it would seem from his yelp, quite gently enough.

"Careful, Mum! I can't afford to become incapacitated, with the restaurant opening in *four* days. As it is I'm going to have to work in gloves."

And sterilize your hands in boiling water before each use, I thought.

"You should have stayed in bed today, son, and had the doctor. I'm sure Giselle wouldn't have begrudged taking her turn waiting on you."

"Of course she wouldn't." My husband swept me into an embracive smile. "But, Mum, when I tell you who it was I met in London today you will be glad I went. Remember Angelica Evangeline Brady, the gorgeous girl who lived at the house on the corner?" Ben outlined the gorgeous parts with his hands. "Well, get this for coincidence." He gripped the table with his good hand and rocked back in his chair. "She is the editor who is working on my book."

"*She* is Mr. A. E. Brady?" I gasped.

"Ellie, she never signed herself Mr., you added that bit."

I did hope in his enthusiasm that he didn't rock himself off the chair; I might accidentally step on his finger.

Hair wisping about her face like bird down, Magdalene

clasped her hands. Was she praying there was still time to get her son's unfortunate marriage annulled?

"Beautiful Angie Brady? She was utterly heartbroken when you went to study in France. Sid Fowler had to take the poor girl out and about to console her."

"Decent of him." Ben quirked an eyebrow at me. "Mum, did Ellie tell you that good old Sid is now living down here?"

"No." A change came over Magdalene's face, but I didn't analyse it. I moved behind Ben so he couldn't analyse mine. Holding the back of the chair I asked in an even voice, "Sweetheart, when did you first know that A.E.B. was an old flame?"

He tipped a little further back, head resting against me, an uninjured finger sidling up my arm. "A few weeks ago. I'm *sure* I said something at the time." He gave a nonchalant chuckle while Magdalene sat summing up the situation.

"No, you didn't." I released the chair.

"Far too small a point to call me on, Ellie." Ben braced himself on the table with his elbows and stood. The set of his shoulders said, Not in front of Mum, Ellie. And my inner voice intoned, A good wife doesn't object to a bit of deceit by default now and then. After all, I had known, on overhearing that pre-Christmas conversation between Ben and Freddy that things were being kept from me—for my own good.

Magdalene picked up the kettle. "If I'm interfering, tell me—but I've always believed that a couple's lives prior to marriage are their own."

Ben's blue-green gaze brushed mine. "Ellie and I concur completely."

What an incredibly vicious thing to say! Strangled by words I dare not say, I backed with outward casualness toward the hall door. This man, to whom I had bared my soul, knew full well that I had not indulged in "life prior to marriage." The handsome lad who had serenaded outside my bedroom window one winter night didn't count. It had been the wrong window. I willed Ben to look at me, to see the anguish in my eyes, but he was donning an apron, urging his mother to tell all while he got dinner, with one hand behind his back.

"Ellie, will you pour the three of us a sherry?"

I pried myself off the doorknob, but Magdalene didn't want a drink, and Ben said it being a special occasion he would join her in not having one.

"Then if you will both excuse me, I will go and check Tobias's medical file and see if he is prone to rabies." My voice wobbled, but it didn't matter. Mother and son were deep in reminiscences.

As I closed the door behind me, I heard Magdalene say, "She seems a decent enough sort of girl, son. I suppose you might have done rather worse these days. She could even be pretty if only she'd do something about her weight."

I seethed all the way upstairs, flung open the bedroom door, and stared myself down in the full-length mirror. The scales kept saying I was losing weight but I didn't believe them. They were a popular brand. Could they be both popular and truthful? Mirror, mirror on the wall, who's the fattest of them all? Surprisingly my blouse and skirt still fit, but I had bought them big so I could wallow around inside and feel extra virtuous. Time to cut back on calories.

Flopped out on the bed, I contemplated telephoning Dorcas and begging her to get herself and Jonas on a plane. Oh, to hear her dear voice saying something wonderfully bracing like, Men will be goats, now and then. But I didn't want Dorcas unhappy, which she would be if she guessed my fear. Was it over—that lovely early glow of our marriage? The cherished belief in Happy Ever After? I had been so sure that marriage was like a diet—you worked at it following the rules of diligence, perseverance, and restraint—it worked.

Ben came into the bedroom about five minutes later. I was back in front of the mirror, head tilted to one side, hair falling over my shoulders. I jumped as his lips brushed my neck. The maroon velvet curtains cast shadows on the reflection of our faces.

"Ellie, isn't it wonderful having Mum here, safe and sound?"

"Wonderful." It was incredible; he was oblivious to my misery, my sense of deep betrayal over Mr. Angelica Brady. He was rubbing my shoulder with one hand, the other dangling by his side. I focused on the need for Dr. Melrose to examine the inflamed finger, so my voice didn't jump around too much when I spoke.

"I am sure your motives were pure in regard to the beautiful Angelica. You probably thought I would leap to all sorts of silly conclusions and wished to spare me."

"That's right." His fingers tightened, his eyes met mine in the mirror. "I don't think you have fully recovered from your

Vanessa fixation. Simply because I once concurred with *your* statement that she was beautiful, you decided I wanted to marry her. Living in Vanessa's shadow, Ellie, has led you to feel threatened by any attractive woman, especially where I am concerned."

How despicably arrogant! How despicably true! My eyes swerved away from his.

"All right, I did care for Angie very much at one time, and I enjoyed seeing her today, professionally and otherwise, but I didn't feel the least twinge of regret for what might have been."

Whoopee! Had she grown taller than he since last they met?

"Ellie, I didn't tell you about her earlier because I felt you already had enough on your plate—this business with Mum and Poppa, Dorcas and Jonas leaving, and"—he pulled me back against him—"your weight."

"We'll have to see about a medal for chivalry." I ducked under his arm and grabbed a pillow off the bed. "Am I correct in assuming you informed your mother that I was at one time enormous?"

Ben paced in front of the fireplace, head down. "Ellie, don't drag Mum into this. She has already been subjected to enough. You and I have been heading for a confrontation. We've been sieving the lumps out of our relationship, trying to keep everything smooth and creamy, and I guess that can't be done." He stopped midstep. "I was wrong, not telling you about Angie, but I'm not exactly ecstatic about the way you conduct yourself with Rowland. Think I didn't notice"—his voice went all cutesy—"the way you almost broke your arm off picking up his pipe when he dropped it yesterday?"

"I did not want a hole burnt in the carpet."

"Sure!" Ben went back to pacing. "And while we are on the subject, do you really go to church for his sermons, or is it the frisk of his cassock as he steps out of the pulpit that pleases you?" A long pause, with both of us staring at the ceiling. "Ellie, if we are going to make this work . . ."

"*If*?" I retreated behind a brittle laugh. "Having your mother here should add a few lumps. In between polishing her halo, she can provide me with endless hours of enjoyment listening to her petty criticisms." My last words lacked total conviction. Magdalene skirted the letter of criticism. In the instance of my skirt, she hadn't said it was too long, she had merely offered to hem it.

Ben, this man I no longer knew, pounced within three inches of the bed. "Don't you speak about my mother that way. She has been through hell!"

"I couldn't agree more, if your father takes after you."

He headed for the door, then turned back. "Since the day you and I met, I have been wading through your crazy relatives. Now, if it doesn't take too much time away from them, I am going downstairs to cook dinner for my mother. Join us if you wish."

Ben bunked down the hallway. I clung to the door jamb, and snarled after him:

"Do we include Freddy among my crazy relatives? Don't you know you two are the talk of the neighborhood? The Dark Horse expects to go bankrupt if you two desist from stopping in for a quick one on your way home from Abigail's!"

Ben swung around. He looked like one of those robots, the vicious kind that sizzle you with their eyes. "I refuse to apologise for stopping in at the pub once or twice a week for a pint and a game of darts. Freddy needs to let off steam about Jill and—"

"Her petulant insistence on marriage?"

"Will you let me finish! I was about to say that the one thing my parents denied me was a brother. Sid sometimes joins us. He's been rather edgy of late, and what are friends for? Marriage isn't intended as a prison, is it? Do you find me interrogating you on each and every one of your activities?"

"I don't have any activities." My smile was the last word in nonchalance. Unfortunately it threatened to tear my face apart.

"Oh, no?" He folded his arms. "Mum mentioned in passing that you were wearing male attire when she arrived and that the trouser cuffs were rolled up, meaning they weren't mine. Mum didn't mention a clerical collar, but even had she, I would not become hysterical."

I closed my eyes and got this lovely picture of me slowly strangling his mother. "There is a perfectly reasonable explanation—"

Ben lifted his hand as though stopping traffic in Leicester Square. "I don't need explanations, Ellie. My feeling for you is based on trust." Whereupon he tapped his watch; this meeting having run beyond its allotted span, he sped down the stairs to dine with Mum.

I doubt he had once looked at his watch while with A.E. Brady. Leaning over the bannister rail I could hear noises from the kitchen. Laughter probably. Never mind. There were still some pleasures to be squeezed from life. Feeling as if I would suffocate, I opened the bathroom door, slid down onto the floor in a huddle, and flung my hair over my face. That way no one would hear me gulping down noisy sobs. I didn't want anyone to feel guilty.

A furry shadow appeared along the wall—Tobias! I put him on the clothes bin, then stood clinging to the shell-shaped pedestal basin until I was breathing almost normally again. My face, alas, didn't recover that quickly. It was red-eyed and puffy. Even Tobias was mildly revolted. "I don't want you to take this to heart"—I splashed on cold water and rubbed vigourously with a towel—"but I have quarrelled with the man of the house. Will you wipe that smile off your face? I didn't say anything about divorce. I am physically and emotionally attached to the man, so the hardest part of all this is that I am going to have to forgive him, after he has eaten his words—the way you are eating the toothpaste."

I removed the tube of McLeans and Tobias's face split into a yawn that went all the way down to his tail. I cradled him against me. "Remember, Tobe, you must not bear our mother-in-law a grudge because she suggested sending you to the big cat farm in the sky whenever—if ever—Ben and I have kittens of our own. Tell me, should I fight the urge to creep downstairs and telephone Poppa, begging him to come and remove her, or would you really hate to miss the chance to use her legs for scratching posts?"

I stooped to put him down and noticed Mr. Digby's suit lying beside the clothes bin where I had left it earlier, uncertain what to do with it. Now I wanted it out of sight. I would roll it up and toss it in the wall cabinet, way at the back. But first I probed through the jacket pockets, then the trouser ones. I wasn't being nosy, merely responding automatically to putting anything away. And, of course, I was killing time. Ah! What was this? From the jacket breast pocket I removed a snapshot and a small coin. A very small coin.

"Look here, Tobe. Bet you've never seen one of these. It's a farthing. Once the smallest coin in the realm. Not so surprising that Mr. Digby didn't want the suit back—if it's that old."

I sat on the edge of the bath; Tobias nuzzled up onto my

shoulder. Together we studied the photo. "Here's the man of mystery, Mr. D. himself. And who else do we have in the shadow of yon tree? A woman in a skirt and cardigan. And a teenager—probably a girl. It's hard to tell with that short hair and leather jacket." I turned the snapshot over and perused the writing on the back. Tobias trod from my left shoulder to my right, meowing for me to continue.

"All right! It says here, 'Eddy, Wren, and Miss Peerless.' And, upon close inspection, the woman in the skirt and cardigan does look like a younger Theodora Peerless." My mind bubbled with possibilities. Reaching up, I patted at the furry face. "What do you make of that, chum?"

Tobias was no help at all. And suddenly sounds of life from below stairs began drifting under the bathroom door. I tucked the photo back in the suit pocket and opened the wall cupboard. I'd have to think of the implications of all this later, when my own life didn't intrude. That *ping* was the telephone receiver being lifted. As I settled a sleeping Tobias in the bathroom basin (one of his favourite nesting places), I strained to hear more. Was Magdalene contacting her spouse in an attempt at reconciliation? I felt a small glow. Perhaps my rift with Ben might not be on public display too much longer. With one last look at my puffy face, I headed downstairs. No one in the hall. Either the phone call had been short or no one had answered. What were the odds that Paris and Poppa were home but wearing their earphones?

The glow flickered and died as I entered the kitchen. Was it blatantly obvious I had been crying? I could say my cold was back. Hand on the doorknob, I heard that sound which so often exasperated but was now Beethoven to my ears. Freddy's voice.

Magdalene murmured something indistinct and then Ben spoke. "Don't get rattled, Mum. Death is not likely to occur before Dr. Melrose gets here."

"He's not the one with a fancy for bumping off elderly women, is he, son? I overheard talk about him on the coach."

My hand fell off the knob. Ben's finger must have taken a terrible turn for the worse while I was upstairs wallowing in self-pity. Would he ever forgive me? Did I deserve to be forgiven?

Freddy was slung hammock-style between two chairs. He cocked an acknowledging eyebrow on seeing me and then closed his eyes. Magdalene was hovering over him, mopping at a red-dish-brown spot on his shirt—he'd been learning to carve roast beef for almost a fortnight now. And Ben was pouring tea, which seemed all wrong in his disintegrating condition.

"Hello, old sock." Freddy sounded like he was suffering from a bad case of wrist fatigue.

"Don't get up for me, Freddy," I said crisply. Magdalene's intake of breath filled the room. Ben turned, and Freddy went right on smiling wanly up at me.

"Come to bid me adieu, have you, Ellie?"

"Better not to talk." Magdalene stopped sponging at the stain. She was hoodwinked, all right. "You need to rest, Frederick."

"You mean . . ." I began.

"I mean I am about to die," replied Freddy serenely. His eyes closed, his hands dragged on the floor.

From the Files of The Widows Club

Monday, 27th April, 7:00 P.M.

President:

Good evening, Mrs. Hanover. Is this a bad line or are your customers having a bit of a singsong around the bar? That's better. You say you had something of a turnup this evening at The Dark Horse? Freddy Flatts . . . Gracious me! That disreputable young man who caused such a stir at the Haskell nuptials. One worries about that poor young woman. . . . Absolutely! One only has to look at her—so dreadfully changed in a few months . . . Oh, quite! Out of the frying pan into the fire when she married that handsome fortune hunter. . . . Has his hair cut a lot, does he? Well, that shouldn't surprise anyone. . . . I do hope Mrs. Haskell wasn't the one who attacked her cousin. One couldn't wonder but . . . Well, that is good news! Now we mustn't keep chatting; we're both busy people. Just wanted to let you know you will be working with Mrs. Millicent Parsnip on the night of the 1st of May, at that Retirement Party we talked about. . . . There won't be too much for you to do, which is good—this being your first assignment. . . . Yes, The Founder is taking a hand in this one. No, no, it isn't the irrepressible Mr. Daffy, but don't worry, he's about to be finally put to rest.

Be assured that the next reports of his demise will not be exaggerated! Now, are you ready for your instructions?

Mrs. Hanover:

A moment, if you please, to wipe one's eyes. Words cannot express how moved and honoured one is to be part of so momentous an event.

President:

Very good. The Subject To Be Retired on Friday the 1st May is . . .

17

. . . "Shot or stabbed?" Hyacinth and Primrose spoke in one voice with intense professional interest.

"Neither. Pinked by a dart thrown by Sid Fowler, who had been so shaken by the mishap that he'd fainted and been in no condition to leave The Dark Horse and bring Freddy home."

"Most unmanly!" Primrose sounded deeply shocked. "How did cousin Frederick reach Merlin's Court?"

"Astride his motorbike. I do not believe he seriously considered dying until he saw the effect his wound had upon Magdalene, whereupon his devious mind flew to the possibilities of the effect on Jill. Someone would break the news to her and she would come rushing to his side. Only, needless to say, she didn't. And by the time her get-well card and recommendation of a honey poultice reached Freddy, he had relapsed into full health. Dr. Melrose's main concern was that Freddy was up-to-date on his tetanus; after which he prescribed an antiseptic cream, then a stiff drink for all of us."

Primrose laid her hand on mine. "What did the doctor say about Ben's finger?"

"Nothing, because he didn't know about it. I didn't speak

up because I told myself I wasn't going to be labelled a meddlesome wife and Ben had a mouth of his own. If he was rendered speechless by fear of having the finger lanced and getting jabbed elsewhere with a needle, his mother could whisper in Dr. Melrose's ear. Magdalene informed me later, at a moment already bleak, that she wouldn't have dreamed of interfering. A husband and wife have their own lives to lead. Famous last words. . . ."

When I awoke the next morning, Tuesday, Ben had already left for Abigail's. He had left something behind: a note cut lopsidedly in the shape of a heart. Fingers trembling, I opened it. *Be mine tonight*, it said. Tears washed down my face. I didn't deserve this. I didn't deserve Ben! I had been such a shrew! How dare I deluge him with my relations, then turn snippy when his woebegone little mother requested the minimum in consideration—a roof over her head until . . . until . . . I swung my legs out of bed. Ah, Ellie, we are going to see some changes made in you! Ben's mother shall reside here for as long as she chooses.

Magdalene was mixing up a fruitcake as I entered the kitchen. The table was lined with pans, but it still reminded me of the headmistress's desk as I presented myself in front of it.

"I'm truly sorry, Magdalene, that I am so late down." The hall clock struck eleven in slow, heavy emphasis. "I didn't get much sleep last night. No special reason, you understand. First, I couldn't nod off and then I kept nodding awake. I do feel dreadful, neglecting you like this."

Raisins showered into the mixing bowl, and Magdalene plunged a wooden spoon, which was too tall for her, round and round.

"Don't worry about me, Giselle, I am quite capable of taking care of myself and Ben. He went off to work with a proper breakfast inside him. Gammon and tomatoes, just the way he likes them. He told me you don't cut the crusts off the fried bread, but we all have our different ways." She was scraping batter into a tin.

Would it make her like me better if I asked to lick the bowl? What were a few extra calories in so good a cause? Obviously she didn't hear me or see my outstretched hands because the mixing bowl went bobbing in the sink.

"If you like to have a lie-in every morning, Giselle, you

won't get a word of criticism out of me." She pushed at the sleeves of her grey cardigan. "I've always had to get up early, so as to get to Mass before the shop opened."

This was getting worse. I needed a calculator to tabulate my sins. Why hadn't I thought to ask Magdalene whether she wanted to go to daily Mass? A splotch of batter stared up at me from the table; I stretched out a finger, then snatched it back. "Would you like to come down to the village when your cake comes out of the oven? The Catholic church is just off Market Street; you could pick up a timetable and have a kneel there while I take care of some things at Abigail's, then I could fetch you over to see Ben and—"

"Have a kneel! I don't think so, thank you, Giselle. In fact"—her lips quivered—"I can't hope to get to church for awhile. . . . We can miss without fear of mortal sin in . . . times of illness, flood, blizzard, and other . . . sincere reasons, such as . . ."

I caught some words that sounded like "fear for life and limb." I should have asked her what she meant. So many things might have been different if I had, but my mind was on my reconciliation with Ben.

If ever a day was a good omen, this one was. The snow had vanished, leaving a vibrant greenness. I could smell the promise of blossom in the air. Deciding against taking the Heinz, I walked to the village. The breeze was nippish, but I didn't mind. Everything was going to be all right. Ben and I would rediscover the bliss of our early married life, my in-laws would discover they couldn't live without each other, and Abigail's premiere would be a mad success.

Mad was the word for the chaos which greeted me as I stepped into the foyer of the restaurant. A glance at the ceiling made me catch my breath. Straddling the second floor bannister railing and some other (invisible) prop was a plank. Tippy-tilting on this perch were a couple of painters, their brushes swooshing the ceiling in a Charlie Chaplin pantomime. A splatter of paint made me dodge sideways and collide with the plumber, who was staggering around in circles, a toilet clutched in his arms.

"What the bloody hell am I supposed to do with this, lady? Your husband had it straight from the horse's mouth that all sales is final!"

"I'm sorry!" I had to shout over the radio music blasting from all sides. Over it, or under it, I could hear the voice of the world's greatest upholsterer—Monsieur Rouche-Babou. I was about to charge into the Bluebell Room and pacify him when I saw Ben emerge from his second floor office and duck around the painters' aerie. The man with the paintpot dangling on his arm seesawed upward. When I opened my eyes, Ben was coming down the stairs.

"I got your note, darling," I said, as he reached me. His lips smiled but his eyes weren't quite focused.

"Good." He moved; my lips grazed his ear. Shuffling a half-dozen menus in his hands, he scowled at the plumber, who set the toilet down and sat on it, arms akimbo.

"Ellie, we'll have a romantic evening. Just the two of us . . . and Mum." Ben's fingers touched my arm as he strode forward, the menus slicing the air. "I want that toilet out of here, Johnson. I don't care if you have to put it in your living room and plant daffs in it. How many stars do you think I will get docked if word ever leaks out that it had been misinstalled in my kitchen?"

I regained his attention, meaning his gaze lit on me in its travels and turned blank. He was surprised I was still here; but pleased. He pointed the menus at the Bluebell Room, nearly taking off my ear in the process.

"Talk to that twerp you hired to do the upholstery, Ellie. Spell it out for him that if he can't get his fringes to lie flat by this evening, he's out on his arse."

"Ben," I said gently, "I can't run roughshod over a man of Monsieur's calibre. I'll bring him a posy of flowers and ask him nicely."

"Whatever it takes." Ben ran a finger across his brow. "Would you also go down on your knees to *your* wallpaperer. Take a look at that area by the front door!"

"What's wrong with it?"

"Come on, Ellie! It looks like a rhino's back."

Maybe I needed glasses. Two inches from the offending section of wallpaper, I couldn't see anything. Wait a minute! My fingers found a hairline crease. Annoying, but due to an imperfection in the plaster.

"Darling," I countered, slipping my arm through his, "let's go into the kitchen. You've been holding out on me with the new menu, and I'm dying to see what you have settled on."

His smile missed me by a quarter-inch, but on entering the

kitchen, he handed me a menu. A special one, in a leather, gold-tooled folder. "Tell me what you think."

"I will, I will. But do let my imagination savour this captivating cassoulet! I can almost smell the bouquet garni in which it is lovingly simmered for three hours . . ." My voice petered out. My eyes did a zigzag down the page and came to a shuddering stop. The words that zoomed out at me couldn't . . . couldn't be.

"What's up?" Ben was moving along the stainless steel counter, assessing how well he could see himself in its surface. "You are not upset that I added an extra veal entree, are you?"

"Not a bit. I am somewhat surprised . . ." My eyes returned to the menu, then flinched away. "I am very surprised by item number four in the luncheon section—the 'D'Ellie Delight.' Not that I want to make a big deal about it . . ." My bright smile slipped and I had to clench my teeth to keep it in place.

Ben was now leaning against the counter, feet crossed at the ankle, laughter dancing in his eyes. Usually I melt like snow on the stove when he strikes that pose.

"Ever thought you would see the day, Ellie, when you would lend your name to such a classy restaurant?"

"That has never been one of my prime-time fantasies, but had I experienced such hopes, I . . . might have pinned them on being featured in the *dinner* section." The menu twitched in my hands. "And I would have aspired to something a little more glamourous than a corned beef sandwich."

Ben's smile went out. "And I"—he swept a hand sideways, sending a glass shattering into the sink—"I thought I was paying you the highest possible compliment in giving your name to a dish which I consider uniquely mine."

"Really!" My laugh turned a nasty little somersault. "No one has ever slapped corned beef between two slices of bread before?"

Another glass almost went the way of the other, but he caught it. "The rye bread is high density, low cal—"

"Terrific. I'm supposed to feel flattered when you proclaim to the world, in addition to your mother, that I have a weight problem?" A voice deep inside me whispered, stop this, you're being petty and childish, but I was like a runaway sledge, out of control. It wasn't just the D'Ellie Delight, it was his leaving that note, luring me down here to be ignored. It was my mildewed stockings. It was my mother being dead when his wasn't. It was . . .

"You're being deliberately thin-skinned, Ellie. I take immense personal and professional pleasure in concocting healthful foods that you can push around on your plate or feed to your cat."

"How noble of you!" I leaned against the opposite counter, but got my crossed ankles out too far and almost overbalanced. I rallied. "What sort of pleasure did it give you to create the Baked Alaska Angelica? Whatever that may be—other than numero uno dessert in the *dinner* section!"

His hiss was like a gas jet coming on. "A baked Alaska, decorated with angelica!" Somehow we were nose to nose; the sparks from his eyes could have burned me to a crisp. "If you ever read anything—other than romantic rubbish about soppy-eyed females and Greek gods with their brains in their pants—you would know that, Ellie." He stepped back, rammed a hand through his hair and smiled compassionately. It was his fatal mistake.

"How soon we do forget, Bentley." My voice, too, could pulsate with pity. "A year ago you would have given your right . . . arm to have your name emblazoned on a rubbishy novel."

"Don't talk bosh!" He snatched the menus from my clutch and held them against his chest. "I had dreams of writing something of redeeming social value. I had it in me to create the greatest blood-and-guts story ever written, but"—he bit his lip and swung around—"we all make compromises."

"Marrying me was a *compromise*?"

"Oh, for God's sake!" He tossed the menus down and pressed his palms against his forehead, pushing hard. "I was talking about the cookery book. You know, Mum was right when she said that—"

An electrician came through the door, spotted us and immediately backed out.

"What did Benny's mum say?"

He paced away from me, then back. "Only, Ellie, that you are supersensitive."

"You can't hurt me." How *dare* she! I smiled at a point six inches above Ben's head. Only the tensing of the facial muscles kept the tears from sloshing down my face. "And I'm not surprised; such is the usual comment of the superinsensitive."

Ben let his hands fall. He leaned, weary and spent, against

the counter. "I wanted you to love my mother! Haven't I always showered your relations with courtesy and kindness?"

"I suppose you have."

"And they're not easy to like, excepting Freddy."

"I don't know about that."

A sigh. "Let's not try and be funny, Ellie."

"I'm serious." A pause, as I realigned the facial muscles. "One of them left you money, didn't he?"

As soon as I said them, I wanted to draw the words back. I wanted to throw myself into his arms and weep that I was sorry. But when he curled his lips and dusted his hands on a dish towel, as though ridding himself of my touch, I took a step backward instead.

"At last we have it," Ben said. Every word a knife thrust. "You are suggesting I married you because I wasn't content with my half of the inheritance. Greedy me wanted yours too."

"Not at all," I replied, digging my grave deeper. "I am suggesting *I* married *you* for *your* half."

And with that I walked, rigid as a tin soldier, from the room.

As I left Abigail's, I could hear Ben on the phone snarling about a case of goblets which had failed to get delivered. To hear him talk, he would be reduced to serving drinks in jam jars. For some, life went on. I made it back to Merlin's Court, without coming undone, by means of adding up all the ways I had violated chapter six of *A Blow By Blow Approach to Fair Fighting*. But it was downhill the minute I entered the kitchen. Magdalene was having a bath, there was no one to save me from myself. I did a disgusting, revolting, unutterably vile thing. Opening up the refrigerator, I piled a plate with every fattening food I could find. When the plate was almost as tall as I, up I went to the bedroom, where I locked the door, climbed into my wardrobe and crouched down with my prey. But are we ever completely alone? Unseen?

As I chewed, my clothes spoke in rustling whispers. She'll have to let out my waist. My sleeves will be too tight again. Back to a quadruple-D cup.

When the plate was empty, I buried my face in my arms and cried. My clothes weren't the only ones that knew the truth about me. I knew: I had a fat mind.

Magdalene commented on my red eyes when I went downstairs, but I explained that I had recently had a cold and was given to the occasional relapse. To change the subject, I brought up her marital situation. She was adamant in refusing to contact Poppa or allowing me to do so.

Under normal circumstances, I would have taken the law into my own hands, but I was swept along on a tide of inertia. Besides, I had Freddy on my hands. He arrived at the house midafternoon, murmuring in a weakened voice that his meals would be cold if I had to carry them to the cottage. Once in the door, he slumped in the kitchen rocking chair, and there he remained all that day, defying doctor's orders that he return to work. Amazingly, Magdalene had taken a fancy to Freddy. Not to bother, she told me, she would get his meals. And she would not listen when I told her she had already elected to do too much. By that evening, the china cabinets had been given a good going through; everything was rearranged so I would never find my egg cups again. The hanging plants were pruned down to stubble. The window ledge was lined with statues. And every flat surface, bar the floor, was covered with doilies. I became convinced that her black holdall contained a false bottom.

When Ben returned from Abigail's that evening, we were frigidly polite to each other. He made only a token protest when I said his mother was cooking dinner. Later I was to wonder if perhaps one of us might have tried to bridge the row, had the timing not been all wrong. But his mother, Freddy, my binge, and Abigail's premiere crowded in on us. Immediately after the Welsh rarebit, which he hardly touched, Ben took himself off to the study. When I peeked through the crack in the doorway later, he was asleep in the leather chair.

That night we lay in bed with an imaginary bolster running from pillow to post. Sometimes a foot would brush mine and I would roll away, clinging to the edge of the bed. Sometimes my foot would stray and he wouldn't move a muscle, compelling me to roll off the bed again to ensure he thought I thought he was the one doing the straying.

Wednesday morning at three o'clock I awoke from the worst nightmare I had experienced since the homicidal hamburgers. This time there had been no visual effects, only a vast blank screen and an offside voice whispering, "Someone's going to die. Guess who? Guess who?"

Struggling up from the pillow, I found the room thick with shadow and Ben sitting on the edge of the bed rocking a baby—no, his arm. I spoke to him, but he didn't answer.

Moonlight spilled over his arm. Hand pressed against my mouth, I slid off the bed. Mustn't cry out and panic Magdalene. I would get to the phone and . . . The door pounced open and there she was in pink flannel, a scapular around her neck and a rosary in her hands.

"Is something wrong, Giselle? I heard noises."

Another time I might have asked my mother-in-law if she knew the meaning of the word knock, but who could think over the low moaning sounds Ben was making? Like a tree trying to prop itself against a daisy, I clung to his mother.

She pushed me away quite gently and bent over Ben. Her hand hovered over his head as she murmured, "My boy, my only child. He's so dreadfully flushed."

"Are you sure? This is that sort of room—maroon tends to give a warm look. . . ."

"Shouldn't you be phoning the doctor, Giselle?" Magdalene's face looked like mine felt. "Don't think I'm taking over, but at a time like this, a child, however old, wants his mother. Better phone Eli, too."

Dr. Melrose answered at the second ring; there was no answer from the flat in Tottenham.

The verdict was blood poisoning. And the blame which I saw in Dr. Melrose's eyes was only a reflection of what I was feeling. As he stashed away his medical equipment, he said, "I realise, Ellie, that Ben may have put up resistance to seeing me, but you could have employed the tactics he used when getting me out to see you. If that finger had been lanced promptly and antibiotics administered, he would be on the mend now. As it is, you must understand his condition is quite serious."

"Oh, I do."

"The cottage hospital is full to overflowing, otherwise I would have him admitted tonight. However"—his lips tightened—"you should manage, Ellie, if you and Mrs. Haskell divide the nursing."

"And Ben will . . . live?"

"Certainly, bar complications." Dr. Melrose clapped on his hat, thumped me on the shoulder, and trod briskly down the stairs, black bag swinging at his side. I kept close behind him. I didn't want him to leave. Magdalene's voice drifted down from the upper bannister rail.

"Don't worry, doctor. I shall be with my boy, reading to him, singing to him."

For the first time I saw a softening of Dr. Melrose's eyes as he paused in the hall. "Don't either of you ladies go overdoing things. Get out for a walk round the garden two or three times a day."

"Not me, doctor." Magdalene's voice quivered above our heads. "Fresh air doesn't agree with me."

It was as well Ben was too ill to realise that his mother had closed not only the bedroom window, but also the curtains. With only one small lamp lit, the character of the room changed. The furniture acquired a hulking look. The pheasants on the wallpaper seemed to fly into each other. Magdalene kept saying the air wasn't stuffy—we had plenty of ventilation from the chimney.

During most of what was left of that awful night, Ben remained sunk in restless sleep, kicking off the blankets and twisting his reddened face upon the pillows; but every half hour or so, he would jerk upright, calling for the painters or ranting at the underchef. We had to keep assuring him that Abigail's premiere would go on as planned.

Each time his eyes opened and he looked at me, the knives of misery and guilt twisted deeper. Every so often I would creep behind Magdalene and open a pane, so Ben wouldn't feel claustrophobic in his sleep. I didn't fight her for pride of place at his pillow. I was consumed with remorse over the row. It helped me emotionally when she would send me downstairs for lemon barley water for Ben or tea for us. What did bother me was that each time I got back she had locked the bedroom door. For fear of Tobias coming in, she'd explain. I was tempted to tell her that closing it was sufficient—Tobias isn't good with handles. And waiting—sometimes for five minutes—for her to hear my knock was becoming a strain. But the rest of that night and the next day were long enough for both of us without our bickering.

By early Wednesday evening, Ben's temperature was close to normal. The antibiotics had taken hold. Dr. Melrose, making his third visit of the day, patted everyone, including himself, on the back. And Magdalene announced it was now clearly a blessing that we hadn't been able to reach Eli. Not wishing to bring her share of the good mood crashing down, I decided not to mention that I had spoken to him that morning to invite him to visit his lost wife and ailing son. He would have come at once but I asked him to wait until the following afternoon so as not to panic Ben that this was a deathbed visit.

Thursday morning saw Ben propped up on his pillows. So far he hadn't said a word to me about our troubles and it was Chinese torture for me not knowing if this was because a) they now seemed trivial in the vaster scope of things; b) he wasn't up to discussing his feelings on divorce; c) his mother was always between us, straightening the bedclothes or tenderly inserting a straw between his lips so he could drink his lemon barley water without lifting his head.

And of course Ben was desperately worried about Abigail's opening night—only thirty-six hours away.

"I know you won't listen to me, son." Magdalene bent the straw for easier swallowing. "But I maintain food doesn't have to be fussy to be good, especially when it's free. Leave it to Mum. I'll make plenty of fishpaste sandwiches, and we can buy lots of bags of crisps."

I rushed to Ben's side. "That would be lovely, Magdalene, but I do think we owe it to Freddy to give him the chance to prove he can cope in a crisis."

"Ellie's right, Mum." Ben leaned weakly back on the pillows. "We don't have any other choice." His voice was grim.

8:00 A.M. I summoned Freddy to the kitchen and broke the news that he was the understudy about to assume the starring role.

"Ellie, believe me, I sincerely wish I could do this for you, but—not to steal Ben's thunder—I have been on the brink of the great abyss myself."

I set Ben's breakfast tray down and began unloading into the sink. "Dr. Melrose assured you, in my presence, that your injury is ninety-nine point nine percent mental."

Freddy didn't look at me; he leaned against the table brandishing a broom at Tobias, who kept leaping to attack. "Old Doc is right. This wound will eventually heal." He tapped a finger to his chest. "But in a far more important way, I am a man scarred for life. I may never play darts again."

"Don't be stupid!"

"I have decided to sue Sid Fowler for physical and emotional anguish." He gave the broom another flick.

"Know what I think?" I dropped, and broke, a cup for emphasis. "I think you are afraid to tackle preparing the food for this party. You're nothing but a coward."

Freddy watched Tobias pounce on the broom. "As you please, Ellie, but I owe it to Jill to turn my injury into a comfortable living."

Grabbing the broom away from him, I pondered whacking sense into him. "You owe it to Ben to get cracking with your little paring knife and start fluting mushrooms for tomorrow evening. If you don't, I'll flute *you*."

Freddy took the broom back, tossed it into a corner, and sank into the rocking chair. "This hurts me, Ellie, more than it does you. Sid's assault has left me, at least for the present, unfit for work. So I will tell the court, and you wouldn't want me to look like a liar, would you? Can you imagine the unfavourable impact of upward of a hundred witnesses streaming into the dock, all ready to swear on holy writ that they had partaken of a banquet prepared by yours truly within days of the alleged assault?"

I trod down on one of the chair's rockers. "Why don't you telephone Mr. Lionel Wiseman and ask his professional opinion?"

"That man! I wouldn't let him represent me. I hear the bugger always inclines to the woman's point of view."

"There is no woman involved in this case, Freddy."

"Yes there is, cousin. His wife Busty—sorry, Bunty—is a chum of yours."

"Enough of this nonsense, Freddy. Either you get to work *now* or lose the perks that go with the job."

Freddy's yawn swallowed his whole face. "You'd try and kick me out of the cottage? Sorry, old sock, you'd have to sue me."

I was saved from ramming one of the hanging plants down his throat by a knock on the garden door. Sid Fowler was on the step. Our unwitting villain held a bunch of narcissi in each hand. Behind him was the milkman, who avoided my eyes and made a production of clanking down bottles in a row.

"All hail, false friend bearing flowers!" came Freddy's ebullient greeting.

Sid's head was sunk into his shoulders. "Hope you don't

mind this early-bird visit, Ellie, but I've a string of appointments starting at ten." He turned his gloomy eyes on the flowers. "One of these is for Freddy, the other for Ben. Okay if I go straight up to the bedroom?"

The milkman kept rattling the bottles. "Six pints enough today, Mrs.?"

I drew in a deep breath. "Make it two dozen. I have rather a lot of cooking to do."

Magdalene agreed to keep mum, but my biggest fear was that Ben would learn that Freddy had thrown in the wooden spoon and left me holding the mixing bowl. I therefore elected to work at home rather than in the sterile sanguinity of Abigail's kitchen with its bevy of ovens and army of appliances. That way, I could hurl off my apron every half hour or so and race upstairs to perpetuate the myth that I was spending the morning catnapping. One thing in my favour was that we did not have a telephone in our bedroom. Ben could not ring Abigail's to check on Freddy's progress.

8:30 A.M. The minutes started ticking off inside my head. I pounded my fists into my hips and blasted Freddy with my eyes as he took his flowers and left.

8:31 A.M. I accompanied Sidney up to the invalid's chamber. Between landings he told me that he was remorseful about Freddy and should have known life would bomb out. It always did when he began getting a renewed enthusiasm for it. I made consoling noises, but again sensed that misery was meat and drink to Sidney. Magdalene acted edgy on first seeing him, but warmed sufficiently to tell him he looked worn to the bone and shorter than she remembered.

My heart leapt. Ben's eyes were asking me to stay. Had the memory of the dreadful things we said to each other merged into his hours of delirium? Did he think it was all a nightmare? But how could I stay? His recuperation depended on his not discovering that the fate of Abigail's was in my hands.

8:40 A.M. Ten loaves of bread multiplied by twenty slices, multiplied by eight made how many mini-sandwiches? And two hundred sausage balls, divided into six batches, times twenty minutes per batch, oven time, took how long?

9:45 A.M. I made a list of items to be prepared and a list of ingredients needed from Abigail's culinary coffers, then telephoned Bunty. She agreed to transport same in her car, on condition that I make thousands of those little chicken tarts everyone was so crazy about at the wedding reception. My pleasure! What could be easier than mushing up chicken with mayonnaise and filling Tom Thumb pastry shells? First, one skinned the chicken, boned it, and cooked it . . . I rang Bunty back and requested she purchase six tins of jellied breast.

10:15 A.M. The hands on that clock could have been arrested for speeding. I rolled up my sleeves and heaved cannisters of flour, granulated sugar, and chopped nuts onto the working surface. Telling which was which at a glance wasn't easy—someone had dressed the cannisters in crocheted cosies. Off they came, but I was not much further forward; someone had washed off the adhesive labels which normally would have advised me whether this white powder was cornflour or icing sugar. Damp finger testing was unhygienic as well as sticky and time-consuming.

Just then Magdalene came in and assembled the scattered cosies into stacks and started to load up a tea tray.

"Well, Giselle, I saw Sidney off the premises and . . . Don't think me interfering, but wouldn't you find it easier if you measured everything out into little bowls before you start mixing up?"

10:45 A.M. I rushed upstairs to let Ben know I was still on the premises, but I couldn't go beyond the doorway because I realised I had white splotches on my cardigan. So near and yet so far. His black hair and convict stubble emphasised the pallor of his face and the hollows under his eyes. I thought about asking Magdalene to give Ben and me a few moments alone. Instead, I embarked on a time-consuming lie about how I was dusting the drawing room and wouldn't be up for awhile. Ben pretended to be asleep and Magdalene looked ready for a good forty winks. But when I suggested she go to her room and take a nap, she acted as though I had suggested putting her out on the ice floe for the polar bears.

11:00 A.M. I shushed Tobias out into the garden and warned him that if he tried to reenter I would guillotine him. Back on with the apron and head scarf. A glance at the statues on the window sill was a comfort, knowing that the saints were with me.

12:35 P.M. I took time for a tea break and surveyed the kitchen. A volcano had erupted in its midst, and for what? The batter that was to produce six dozen choux pastry puffs had produced seventeen lone items. Skimpy ones at that.

Footsteps on the stairs! I quailed. Had Magdalene dozed off? If this was Ben, the sight could kill him.

Whooh! False alarm. It was Magdalene. She surveyed the whitened floor and the working surface which would have to be chiselled clean, but didn't say an unkind word. Would it, I wondered, be easier to like her if she weren't my mother-in-law?

12:45 P.M. Into the oven with the cheese straws. They looked like worms, but that didn't mean they would taste like them. Hark! The front doorbell. Bunty at long last. What might it take to bribe her into helping me roll out pastry? I skidded across the flagstones in the hall. Was it futile to hope I could contain the flour upon my person, so as to prevent its absorption into the air? Another peal of the bell. Were Bunty's arms so full of boxes and bags that she had to lean on the bell with her nose?

I must have looked like an overworked pirate as I flung open the door. But it wasn't Bunty on the step. Mrs. Amelia Bottomly, gargantuan in cape and deerstalker hat, stood there. She was flanked by the beaming ladies of the Historical Society.

"Hello, hello! Dear Mrs. Haskell!"

"What . . . what a lovely surprise!" I gasped

"It shouldn't be. I telephoned last weekend and your charwoman assured me she would convey the message. She did, I trust?"

"Oh, certainly!" I brushed at my apron and the air whitened. Roxie had conveyed that message when my brain was all stuffed up from my cold. I had never given another thought to this invasion.

"Splendid." Mrs. Bottomly surged inward and onward. At the lift of a ring-laden hand, a swarm of angora berets and assorted hats followed suit. The hall buzzed. I was surrounded by cameras, notebooks, and pencils. Could I throw my apron over my face and refuse to come out? I did not have time for this. I had Ben to consider. Still, this calamity might not be without its silver lining. It did, after all, provide me with a viable excuse for not spending the afternoon with my recovering husband.

I stepped backward to avoid being trampled, then ducked,

so as not to be clumped in the face by a free-swinging Kodak camera.

"Super to have you all here." I gave the scarf a pat as though it were the latest thing in headwear for the mistress of the manor. "But there is one smallish problem."

"Yes?" A dozen pairs of eyes fixed themselves on me. It occurred to me that I might be in danger of being lynched if I failed to let the tour proceed.

"My husband Bentley is ill in bed, so I would appreciate your being as quiet as possible while taking a peek into the rooms on the second floor. I will show you which door not to enter, and—"

"I wonder if they share a bedroom?" came a voice from the foreground.

"What about the dungeons?" demanded an anemic-looking woman in the accusing voice of a reporter.

"Sorry. Dungeons are one medieval convenience we don't have at Merlin's Court."

A rustle of disappointment. Two women lifted eyebrows in unison, tightened their coat belts, and stalked out. But as they exited, two others came in. One was Miss Gladys Thorn.

"Mrs. Haskell, such a thrill! I have been unable to sleep for nights." Miss Thorn went into one of her curtsy dips. I also spied Mrs. Hanover from the pub and Froggy—pardon me, Shirley—Daffy, wife of Vernon Daffy, estate agent. Was she here at his behest, in hope of persuading us to sell?

The group broke into twos and threes and wandered around the hall as though it were a museum. Every table leg was respectfully surveyed. Mrs. Bottomly stage-whispered in my ear. "Decent of Millie Parsnip to accompany Shirley Daffy, don't you agree?"

"Frightfully." Goodness knows why, but agreement was so much speedier than questions, and speed was vital when . . . the cheese straws! They would be burned to a crisp!

"One has to applaud Shirley for staying in the mainstream at a time like this."

Mrs. Bottomly drew me toward the bannister and Rufus, the suit of armour.

"Mrs. Haskell, you did read in Tuesday's *Daily Spokesman* that Mr. Daffy has disappeared? He went out jogging and hasn't been seen since."

"I didn't know." An awful phrase popped into my mind

—third time's the charm. Dreadful! Poor Mr. and Mrs. Daffy! Even more dreadful was the realisation that at that moment, I was marginally more concerned about my cheese straws than a neighborhood tragedy. If they were burnt, could I curry them?

1:08 P.M. I sped down the stairs after breaking the news to Magdalene that a couple of dozen women were rampaging through the house. All she said was, "We all live our lives differently, Giselle." Ben, thank the blessed saints on the windowsill, was still asleep.

"Do continue to make yourselves at home, ladies. I have taped a piece of paper to the door of my husband's bedroom. And the kitchen is also off-limits because I am whipping up a few cakes for tea . . . in case the vicar should chance to call."

I slipped around Millicent Parsnip and past Mrs. Daffy. Mrs. Bottomly was posing for a photo, her arm around Rufus. I hoped she wouldn't crush him.

1:13 P.M. Bless Bunty's blond head. She had let herself in the back door. Dressed in a leopard-skin waistcoat over a black leotard, she was shaking cheese straws off their baking trays onto cooling racks. I wondered if I should throw her an apron as a hint she was welcome to stay on for the next couple of hundred stuffed grape leaves?

"Hey, El, this is kinda fun. And Li will be so proud of me; he's got such lofty ideals about helping the oppressed!"

1:35 P.M. All that exuberance had me fooled. Bunty wasn't any better at this than I was. So far, we had sixteen spinach balls the size of golf balls, thirteen the size of walnuts, and forty-one pellets.

2:00 P.M. Bunty and I were discussing where we might locate a suitable pop-up cake for my role in the Aerobics Follies, when a voice caroled, "Don't mind me. I couldn't resist a peek at the kitchen and . . . my, isn't it . . ."

2:01 P.M. Shaking with flour and fury, I marched into the hall to speak to the Historical Society. Typically, my timing was off. The women were all clustered around Rufus. All, that is, except Millicent Parsnip, who stood in the middle of the Turkish rug, saying, "Smile!"

The camera flashed. There were the usual complaints. "I wasn't ready!" "My mouth was open, I'll look like I was catching flies!"

I tiptoed behind Mrs. Parsnip, lest I be invited to be in the photo. To subdue my frustrations, I tapped on the ledge of the niche by the drawing room door. The Egyptian urn that once reposed there had been replaced by a statue of an unfamiliar saint who looked nearly as unhappy as I.

"Everyone set?"

A pang, as I remembered Dorcas taking our wedding pictures. Then, a gasp—I'm not sure if it was mine—widening to a ripple of consternation. Mrs. Bottomly swayed, caught at a bannister rung and, amid screeches of alarm, disappeared, taking with her a section of the floor, Rufus, and the two closest ladies aboard.

It was a distressing moment. The scramble of the rest of the party to terra firma! The shrieks of distress. And the sound I dreaded most—Magdalene, calling over the railing, "Giselle, would you mind asking your friends to be a little more quiet? My boy is trying to sleep."

It isn't enough to say I was numb. I was standing outside myself, watching this other Ellie Haskell go straddling over the legs of those women who were prone on the floor.

"Excuse me, please!" said this Ellie as she joined the braver members of the Historical Society in staring down into a dark void approximately three foot square—or to simplify, the size of one flagstone. A whisper stirred through the group, but there was silence from the grave . . . I mean, below. The other Ellie opened her mouth, then closed it. A section of flagstone was sliding out from the under belly of the floor. Horribly, instantly, there was no more void. The silence that Magdalene had urged now engulfed the hall.

I was stunned, but my extensive reading in the field of gothic novels was decidedly in my favour. I sensed what sort of gadget I was up against and summoned up a mental picture of where the ladies of the Historical Society were standing at the crucial moment. I had been alongside this niche, my hand on the stone ledge. Repositioning myself exactly, I thought back . . . yes, my eyes had been on Mrs. Bottomly as she clutched the bannister, the second bannister up . . . The loose bannister! The one first brought to my attention by Mr. Vernon Daffy at the wedding reception and the source of many Roxie complaints. But surely the bannister of itself could not be the catastrophic catalyst? Were it so, the hall floor would be forever dropping out from under. No, the bannister had to work in conjunction with something else. My fingers clenched the stone ledge; I felt a give and in that moment had the answer.

"Mrs. Parsnip," I called across the room, "would you kindly twist the second bannister from the bottom?" As she did so, I depressed the ledge. Seconds later, a ripple of wonderment washed through the hushed group. The void had reappeared.

Millicent Parsnip cupped her hands around her mouth and inquired tremulously, "Anyone down there?"

Silence. Then a flicker of hope. Way, way down in the blackness we could see a tiny splurt of light. Could it be . . . ? Yes. Someone had struck a match; voices set up a cheer.

"We're alive! Uninjured! Not even a dent in the armour!" There was a sound of pulleys churning, and the tiny flame glowed brighter. The survivors were being elevated to the surface.

"And," boomed Amelia Bottomly triumphantly, "we have found the dungeons!"

There were those in the group who made it plain they were convinced I had known all along about the secret entrance. But they managed to work off their irritation by discussing what a vast improvement ours was on the oubliettes of old, which provided no safety net when the floor dropped out beneath the hapless victims at the whim of any sheriff, duke, or king who didn't have better things to do with his time.

"Come now, Mrs. Haskell," Mrs. Bottomly's eyes were like suction cups. "There has to be more than twiddling a bannister. I swear I cannot leave this house until you tell me the nature of the Open Sesame."

Were she to carry out this threat I could have ended up with her in one turret and Magdalene in another. But something—call it stubbornness—stopped me from assuaging her curiosity.

"I'm sorry, but where would be the fun of having something like this if its secrets weren't—secret?"

The chins quivered in disappointment, but Mrs. Bottomly made a valiant effort. "Never mind, Mrs. Haskell. Merlin's Court will still be added to the Historical Society's permanent register—meaning, we will be back next year."

I was tempted to suggest that if they left right now they wouldn't have to rush.

* * * *

As the door closed on the last beret, I was torn between fatigue and elation. I should have realised that local legend spoke true. Wilfred Grantham had been too much of a purist to build his castle without that most basic of requirements, a dungeon. Had everything been different, I would have raced upstairs to tell Ben. As I passed the telephone, I even felt an urge to ring up Mr. Edwin Digby. He might be interested; after all, he had featured a dungeon in that book of his about Ethel the pickler, and he had a link with the mad-hatter doings of Wilfred Grantham, on account of the Misses Lucretia and Lavinia.

4:27 P.M. I returned to that chamber of horrors, the kitchen. The ticking inside my head was getting louder. No Bunty. Her apron was discarded on a chair; scrawled in the floured surface of the table was *Gone home to slip into something comfortable—a bubble bath*. Well, this explained why she hadn't come out into the hall to see what all the commotion was about. But she had finished the last batch of chicken tarts. They looked nice, even the ones we had to make out of tuna because we ran out of jellied breast. Everything else looked subtly nongourmet, but the refrigerator was now full.

Too full. As I brushed past it, I heard a crash from within. The top shelf had collapsed. Hours of work reduced to pâté.

I wanted to kick off my shoes, lie on the floor, and turn up my toes, but there was a knock on the garden door. Freddy come to beg forgiveness? Thoughts of pressing his face inside the fridge revived me somewhat.

But the man on the step was short and stout with deep brown eyes, a bald spot, and a fluffy white beard. Two suitcases and a yippy little dog were by his feet.

"Ellie, is my son dead?"

His question revived me like a slap in the face. My father-in-law, Elijah Haskell, threw his arms around me and we both began to sob.

"No, Ben's much better." I wiped my face dry and stepped aside to let him and his dog enter. Tobias wouldn't be pleased about the dog, but we are all called upon to adjust.

"My wife, she's bunked off to another convent?"

"No, but . . ."

"Then, what's to cry about?" Poppa asked over the dog's yapping. His eyes took in the culinary turmoil. "This is a nice place you've got here. A Star of David on the wall, and it could look like home." He put his luggage down and began unwinding the little dog. "Take me to see my family, Ellie, then tell Poppa how to help."

Now was the time to inquire if Ben's culinary skill was a genetic fluke, but I was put off my stroke by his suitcases. They didn't look the weekend sort.

I gave a casual, hiccuping laugh and found myself thinking of the handmade furniture in the flat in Tottenham.

"You can make me a cake, Poppa, one I can leap out of on the night of Bunty Wiseman's Aerobic Follies at the church hall."

From the Files of
The Widows Club

MEMO: From Executive Board to Mrs. Geraldine Stropp, Correspondence Chairwoman.

Thursday, 30th April

Please arrange to have two dozen yellow roses sent on Saturday, 2nd May, to Mrs. Ellie Haskell of Merlin's Court, Cliff Road, Chitterton Fells. Card to be enclosed. Message to read: "Sorry." No sender. Please be sure and bill Treasury before the first of the month.

NOTE: This action was not presented to the members at large. It is a direct order from The Founder.

. . . "My poor Ellie, what an agonising day! If only we had known . . . known you!" Primrose sighed. "We could have helped by sending Butler over to make little sausages on sticks. You would have been pleased to do so, would you not, Butler?"

The man removed plates scattered with toasted teacake crumbs. "Certainly, madam. Although not as much as I h'enjoyed breaking into The Peerless Nursing Home. Surely Mr. Freddy . . ."

"Please!" Hyacinth's black brows zigzagged together. "We do not wish to hear that name. . . ."

In all fairness, a certain person did knock on the front door Thursday evening to sob his apologies through the letter box. If Eli's dog had been handy, I would have whispered, "Postman!" in her ear and flung wide the door.

"Ellie, old sock, did I by chance forget to mention that one of the deep freezes at Abigail's is crammed with bite-sized morsels prepared during my training sessions with Ben? Of course, I never dreamed that they would go public—we have been eating them for lunch. But it occurs to me that in a pinch . . ."

I almost went through the letter box. To have suffered the horrors of the damned while a deep freeze had everything at the ready! A moment's quiet reflection, however, brought me to realise that Freddy was not totally to blame. Had my husband and I been properly communicating, I would have recognised that while Ben lay blank-eyed on the pillows, he wasn't fretting whether Freddy would recall the precise ratio of air to solid in a mousse, but whether he was up to proper thawing.

Freddy rattled the letter box to recapture my attention. "Of course, Ellie, you might like to make some chicken tarts. They're a bit simplistic for Ben or me, but—"

"I know, they were a great hit at the wedding reception." So, the chicken tarts weren't wasted, but nothing could give me back the hours I could have spent with Ben, or undo the fact that he thought he came a poor second to dusting the drawing room.

When I brought Poppa up to see Ben, I could tell that the dent in our marital relationship had deepened into a bottomless pit. My own husband had to snap his fingers a couple of times to recall my name. And if I didn't have enough problems, the little dog, misnamed Sweetie, took a snarling dislike to me. I couldn't think of a thing to serve for dinner except ruined hors d'oeuvres. And, for all his pleasantness to me, Poppa soon made it plain that his desire to see his son did not include a willingness to speak to him. Honour must prevail. The possibility of instant reconciliation between my in-laws also went out the window like a loose canary when they met across Ben's bed.

"You're looking fatter, Eli."

"You're looking thinner, Maggie."

"I will not turn my son's mansion into a battleground."

"Won't seem like home, will it?"

She smoothed down her grey cardigan, he rubbed his bald spot, and that was that.

From then on, the house turned into a revolving door. Each time Magdalene saw Eli, she crossed herself. Each time he saw her, he chanted something in Yiddish. I grew dizzy wondering how long this might last. And, to add zing to the tension, Sweetie was trying to drive me off her territory. Tobias went into hibernation. Occasionally I would espy a dangle of fluffy tail out the door of a high cupboard but, in my time of need, the comfort of a warm furry body was denied me.

How long would Poppa stay? My suspicions became confirmed when he requested a room with a view, enquired as to the location of the nearest synagogue, and wanted to know whether I was aware of any chess societies in need of new members.

Within hours of Poppa's arrival, I began to perceive unnerving signs of a different sort. He wasn't making himself at home; he was making *my* home *his* home. Candlesticks bearing the Star of David and portraits of rabbis began springing up all over the house in direct competition with his wife's statues, pictures, and the holy water fonts she had placed beside every door—from the refrigerator to the drawing room. What would Dorcas and Jonas think were they to walk in now?

Never had I missed my dear friends more than that long Thursday evening. How much more could I take of Poppa not talking to Ben (except with his eyes), Poppa and Magdalene not talking to each other, Ben not talking to me, and me . . . doing all the talking. With fond nostalgia I thought of the Aunts Astrid and Lulu, dear Uncle Maurice . . . stopping short only at Vanessa. But mostly I thought of closing the kitchen door on chaos and sinking into a deep, deep sleep. But to reach this utopia I would have to get into bed with Ben, who had summarily rejected the cup of tea I offered to fetch him; his mother was bringing him hot milk.

To sleep on the chaise lounge now that he was better would make me look silly. To retire to a separate bedroom would be wrong. Magdalene would know. Turning off the bedside light, I slid planklike between the sheets. I had worked off just a little of my remorse.

"Forget something, darling?" Ben's voice broke into the darkness.

I wasn't too tired to smile. "What?" I edged a millimeter closer to his warmth. Statistically, what were the chances of the bedroom door flying open?

"Your duster. Oh, and Ellie . . ."

"Yes?"

"I promise not to wake you if I die in the night. I know you need your beauty sleep."

I felt him fold a pyjama'd arm over his face and close his eyes. Cruel! Cruel! How could I sleep? What if he died in the night and I were not awake to revive him? Dr. Melrose had assured me that all that was needed now for complete recovery was a few days of bed rest and medication. But I knew Ben when he was intent on making a point.

Tomorrow is another day, I thought, ripe with promise. The promise of continued hostilities, Roxie giving me hell on account of the kitchen, and Sweetie, the dog with the yap that went right through you, scratching her toenails as she hurtled across parquet and stone floors, wetting every time someone laid down a newspaper. Why didn't I remember meeting the little dear on my visit to Tottenham?

Sweetie, so Poppa informed me the next morning, was new. Secondhand new, that is. He had purchased her from a man boarding the same London train yesterday, who, after much fumbling in his pockets, discovered he did not have the money for her fare.

"Is she a present for your wife?" I attempted a smile at Sweetie, but had to snatch it back.

"Maggie hates all dogs."

Sweetie must not have heard him. When Magdalene entered the kitchen at eight o'clock and Poppa went out into the hall, the dog skittered toward her, whimpering and darting looks over her ratty shoulder at me.

"Poor neglected mite." Magdalene squinted as though unsure precisely what the mite was, but ten seconds later the wee brute was halfway up her leg and into her heart.

And to give the devil her due, Sweetie did get Magdalene to set foot out of the house. My mother-in-law set the fuzzy scrap down, took one look at the dishes rising like the Tower of Babel, and pressed her lips firmly together. She was not going to say a word of criticism. She donned her coat and the damson beret, attached Sweetie to a length of string, and with a squaring of her birdlike shoulders, informed me that she refused to be a victim any longer to her nerves.

"I don't expect you to understand, Giselle, but I've been hiding from shadows."

"Have you, Magdalene?" I felt a surge of closeness, all tied up with the Raincoat Man and the hamburgers that chased by night. I wanted to ask what her shadows looked like, but Sweetie was standing cross-legged by the garden door. Out they went and in came Roxie. Half an hour early. Blast! I could have hidden the mess and the kitchen itself, given time.

I put on two aprons—one for the front, one for the back—and started tying strings. "Feel free to develop a crippling headache, Roxie, and go home."

She smacked her red butterfly lips together and, without removing the velvet hat with its sequined brooch, tossed both ends of her feather boa over her shoulders and rolled up her coat sleeves.

"I hate to think what the health inspector would say if he was to pop in. A good thing Roxie Malloy can keep her mouth shut." Her record for that feat was 1.024 seconds.

I flushed water into the sink and said I would naturally pay her extra.

"I wouldn't dream!" She fluttered purple lids. "What with the day you had yesterday, the Historical Society all over the house, falling into dungeons! Couldn't hear the numbers at bingo for all the talk about it. Course, if you should choose, Mrs. H., to slip a little something extra into me hand when I'm not looking, there's not much I can do to stop you, short of giving offense. And with your mother-in-law visiting you too, I gather—"

"Did someone mention me?" Magdalene came through the garden doorway, nose reddened by the wind, beret pulled over the ears, Sweetie trying to outrun the lead so she could gnaw my legs.

"I thought I heard the kettle whistle, Giselle, and I always have a cup of tea about this time. Oh, it's not even on—never mind, I'll manage without. What I have to tell you is I've changed my mind about tonight."

"That's nice. Magdalene, I'd like you to meet Mrs. Malloy."

"Very pleased," said Magdalene. "Perhaps you won't need to come in as many hours now I'm here." She blinked a smile at Roxie. "Yes, Giselle, as I sat on a bench looking at God's lovely trees and thinking how they needed pruning, I came to know my duty. I must be at this party to see that my only son's restaurant gets off to a decent start."

I am ashamed to say I didn't like Ben's mother excessively, but I couldn't fault her courage.

"Pleased to meet you, madam," Roxie huffed at Magdalene. "Now if you'll scoot sideways, I'll mop around you. I hope Mrs. H. informed you that I don't clean up after dogs." The words were barely out of her mouth when Sweetie went into a squat. That animal had to be two-thirds water.

* * * *

4:28 P.M. I wriggled around inside my black dress, trying to get the shoulders to sit right. I had found my pearl earrings, but I still had to locate my flat shoes with room for swelling. Knowing they were in my bag would make my feet hurt less. I dreaded going upstairs to say good-bye to the men. On my last excursion into the bedroom, Ben accused me of being in collusion with Dr. Melrose. My husband's hollow laughter still rang in my ears: "I will not be kept away from the most important event of my life!" So much for our wedding.

4:34 P.M. Up the stairs, one slow foot at a time. I opened the bedroom door. Within, all appeared tranquil. Poppa was seated in the Lloyd Loom chair by the window, carving the wooden icing for my cake. He had not taken kindly to my suggestion that cardboard would do. The atmosphere was like Delacorte Antiques: too idyllic. I got the nasty feeling that the moment the car disappeared in a fog of exhaust fumes, Ben would be out of bed and phoning for a taxi to take him to Abigail's. And in such a crisis, Poppa would be useless. Even to cry, "Halt!" would be a violation of his principles.

I crept across the floor, turned the key in the lock of Ben's wardrobe, then slipped it into my bag. Eli glanced up; I waved at him, kissed the air inches above my husband's face and tiptoed out.

4:45 P.M. It was raining as I crossed the courtyard to the car. Magdalene was in the front passenger seat holding the silver punch bowl, wrapped in newspaper, on her lap. The smile she gave me as I yanked the door closed was a little frayed at the edges. She kept fingering the bowl. I was sure second thoughts had been attacking her since the sky began to darken. Would she have stayed at home if she hadn't overheard Poppa telling me to keep my eye on her at all times because she wasn't used to rich food and alcoholic beverages?

Roxie was in the back seat with the chicken tarts. She had kept finding things to keep her busy until she missed the bus and required a lift into the village, but she wouldn't hear a word about my running her on home. Why was she so determined to work this evening, unless it was all the behind-the-scenes booze?

Magdalene made little whispering noises beside me. I started a prayer of my own. "Please God, let Heinz have benefitted from his latest treatment at the garage. Grant that we may make this journey without doors or wheels flying off." I turned the ignition key. Noises—harsh, grinding noises. Magdalene clutched the punch bowl. I grasped the wheel, pressed down hard on the accelerator and blew on the windshield to defrost it. My best hope was to outrace whatever was about to succumb to gravity.

Waves of Attar of Roses as Roxie leaned forward to tap Magdalene on the shoulder. "Want to know what put me off the Catholic Church for life? Well, I'll tell you irregardless. It was all that talk about coming together and then Rome knocks off St. Christopher, the only one of the lot that nonbelievers like me thought did his job."

5:00 P.M. Two waiters, impeccable down to their smiles, greeted us at the door of Abigail's. Each took a tray of chicken tarts, but Magdalene was adamant about retaining control of the punch bowl. They preceded us up the Persian carpeted stairs to the second floor hallway. Facing us a few feet to the right was the alcove leading into the reception room. Standing within was a sight to make my blood boil. Freddy!

To my revulsion, he dropped to his knees and groveled forward to clutch at the hem of my dress. The waiters exchanged a significant look.

"Ellie, forgive! I have come to my senses. I want to work. Or at least get paid."

"Stop it!" I tried to shake him off, but he was like static cling. Magdalene gave a little yelp. Pressing down on the newspaper covering the punch bowl, she exclaimed, "I'll put this where it's supposed to go." With a bobbing flit, she headed down the hall like a sparrow trying for lift-off. The waiters, smiles back in place, followed. Roxie didn't budge. Freddy gave her a wink.

"Ellie, I know I've made you wretched. You look a hundred years old, but maybe it's the dress; not telling its age, is it?"

This gorgeous original (only two others on the rack) bought for the honeymoon I never attended! I eyed my watch. Was there time to dash home and change? Absolutely not. Not even time to push Freddy down the stairs.

6:15 P.M. I stepped through the alcove into the reception room and savoured a moment alone. All was magnificence. The tables flanking the walls were covered with white damask cloths and laden with the sort of spread commonly glimpsed only on the pages of magazines where the meals coordinate with the decor. Wall sconces added their brilliance to the gloss of panelling, the sparkle of silver and crystal. There were flowers everywhere; the air was scented like a springtime country garden. Raindrops spattered the tall latticed windows overlooking Market Street. Pretty, but would the room be warmer looking if I drew the Jacobean print curtains? My hand brushed the fabric. From here, the cars and buses below looked like they were playing tag, sending up sprays of slush. People scurried along, umbrellas and raincoat collars up. A shiver decided me. But before I could pull the curtains, one of the waiters came in to speak to me about the positioning of the punch bowl.

6:25 P.M. Five minutes to go. Was Ben lying awake and tense, listening for the striking of the hall clock? Should I phone home? Yes. I rushed into the office, two doors to the right of the reception room. Since there was no phone in our bedroom, I would only get to speak to Poppa. My fingers stumbled as they dialed. Surely he would write down my message and hand it to Ben. What shall it be? A triumph is in sight, or simply, I love you. The phone rang at least twenty times; my panic escalated with each *brrp, brrp*, until I remembered that Poppa must have had his earphones on. I quickly hung up before Ben decided to crawl out of bed to silence the phone.

6:30 P.M. The waiters were stationed at the foot of the stairs. Magdalene and I positioned ourselves at the top like characters in a Jane Austen novel. I fully expected to hear the words, The Dowager Duchess of Plooth and Her Daughter Esmerelda, floating up to us. I unhooked and rehooked my belt. Magdalene straightened her black lace mantilla. Like me, she was wearing a black dress. We should have discussed our ensembles, I thought.

Mr. Howard from the bank and his wife Cynthia, their coats darkened with rain, headed toward us. "So pleased you could both come. I would like you to meet my mother-in-law Magdalene Haskell. Unfortunately my husband . . ."

They passed on by, as did the Wilsons and the Peckworths. I kept eyeing Magdalene to see if she was enjoying herself. Her expression was intent, but she addressed Mr. Bremmer as Mr. Barking. Now came someone whose name provided august emanations—Lady Theodora Peerless in a check raincoat. Her peach lipstick emphasized her protruding teeth. I liked the effect; it made her look warmer. What was she like before life turned her into a brown paper parcel, giving little hint what was inside?

"I'm sure, Ellie, you will do fine. Your husband, and your mother-in-law"—a nod—"will be proud of you." There was a hint of something winning under her smile; perhaps underneath she might be as colourful as her history.

My eyes strayed after her—how did she come to be in that photo with Mr. Digby and his daughter, Wren? Mrs. Melrose introduced herself, reminding me in a voice as strident as her mustard and plum tweeds that this was the doctor's night at the hospital.

"Good to hear, Mrs. Haskell, that your man is on the mend. Mine needs his sleep, you know."

Behind her came Charles and Ann Delacorte. She was the picture of World War II elegance in the emerald green dress she wore for my wedding; he was as glacial as ever. I turned to introduce Magdalene, but she was gone. Probably to the loo. Ann and Charles moved through the alcove and I saw two people I had not anticipated would come when I added their names to the guest list: Jenny Spender and Dr. Simon Bordeaux. Black cashmere coat hanging capelike from his shoulders, a white silk scarf streaming down the front of his dinner jacket, the doctor looked as though he ate only caviar for breakfast on his toasty wheats. A patron to be cultivated. Jenny's hair wasn't in plaits tonight. It was held back by a satin band that matched her turquoise dress. Why didn't someone encourage her to dress like a teenager? I thought of the invalid mother and the old-world nanny. Would it be thought interfering if I offered to take Jenny shopping?

"It is good of you both to come."

Dr. Bordeaux's deep-set eyes flickered across my face. He ignored my outstretched hand. "There is nothing like a hint of infamy to push one to the top of the social ladder, Mrs. Haskell."

What an arrogant man to think I had invited him because he was suspected of callously murdering old ladies!

Jenny glanced up at him, smiled, and touched the white plastic raincoat folded over her arm.

"We can't stay long because Nonna tends to doze off in the evening. It was kind of you, Mrs. Haskell, to include Mummy's name on the invitation card, but you do understand, she doesn't go to parties—or anywhere."

Dr. Bordeaux interpreted the question in my eyes. "Except once a year when Jenny and I take Mrs. Spender to a nightclub in London for her birthday celebration. For a few hours we watch her come alive again."

What a pathetic situation. Did I detect repressed passion in his voice? Was the invalid Mrs. Spender once his lover? Was he still ensnared by the memory of what they had shared? I dragged my eyes away from him and Jenny. Surprise! Magdalene was back.

Another couple moved to the top of the stairs. And another. Would anyone notice if I kicked off my shoes? "So pleased you could come. . . . Yes, there is a room for coats at the end of the hall. . . ."

My voice just went down the wrong way. Coming toward us was Vanessa, her mink-clad body entwined around Rowland Foxworth's arm. He surely was horribly embarrassed. What man wouldn't be? Family decency had decreed I invite my relations, but only she had taken the embossed white card literally.

"Darling Ellie!" She closed in, her eyelashes brushing my face. "You look ravishing. I could count every one of your ribs from downstairs. Can you believe the change, Rowland?"

Instantly I gained a stone. A good thing I was not bothered about what Rowland thought of my feminine appeal. A married—happily married—woman doesn't need that kind of reassurance; besides, I had more important things on my mind. Magdalene was gone again.

Rowland patted his pockets for his pipe, dislodging (unintentionally?) Vanessa's hold on him.

He turned to her. "Ellie never changes in my eyes."

An intake of breath. Was it mine or Vanessa's?

"How's Ben?" Absently Rowland touched a hand to his silver hair. Vanessa studied her fingernails. Magdalene's face wavered at my left. I introduced her to Rowland. Those grey eyes of his, that beautiful mellow voice, touched me physically. I experienced, to my eternal shame, a thrill of adulterous pleasure, in addition to the lesser sin of cousinly conquest.

"Quite a pretty girl." Magdalene squinted for a better look as Vanessa and Rowland passed down the hallway. "A bit like Angelica Brady. This one's your cousin, you say? Did Ben meet her before or after you and he had settled things?"

7:15 P.M. The party was a smashing success. Cigarette smoke beclouded the air, as here and there someone emphasised the point in a witty monologue with a fiery tip. Freddy kept popping into the room to take little bows. With his hair up and under his chef's hat, he looked borderline respectable. From all sectors of the room came accolades about the food.

Freddy was doing a backbend to hear what Gladys Thorn was saying to Millicent Parsnip about the flaming cheese. Would someone please mention Ben's name! I was miserable that he wasn't the focal force here this evening, wretched about the rift between us, guilty that things had gone well without him, angry that I should feel guilty when I already had enough on my plate, and—this is the bad part—fully aware that the aforementioned guilt was an emotional blanket caused by the knowledge that I had looked upon the Reverend Rowland Foxworth with lust aforethought. That the experience lasted a scant fifty seconds was no consolation. I had eternally dishonoured my wedding vows.

Vanessa glided up to me and said we ought to have a little talk on a subject whereof she was an expert and I a beginner —men.

"You'll destroy your marriage, Ellie, if you don't stop ogling Rowland in public. And I'd hate to see you lose Ben. One doesn't meet men like him every day—er—at escort services."

She glided off to stand near the windows, best profile on view. I stopped grinding my teeth, as I realised how long it had been since I'd opened up a magazine and had to close it on her face.

Rowland was at the punch bowl next to Charles Delacorte, who was picking his way through the sandwiches. I crossed the room toward Amelia Bottomly and Millicent Parsnip. I could not look at Rowland without seeing into my soul and knowing that, despite my sense of shame, I didn't want Vanessa or any woman to have him. Rowland must keep only unto me, his heart a shrine to my unattainability. It was devastating to discover, at twenty-eight, that one was a low woman.

7:30 P.M. I sat by the desk in the office, holding the phone, listening to the *brrp-brrrp*. No answer. Common sense told me that if Ben had suffered a relapse, Eli would have telephoned. But guilt had a louder voice than sense. It told me I was being punished. Something was wrong.

7:35 P.M. The party hummed along. The smoke was making me feel sick. I went the long way around Vanessa to the windows, intent on opening one, but Magdalene, in the midst of talking animatedly to Sidney, was apparently struck by the same idea. She parted the curtains, reached for the latch, then froze. What was it? An attack of some sort? Arthritis, perhaps.

"Ellie, dear"—Sidney gripped my arm as I started after Magdalene—"I want you to be one of my first customers to know that my life is suddenly in bloom. I'm floating on air. Bound to crash sometime, but might as well dance in the sun while I can! Some months back I put an advert in the classifieds of *The Daily Spokesman*, expressing my heartfelt wish to meet a female who thinks personal hygiene and bingo important—"

"Sidney, I think I read it." I peered between heads searching for Magdalene, who had again disappeared.

7:40 P.M. I nudged the punch ladle against the the floating ice ring garlanded with fruit flowers. Roxie passed me carrying a tray of munchie-morsels; she walked with exaggerated care along an invisible line. Someone tapped me on the shoulder and I jumped. It was Froggy, I mean, Shirley Daffy.

"Mrs. Daffy, I do hope you will have good news soon concerning your husband. It is, after all, only a few days since . . . he went out jogging."

Her eyes popped with emotion. "I'm being sensible about it. It doesn't do any good to get in too much of a fidget over what you can't alter. And I make myself get out as much as possible." She touched the brooch puckering the front of her brown crepe frock.

"How pretty!" I said to fill up a pause. "What is the significance of the blackbirds?"

"Crows, actually."

"Really!" I started to say more but Mrs. Bottomly appeared and rather rudely snatched Mrs. Daffy away. I found Mrs. Hanover beside me, replenishing her plate.

"Any more of the chicken tarts left? Oh, goody! One does find them tasty." She helped herself from the now scanty array. I would have to do some artistic interspersing with parsley.

"Mrs. Haskell!" Her very false teeth made her smile a bit unreal too. "We do so miss your husband of an evening. Such a lovely pair, him and Frederick! I can't tell you how relieved were all the regulars when that dart incident didn't turn out serious. A bit of a *dark horse* is Sidney Fowler. But I wouldn't think, not for a moment, that he meant to hurt Frederick. Would you, Mrs. Haskell?"

7:45 P.M. I was getting almost as edgy about Magdalene as

I was about Poppa not answering the phone. I would have asked Sidney to look for her, but he was talking to Mrs. Bottomly on the far side of the room. From her gestures she appeared to be unhappy about something. Last week's wash-and-set? The towering pompadour did look a bit top-heavy.

Roxie paused at my shoulder. "How's it going, Mrs. H.?" She thrust her fingers into the midst of her silver tray and bunged two sausage whatevers into my hand. Not to make the guests feel left out, she did the same to the man with the handlebar moustache standing next to me. "Makes a person do some hard thinking, doesn't it, Mrs. H.?"

"About what, Roxie?"

"The horrible abomination of human nature. For instance, that Miss Thorn, over by the fireplace, born with her knickers on."

"Shhhhh!" Luckily, there was no one else at the buffet table. Handlebar moustache had gone.

"As for our Mr. Sidney"—she minced out the name—"people think they've got him pegged. Don't you believe it!" Roxie popped a sausage thing into her mouth. "Now what I want to know is why you invited that Dr. Bordeaux. Mark my words, that hollow-eyed look comes from sleeping on a marble slab."

"Shhhhh." I couldn't get the parsley to sit right.

Roxie rammed herself against my elbow. "Believe you me, he's no social asset. Only look—every time he and that kiddie with him take a step close to Ladyship Peerless, she footsies the other way. Course, who can blame her, Mrs. H. Him turning her ancestral home into Bedlam!"

"Nonsense!" I gave up and ate the wayward sprig of parsley. "The Peerless is a private nursing home for nervous disorders. And Lady Theodora is a sensible woman. She has no grudge against Dr. Bordeaux. He didn't steal the place. Her brother sold it."

Guests eddied past. I smiled, exchanged a few words, and poked at the roses in one of the silver vases. A waiter held a champagne bottle over the punch bowl. Roxie shifted her silver tray to her other hand and slid her lips around to reposition her lipstick.

"When it comes to that Charlie Delacorte, Mrs. H., I wouldn't buy a button from him. Although, to give Lucifer his due, I don't believe what's said about him carrying on behind his wife's back. I'd lay me bingo money that Mr. Delacorte's vital organs have been in cold storage for years."

"Really, Roxie!"

I focused on Charles Delacorte, who was in the middle of the room gingerly eating around the edges of something. He was alone. I hadn't once seen him and Ann standing together this evening. Was this her, coming up to him now? No, it was Millicent Parsnip, very smart in a black pillbox hat. Her pussycat face all atwitch, she opened her evening bag and brought out a flutter of papers.

Roxie swayed left, whether accidentally or to gawk I don't know. "Getting him to sign some petition, she is, Mrs. H. Probably that one to save the lighthouse."

Apparently Millicent was some spokesperson. Charles handed her his plate and uncapped his pen, his face solidified boredom. Poor Ann. Does she love him? Frightening to think she may have when they first married. My eyes sought her out—over in a corner by herself. Roxie veered off to the kitchen, ostensibly to refill her tray.

Ann was staring into space. No, she was looking at Lionel Wiseman. I remembered the day she came with me to his office. Was it dislike I sensed behind her composed manner? No, something more smouldering. Fear? Lionel was quite a big fish in the Chitterton Fells pond. Was there some problem, say, a financial one, with the antique shop? If Ann would confide in me, perhaps Ben and I could help. I started across the room. Through the press of people and the smoke, I could see Ann. Her dark eyes were once more as smooth as her rolled hair and draped emerald dress. One of the men in the group turned to me.

"Compliments to your hubby. Fabulous affair."

At last someone had recognised the genius at work here. I must get to a phone.

Mrs. Hanover from The Dark Horse had joined Millicent Parsnip in talking to Charles Delacorte. Ann hadn't moved. I smiled myself away from the man who spoke kindly of Ben and saw Bunty come up behind Lionel. She placed her fingertips on his broad shoulders and mouthed "Boo" against his neck. Almost in slow motion, he turned toward her. A smile lightened his strong-jawed face and the ticking inside my head picked up the tempo. What I saw was a unit of three people, not two. The ticking got louder until it was tapping out a message. If Ann Delacorte feared Lionel Wiseman, it was because she loved him passionately, obsessively.

A touch on the shoulder surprised me; a shudder jolted my spine. I turned to face one of the waiters, trampling on his foot.

"Mrs. Haskell, forgive me for startling you."

"Yes?" I looked up at him, then away—there was some sort of commotion going on to my right. Had a chance spark from a cigarette ignited something or someone?

"A gentleman waiting beyond the h'alcove wishes to see you, Mrs. Haskell."

All sound faded. People bumped up against me in passing—Millicent Parsnip and, I think, Mrs. Hanover. With them was a man with his head thrown back. And then they were gone. I couldn't move. The gentleman in the hall had to be a policeman, here to inform me that Ben had suffered a relapse. A fatal one. Never would I get to tell him how sorry I was for being so nasty about the D'Ellie Delight. Never would I get to tell him how much I loved him and that Rowland was only a fleeting thought.

"The gentleman won't give his name, Mrs. Haskell. But I do not believe he is a gate-crasher. We've h'already dealt efficiently with a few of those, one in particular not being at all the sort to add tone to the proceedings."

The waiter and I were jostled together, then thrust apart, as we headed for the archway. A new thought wedged in my throat. The person waiting for me could be Poppa. Voices flowed over and through me.

"I'm sure he will be fine. Millie Parsnip and Mrs. Hanover did the right thing getting him out of this crush to a place where he can breathe better. Millie was a nurse, you know."

"That's a comfort; and look—Amelia Bottomly is chatting with his wife. No need for her to know and get concerned."

At any other time I would have stopped and asked questions. Had the man come over the worse for drink or smoke? I would have wanted to know what I could do to help. As it was, I said nothing. Emerging from the alcove, Teddy Peerless and I collided. I did register that she looked odd and that her apologies were as disjointed as mine, but my heart was hammering its way out through my ribs and my very next step sent me into a second collision—with Mr. Edwin Digby.

"Mrs. Haskell," said the waiter, "this is the gentleman who wishes to see you."

The waiter turned tail and I blinked at Mr. Digby, my relief so violent I felt sick. He was wearing a top hat, a velvet-collared coat, and was royally, imperiously, drunk.

"How good of you to come."

He stroked the goatee, then held up a purple-veined hand. "Don't flatter yourself that you are irresistible as a hostess, Mrs. Haskell." Every word was a blast of boozy breath. "I happened to be passing and elected to stop inside to alert you that I have changed my mind. I wish my pin-striped suit returned."

"Mr. Digby, I had planned to return it." I wanted to laugh madly, joyously. The evening was almost over. No disaster had befallen. My fears for Ben were absurd. Abigail's premiere was a triumph!

"You haven't done something officious, such as sending the suit to the cleaner?" Something in Mr. Digby's manner sobered me.

"Of course not," I said primly.

He pressed his hands together but was unable to stop their tremor.

"Spare me your womanly sympathy, Mrs. Haskell. It is merely that the suit is . . . of sentimental value."

He must be very drunk to be this honest. I wondered when he remembered the photo in the pocket.

"Mother gave you the suit, I suppose."

It was the right thing to say. The beard parted in a smile.

"Ah, Mother! I left her outside this front door—I trust t'was this one. I must needs now"—he stumbled over the words—"go hence and explain that this visit was extended through no fault of mine. If you will graciously place that suit in a paper bag, I will call for it tomorrow."

He swayed toward the stairs and I started to ask him to stay, at least for a cup of coffee. But then, with terrifying suddenness, the bottom plummeted out of everything. I heard a gasp and saw Teddy Peerless leaning against the office door, her face ashen. My mind took a leap to the man who had been led from the room a few minutes ago in search of fresh air. And then another leap: Should I have put the chicken tarts in the refrigerator instead of the pantry?

I took a step toward Teddy and almost went sprawling. Sweetie bundled over my feet and streaked into the reception room. Shouts. Shrieks. Laughter. A lone cry of "How unsanitary!" Teddy was feeling her way along the wall and Magdalene was wrenching at my arm.

"I brought her in the punch bowl for a little company. Oh, Blessed Mother, what will Ben say?"

She was about to find out. The front door opened wide—Mr. Digby exited; Ben and Poppa entered.

"Your foolish husband got up when my back was turned," shouted Poppa. "He skulked down to that cottage, helped himself to your cousin's clothes, and phoned for a taxi, which broke down coming up the hill. So we waited and waited for another. Your husband is worn out. What about me?"

I didn't have enough arms, enough feet. I tried to reach Teddy with my free hand while watching in horror as Ben staggered, white-faced, up the stairs. He collapsed at the exact moment that Teddy's cry rang out: "Charles Delacorte is in the office! Dead!"

From the Files of The Widows Club

Monday, 3rd May
Memorandum to President:

I am pleased to report that on the evening of Friday, 1st May, all went according to plan. At 7:36 P.M. I engaged the Subject To Be Retired in conversation and under cover of asking him to sign the Lighthouse Petition (it is an ill wind, etc.), made the prearranged substitution. Whereupon I did feel concern that he might not eat what was put before him. Happily he did and began wheezing almost immediately. Mrs. Hanover stepped forward and assisted in propelling the S.T.B.R from the room, offering assurances that all he needed was a little fresh air. We then took him to the office two doors down from the reception room and sat him in the desk chair. After assuring him there was no need to summon his wife—the less fuss the better—I went to fetch his inhaler from his coat. Ten seconds later Mrs.

Hanover left to telephone for medical assistance, after which she proceeded to inform subject's wife, he had been taken ill.

I deliberately failed to find inhaler until I had searched twenty-four pockets, as suggested on my receiving this assignment. When I came out of the cloakroom, with aforementioned in hand, the news was sweeping the building that S.T.B.R. was dead.

I wish to commend Mrs. Hanover for her splendid cooperation. Also, many thanks to the other members of The Widows Club for their moral support during the evening. The speed and efficiency of The Founder speaks for itself.

In response to the request that I voice any feelings of distress I may have experienced since the retirement, let me state that distress is too strong a word for the vague unease I have felt, since the night of 1st May. This is not associated with subject's death but with the admission of his widow (upon my nomination) to our membership. I now feel (without being able to define) that she does not fulfill the lofty standards that are the rock upon which The Widows Club is built.

Respectfully submitted,

Millicent E. Parsnip

PART THREE

At last my story was over. I had told these strange women my macabre tale and now must go home to my husband.

"The important thing is that Ben is going to be all right." Hyacinth interrupted my thoughts.

"The important thing," I contradicted, "is that Charles Delacorte is dead. And by my hand. He was allergic to seafood as well as other things such as cats. That was why he was always picking through the sandwiches and occasionally sniffing them for good measure. But I outfoxed him. I made some of my chicken tarts with tuna, remember?"

"My dear, dear Ellie." Primrose proffered the smelly salts. "Of course we remember. And you should remember that although these club women may not be our sort in some ways, they are not stupid. They would never have banked on your running out of chicken. No, indeed! One of them will have brought along something fishy in disguise—possibly a look-alike tart—and fed it to Mr. Delacorte when he wasn't looking. You had received many requests for them."

My shoulders sagged. "Even so, Charles Delacorte may

well have eaten one of my tuna tarts before he got to theirs. I can never be certain I didn't cause his death."

Hyacinth snapped the green book closed. "Stop wallowing, Ellie. If we all went around worrying about who we might have accidentally killed, we would never get any work done. And set to work we must."

That was, I trusted, the royal we. Shifting in my chair, I stared at the clock on the wall. Nine o'clock. We had sat in the rose and green coffee room at Abigail's for hours. We had drunk innumerable cups of tea and dispatched William Butler to the kitchen so many times he was undoubtedly dizzy or asleep. I wanted to go home to Ben.

On the morning after The Death, Dr. Melrose had come out to Merlin's Court and confirmed my diagnosis of a relapse. Ben was now suffering from a viral condition contracted while in a weakened condition and aggravated by gate-crashing his own party.

Generally speaking, I think Ben was pleased with his setback. Now he could call a halt to conversation simply by closing his eyes.

It had been a bleak moment when I had confessed to him about the fake chicken tarts. What I had done violated the fundamentals of his professional code. He was sorry about Charles, but it could not be said he felt his loss keenly. Momentarily hope had flickered in Ben's eyes. If I were to keep quiet at the inquest and let it be thought that Charles had absentmindedly scoffed a tuna toastie . . . but Ben was pulled up short by his conscience and I by the memory that Bunty had been present when I made the tuna/chicken tarts.

The ruin of my husband's dreams stared me in the face. His professional integrity was in question. No one would patronize Abigail's; no one would buy the cookery book. Ben would become the butt of such jokes as, Chicken by any other name is not the same. Perhaps if we were to flee the country and start afresh under an assumed name, things might improve. But for the present, all I could do for Ben was not to burden him with my guilt and misery.

I insisted he obey Dr. Melrose's orders not to attend the inquest. I even talked glibly about what I would wear to the funeral and whether we should send a wreath or a cross. On the plus side, I felt glad the pressure of having me as a daughter-in-law was bringing Magdalene and Eli closer together. They eyed each other sometimes over my head. Ben closed his eyes a lot. I was glad that he bought the notion that I was shrugging the matter aside. At the same time, I resented his not seeing through me.

But did he? Had we been deluding ourselves that ours was a grand passion because the circumstances under which we had met had been so romantic? To say nothing of all that romantic money. I kept remembering the wedding reception and those whispers in the hall.

"A shame she didn't marry the vicar." "This one is much too good-looking." "She's bound to get fat again. People do when they're happy."

"Poor Ellie." Primrose leaned across the seersucker tablecloth and touched her papery hands to my face. "Indeed I know how you must feel. Every time I step on a beetle I anguish, but it is our duty as Christians to combat grief with work."

"Which," Hyacinth cut in briskly, "offers the additional advantage of being an excellent means of getting things done. Ellie, should you sincerely wish to redeem Ben's reputation and your own self-esteem, I urge you to help Flowers Detection in the noble endeavour of uncovering the identity of the founder of this widows club. In so doing you may find that Charles Delacorte's allergy to fishy food didn't kill him per se; it was used to reduce him to a state of helplessness so that someone hidden in the study could step out and quickly and easily smother him without suspicions of foul play being aroused. Someone could have had a plastic bag in her pocket."

Hyacinth stopped and her eyes snapped me to attention, but I went almost immediately back into a sag. I wanted to believe . . . and true, I needed a bit of nobility in my life right now, the sort of stuff that would bring Ben running to me on his knees. But was I fully convinced that this evil organisation existed? And supposing it did, what could I, the notorious bungler, do about it?

Tapping the green notebook on the table, Hyacinth fixed me with her dark eyes. "You want proof, don't you? Well, for starters, Mrs. Daffy told you at the party that those black dickybirds on the brooches worn by the women are crows."

"So?"

"Don't you find it suggestive, Ellie, that she had scarce uttered the words when Mrs. Bottomly snatched her away?"

I placed my bag on the table to signify that I was about to

snatch myself away. "Presumably Mrs. Bottomly had someone she wished Mrs. Daffy to meet."

Primrose shook her head of curls, tut-tutting gently. "I fear, Ellie, that you slept through some of your school days, as I did. The proper terminology for a line of crows is"—she paused theatrically—"a *murder* of crows."

I stared at her in horror.

Primrose nodded at her sister. "We imagine that Mrs. Daffy, in a flash of self-importance at becoming a new member, forgot she wasn't supposed to reveal the species of the bird. The brooches are so small that people on the outside are likely to think, as you did, my dear, that the birds are of the four-and-twenty kind that got baked in the royal pie."

I looked from Primrose's faded flower face to Hyacinth, with her hooded dark eyes and cone of black hair, then set my bag down on the floor. "Have you asked any of these women what the brooches represent?"

Primrose smiled at my curiosity. "Last Tuesday at the post office, I trod on the foot of a woman wearing one. Understand, Ellie, I did not press hard, only enough to enable me to apologise and start up a conversation. One does not wish one's profession to make one ruthless. And she was really such a charming woman. She'd had an uncle who had gone out to India, I remember . . ." Hyacinth winced and Primrose collected herself. "To put it in a nutshell, she admitted quite freely that the brooch was an insignia of a widows group, the birds symbolic of women closing ranks in the struggle to rebuild the nest."

"Sounds logical. Birds, crows, and the rest of the fowl of the air must go through the same struggle with the grief process as the rest of us." I pushed back my chair. "This conversation has been extremely stimulating, but as you know, Ben is not fully recovered, and if I don't get home soon, Magdalene will have slipcovered all the furniture and Poppa converted the dining room into a workshop."

"Sit down, Ellie." Hyacinth was firm.

I sat.

"Please do not think I am applying the thumbscrew, but do consider—if you do not help us, you may find yourself begging your in-laws never to leave because the thought of life alone with Ben is untenable."

I wavered, but somehow managed to drag a rabbit out of the hat. "Dorcas and Jonas will be returning soon."

Primrose nodded at me sadly. "Your dearest friends will immediately intuit that something is supremely wrong between you and your spouse. They will suffer with you. My dear, friends are never an escape."

I twisted a corner of the tablecloth into a point. Tomorrow I would airmail a note to D. and J. telling them I was frightfully busy entertaining Ben's parents and the house seemed unbelievably crowded. It was the kindest thing I could do.

Hyacinth pushed back her chair. "Ellie, the brooches are indicative, but they do not prove that this murderous organisation exists. However, I believe that Flowers Detection can convince you."

"You needed me, madam?" Unnervingly Butler made no sound on entering.

"I did. And next time try to be a little more prompt. Did you fetch what I asked for?"

"Is rain wet, madam?" Expressionless, he handed Hyacinth a book in a white-and-red jacket.

"Splendid, Butler." Primrose beamed up at him. "You also took care of that other small matter?"

Butler inclined his head. "I found the party at home and agreeable to visit at the time you suggested."

As the door closed, I said, "Who, if I may ask, is the person he has invited to visit you? Or should I say us?"

"First things first." Hyacinth held up the book Butler had handed her. The red splattering on the white background was an artist's rendition of blood. The title was *The Merry Widows*. My bag slid off my lap, spilling its contents all around my chair. My voice cracked. "Edwin Digby, alias Mary Birdsong, wrote that book. I stumbled upon it in his study."

Hyacinth's orange lips curled in a smile. "You told us so in describing your visit to him."

"While I was requesting Butler to fetch more toasted tea cakes"—Primrose adjusted the curls upon her forehead—"I whispered to him that it would be extremely helpful were he to admit himself to The Aviary and fetch the volume, which, needless to say, we will return in the condition we received it."

"What if he had collided with Edwin Digby?"

Hyacinth waved a nonchalant hand. "Butler has his ways, which we never probe. I think he may have been somewhat concerned about colliding with Mother, but happily all went well." She tapped on the book. "We knew about this through our research." She held it out to me. "Do you wish, Ellie, to read the plot outline on the inside flap of the jacket?"

"Certainly."

Primrose edged her chair closer. "I would appreciate your reading out loud, Ellie."

I cleared my throat.

From the pen of Mary Birdsong drips another tale of icy terror. This time the locale is the picture postcard village of Nettleton Byways, where a group of ladies, wholesome as wholemeal bread, have formed a club. A club for would-be widows. Women who choose windowhood over divorce. This organisation has been operating successfully for many years and provides the following services:

1. *Elimination of adulterous husbands, with an emphasis on the death appearing to result from natural causes, an accident, or suicide.*
2. *Emotional support in dealing with subsequent guilt or remorse.*
3. *Social activities, which include a monthly luncheon meeting, bridge, whist, gardening groups, and charitable works. Board meetings are held in closed session.*

Deaths are prescribed by the club's founder. Members of the board are encouraged to assist in implementation. The identity of The Founder is known only to charter members who are no longer active. His/her instructions are issued by telephone to the current president, who sees they are carried out. The heroine of this tantalising novel . . ."

My hands trembled so violently the book fell. "Are you saying that Mary Birdsong is our man?"

Primrose pursed her lips. "My dear, Ellie, don't you think he's a shade *too* obvious?"

I ran my fingers through my hair, causing it to slide down my neck. Speaking through a mouthful of pins I said:

"I think Mr. Digby's background—which, from what Roxie said, has been marked by tragedy—should be checked. But drunk or sober, he isn't a fool. The fact that everything points to him—this book, the brooches (he is an ornithological enthusiast)—suggests to me that The Founder has set the stage so that if the blade of the guillotine ever falls, it will land on Mr. Digby's head."

Hyacinth looked from me to Primrose and back again. "The possibility should be considered that he wishes to be caught. But let us remember that even if *The Merry Widows* is still in print, which I doubt—seeing that it was published twenty years ago and Mrs. Malloy said his early work is unattainable—no one would connect it with a real club. Except the widows themselves. And they can not be sure that Edwin Digby is involved in any way, other than an inspiration."

Primrose drew her shawl tighter. The room was growing shadowy. "Ellie, I know you have been busy with such distractions as death and illness, but have you talked with Lady Theodora about why she went into Abigail's office and discovered Charles Delacorte that fateful night?"

"I haven't spoken with her. I saw her as I was coming in here this evening, but she pretended not to see me and crossed the road. My knowledge of what she told the police is reported in *The Daily Spokesman*."

"She said that she entered the office, mistaking it for the bathroom." Hyacinth tapped on the green notebook with a ruminative finger. "Not quite plausible, but so often the truth is not. By the way, Ellie, did Mr. Digby ever collect his pin-striped suit?"

"Yes, the morning after the death. You think his haste unseemly under the circumstances, that he was desperate to recover that photograph?" What was wrong with me? I wanted Abigail's name cleared at all costs, didn't I? And surely someone would take Mother in if Mr. Digby were sent to prison.

Primrose's blue eyes met mine. She exchanged looks with Hyacinth and said, "Butler must begin a full-scale investigation of Mr. Digby, tomorrow at the latest."

"Agreed." Hyacinth lifted the teapot and poured a trickle into each of our cups. "He will also check out Lady Theodora; likewise Lionel Wiseman who, so says his wife, is especially sympathetic to his female clients! And Bunty Wiseman—married (although gossip says otherwise) to a man old enough to be her father. Is the attraction love, money, or something more Freudian? And I mustn't have Butler forget Mr. Sidney Fowler, whose father deserted him as a boy, had a reputation as a Casanova in his youth, and—"

"—And may have locked Bentley in the potato bin during a childhood game of hide-and-seek," Primrose contributed.

Hyacinth moved our cups toward us. "I will conclude this summation, thank you, Prim. Roxie Malloy's references must be rechecked. The Founder is a person with both ears to the ground and the opportunities inherent in Roxie's work are boundless." Hyacinth stopped and looked toward the door. "Am I hearing things or was that the doorbell?"

Standing, I pressed my hands on the table. The cups and saucers did a slow slide. "Isn't it a strange coincidence that all of these suspects are known to me?" I took a steadying breath and the crockery came to a standstill. "We cannot assume simply because these people have cropped up during the course of this evening's conversation that one of them is The Founder. He/she and I may never have crossed paths, let alone spoken to each other!"

Hyacinth's black eyes burned into me. "My dear Ellie, I don't assume. I *know*."

The orange lips smiled complacently. "Did you receive a bouquet of roses the morning after Charles Delacorte's death?"

"Yes."

"Enclosed with them was a card, am I right? Inscribed with the words, *I am sorry*. There was no—"

"—signature." That moment seeped back.

. . . I am standing in the hall at Merlin's Court, the yellow roses in my hands. . . . I feel such elation at the belief that Ben has sent them . . . then I see his stony face when I come running into the bedroom with them. "The gallant Rowland strikes again," he said. . . .

I sat down.

Primrose touched my hand. "My dear Ellie, Charles Delacorte *had* to die that evening at Abigail's. The occasion was too ideal to be missed. But, small consolation that it is, someone regretted the necessity of involving you. Someone who knows you, likes you, and quite possibly admires you."

"The signature could have easily been omitted by mistake," I protested. "But how did you know about the roses?"

"Our discovery of the flowers sent to you was fortuitous." Primrose stretched the edges of her shawl over her arms. "We thought it might be of interest to know who sent wreaths to the funeral, so we instructed Butler to check the florist's order book, which he did last midnight—" Primrose coughed behind her hand—"not wishing to intrude upon working hours."

"Most considerate." Belatedly, I picked up my scattered possessions off the floor and replaced them in my bag. Would that I could collect my scattered thoughts that easily. The analysis of the suspects, my supposed connection with The Founder, was leading straight as a homing pigeon to the moment when the Tramwells would reveal what they wanted from me. Part of me determined that whatever it was, the answer was NO! Another part kept stuttering, but think—this may be your one chance to put things right for Ben and Abigail's, to say nothing of saving the lives of countless erring, unsuspecting husbands. What was a little danger, a little terror, in so good a cause? If only I were the stuff of which heroines are made.

"If there is a Founder," I said, "I'll put my money on Dr. Simon Bordeaux. He must know what is behind all those nervous breakdowns at the Peerless. He cannot be totally evil because he is taking care of Jenny Spender and her mother, but he is creepy."

Hyacinth squared her shoulders. "Ellie, the most vital thing we have learned concerning The Founder is that he or she is diabolically clever. Dr. Bordeaux may be diabolical, but clever—no. Otherwise he could have managed to bump off a few helpless old women without causing a ruckus."

"He was never brought to trial on any charges," I reminded her.

"He may not have been guilty of anything. Those women who remembered him in their wills may have done so by desire. To earn an undeservedly sinister reputation doesn't smack much of cleverness, does it?" Hyacinth closed the green book and laid it on the table.

My heart thudded. My hands felt as though they were smeared with cold cream. The sisters were bracing themselves to appeal to my nobility of character. They were going to ask me to risk everything that mattered most to me. Grabbing at the first thought that came into my head, I said, "What about Miss Gladys Thorn? Isn't she as suspect as any?"

The parlour door opened and closed; I heard Butler's tentative cough, but kept talking. "*The Maiden Voyage*, a book on the subject of repressed feminine sexuality, strongly suggests—"

Primrose smiled gently. "Dear Ellie, why not talk to Miss Thorn herself?"

I could not move my eyes, let alone anything else. Butler was walking Miss Thorn across the room. Now he drew out a chair for her. She twitched a smile at me and I strove to indent my face in response.

"Tea, madam?" Butler spoke through his nose.

"Oh, that would be nice, thank you so terribly much."

As the door closed behind him, Miss Thorn straightened her glasses, fumbled with the tablecloth, then locked her bony hands together. "Mrs. Haskell, you now know all. I do beseech you—if you feel some particle of charity in your heart—not to tell the dear vicar. He would be so grieved."

"I imagine he would be aghast," I said hoarsely. "To know that men of his parish are being murdered in record numbers—"

Primrose coolly interrupted me. "Quite, my dear Ellie. Mr. Foxworth might feel that his sermons weren't getting through." She patted the church organist's hand. "Do you recall, Ellie, our telling you that Flowers Detection was brought into this investigation through the efforts of someone personally affected by the number of men in this locality meeting untimely deaths?"

I responded a little impatiently. "Absolutely. You described her as the Other Woman in so many ill-fated affairs that she had contacted an insurance company—" My eyes met Miss Thorn's. She was blushing.

"I fear, Mrs. Haskell, you are looking at her." Her mushroom eyes swam behind the glasses. "How can I hope to make you, an ordinary woman of pure impulse, understand the curse of one born with an animal magnetism, a musk, if you will, which draws men willy-nilly? My reason for not marrying—although I have had more proposals than I can count—is that I know"—she touched her forehead, now glistening with perspiration—"that it is physically impossible for me to confine myself to the passions of one man. Those others out there wouldn't let me. And does not the dear vicar so often say we must use our unique gifts for the enrichment of others?"

She was wringing her hands so tightly I thought they would start dripping. The nerve of her. Speaking about marriage that way as though it, and people like me who settle for it, were incurably dull. And yet . . . hadn't Ben awakened on our wedding night shouting out Miss Thorn's name? I had thought he was having a nightmare. *Et tu*, Jonas. Hadn't he once said he got all hot under the collar when looking into Miss Thorn's eyes?

"Can it be true, Mrs. Haskell, that you never suspected?" Miss Thorn's eyes shuddered away from mine. "Vernon Daffy, may he rest in peace, refused to leave me alone. At your wedding reception he followed me upstairs, and after we had . . . delighted in each other, he begged me to play the piano for him, and I was so transported that I didn't notice that his wig had come off until the cat started playing with it. The next moment you entered, and Vernon hid under the bedclothes."

Hyacinth thumbed through the green book. "Mr. Vernon Daffy made the fatal mistake of asking his wife for a divorce, so he could marry another woman."

"My men, God bless them,"—Miss Thorn closed her eyes—"have always respected me too much to reveal my name, but some suspicions must have been aroused because—" She stopped, digging her fingers into the edge of the table. "I heard rumours, shocking, unfounded rumours, that I was having an affair with a gentleman whom—although I never disliked him as much as many people did—I was never once tempted to visualise . . . naked."

Primrose closed her eyes.

"Ellie," said Hyacinth. "Miss Thorn is speaking of Charles Delacorte. Granted, he may have been having an affair with some unknown woman and used Miss Thorn as a scapegoat. But, what if he were guiltless of all wrongdoing, other than being an extremely unpleasant human being?" She paused for emphasis. "Something tells me we may have encountered a motive for murder different from the norm here. In other words, Mrs. Delacorte's reason for wishing to be a widow may differ from that of the other club members."

I tried to grip the seat of my chair, but my hands kept slipping. "You're thinking Ann may have wanted Charles out of the way because of what I told you about her feelings for Lionel; but that doesn't add up." We were talking about a friend of mine. The sisters nodded and Gladys Thorn's mushroom eyes magnified behind her glasses.

"Bunty's still in the picture, you mean?" Hyacinth stood, paced for a few seconds and sat back down. "A stumbler, but Ann Delacorte may be banking on her allure as a heartbroken widow. And Flowers Detection must bank on her loyalty to the club not equalling that of her sisters, making her a little more approachable, a little less guarded if someone—"

She stopped significantly. I finished for her. "If someone attempted to infiltrate the group." I picked up Edwin Digby's book, *The Merry Widows,* then dropped it, as if it were white-hot. "I can't do it; I can't phone Ann and tell her I've just begun to realise how much we have in common—that I, too, want to murder my husband. What if something went wrong? What if I got in too deep and couldn't get out?"

The pink bows in Primrose's silvery curls and the Mickey Mouse watch were suddenly at odds with the sternness in her blue eyes. "Ellie, men are being *murdered.* Can you live with yourself knowing that?"

"I'm not at all sure that they are," I flashed back.

"Then, my dear, nothing terrible can happen, if you just have a little chat with Ann about your unhappy marriage and how you are desperately seeking a way out."

I couldn't answer her. I didn't have any words left. I opened up *The Merry Widows* and continued reading from the jacket where I had left off.

The heroine of this macabre tale is a foolish female who eventually gets what is coming to her.

"And now, my dear Ellie," said Primrose, "it's time to assign Bentley a paramour. Remember, to meet the eligibility requirements of The Widows Club, you must accuse him of conduct unbecoming a married gentleman."

Miss Thorn raked fingers through her hair. "Anything I can do in the line of duty?"

Hyacinth froze her with a smile. "Without doubt, cousin Vanessa is the ideal choice. Her attentions to the vicar can so easily be made to look like camouflage. Now, Ellie, as to contacting Mrs. Delacorte and requesting she put you up for membership in The Widows Club, I suggest you allow a decent interval to elapse, say, a few days. Perhaps you could use the interim period to do something about eating sensibly?"

Miss Thorn twitched agreement. In addition to her other shortcomings, she undoubtedly ate like an elephant and lost rather than gained.

At midnight, after that marathon talk with the Tramwells, I crept into Merlin's Court like a thief.

"Ellie." Ben came out of the hall shadows and crushed me

in his arms. "I thought you had left. And I was desperately worried about you; I didn't think you would like being a nun." He attempted a laugh. "I couldn't blame you though if you'd had enough. I've failed you miserably." He kissed my neck, my weakest spot. "My illness is no excuse. . . ." Something in his voice told me he hoped it could be. "My treatment of you has been unforgivable."

I wasn't the innocent I had been when we married. I knew now that unless one chooses to join the ranks of the divorced —or worse—a spouse has, at times, to forgive the unforgivable. And Ben was compounding all the horrors of my situation by being utterly desirable. I stood there, my nose against his ear, arms rigid at my sides.

"Ellie, I know that even without what happened to Charles Delacorte, this has been a time of adjustment for you. First Mum, then Poppa descending on us with their problems, but in the end nothing counts but our love for each other. That is still so, isn't it? We would have married even if so doing had cost us the inheritance. The house, and the money is just the *fondant françois* on the cake."

This from the man I was plotting to murder! That I was doing so in a just cause and did not plan to bring the matter to fruition seemed, as the shadows in the hall stealthed the walls, to be splitting hairs. Ben had every right to know about my involvement with Flowers Detection; he was crucially involved. But if I told him everything . . . anything, he might be consumed by guilt, thinking that he had reduced me to this state of lunatic credulity. And . . . he might respond with heavy-handed chivalry and demand that I stop. A big chunk of me wanted to stop. But what if no one combatted the widows? What if they expanded their horizons? Did I want to raise children in a world where it was off with the heads of grannies who wouldn't babysit every other Saturday or teachers who didn't give all A's?

In such a frame of mind, how could I go freely into my husband's arms? That night I did not worry about the absence of violins; my head was filled with bells knelling. That sort of thing makes a woman frigid in a hurry.

There was, however, a glimmer of help for me. Ben blamed my abstraction upon his mother, who spent half the night pacing in her turret room. Even now we could hear every step, every chink of the rosary beads.

Poppa, on the other hand, caused us daytime audio problems. The next day and the next, the sound of his saw was enough to send anyone into orbit. He had turned the loggia into his workshop, and sawdust rose like a Sahara sandstorm. I tried to look pleased. He was, after all, engaged in making the cake from which I was to leap the night of Bunty's Follies —now only a few weeks away. I had expected something disposable, but this was a magnificent edifice, good for the wear and tear of the next three generations. Not that my crystal ball showed any future generations.

Monday morning, three days after Charles Delacorte's funeral, I determined I could do something about my marriage. I could eat the attractive, delicious, well-balanced meals Ben prepared. And if in so doing I gained a pound, so be it. Somewhere along the pathway to becoming the perfect wife I had forgotten that I had needed Ben's help to keep trim; I had stopped letting him support me in this very important area of my life. We had been more of a team, more married, in the days when we were friends.

If only . . . if only we could have a second chance. I made a second determination. At nine-thirty, give or take an hour, I would pick up the phone and dial Ann's number.

Magdalene and I were alone in the kitchen, but I was barely aware of her until she said, "If it's something I've done to upset you, Giselle, I'd rather you told me straight out. Don't worry about hurting my feelings, I'm not as frail as I look." She picked up the milk jug with both hands. "I draw strength from doing for others."

I believed her. The kitchen was a changed place. Strung above the window were brightly painted egg shells sprouting tiny plants. A patchwork rug lay on the floor, a doily draped over the back of the rocking chair, and a new army of statues topped one of the cupboards. But the biggest change was in Magdalene herself. She wore a secret glow that perked up her dusty sparrow face. She and Poppa still weren't speaking beyond essentials, and she continued to cross herself every time he came into the room. But there seemed something different about the way she did it. Had Charles's untimely demise brought home to her the temporary nature of all things, including extramarital flings?

"You haven't done anything to upset me, Magdalene. I'm

just a bit preoccupied." A nicer person would have reassured her with a hug. My uncooperative arms dangled at my sides. In a few minutes I must take that long walk to the phone.

"You'll just be saying that, but it's not in my nature to poke and pry." Opening the garden door to admit Sweetie, her expression clouded. "Hm! Here comes Mrs. Malloy."

"Morning!" Roxie rattled the supply bag at Sweetie. "Not another in the world like the little moppet, is there? Only scratches to come in when she has to go."

Magdalene and Sweetie bristled. Hurriedly, I mentioned the post Roxie had in her hands.

"Don't get excited, Mrs. H. Nothing of interest." She licked her index finger and continued to flip through. "Nothing but bleedin' bills, by the looks of it." She whapped the envelopes on the table and prissied her lips at Magdalene. "We can't get letters from France every day, can we, Mr. H.'s Ma?"

My mother-in-law hadn't mentioned any foreign correspondence. She avoided my eyes and got busy stroking Sweetie; her lips were tight. Roxie dumped the supply bag on the table and gave me a lavish smile. "How's Mr. H. and the restaurant coming along?"

"Ben's at Abigail's now. It's going to reopen for lunch tomorrow." I leafed through the envelopes and put them in the wire rack. I didn't want either of the women to realise how scared I was that he wouldn't be given a fair chance to live down the . . . my past.

Roxie unstoppered the all-purpose bottle. "My guess is things'll be all right. There's always them what like to live dangerously."

Spoken from firsthand experience? Did that two-tone hair and madam makeup hide a face I didn't know?

"Mr. Flatts's back on the job, is he? Not nursing his dart wound so he can sue Sid Fowler?"

I started to say that Freddy was again an employee, but was cut off by my mother-in-law.

"Mrs. Malloy, this isn't my house but—"

Roxie looked right, then left. "You could've pulled the wool over my eyes."

"—and I'm never one to criticise, but the last time you were here you did miss three finger marks on the left side of the cooker."

"Ooooh!" Roxie snarled a breath which tripled the size of

her bosom. "Begging your royal pardon, I must not have had the time. I'm that busy these days putting fresh water in all them little birdbaths you've got dotted around the house. And there's not even a budgie in the house!"

Magdalene crossed herself.

"And another thing!" Roxie smacked her lips. "Haven't I been telling Mrs. H. until I'm purple as this hat that I don't dust little graven images."

A blessing on my house. I was driven from the kitchen, driven to phone Ann. Out in the hall I seized the telephone off the trestle table and trailed its cord into the drawing room. Closing the door, I deposited the phone on a chair, shoved another chair against the door, and paced the room. Ready or not! Hands shaking, I picked up the phone, put it down, picked it up again, and dialed. Ann answered at the second ring.

"Ellie! Lovely to hear your voice."

"And yours." I was appalled at how calm I sounded. "How are you feeling?"

"Serene. In so many ways this has been harder on you than me."

Indubitably true, if the suspicions of Flowers Detection were correct.

"Ann, you are incredible." My voice splintered. "You make me ashamed of myself. There you are getting on with your life while all I'm doing is making the most terrible botch of mine." Again, true.

"Ellie," her voice rang with sincerity. "Clearly you need to talk, really talk. Would you like to come over here?"

"Now?"

"What better time?"

I had to wash my hair, grow my nails . . .

I drove, rather than taking the bus, because the odds as always were excellent that the Heinz would break down midway. That damn car!

Ann met me at the door of the shop, put up the Closed sign, and led me through the amber velvet curtains, across the storage room, and up a flight of varnished stairs into the flat. On first coming here I had been intrigued by Ann's collections. Music boxes, clocks, crystal, jade, salt cellars, and inkwells crowded the sitting room. Now the place had a narcissistic look. The many photos were all of herself, most of them taken in childhood with some singer of forgotten fame. Several were inscribed, Me with the wonderful so-and-so. My misgivings intensified when I saw, newly pinned to the collar of Ann's white crepe blouse, a blackbird brooch. She closed the door. The very ordinariness of her smile made my skin prickle.

"Would you like a sherry?" She moved to a table covered with a tapestry cloth and crammed with decanters, some with price labels on them.

"No, thank you." My fingers brushed a silver frame surrounding the image of little Ann gazing idolatrously into the face of the songbird Sylvania. "I . . . I am avoiding alcohol at present on account of its being a depressant." Far smarter not to think about what I was going to say or the consequences. Get on with it and get out of here.

"I understand." Ann smoothed down the sides of her maroon and black skirt and perched gracefully on the arm of the horsehair sofa.

"No, you don't!" I crossed to the window and flung my arm around my eyes. "You're too good, too decent to have any idea what is going on inside my head. All the anger! The feeling that all men are beasts!" Was the great Sylvania smirking at me?

"May I hazard a guess as to what is distressing you so? You feel guilty because you don't pity me . . . you envy me."

My neck came up, almost snapping off my head. Thank God for long hair. It is forever tumbling down and providing something to do for one's hands.

"Ann, I don't know what you mean."

"Yes, you do." She crossed her ankles, inserted a cigarette in a jade holder, and lit up. "This, for instance." She blew out a curl of smoke. "When Charles was alive, I couldn't have a cigarette in peace. I couldn't do *anything* in peace, even dislike him." She leaned back and exhaled. "There, I am finally telling you the truth. All the other stuff I told you regarding my relationship with him was rubbish, invented according to the rules of . . ."

"Yes?" A hairpin dropped down the front of my shirt.

"The rules of . . . the stiff-upper-lip club." Ann tapped away ash. "Strangely enough, I never hated Charles. He wasn't man enough to inspire that deep an emotion. But even from a distance I can see Ben is different. He is virile and dynamic, and you are in love with him, you poor fish."

"Why else would I marry him?" I turned back to the window.

"Not for the reasons he married you. It isn't necessary for you to tell me anything, Ellie."

How convenient, considering my lips were hermetically sealed.

"It was crystal clear to me the day of your wedding that Ben was nothing but a handsome rogue. That service, a *menage à trois,* and the reception crammed with his debauched friends. Where did he dredge up that woman who did obscene things to the suit of armour? And that paunchy man who kept chasing the woman in paisley up and down stairs! Small wonder his parents refused to come. Ellie, dear," she continued serenely, "everyone felt frightfully sorry for you, especially when the policeman dropped in and Ben was so cavalier. 'Just a little private business.' " Ann mimicked his voice so closely that I almost wrenched the cigarette away from her and stubbed it out in her face.

She leaned toward me. "Sweet, innocent Ellie. When word got out that you had hooked up with him through an escort service, no one was surprised or thought any the less of you for succumbing to his fortune-hunting charms. Your being overweight made you an easy mark."

"I was fat, actually."

"Yes, well . . ." Ann touched her fingertips to her smooth dark hair. "Poor dear." She sounded as though I had said something a little coarse.

"Happily you are a resilient person, Ellie. I imagine you would have continued to endure being used if only Ben had exercised the decency to be discreet in his relationship with your cousin."

Incredibly, Ann was speaking the lines assigned to me by the Tramwells, making everything so much easier, but I forgot I was playing a role. "Not true, there is absolutely nothing going on between—"

Ann rose from the sofa and placed a hand on my arm. "Ellie"—her voice throbbed with sympathy—"you know it is true. Don't hide behind passive misery. Feel anger! Feel murderous rage! Think of all you have done for your cousin—giving him a job, letting him live in your cottage."

Him? She wasn't talking about Vanessa. My eyes dilated.

Ben and . . . Freddy! Those two would collapse with laughter if they heard this. But my mind went into reverse. I was back at the wedding reception, overhearing snatches of conversation puffed on the air.

"A fairy story in the true sense of the word." "Extremely good-looking, but then they so often are. More unfair, I always say." "Best man a hairdresser . . ." And later, Ann herself had talked about it's being worse when the Other Woman was a man.

I sank into an armchair. It made grotesque sense. Freddy's masquerade had set the spark and eager tongues had fanned the flames.

"Ellie, do you feel faint?" Ann was all solicitude.

"No, I'm fine." And so I was. Blood surged to my brain. I was angry—for Ben, myself, and Freddy. Whatever my cousin's failings, he would never have stooped to setting his cap at my husband. I didn't doubt that the most venomous of the gossips were those same women who were bumping off their husbands right, left, and center.

Eyes closed so their expression wouldn't give me away, I groped for Ann's hand. "What a coward I have been! I haven't wanted to face the truth about those nights when Ben and Freddy stopped for a drink after work, the hours they spend engrossed in each other, talking about secret"—I had to do better than recipes—"things." Then I let my anger work for me. "Ann, I can feel it! The beginning of that murderous rage!" I pounced out of the chair and paced the crowded room. "They have taken me for such a fool! I could kill them! Kill them both!" My voice spiralled. I could feel the heat of Ann's eyes on my back.

She gave a light laugh. "Wouldn't one of them be sufficient? It does, after all, take two to have an affair. Ellie, have you ever heard of a novel called *The Merry Widows*?"

I tensed. So this was how the approach was made. "I . . . I can't say I have."

"Not surprising. It's been out of print for years; a book that sank without a ripple. We get boxes of such in the shop and end up using the paper for packing. This one's by Edwin Digby actually and is about a group of wives who form a club, the purpose of which is to murder off their adulterous husbands. The especially nice thing about the scheme is that one doesn't plunge the knife or the poison . . . into one's own mate. The necessary steps are taken for one, and afterward, an abundance of emotional and social support is provided."

Silence.

"Amusing, don't you think?" Ann peeled a price tag off a decanter.

"I think . . . it's a pity there isn't something like that locally. I could divorce Ben, but then he would get a share of the inheritance and I . . . I can't bear the thought of him walking away with more than the clothes on his back." Pressing my fingers to my brow, I waited.

"What if there were such a group?" Ann circled around me, fingers trailing the furniture.

"I suppose . . . I wouldn't be eligible. After all, mine isn't a case of another woman." I fought a feeling of sickness.

"Oh, I don't think that—it's only a technicality. The important thing is knowing the right people." Ann brushed my arm. "And, of course, we *are* talking about fiction."

I moved away from her to stand in front of a Victorian standing lamp. "Fictitiously speaking, how would someone apply for membership?" The room seemed to dim.

"Come here." Ann pulled a chair away from a table with claw feet. "Sit down and tear a sheet off that pad of paper, and yes, there's a pen behind this vase. You are going to write a letter."

"I am?" My heart pounded.

"Yes, to Dear Felicity Friend." The paper nearly blew off the table. Ann stood in front of me, tapping out a beat on the table. "Wisest, I think, to keep the message short and sweet: Dear Felicity Friend, Please help me get rid of a terrible problem—my husband." Ann picked up a cigarette and flipped it between her fingers. "Sign it with your full name and a code."

The pen dug a hole in the paper. Could I assume that Felicity Friend was The Founder, or was Felicity merely an unwitting instrument? "Why a code?"

Ann touched a cold finger to my cheek. "Why, Ellie, so Dear Felicity can answer you in the confidential column. Let's see, how about something charmingly traditional like Heartbroken. That's it! Write it down." When I had done so, she tweaked the paper out of my slack grasp and folded it in two. The urge to snatch it back made my throat hurt.

"What next?" I managed. ". . . if this were fact, not fiction."

Ann folded the paper again. "I would take this to the president of the club and urge your admission to our . . . the ranks."

"The president being . . . ?"

"Let us say Mrs. Amelia Bottomly, although I don't suppose I should be saying anything of the sort. But we don't have to be terribly discreet, do we, as this is only fiction. She would then get in touch with the founder of the organisation, who would make the decision as to whether or not you were eligible." Ann straightened the Sylvania photo. "Then if you got clearance from the top, you would be contacted by telephone and asked in so many words if you wished your husband murdered. If you answered yes, you would be told the amount of dues payable and where to deposit. Simple, isn't it?"

"Admirably." My hands relaxed. No need to snatch back the letter to Dear Felicity. It only constituted an application; it was not a signing of the contract. I was ready to get out of here.

Ann held the paper between a finger and a thumb. Her eyes gleamed.

"Would you want me to tear this up if this were fact?"

"I . . ." Remember two important things, Ellie, I thought. You are not endangering Ben's life and you are serving mankind. If you proceed to Point B—the telephone call—you may help accumulate enough evidence to call a halt to these vile murders. "Widowhood certainly becomes you, Ann." I stood up.

She tapped the paper to her lips, picked up a black suede handbag, and dropped the paper inside. Then she went to stand by the fireplace, looking up into the gilded mirror. Her reflected eyes met mine.

"Life is what we make of it, don't you agree, Ellie? If there were a Merry Widows Club, I would have had to worm my way in because my marital situation wouldn't have met the admission requirements. Charles was incapable of having an affair, that is, with anyone except himself. But rumour, goodness knows who started it, buzzed it about that he was carrying on with Miss Thorn, of all pitiful people. I have always thought that lies are so much more credible when far-fetched. Although Charles did seem to rather like the poor wretch."

Ann turned back to me, her fingers stroking the blackbird brooch. "My only regret concerning this death was your involvement. I like you, Ellie, and I don't like most women."

"Bunty Wiseman, for instance?"

"You noticed."

"Could it be that you are in love with her husband?" When would I learn to be discreet?

Ann's smile vanished. She stared at me, perhaps without seeing me. I had gone too far.

"You're right," Ann said softly. "Lionel Wiseman affects me as no man ever has, and he was showing definite signs of being attracted to me before he went and married that piece of candy floss. The day you and I went to his office, I felt the room begin whirling the moment he entered. Here's something amusing. I wrote a letter to Dear Felicity myself several weeks ago, just to cool off. I told her that I had this uncontrollable urge to rush into Lionel's office and fling off my clothes."

"I have the feeling I read that," I murmured.

Ann gave no sign of hearing me. She removed a black hat from a rack on the wall and stood in front of the mirror, tilting the brim over her brow. "Of course, that was before I knew that there were other, more valid reasons for writing to Dear Felicity." She adjusted the hat to another angle. "Ellie, I do hope our little chat has helped clear your head. It has mine. If there were a Merry Widows Club and I had my suspicions as to the identity of its founder, I might decide that I had waited long enough to approach that person and request a small favour. Widowhood is pleasant, as I have said, but I don't think I want to make it a way of life." She stopped talking to herself in the mirror and addressed me. "How about lunch, after which I do have an errand to run . . ."

Run was what I was going to do, run to the nearest telephone kiosk. Ann's last words were fraught with ominous possibilities. I stammered that I couldn't make lunch. I had to get out of this room. But suddenly it was a long way down the stairs, through the amber velvet curtains, across the shop floor to the fresh air of the world outside.

"Miss Hyacinth or Miss Primrose Tramwell, please." I stood in the telephone kiosk at the corner of Market and Herring streets, convinced I was being photographed by hidden cameras.

"Sorry to keep you, love," said the female voice from the Pebblewell Hotel. "Our gentleman at Reception says the ladies left word they'd be out all afternoon, fishing."

Hair curtaining my face, I stepped into the pedestrian flow. Out baiting their hooks, were they? The tower clock struck noon. My conversation with Ann kept scraping round and round in my head, with certain names making the loudest noise. Bunty and Lionel Wiseman. I stepped back into the kiosk and dialed Bunty's number. What would I say to her? Ann Delacorte is out to get your husband . . . and maybe you too. No answer. I hung up.

Another name bounced out at me. Teddy Peerless. She had found Charles's body. She was in that photograph with Edwin Digby and the young woman I presumed was his daughter, and Teddy was closely acquainted with both Wisemans. I had no idea what rivers the Tramwells might be fishing, but I would tackle the pond.

Pushing open the street door, I mounted the bottle-green staircase to the offices of Bragg, Wiseman & Smith.

"Hello, Teddy."

No answering smile. Her hands kept moving, ruffling through cardboard folders in the file cabinet. "You made me jump."

"I'm sorry," I said to the back of her head. Why this feeling that she had been expecting me for some time? I came further into the room, put my hand on the desk, and took it off again. "I see you're busy, but if you haven't had lunch, Teddy, could we go somewhere—not Abigail's—and talk?"

"I can't." Teddy finally turned to me, a folder held to the front of her cardigan. It struck me that she looked more beige than ever. Her prominent teeth bit into her lower lip, but otherwise her face was expressionless. Bunty had provided a detailed account of *what* Teddy Peerless was—daughter of an earl, neglected sister, dedicated secretary—but did even Bunty know *who* Teddy was?

"Are you afraid to be seen with me because people are making nasty jokes about Charles's death?"

"I am not." Her voice was flat, but something stirred in her face. I thought I saw sympathy, the desire to tell me something.

"Liar!" squalled a voice. I jumped. I had forgotten the parrot. It pranced gleefully upon its perch. Avoiding his knowing eyes, I said, "How about a half hour, Teddy? You have to eat sometime, and I need to discuss that night at Abigail's."

Her face had gone neutral again. "Mrs. Haskell, I have a will that has to be typed immediately."

"Liar!"

Lady Theodora—I couldn't continue thinking of her as Teddy when I had ceased being Ellie to her—closed the file cabinet and began organising stray paper clips on her blotter. I sat down because I didn't know what else to do with my legs.

"I'll talk fast," I began. "I've been trying to put together all the higgledy-piggledy pieces of the night when Charles died. When I was leaving the room to talk to a man—who turned out to be Mr. Digby"—her hands stopped moving—"you and I collided. And even though my mind was on other things, I was struck by how agitated you looked. Mrs. Malloy, who works for me, had mentioned earlier that you seemed bothered by the presence of Dr. Bordeaux—"

"I can understand, El . . . Mrs. Haskell, that what happened was a distressing experience for you and your husband, but really, you sound irrational on the subject." A paper clip landed in a tin with an earth-shattering ping. "A man unfortunately died. What do I have to do with that?"

"I want to know why you found him, why you went into the office."

"Bite your tongue!" screeched the parrot.

Teddy was now taking the paper clips out of the tin. "As I told the police, I simply mistook that office for the powder room."

"Why?" I stood up. "There would have been a sign—one of those stiff girls with the triangular skirts—on the door."

"Please excuse me." Teddy crossed to the far side of the desk. The protruding teeth gnawed at her lower lip.

"Did you see Mr. Digby?" I asked. "Were you upset and wanting a place to escape for a few minutes? Is Mr. Digby your brother, returned here under an assumed name . . . and a beard?"

"Kill, kill!" shrieked the parrot. "Drown the pretty damsel in the nearest sea!"

"Silence, you old barnacle. And how do you do, Mrs. Haskell." Lionel Wiseman filled the small office, not only on account of his height and powerful build, but because he was (with full apologies to Ben) powerfully handsome.

"Abigail's lease holding up?" He was still clasping my hand and I didn't know whether it would be ungracious to remove it or inappropriately friendly to leave it there.

"The lease is doing splendidly. I came to ask your secretary to lunch—but another time. I did phone Bunty, but she was out."

He held the door for me, his gold cuff links gleaming. "My wife keeps herself entertained. I count myself fortunate if I find her at home in the evenings."

Teddy was back at the files. As I went down the stairs and out into Market Street, I remembered Roxie saying the village gossips didn't believe the Wisemans were married. What, I wondered, was Bunty's real name? Something awful she had said. Something . . . beginning with a 'W'?

* * * *

When I entered the kitchen at Merlin's Court, Magdalene and Poppa were at the table having lunch, the earthenware teapot between them. Sweetie lay across Magdalene's feet, grunting out little snores. Tobias was a mere dangle of tail from an upper cupboard. My in-laws weren't talking, but the silence was of the sort that binds people together.

"Back with us, are you, Giselle?" Magdalene flitted up from her chair. "I don't suppose there's any point in asking if you want a sandwich."

I stripped off my gloves and unbuttoned my coat. "I would like two, please, and some of that soup." As Magdalene disappeared into the pantry for bread, Poppa's voice spoke in my ear.

"Such a feisty one, that woman! Doesn't look a day over sixty-five, does she?" Was this the man who had talked about Mrs. Jarrod with a similar gleam in his dark brown eyes? Could it be that he was over that woman? I hung up my coat in the alcove. In his favourite red cardigan and leather slippers, Poppa didn't look like a lecher and even less like a man who would decide to revitalize his marriage by injecting a little jealousy. But then did Miss Thorn look like a vamp? Or Teddy Peerless a woman with a secret? Or the Tramwells detectives? Did I look like a woman who could inspire a grand and undying passion in a breathtakingly handsome man? Well I had, which goes to show that you can't tell anything about anyone, especially murderers.

After lunch, all three of us did the washing up. I had just put away the last cup and Magdalene had rearranged the handle when the phone rang. I didn't think the Tramwells would ring me; we had arranged it would be the other way around, but out in the hall I dropped the receiver before getting it to my ear.

"Did I tell you this morning how much I love you?"

"I believe so, thank you, and . . . ditto."

"Is one or more parent lurking in the immediate vicinity?" Ben's voice dropped to a stage whisper.

"That could be so." Apart from Rufus and his mate, I was alone in the hall, but the memory of my visit to Ann stung, and what's one more lie in a healthy marriage?

"I've been thinking, Ellie." Holding the receiver was almost like touching him. I could see him, the dark brows coming together, the intensity of his blue-green gaze. One of the more unsettling features of frigidity is that it leaves you at the worst possible moments.

"What have you been thinking, Ben?"

"That it may be time to give the parents a nudge. I am sorry about their problems, but I am not sure coddling them is the answer. Living with us is like living in a hotel for them. They are together without ever meeting, if you know what I mean."

I knew exactly what he meant.

"Ben, we can't hustle them. For starters, your father hasn't finished my cake. It's turning into a drawing room conversation piece. Also, I am sure there is more to their marital difficulties than Mrs. Jarrod."

"You don't think that Poppa could be . . . one hates to suggest such a thing about one's own father, but . . . well, impotent, and he's been trying to give himself an out?" Ben's voice dropped lower. "If it is *that*, I hope it isn't . . . hereditary."

"Ben, it doesn't do to make wild guesses."

"You're right. And I should worry about my own life. Ellie, there's more to *our marital situation* than I can put my finger on."

Oh, the folly of marrying a man of above-average intelligence!

"Sorry, Ben, but there goes the doorbell. I have to go."

"Let Poppa or—"

Pretending not to hear, I hung up. Chalk up another lie; I hadn't even asked Ben if the luncheoners at Abigail's had included any patrons other than himself and the staff. I whispered into the empty hall. "All for your own good, my darling. You will thank me for my strong-mindedness when single-handedly (give or take Flowers Detection) I unmask The Founder and restore your professional reputation."

The phone rang again as I was prying my hand off the receiver. Don't let it be Ben. I might lose all control and beg him to abscond with me to a desert island.

"Ellie, such a thrill finding you at home." Vanessa's voice breezed into my ear. "I'm at the London flat, but I plan to come down to Chitty Chitty Bang Bang next Saturday and wonder if you and I could get together for a cousinly chat?"

I didn't like this. Was she out of work and forced to pawn one of her furs? With so many illusions already stripped away—Ann, Miss Thorn; and big questions raised about Teddy and . . . Bunty—I wasn't ready for anything that would put a crimp in a lifetime of loathing Vanessa.

"Is something wrong?"

"What a foolish question. Life for me began to fall apart when you got married and I realised that none of the important things—looks, charm, style—counted for anything."

"Does Rowland fit into this?"

She smirked audibly, said, "See you Saturday evening," and hung up.

I almost wished the phone would ring again. The prospect of nothing to do stared me in the face. My thoughts weren't good company. Had I read too much into my conversation with Ann? She had admitted she hadn't loved Charles and that she wanted him dead. We had discussed a book by a local author and played a silly charade of writing to an advice columnist. I had felt concern for Bunty as the wife-in-the-way; but as it seemed highly unlikely that a wife-murdering organisation had set itself up in competition with The Widows Club, Ann would surely be content with trying to break up the Wisemans' marriage. An anonymous letter here, a venomous word there . . . I paced the flagstones in the hall.

Desperation, it was once said by my mother, makes geniuses of us all. Inspiration struck as I foresaw an afternoon—alone—of listening to the clock tick.

The Peerless Nursing Home. Confirmation or negation could be found there. So, alas, could Dr. Bordeaux. Grabbing the telephone before I could lose my nerve, I dialed directory enquiries, got the number, and stuffed a finger, which felt big and boneless as a sausage, into the dial hole. In that moment I empathised deeply with obscene callers everywhere.

"The Peerless Nursing Home."

"Gggg." In deepening my voice it went so low I lost it. Start again. "Good afternoon, this is Nurse Jones"—oh, come on!—"from the Cottage Hospital. Our Dr. Brown . . . ing is having some problems with a patient in Psychiatric—a woman with sixty-one different personalities, a record, Dr. Browning believes, and he wonders if Dr. Simon Bordeaux would be free to come over immediately and offer some helpful hints? The case promises to be written up in all major medical journals."

"I'm sure Doctor would have been only too pleased, Nurse Jones. But this is Doctor's afternoon off. He has already left the premises. If another time would suit Dr. Browning?"

"I don't think so; the patient isn't expected to live more than half an hour. A once-in-a-lifetime opportunity, so to speak."

His day off! What luck! My breath exploded in a whoosh of relief as the receiver hit the cradle. What did I have to lose on entering The Peerless and making contact with one or more of its patients? Other than my life, that is. And if I played my part well, the part of a would-be patient checking out the nursing home to see if it offered the right . . . no, the wrong facilities, I should not only be safe, but informed. I smiled up at Abigail's portrait. She appeared to wink, but it may have been a shadow hitting the portrait from the window.

There are advantages to having seen fatter days. I did not have to search far in my wardrobe to find a garment with stretch appeal. The dress which I held against me and surveyed in the mirror had huge white spots on a red background. Not ideal. With my coat gaping open, it would be possible to see me coming or going for miles around. But I decided I liked the dropped elastic waist more than I disliked the spots. Now—a major decision. Should I use a pillow? No, too big. A chair cushion worked but didn't provide the look I wanted. I wished to appear so imminently pregnant that no starch-crackling nurse would dare raise her voice above a whisper to me. I wandered about the bedroom, practising maternity posture. What would make the ideal baby? Oh, for Dorcas! She would have come up with a bright idea. Bright, that was it! I sped along to my friend's old room, sniffed the air nostalgically for a whiff of Athletic Woman's Talc, and found the bag of balloons, the remains of those she had strung up for the engagement party. Dear Dorcas, everything in its place and a place for everything. I could almost hear her voice: "Frightfully spiffing of you to attempt this, old girl." Mmmmm. She might not think it so spiffing if she came home from the States to find me not in my place.

The balloon looked great, but being light, it tended to shift. A problem easily solved by filling it with water. I decided against wearing it while driving the car. Into a carrier it went. On with my camel coat, over the shoulder with my bag, and down to tell Magdalene and Poppa that I had some shopping to do.

"Nice to have so much free time on your hands, Giselle." Sunshine sparks flew off Magdalene's knitting needles; the jacket she was making for Sweetie grew even as I watched.

It seemed a safe kindness to ask her to join me. Since the

fateful evening at Abigail's, Magdalene had stayed close to home, although she was no longer fanatical about locking windows and doors.

Poppa looked up from his cake carving and smoothed his bald spot. "Go, Maggie, why don't you?" His voice sounded . . . creaky. And why wouldn't it? He spoke to her so rarely.

The needles slowed.

"On second thought," I said, feeling as if I had offered a sweet to a child and snatched it back, "it is still unseasonably chilly."

"Wouldn't do, then. Maggie's always had a chesty chest." Poppa cleared his throat and got back to carving.

As I crossed the courtyard to the car, I heard a creak behind me and felt a presence, but I didn't slow my pace. I wasn't going to give Tobias the pleasure of thinking he could scare me out of my wits, not that easily. And I wasn't much concerned about the Raincoat Man. The average person only has the capacity to be petrified of one thing at a time. Besides, I had strong suspicions that the Raincoat Man was Butler, out on surveillance, even though he had responded to the suggestion with—"Me, madam? But I h'understood you to say the fellow had 'orrible teeth." My one concern was that the balloon might burst before I got to The Peerless. Nose pressed to the steering wheel, I bounced down Cliff Road.

As I rounded the first bend, I spied Mr. Edwin Digby and Mother coming toward me. Her feathers had an icy gloss to them, and she was poking him along with her beak. Dropping down so that my knees grazed the car floor I concentrated on neither seeing nor hearing when Mr. Digby's voice was blown in my face by the wind.

"Incomparable weather for a stiff neck, Mrs. Haskell."

Ditto a stiff drink at The Dark Horse. I wished I didn't have this sneaking liking for Mr. Digby. I wished I didn't suspect him of being the evil force behind a murder network. I wished . . . that life wasn't littered with foolish wishes.

The Heinz showed its true colours as I exited the village. Its whine turned fretful, eerily echoing the wind. A couple of times I swear it tried to go backward. But the secret was never to let it get the upper hand. I had just given the gear knob a vicious twist when I beheld the long, high wall of the nursing home. A yellow van inched around me, then a dark green car slashed past. The steering wheel vibrated in my hands, but my eyes were on the stone eagles atop the pillars. I passed through the entrance and down the avenue until—there loomed the mammoth stone house. At that point, I fervently wished the avenue could have gone on to John O'Groats.

I stopped, positioned the balloon, then drove forward a few more yards to park in the middle of the gravel semicircle. Sneakiness oft draws attention to itself, and if matters went awry, I needed to be able to leap from the top of that flight of steps into the Heinz. Telling myself that all the signs were favourable (the bloodhounds Sin and Virtue weren't out and about today), I gathered my courage in my clammy paws, got my legs going, and lifted the door knocker. It fell like a lead . . . balloon. All too promptly the door opened. Facing me was a large nurse in a small frilly cap.

"May I help you?" She had eyes like pellets and a face which had been chiseled into shape. She breathed Detol the way Roxie breathed Attar of Roses.

Pressing both palms against the small of my back, I stepped inward, forcing her to step back. "I'm—Mrs. Heinz. You are expecting me, I hope? My doctor sent me to have a look at the place to see if I could be comfortable here during my confinement."

The nurse stared at me. Had I blown it too soon by using a word no longer in maternity jargon? I moved my hands to place them protectively on the protrusion jutting through my gaping coat.

"We don't *confine* people here." The nurse's face bleached out to match her white cardigan. "I don't know what you've been told, but this most certainly isn't a prison."

"I can see that, indeed I think the place looks most inviting." Taking another step forward, I fixed eager eyes on the black-and-white checkerboard floor, the white walls rising to a lofty and ornately plastered ceiling. The staircase, also painted white (criminally, in my opinion), rose at the end of the hall, facing the front door; it went up steeply for a dozen steps, then divided.

"Mrs. Heinz?" The nurse jammed the door shut. "Are you having a nervous breakdown?"

"What, in my condition!" I clasped a hand to my throat. "Dear Dr. Padinsky"—if he was good enough for Magdalene, he was good enough for me—"has warned me repeatedly that trauma of any kind could be hazardous to the baby, which is why he insisted I look this place over."

"Mrs. Heinz," the nurse replied in a harsh, cold voice, "how will visiting a nursing home for emotionally disturbed women help you to a problem-free delivery?"

A chair, painted white, was at hand. Legs spread, back arched, I lowered myself into it. "Don't tell me," I bleated, "that this isn't Chitterton Fells Maternity Home?"

"It is not." She had the door open. "You haven't come much off course. Turn left on the Coast Road, proceed two miles, and you can't miss it—a modern, red brick building." She was close to smiling at the prospect of being rid of me.

"Why silly me!" I gave a light laugh which tapered off into a most satisfactory "ooo-ooch!" Gripping my hands to my balloon stomach, I rolled my eyes and lolled my head sideways.

Nurse let go of the doorknob in a hurry. "What is it? Do you think you are in labour?" Her eyes were almost kind, but I wasn't fooled. That was a blackbird brooch protruding from beneath the white cardigan.

"I've been having these twinges. Dr. Padinsky says they are warnings, that I must rest." A small shudder. "Oh, what would he say if he knew I must get into my car and drive when feeling like this?" I addressed her nose. "Would it be possible for me to lie down somewhere quiet? These episodes usually last only half an hour . . ."

She glanced, furtively it seemed to me, around the antiseptic hall.

"I can't risk hurting the baby or having Dr. Padinsky cross with us—I mean, me." Although I had quickly changed that last word, the plural had done its job.

"No, of course not. And we do pride ourselves on our personal approach at The Peerless." She sounded conciliatory, almost jolly, as she placed a hand on my arm. "This is Dr. Bordeaux's afternoon off, otherwise I know he would have been only too pleased to examine you."

"That would have been wonderful."

The nurse's strong fingers handcuffed my wrist as she led me under the righthand sweep of stairs into a room that in the days when this was a house and not a nursing home had probably been a parlour. French doors led into the garden, and I could see a corner of the Dower House. With a pang, I thought of Jenny, her invalid mother, and the old nanny. It was easy to say they would all be better off when removed from the doctor's criminal clutches, but the shock of disclosure would be shattering.

"This is the visitor's waiting room." The nurse helped me onto a tweedy brown couch. "I will just take your pulse and blood pressure."

"Please, I really don't feel up to that sort of thing."

"What if I fetch a glass of water?"

"That's very kind, but I would prefer to be left completely alone for that half hour. I can never relax if I think someone is going to come into the room just as I am drifting off to sleep."

"Very well." She straightened an embroidered chairback, which looked as though it had been an occupational therapy project, and left the room.

I forced myself to wait a full minute after the door clicked shut before tiptoeing up from the couch. The door handle, when I lowered it, made a fearsome noise, but when I pressed an eye to the thin strip of opening, the hall looked deserted. Crossing it, however, was like swimming the channel.

My dash up the stairs to the third floor felt like scaling a wall. Drying my palms on the sides of my coat, I tapped on the door immediately to my left, then, allowing a scant second for a response, depressed the handle. The door didn't budge.

"Nurse, is that you?" wheedled a voice. "I'll let you have my sago pudding for a week if you'll talk Doctor out of giving me any more injections."

"Hope you're feeling better, Mrs. Freebrun." I read her name off the doorplate. Was her door locked because she was an especially difficult patient, clinging obstinately to remorse? Or did she pose a danger to her doctor, should she escape and denounce him as a villain?

I tried the doors of Mary Wallace, Doris Barch, Ida Parkhurst. The same; no admittance. Would I be wasting valuable time were I to attempt a conversation through one of their keyholes? And how could I inspire instant trust?

"Ida, I am a missionary worker. Will you help me reach my daily quota of redeemed souls?"

No answer from Ida, but what was that noise? The handle slid wetly out from my grasp. There it came again, identifiable now as footsteps mounting the stairs. Caught with my neck in the rope. No escape, except by leaping the bannister railing, and I couldn't take that route; not in my condition. Breaking into a fog of perspiration, I grabbed the next handle down the line, bracing myself for what was to come. Amazingly, this door opened. Quicker than one can say, "Nurse," I was inside. It was a household cupboard, crammed with mops, buckets, brooms, and the reek of disinfectant.

All this I saw at a glance from the ruddy glow of a cigarette lighter.

"Hello, my love," said the other occupant of the cupboard placidly.

She was seated on the base of a Hoover, lighting up a cigarette. She looked a nice enough woman, meaning she wasn't dressed as a nurse, but I eyed her in horror as I pressed a finger to my lips. If the person on patrol smelled smoke or saw it creeping out from under the door, we were done for. The same applied if the fiery tip of the cigarette got any closer and I popped. I held my breath. The lighter snapped shut. The footsteps drew level with the door, then passed on. Tomorrow I would take out stock in disinfectant.

"It's young Mrs. Haskell, isn't it? I've seen you about in the village." My companion's voice spoke into the darkness.

"Yes, and you are . . . ?" The smoke, the close quarters, and the possibilities of the situation were all combining to suffocate me. The lighter flared and I was looking down at a face that might have belonged to a kindly middle-aged sheep.

"Beatrix Woolpack. This is such an unexpected pleasure. Although, come to think of it, you are the second person I have bumped into in this very cupboard. The other was a man named . . . now what was it? Butcher? Baker?"

"Butler?"

"That's right." The fiery tip of her cigarette danced. "He was so interested when I told him about my late husband being a locksmith and how I had worked shoulder-to-shoulder with him all our married life. Sad, isn't it. To think that all I got out of marriage, other than two quite nice children, was the know-how to get me out of my room here for a change of scene and a Players."

"Very sad."

"The same tired old tale, isn't it, my love. A woman living for her husband by his rules, staying home to raise the children because he said a woman's place was in the home, and then being slapped with the news that he'd found someone younger, better-looking, and with the gumption to be her own person. The wonder isn't that I joined The Widows Club, but that more women don't pawn their engagement rings to have their husbands killed."

"Quite." I backed against the wall. One of my feet landed in a pail; a pole rapped me on the head.

"What will you be thinking of me?" came her voice. "I haven't asked if you mind me smoking."

"Not a bit."

"His car went over the cliff, if you remember. Relatively quick and painless. I wouldn't have wanted him to suffer. He wasn't a bad man, just a bad husband. So often the case, isn't it?"

"Yes." My ears were on the alert for more footsteps.

The red dot vanished. Mrs. Woolpack must have stubbed out the cigarette. "This has been so nice, Mrs. Haskell. We must do it again some time, mustn't we? But now I shall be getting back to my room. It's quite cosy, you know. I have photos of my dog George and my cat Minx; my daughter has given them a temporary home. I shall be out of here soon."

"That will be lovely. Mrs. Woolpack, before you go, do you know the name of the person who founded this Widows Club?"

"I don't, my love." She was inching the cupboard door open. "But if I did, I wouldn't say. To thine own club be true, isn't that right? As it is, I can never make it up to my dear friends for my wickedness in rescuing that wretched Mr. Daffy from that train." She picked up her cigarette stub from the floor.

We tiptoed to her door. Drawing a knotted wire from her pocket, she deftly inserted it into the lock. I was halfway down the stairs when it struck me that she hadn't asked what I was doing in her cupboard.

The hall seemed to have doubled in size since I left it. Could I get across to the waiting room and my invalid couch without being discovered by my least favourite nurse? Maybe. Things looked hopeful as I came off the last stair. Not a twitch of a uniform or any other sign of human, make that inhuman, activity. I traversed the black-and-white tile without hearing a sound save my own footfall.

"Mrs. Heinz, where have you been?"

Pivoting toward the accusatory voice, I gripped my balloon stomach in a last sympathy pitch and heard a *thuwpp*! I could feel myself deflating, feel water gushing down my legs. Eyes glued to the face of the nurse, that same sweet soul who had admitted me, I wondered if I looked as aghast as she.

Her voice shook. "It appears that your water has broken."

"Oh, is that the problem?" Mesmerized, I studied the spreading puddle. "I felt a bit odd and came to find you. I should never have attempted the stairs, I know, but—could you please telephone?"

"A Dr. Padinsky, I believe you said, but perhaps Dr. Bordeaux has returned to the Dower House."

"No. Absolutely not. I won't see anyone but my own doctor."

"Very well." She looked relieved. "I will make the phone call immediately after I take you back to the waiting room." She reached for my arm.

"No." I shook her off. The situation permitted extreme agitation. "I will go and lie down. You phone Dr. Padinsky immediately."

I was within a couple of yards of the waiting room. I grabbed the door, closed it behind me, then raced for the French windows. Could I make it around the side of the house to my car before Nurse got off the phone? Was she suspicious? Was she even now speaking to Dr. Bordeaux, listening to his instructions, preparing to arm herself with a poisoned syringe and pursue me at full tilt? Or had she swallowed the situation because she had let me into the building, and Dr. Bordeaux might be very, very annoyed with her if anything were amiss?

Ducking across the lawn, I felt weighed down by hopelessness. The doctor could appear at any moment, the dogs panting at his heels. And menace there already was aplenty. The wind dragged at my hair like an outstretched hand and sucked in gloating breaths. The trees kept breaking through the tattered mist to stand directly in my path. My hip whapped into a bench. Inside the house, the dogs Virtue and Sin began to bark.

Immediately ahead now was the Dower House. No sanctuary to be found there even if the doctor were absent. Jenny was only a child, her mother helpless, and the nanny ancient. Dr. Bordeaux was their patron, probably respected. Possibly loved.

I was now level with a set of French windows similar to the ones I had just exited. Panting, I peered through the glass and saw two people. Clinging to a web of ivy, I strove to catch my breath. The couch was empty, unlike the time when I was in this room and the invalid lay there. Jenny was in the middle of the room with her back to me, her hair—more auburn than sandy under the electric light—spilling loose about her shoulders. It struck me that something was different. Her dress, a green silk sheath, was for once not too young, but too old for her. The other person in the room was Dr. Bordeaux. I couldn't see much of his face because Jenny kept moving, blocking off my view, her gestures angry. Clearly some sort of altercation was in progress. Good for me, but I was sorry for Jenny.

Nipping past the window, teeth chattering, I slithered around the side of the house and raced towards the gravel semicircle. Virtue and Sin waited, bowlegged, muzzles at the ready, directly in front of the Heinz. I expected to freeze with stupefied terror, but the stupefying part was, it didn't happen. Perhaps life with Sweetie had toughened me or perhaps as adversaries I would take the dogs over the nurse. Teeth bared in a playful smile, I hurled a shower of pebbles into the air. With canine shrieks of glee, they leapt into the air, tongues lapping, paws flapping, while I made the last desperate hustle toward the Heinz. Would a hand reach out from behind me and twist my neck into a rope? I jabbed the key in the ignition, my eyes riveted to the door of The Peerless. Foot on the accelerator, I begged, "Heinz, don't fail me now." Then I rammed into reverse and whizzed backward down the avenue. I couldn't risk the precious minutes necessary to turn the car around.

Not only had I to get away from here, I had to get to the Tramwells. I had to tell them that my visit to The Peerless had convinced me, as nothing else could have done, that The Widows Club was a matter for the police. Yes, the men in blue had been unreceptive at first, but I would accompany the sisters to the station house and offer all the information I had garnered. But I couldn't—wouldn't—play amateur detective any more. The risks were too great. I wasn't going to end up in a broom cupboard, and I wouldn't have Ben involved. I couldn't shake off the feel of the nurse's hand on my arm or the look in those pebble eyes. And if such a woman was afraid of Dr. Bordeaux, God help us all.

I sat shivering in a maroon leather chair in the reception room at The Pebblewell Hotel from four that afternoon until six in the evening, drinking countless cups of coffee and whiling away the time by counting people going up and down the red carpeted staircase. Soon they all wore grey woolly coats, had faces like Mrs. Woolpack, and talked in sheep's voices. When I awoke, the Tramwells still hadn't returned. What if they didn't come back? What if they had decided they were not equipped to handle a murder investigation and had returned to their pastoral village? Panic broke in icy waves through my skin. What if Ann were hit by a car? Her belongings would be examined by someone in authority who would find the damning note I had written to Dear Felicity Friend. What precisely had I said in that note? Forget the police! What if Ben somehow got hold of it? I began pacing the space between the two couches, bumping every third step into the oversized coffee table. The receptionist had her eyes on me. Mine kept time with the onyx clock on the mantel. Still the sisters did not return. When two elderly gentlemen, newspapers tucked under the arms, invaded my territory with talk of grouse shooting, I had waited long enough.

The Heinz, marvel of marvels, started right up. I drove through the dark blanket of evening into Chitterton Fells and along Market Street. I had to get that piece of paper back. A streetlamp spread a silvery sheen outside Delacorte's Antiques. I drew up at the curb, opened the door to step out and jumped when something brushed against my calf. Looking up at me was Mother. She honked, eyes bright with hope. Mine scanned the street but I could see no sign of Mr. Digby. He must be swilling it back at The Dark Horse.

"Unlike you, old faithful, to leave your post," I said to Mother. "Seen someone you know?" I stroked her head. "Some people don't deserve to have geese." She looked defensive, then forlornly scooted away.

The shop sign said Closed, but Ann might not yet have locked up. She hadn't. I entered to greyness, dramatised by shadowy humps of furniture and the *William Tell* Overture.

"Ann," I called, fumbling for the light switch. The room sprang to eye-smarting brightness. "Ann!" No answer. The shop looked different at night, less cosy, but something was wrong . . . no, more like—missing. And why not! After all, everything here was for sale except the cash register. I shook myself, but the day's events crowded in on me. Would there be repercussions to my visit to The Peerless? What would I say to Ann? Could I persuade the police that Bunty might be in peril if the widows were prepared to bend the rules? I crossed the shop, telling myself that I would walk up those stairs and knock on that door. My hands reached for the amber velvet curtains and pulled them apart. . . . I would say, Hello Ann, I've been thinking about that little charade we played. . . .

Something brushed against me and I was so startled I toppled over. When I opened my eyes and grovelled to my feet, I found myself looking at Ann. Her eyes were opened wide, her hair and fortyish clothes as elegant as when I had seen her that morning.

There was only one real difference. She was dead. Two arrows pinned her jacketed shoulders to the wall under the left-hand curtain. A third was punched into her chest.

I had been right: there was something different about the shop. The crossbow was missing from the wall behind the register.

I was standing there looking at this woman who had been my friend when I heard again the tinkle of the *William Tell* Overture.

From the Files of The Widows Club

Minutes of Board Meeting, Monday, 11th May

The minutes of the March meeting were approved as read. Treasurer, Mary Ellis, reported a current balance of £139.71 and fended off an accusation by Betty White that £2.13 had been misappropriated for the purchase of fertilizer for the gardening committee. Activities Chairwoman, Martha Grub, made a motion that a trip to Hampton Court be made an annual event. Motion seconded by Mrs. Shirley Daffy and unanimously approved by the Board. Mrs. Agnes Levine, Membership Committee, circulated copies of the updated standard Telephone Approach To Prospective Members. Two spelling and three typographical errors were called to the Board's attention, but the document passed by a two-thirds vote for immediate implementation. Corrected sample attached. Refreshments of currant buns and cocoa were served. The meeting concluded abruptly at 9:36 P.M. when the news of Ann Delacorte's death was received.

Respectfully submitted,

Millicent Parsnip,
Recording Secretary

The Widows Club
Telephone Questionnaire

Membership Committee Member:

Good day, Mrs. Jane Smith (fictitious name). I am telephoning at the request of a mutual friend who tells me you may seriously be considering the possibilities of becoming a widow.

Mrs. Jane Smith:

a. I am indeed.

b. Is this an obscene phone call?

(If the response is *b*, pretend you have the wrong Jane Smith, on whom you are playing a practical joke, and hang up. Otherwise proceed.)

M.C. Member:

Let us be sure we fully understand each other. You *do* dream of having your husband murdered?

Mrs. J.S.:

I can't think of anything nicer.

M.C. Member:

Well then, Mrs. Jane Smith, you are exactly the sort of woman we want in The Widows Club, a local organisation that offers a vast assortment of social and cultural activities along with its guilt management services. Your sponsor will be happy to discuss them with you, if you decide to join us.

Mrs. J.S.:

When may I be admitted to your ranks?

M.C. Member:

That I cannot tell you. The admittance procedure varies anywhere from a few days to a few months. We do ask that you begin preparing yourself emotionally. Get plenty of rest and exercise to control nerves. Endeavour to treat your husband as though you were readying him to go away on his holidays. A little kindness now is an investment in both your futures.

Mrs. J.S.:

I cannot wait to begin.

M.C. Member:

Good. Now we come to the matter of the initiation fee. The Widows Club realises it is difficult for many women to come up with one thousand pounds cash. If you can, splendid; otherwise we ask that you make a contribution of jewelry—your engagement ring, gold watch, etc. The Widows Club does not discriminate on the basis of economic status. On payment of your fee it is required that you enclose a brief, handwritten application. This, along with the note you recently wrote to an advice columnist, will be kept on file.

Mrs. J.S.:

How and where shall I deposit the membership fee?

M.C. Member:

The current depository is the statue of Smuggler Jim in St. Anselm's churchyard. The left boot contains a crevice ideal for the purpose. Please deposit the fee between midnight and four A.M. during the next forty-eight hours. On the remote chance that you are seen in the churchyard, say you felt a need to come to terms with death.

Mrs. J.S.:

And then?

M.C. Member:

Relax and wait. You will receive notification of approval through the confidential column of our local advice columnist, Dear Felicity Friend. Mrs. Jane Smith, it is my privilege and pleasure to assure you that your husband will be detained on earth no longer than strictly necessary. I look forward to that happy day when you join us at one of The Widows Club's general meetings and receive your membership badge.

22

Primrose was, I think, disappointed that I didn't faint dead away or, at the very least, go into hysterics when she and Hyacinth entered Delacorte's to find me in the most compromising of positions, inches away from Ann's body.

"My dear Ellie," she said, as she propped me against a bureau, "what a very nasty shock for all of us. I have for years considered bows and arrows one of the menaces of modern society, but, on the bright side, we must remember that Mrs. Delacorte was hardly a person you would have wished to keep as a friend."

"True, but I didn't kill her to get her off my guest list."

"Of course you didn't," Primrose soothed. "This wasn't a murder, it was an execution. Oh, the thrill, Hyacinth, of being proved right!—professionally speaking."

I wished she would keep her voice down. I could not shake the feeling that the murderer might still be here, lurking behind a piece of antique furniture.

Hyacinth lowered me onto a chair. "I couldn't agree with you more, Prim. We suspicioned (did we not?) that Mrs. Delacorte had used The Widows Club for her own ends. But there has to be more. She must have taken some action to precipitate this."

I pressed my fingers to my eyes, trying to shut out the horror of Ann's unflickering gaze. "Life is what you make of it," she had said. "If you want something done, an obstacle removed from your path, it is best to go to the top." I heard myself giving the Tramwells a fractured account of my visit here this morning.

Primrose fluttered in circles like a moth. "Somehow Mrs. Delacorte discovered, or guessed at, the identity of The Founder. After you left her, she went to see him or her. Putting you up for membership would not have sealed her fate, so my belief is she requested that Bunty Wiseman be eliminated; perhaps she even put the squeeze on The Founder. But that is neither here nor there. Mrs. Delacorte placed herself in a very perilous position and it was decided she had to be removed. It most assuredly would not do to have members of the club stepping outside the club's charter. Oh, dear me, no! The results would be murderous mayhem."

"Absolutely," said her sister. "But I feel very strongly that the swiftness of the response indicates a breathless kind of fury, due to the fact that Mrs. Delacorte's desired victim was a woman and one whose husband she coveted. We have much to discuss—why we are all here, for instance—but now we must do the courteous thing and telephone the constabulary."

"Not for a few minutes, please. I have something I must retrieve from Ann's bag." I pried myself out of the chair.

"Dear me, of course!" fluted Primrose. "The note you wrote to Dear Felicity Friend! Who is, as Hyacinth and I have been meaning to tell you, none other than Edwin Digby, under the guise of another female pseudonym—"

"We can go into all this later," Hyacinth interrupted, but Primrose swept on.

"Butler has confirmed the suspicions aroused, Ellie, when you spoke of the page you saw in Mr. Digby's typewriter. The writing had the cadence of something from an advice column. And when Mrs. Malloy arrived at The Aviary that day she mentioned that she had seen him entering the . . ."—Primrose stumbled over the next word—"Gentleman's. Her hints that she could keep her mouth shut suggested that this observation had been made somewhere other than The Dark Horse. Earlier she told you, Ellie, that she had cleaned the executive toilets at

The Daily Spokesman and knew the identity of Felicity Friend. Am I making myself clear?"

"You are making yourself *long*." Hyacinth tapped on a Victorian desk. "We must look for that note at once, although Mrs. Delacorte may have already passed it on. Indeed, she may have used it as an excuse for her fatal visit. Ellie, your contribution to our efforts is magnificent and I regret you have been forced to spend the remainder of the day aimlessly awaiting our return from London. When we arrived back at the Pebblewell Hotel we were told that you had just left the premises. We followed at top speed and spotted your car."

"My dear," scolded Primrose, "you were saying that *I* was talking too much. The police tend to be nitpicky over such questions as 'When did you enter the premises and discover the body?' " She touched my arm. "We will say that you fainted, Ellie, and we dithered about reviving you. However, two minutes is all I think we can allow ourselves to search for the handbag with the note."

"Are we going to tell the police about The Widows Club?"

"Indeed not. Think how galling if they were to step in at this late stage, solve the case, and scoop the credit. I think I would weep after the exhausting day we have had browsing in Harrods, waiting for Butler to get finished checking up on Edwin Digby's genealogy at Somerset House. And all for naught. It seems Digby isn't his real name either. Oh, and Ellie . . . Put your gloves on, dear."

I went through the amber curtains sideways so as not to brush against Ann's body, then up the stairs to the flat. I had to find that note. If the police got their hands on it, I doubted my marriage would survive, and prison decor had never excited me. As things stood, the police would surely put me under the microscope. This was my second body in less than a month. First the husband, then the wife.

Switching on the light, I lifted Ann's coat from the chair where it had been tossed, but the bag wasn't underneath. Hyacinth's voice sliced through my jumping nerves. She was telephoning the police station. I could count on a minute at most.

How ironic to realise that less than half an hour ago I had *wanted* to talk to the police. I had pictured a kindly detective patting me on the arm and saying, "Thank you, madam, the boys and I will get right on it." Alas, how a corpse alters the case. Now I pictured a different look on the inspector's face as I babbled away about a widows club while Ann's body was pinned to a wall. I *had* to find that note.

The scream of the sirens ripped into my head just as I discovered Ann's black suede bag on a bookcase. Hands shaking, I snapped open the clasp. Comb, mirror, purse, cheque book, oh, please . . . My fingers were stiffening up. But there it was, the folded square of paper. I opened it just to make sure. Yes. I moistened my lips and placed it on my tongue. I always said I could eat anything. Then I flicked off the light and, chewing madly, stumbled down the stairs.

I wasn't alone in the narrow dark. The what-if demons pressed in on me. What if Ann, even though she had not passed on the note, had mentioned my interest in becoming a member of The Widows Club? What if the nurse described me accurately enough to Dr. Bordeaux that he recognised me? What if I broke down under police questioning? I took the last step and edged the curtains apart.

Hyacinth was on her knees half under a table; Primrose was atop a stepstool.

"There, there, ladies," came a comfortable male voice. "You can come out of hiding. You are perfectly safe." The shop was crammed almost as full with policemen as it was with merchandise. I swallowed hard.

"Well, that didn't go too badly, did it?" remarked Hyacinth. Primrose had driven the hearse around the corner from Delacorte's. She now proffered a bag of extra strong peppermints, saying they would warm us up. I liked the way they killed the taste of paper and ink.

Didn't go too badly? I sank low on the seat. Please don't let Ben amble this way and see me! There was no reason for him to walk in this direction on leaving Abigail's, and if he had any dinner customers, he was probably still at the restaurant. But the last hour and a half seemed to lead inexorably to the moment when I must break it to my husband that I had spent the evening with a dead body and the police. And he must be warned to brace himself for the newspapers' gleeful rehashing of Charles Delacorte's death.

The inspector had suggested that one of his men get in touch with my husband—"You've had some nasty experiences recently, haven't you, Mrs. Haskell?"—but I had declined. I preferred to tell him myself, at home. A constable had been stationed outside the shop to disperse the crowd which had gathered with the arrival of the police and the ambulance. He was told to give out the information that Mrs. Delacorte was dead and that the till appeared to have been raided. Better that, the inspector had intimated, than a panic spread that a maniac killer was on the loose in Chitterton Fells.

"Ellie, I don't feel that this murder can fully account for the distress and agitation I sense in you." Primrose handed me another peppermint. "Tell us, my dear, what else happened today?"

"I went to The Peerless Nursing Home."

When I finished my account of that little visit, Primrose ecstatically pressed her hands to my face. "So brave, so ingenious! And I do feel you should put aside your little fears about the nurse going to Dr. Bordeaux and confessing her stupidity at leaving you unchaperoned. Even were she so lacking in self-preservation, you don't *look* like a Mrs. Heinz."

"But if she gave an accurate description of my car . . ."

"How could she?" Hyacinth flexed her pencil. "Isn't its right side an Austin, the left a Rover, the right door a Vauxhall? Let us proceed. You say Jenny Spender seemed to be remonstrating with Dr. Bordeaux as you passed the window?"

"Yes." I pressed my hands against the back of my neck and rubbed my feet together to stop a creeping pins and needles sensation. "I *have* to go home."

"We can all do with an early night, Ellie." Hyacinth's voice was reproving. "We have arduous days ahead. It is surely folly to think that the police won't wish to interrogate us further." She made another notation in the green book.

Primrose fussed with a button at her throat. "I do believe we have so far been a credit to ourselves. Was I not splendidly tiresome in explaining how we had missed an appointment with Ellie, raced in pursuit of her—without speeding, of course—and entered Delacorte's just in time to see her collide with the corpus delecti?" Her eyes sparkled, then sobered. "Ellie, you seem so constrained. Is it possible you felt obliged to tell the inspector certain small untruths and now feel guilty? For instance, when he asked whether you had noticed anyone in the vicinity of Delacorte's as you were about to enter—"

"I didn't see anyone; I saw a goose—Mother Goose. She was only a few yards from Delacorte's. Mr. Digby must have been in The Dark Horse, and I wondered if she had seen anyone she knew to make her cross The Square like that."

"You handled the entire situation commendably," approved Hyacinth, her earrings swivelling.

"Given my growing reputation," I said, "the inspector was pleasant. And now"—I opened my bag and took out the car keys—"before I leave, I do have something I must tell you. I can't help you anymore. I'm a coward, not a heroine. Seeing Mrs. Woolpack changed things. She made it all real, and I'm afraid that if I go on attempting to infiltrate The Widows Club, something may go wrong. Something could happen to Ben, such as his name ending up in the wrong file."

"Oh, what a dreadful thought!" Primrose reached into her handbag. "Do have a sip of brandy."

For the briefest moment I was distracted by the enchanting little flask with the minute silver cup chained to the stopper.

"I do urge you to reconsider," said Hyacinth. "Thanks to Mrs. Delacorte's death, we would seem to be on the verge of a breakthrough."

"One would like to think that the woman is at peace, but I rather fear"—Primrose lowered her eyes—"that where she has gone, her troubles are just beginning. However, we at Flowers Detection must always feel gratitude toward her because, in dying, Mrs. Delacorte showed us how to entrap The Founder." Her silvery curls shone in the electric light. "Is it too much to ask, dear Ellie, that you display that nobility of character which we know you to possess and act as the scapegoat?"

"Me?" I had guessed this might be coming. "I am the girl who is frightened of food, remember! Besides, my life is full enough as it is with inquests and funerals and the imminent possibility of being arrested."

Primrose dabbed a lace hanky to her eyes. "We do have our way to make in the detective world, you know. And the lives of countless husbands are in your hands."

Those words buzzed in my ears like a bluebottle the next few days when I wasn't giving way to more dismal thoughts.

On the night of Ann's murder, Ben and I arrived home within minutes of each other. He was aghast when I broke the news to him. I was aghast by the sincerity of my lies.

"My poor darling." He cradled me in his arms. We were in the hall, still in our coats. "You go to visit a friend to see how she is surviving the death of her husband and find her dead. It's unspeakable. Those two old ladies who came in the shop immediately after you—were they shoppers?"

I wanted to tell him everything. I wanted us to have been married for fifty years so nothing I might do could shock him. But I was afraid that the truth, the whole truth, spilling from my lips would send him thumbing through the telephone directory for the name of a solicitor specialising in divorce. Ben didn't know the Tramwells. He couldn't be expected to view them as anything but oddities. Dangerous oddities with whom I had been in communion for some time, without mentioning it. He would begin watching me over the rim of the morning newspaper, wondering how it was that he hadn't recognised sooner my strong resemblance to my wacky relations. The lights glinted on Rufus's visored face; memory came of him in Aunt Astrid's arms, her hand on his metal thigh. And then there was Aunt Lulu pocketing ashtrays, and Uncle Maurice panting after the woman in paisley, and Freddy—the sanest of the lot—threatening to sue Sid Fowler. My fingers dug into Ben's shoulders. I couldn't risk giving him anything but an expurgated version of this evening's events. My faith must be in the police; they would do a little digging and come up with a lot of skeletons. The Widows Club would come to light eventually, without my holding the torch. If the Tramwells were determined to proceed with the case, then so be it. I couldn't put a host of anonymous, adulterous males ahead of my husband, my marriage. A good wife gets her priorities straight.

"Darling, this is bound to be rough on you." Ben smoothed my hair. "But this time I will be with you. If the police need to speak to you again at the inquest, I'll be there all the way."

He was making this so hard for me.

"So, the motive was burglary, and Ann walked in on it." Ben helped me off with my coat. "I wonder if the murderer had ever used a crossbow before. That sounds like good marksmanship to me, getting her through the heart and pinning her to the wall so she'd stay propped behind that curtain. Quite the theatrical touch."

I pressed my fingers to my eyes, only sharpening the gruesome image, but I did feel heartened in one respect. If Ben was questioning the use of weapon, so would those trained in detection.

"I'll get you a cup of tea." Ben drew me toward the kitchen, where we found Magdalene and Poppa. The whole story to be gone through again! And I knew exactly what my mother-in-law would think: All the girls my son could have picked, and he marries one whose life path is strewn with bodies!

That week moved forward, as excruciatingly slow as babies in a crawling race. *The Daily Spokesman* headlined first the announcement of, then updates on Ann's murder. According to the reports, the police were pursuing several leads. The good news for me was that the medical examiner decreed death had occurred during that time when I was within full view of eyewitnesses. But I still thought the Tramwells' alibi might be iffy.

On Thursday morning Ben and I went down to the police station and I read over my typed statement and signed it. No one gave me any funny looks. Afterward I insisted that Ben return to Abigail's. As I walked into the house I was trying to cheer myself up with the thought that I was down to two unwelcome engagements. Ann's funeral was set for Monday at 4:00 P.M., and the inquest would be as soon as the coroner's court convened. After that, my calendar was a social vacuum.

I was passing through the hall on my way upstairs to put away my coat, wondering where Magdalene and Poppa were, when I saw Magdalene by the trestle table. Her hand was on the telephone receiver; her eyes reminded me of Ann's—unblinking, fixed.

"What is it?" I rushed to her.

"Nothing!" She covered the receiver with both hands as though trying to hide it.

"Is telling lies a mortal or a venial sin?" I plonked her down on a chair. Poor little wispy person. "You've had a crank phone call. No point in denying it, I know the look. I had a similar experience once."

She stared up at me with unseeing eyes. "I was just offering it all up for the souls in Purgatory."

"What did this person say to you? Something vicious about the murder? About me?"

"The . . . the word murder was used."

"Where's Poppa?"

"He took your cake over to the church hall in the wheelbarrow. I couldn't go with him, not without a special dispensation, because of it being *that* sort of place. I'm from the old school, before Vatican Two." Her voice faded.

I had to snap her out of this. I suggested we do a little weeding in the herb garden. Reluctantly, she agreed. But I continued to worry about her; she wasn't her usual prickly self. That evening, when I mentioned the phone occurrence to Poppa and Ben, she refused to talk about it, and when Freddy climbed through the drawing room window at a little after nine, she came out of her chair as if hooked to a spring.

"It's only me, Maggie dear, not the Chitterton Fells murderer." Freddy eyed the tea tray. "What, no cake! This may cease to be my favourite eating place." He threw himself prone on the sofa. "And what's up with you, Ellie? Been finding the last day or two deadly dull?"

"Freddy, put the gag back in your mouth." Ben emphasized his displeasure by snatching away the dish of chocolates before my cousin got his fingers in it.

Poppa said, "You look exhausted, Mr. Flatts. Must be the short hours you young people work."

Magdalene was silent. I said I would fetch Freddy some Madeira cake. I wasn't being nice. I was grabbing at an excuse to get back to the kitchen and have another search for my engagement ring. Before going out to weed I had stood right by the sink and was certain (twenty percent so) that I had put it in a flowerpot saucer on the window sill. Could Tobias have gotten his paws on it and knocked it flying? I crawled around the floor. No luck. Had this happened at any other time, I would have gone to bed on a stretcher. The memory of Ben placing that ring on my finger was particularly sacred because I couldn't remember his doing the same thing with my wedding ring. I had developed an arthritic-looking hump to that finger and had worked at becoming left-handed so as to flash that diamond shine.

But murder alters people. I was distressed, but not distraught. The ring was bound to turn up. I returned to the drawing room with the Madeira cake. Magdalene and Poppa had gone to bed. Ben and Freddy were discussing the cookery demonstration Ben was giving to the Hearthside Guild between noon and 3 P.M. on Saturday, the 16th May. Why . . . that was this Saturday! I had forgotten all about it, but I imagine the fortnight I had recently undergone would have put most people off schedule. Thank God, Ben had remembered.

"Really, mate, I don't know why you are lowering yourself." Freddy rolled over on the sofa and hung face down over the edge. "I can't credit the gross insensitivity of those women, asking you to create a stew *á la difference* in a pressure cooker! Where's the magic? Where's the mystique? Aren't those the things where you just bung everything in and cover your ears?"

Ben scowled. "Will you lay off? The spokeswoman for the group didn't ask me what I wanted to do, and I didn't want to be temperamental. I thought myself lucky not having been struck off the list of coming events." He halted. "Ellie, I didn't mean—"

"Yes, you did," I said, "and it's all right."

A smile crept into his eyes, then vanished. "I would have liked to have done something more challenging, especially as"—his voice picked up speed—"Angelica Brady, the editor from Brambleweed Press, indicated she might come down for the demonstration. She thinks the book's appeal may be enhanced if the jacket contains a spiel about the charming little doings of charming little Chitterton Fells. She had me send her some copies of *The Daily Spokesman* and claimed to be enchanted by our rusticity." Ben looked down at his plate of cake, then came and sat on the arm of my chair. "Ellie, is something wrong?"

I thrust the thought of my engagement ring out of my head. "No. I'll enjoy meeting Miss Brady." I picked crumbs off his plate, then put them back. "I was just wondering about Abigail's."

Freddy sat up, blew on his fingernails, and rubbed them against the lapel of his suit jacket. As usual, he wasn't wearing a shirt. "Yours truly will manage alone and undaunted, even if we are mobbed by more than six customers." He shook back his hair. "Business, Ellie, has been picking up by leaps and bounds this week. We had four people today, if you count Mrs. Bottomly as two."

I hardly slept that night. I lay looking into darkness, afloat with wide-open eyes. I spotted those of Charles Delacorte, Vernon Daffy, Ann Delacorte, and—I had to squint to be sure—Poppa's dark brown ones. What if some of the husbands, dead or soon to be dead, were one-time sinners like Poppa? I turned over all in one movement so as not to disturb Ben and buried my face in the pillow. Had I lowered my moral standards to the point where I was prepared to concede that in some cases the crime merited the punishment? I wanted so much to shake Ben, wake him up, tell him that I was an accessory before and after the crimes. Moonlight washed into the room, showing me his face—peaceful, unsullied. I had to get up, pace around, think. The illuminated face of the bedside clock said four-fifteen. Shifting silently off the bed, I grabbed some clothes, including a sheepskin jacket, and stole into the bathroom to dress. A brisk walk would either clear my brain or numb it.

The night was like a jeweller's window; the moon a silver salver displayed on black velvet studded with diamonds. Spring, it would seem, had come in on the back of a snowbird. The air was filled with innocence. I didn't think about where I was going. I was doing battle with the demon. Me. Why is the easy way out never all it is cracked up to be? When my feet brought me to the churchyard railing, all I had settled upon was that I would talk to the Tramwells again . . . sometime soon. I was coming through the lich-gate when it suddenly struck me that Sweetie hadn't set up the alarm when I left. I would have expected her to drag me back upstairs by the cuffs of my slacks and deposit me like a trophy outside Magdalene's door.

Speak of the dear little doggie, a yap shrilled the air and a splodge of shadow leapt at my leg. I started to shake it off, then let it hang. Coming toward me through the purple haze was either a ghost or my mother-in-law. She was wearing the damson beret that made her ears stick out and she showed neither surprise nor pleasure in seeing me. Her eyes were those of a ghost. She reached out and curled her fingers around a tombstone, but she didn't speak. Sweetie, on the other hand, was making enough noise to disturb the dead. I moved my palm in front of Magdalene's eyes. Could it be?

Her voice startled me. "Giselle, I won't think you're interfering if you tell me I'm sleepwalking."

"It runs in the family." I put my arm around her. "Let's go home."

Magdalene spent most of Friday in her room. When I passed her door, I heard Poppa reading to her, something about the power of faith. I couldn't tell how far their reconciliation had come; they still spoke little in my presence. So many half-knowns. So many loopholes for fear.

Roxie arrived Friday morning and was bringing out the all-purpose bottle from the supply bag when I noticed, snagged on her sleeve, a brooch. A blackbird brooch. To stop my hands shaking I unsnagged it. Roxie was not one whit abashed.

"Like it, Mrs. H.?" She slopped liquid onto a rag. "Keep it."

Three—or was it four—husbands she had gone through?

"No, really I couldn't. These are crows, aren't they?"

"Are they?" She dusted Sweetie off a chair. "Well, suit yourself. I like a nice brooch but these are a bit on the common side, aren't they? You see them everywhere. I picked this one up on the street."

A likely story. So likely it could be true. I escaped with *The Daily Spokesman* to the drawing room. Nothing about Ann today. My hands took me directly to the Dear Felicity column. Edwin Digby's face loomed in my mind's eye. Was he the evil force or the dupe of the evil force? Unwillingly, my eyes scanned the column . . . *Dear Heartbroken, your problem will soon die a natural death.* I could not breathe. It couldn't be . . . but Heartbroken was the code name I had used on that damning note.

I began to pant and then, miraculously, euphoria burst upon me. Not only had I retrieved that note, but Ann had explained to me that it represented only an application for membership. A woman wasn't admitted to the club until after a telephone call, asking—in so many words—do you want your husband murdered? And I hadn't received such a telephone inquiry. I would have remembered.

Saturday. Ben's big moment before the Hearthside Guild. The church hall was a long room with plank flooring, brick walls, a stage at the north end, and a kitchen at the south, behind whose green accordion doors Ben was now making ready. He had brought all his equipment from home except the pressure cooker. He didn't own a pressure cooker.

Magdalene, wearing a little brown hat with a feather, and I, in a black leather coat and boots, had accompanied him. We were now trying to get out of the way of the women who were either setting up rows of folding chairs or sticking Reserved labels on them. I glimpsed the back of Millicent Parsnip's head, got a side view of Mrs. Hanover, and a full view of Mrs. Daffy's rear end as she unfolded a wooden seat. A huddle of men stood against one wall, voices a little too loud, making it clear the speakers weren't the least embarrassed at being dragged to this sissy affair by their wives. My heart began knocking. Could that be Dr. Bordeaux on the edge of the group? A chair was lifted in front of my face, and when I looked again, none of the dark-haired men resembled the doctor. It was Sidney I saw standing on the fringe. He had a red rose in his lapel and his hair appeared to have been set in rollers. He still looked like a caveman, but one considerably ahead of his time.

"Eli never could face any of the little plays Ben was in at school. It was always the same. He would come down with stage fright just as we were leaving the house." Magdalene had her hands on two chairs as if restraining them from walking away. She looked better for her day of rest yesterday. Still perhaps a little shadowed under the eyes, but otherwise recovered from the shock of her sleepwalking experience.

"Poor Poppa," I said.

"Men don't have our stamina. It comes of having one less rib."

Millicent Parsnip knocked a chair against me, and through every detour of her apology, I kept my eyes on hers. I didn't want to know if she was wearing her blackbird brooch.

"Such a pity Reverend Foxworth decided to go on holiday today instead of tomorrow, as he had planned. It would have been so nice if he could have opened the occasion with a prayer, but I understand his mother phoned and asked him to make the change. Well"—Millicent's pussycat face spread into a smile—"looks like the big moment is almost upon us." She moved off along the row. The curtains had parted a foot. I could see a man, or rather part of a man's suit, going through. I could hear Roxie's voice.

"Should you require an assistant, Mr. H., I'm your woman. And I won't charge you more than a couple of quid."

The steam from Ben's voice reached me. "Move my salt! Move my pepper! Move an inch and I'll kill you." Curtain. Magdalene was rearranging her chair when the advent of Mrs. Bottomly obscured all else from view.

"A marvellous afternoon to you, Mrs. Haskell." The chins swayed. "We"—she sloshed out an arm to include the rush of women—"we are *all* so much looking forward to this. And you, my dear, must relax and savour every moment!"

She was gone without a glance at Magdalene. She was sitting with her eyes downcast, her hands clutching her bag, murmuring, "He will be just fine, and if he isn't, I don't need to tell anyone."

I was about to sit down beside her when I saw a young blond woman coming through the door with a red rose in the lapel of her silver-grey suede jacket. At first I thought she was Bunty. The height was similar, but this woman was strikingly beautiful, whereas Bunty was merely striking. Could there be any doubt who this was? Parents who name a child Angelica have something like this in mind. She saw me staring and with long strides, alligator briefcase swinging alongside her midi-skirt, came over.

"Greetings! Hope I'm not frightfully late." She had a slightly raspy, more than slightly sexy voice. "I'm Angelica Brady and you must be Ellie because this certainly is Ben's dear mum." She extended a gloved hand, breezily friendly. Then . . . bingo, her eyes glazed. Magdalene was half out of her seat; was Miss Brady shocked by the changes time had wrought in my mother-in-law? Or was there something about me she found instantly repellent? I started to say how pleased Ben would be at having her here, but neither of us was listening. Miss Brady was staring into space—a space occupied by Sidney Fowler. The roses worn by each were as alike as two red roses can be. So were their facial expressions.

"Angie, didn't my Ben tell you Sidney also lives here?" Magdalene asked.

"No, but I have only myself to blame for that." Miss Brady's voice could have been produced by remote control. "One of the first things I said to Ben was that I didn't want Sid's name to crop up in conversation."

Sidney moved, but not toward us; he stumbled about on his heel and made for the exit door.

"Say hello to Ben for me," whispered Miss Brady, then she too was gone.

"I'm beginning to be glad Ben didn't marry her." Magdalene sat back down and smoothed her skirt over her knees. "Shush. I think my boy's performance is about to begin." Out came her rosary. The last of the seats filled up and Bunty squeezed into the row in front of us.

Music flooded the room, golden, effervescent, like sunlight. At the piano in front of the stage was Gladys Thorn. Her dress had baggy silk sleeves, turning her arms into great moths, darting, floating. The curtains were opening. I tensed. The inexplicable behaviour of Miss Brady and Sidney was forgotten. Magdalene and I hitched our chairs close together, hands brushing as we placed them on our laps. Behold a narrow hospital-green kitchen. Behold Ben (my hand inched up in a wave), television handsome, behind a table lined with all the makings of a stew, his backdrop a surgical-steel cooker and sink.

"Good afternoon, ladies and gentlemen." Since last I had seen him, he had acquired a trace of a French accent.

Magdalene kept whispering to herself. "Shoulders back, son. Talk up, and don't lick your fingers."

Millicent Parsnip stepped out of the wings, a small piece of paper held out in front of her. Beaming, she read from her notes.

"Dear friends, it is a pleasure and a privilege to have with us today Mr. Bentley Haskell. His theme is Cooking Under Pressure." Mrs. Parsnip's laugh got only one echo from the audience. Ben stood with a receiving smile on his lips. Miss Parsnip skipped page two of the notes. "And so, without any more ado, on with the show!" A round of perfunctory applause as, plaid skirt twitching, she exited. I bit down on my thumbs.

Ben held up a piece of meat shaped like Australia. "A stew by any other name is . . . a ragout." The meat sailed up in the air. He caught it with one hand and began squirting with lemon and peppering away. "The integrity of this recipe is dependent upon a refusal to allow the beef to dominate the vegetables." I stopped listening. Hands shot up throughout the hall. I sat up tall in my chair. My husband had his audience in the palm of his hand.

"Yes?" He arched a black brow, tossed a dollop of butter in the pressure cooker and set it to sizzle on the burner.

"Aren't you going to coat the meat with flour?" demanded a voice belonging to the hand in the front row.

"No." Ben blew out the word and slashed into an onion.

I sank down in my chair until my head was level with Magdalene's. Would it be cheeky to ask if she had another rosary? The show went on, fired by commentary from the audience and rebuttal by the star. Ben was locking the pressure cooker handle, explaining he would now prepare a couple of loaves of hurry-up bread, along with a cinnamon custard. I was thinking, we're on the home straight now, when it happened. A monumental bang.

My immediate reaction was that the room had exploded, but as steam fogged the kitchen, I knew. The pressure cooker had blown up. Ben! The audience was in a shambles, screaming, knocking over chairs. A voice from the kitchen bellowed, "Stay back! Everyone stay back!" The green accordion curtains swished shut. Magdalene was dragging me down as I dragged her up. I could see her mouth opening, but her screams, like mine, were lost in the hubbub. My hand tightened on hers, the rosary beads knotted between us.

A great weight came down on my shoulder. I wrenched my neck round to see Mrs. Bottomly, her face cracked in two by a consoling smile. "Relax, Mrs. Haskell, Dr. Bordeaux is with your husband now; so fortuitous that he happened to be here. He will take Mr. Haskell down to the nursing home in his car, and if necessary, keep him overnight."

Her eyes were sending me a secret message. I felt myself falling into nothingness. I didn't understand, and yet I knew what was happening. I must get to Ben! Once that was accomplished, I could fight the doctor off with a carving knife. Magdalene was on her feet. "No one will stop me seeing my son. Didn't I almost die three times giving him birth?" We were surrounded by a wall of concerned faces. My hands clenched into fists, but I thought better of punching my way out. I stood a better chance of making it if I ducked down and crawled. I was half up, half down, when I saw the hall's entry door fling open, saw a man's trousered legs, and a swatch of raincoat.

"Sorry to break things up, guys and dolls, but I'm from the police!" a deep voice grated. The circle crumbled. I clung to Magdalene's hand. Later, I would experience exuberance, incredulity—right now, nothing mattered but reaching Ben. I yanked my mother-in-law past dozens of disappointed eyes. A husband, my husband, was about to be snatched from the jaws of death—otherwise known as The Widows Club. Whatever the explosion had done to Ben, I would put him back together—or love him the way he was. A sob of relief, he wasn't in pieces! I could see my darling lying half on, half off, a metal serving cart. Dr. Bordeaux stood nearby, his fingers steepled out from his chest.

"Mrs. Bentley Haskell." The man in the raincoat cut a path through the crowd. He wore a hat with the brim pulled low and had greasy black sideburns. "I've been sent to fetch you down to the station to answer a couple more questions about the murder." He reached into an upper pocket, flashed a leatherbound square of cardboard and intoned, "Homicide. We'd like you to bring your mother-in-law with you"—he tucked the folder away—"to make things a bit more comfortable for you."

I didn't ask how he knew I had a mother-in-law and that

Magdalene was she. He had a bulge in his raincoat pocket that looked like it could be a gun, and his teeth were rotten. I played along.

"We'll . . . we'll have to take my husband home first. He's had a cooking accident." I moved in with agonising nonchalance to the serving cart and reached for Ben's hand. Thank heavens, it felt alive. Was that funny smell chloroform?

Dr. Bordeaux's voice chilled the back of my neck. "No need for that, Mrs. Haskell. You go along with the policeman and I will take—"

"Oh, no, you won't," snapped Magdalene, "because I won't budge from here without my son!"

The Raincoat Man swaggered toward me, hand in his pocket. "You'd best get your husband rolling, Mrs. Haskell. As for you, Doc, I'd start giving first aid to some of the others here."

Butler! It had to be he, playing his part brilliantly. I had to crush down my elation, to prevent it bubbling out of my throat in hysterical laughter.

"Excuse me." I addressed Mrs. Bottomly's chins, my hands gripping the handle of the cart. "Coming, Magdalene?" The horrid faces of these women! Mrs. Parsnip backed away from me, her eyes immobile.

"Sorry everything went so wrong," I babbled, thinking it prudent to pretend a kind of normalcy, but the possible interpretations of my words abruptly sobered me.

The menace in the hall had been so strong that I had been afraid that of itself it might prevent our leaving; once outside, I clung to Ben's hand, trembling. We stood on the gravel path, the elms casting green shadows over our faces. A bee buzzed close to my ear. "What now?" I asked.

The Raincoat Man withdrew his hand from his pocket and with it a gun. He rubbed the barrel against the bridge of his nose, then pressed it against the base of my throat. "We take your car, sweetheart, and we drive away from the village."

"So we aren't going to the police station?" Magdalene pulled her hat down over her ears.

"Not within a mile." He drew the gun back a few inches. The rotten teeth were very much in evidence. "Sorry, old woman, but you don't get to drive down busy streets and toss a shoe out the window with a message inside."

Something was seriously wrong with his speech. Not a

wink, not a word that he was Butler. Ben made a grunting noise and his arm lolled off the cart. I prayed he wouldn't wake up. This rescue was deteriorating with every step. Silently, Magdalene got into the back seat of the Heinz. The Raincoat Man watched with a sardonic smirk as I manoeuvered Ben, by means of a modified fireman's carry, alongside her.

"Well, Reggie Patterson," my mother-in-law snipped. "I must say this is a lot better than knowing you were out there somewhere, watching. You nasty boy. And don't go taking on airs thinking I'm frightened. What, me frightened of anyone as stupid as you? I remember well when you used to come and collect your father's rents. It was said up and down the street that all his money couldn't do for you what nature hadn't. You're stupid and a coward!"

"No, I ain't."

Magdalene's lips ruched into a smile. "Those that were short on the rent put their dogs out the minute they saw you coming—even Mrs. Rose with her Pekingese. And those who didn't have dogs had their kiddies bow-wow at the window. My Ben"—she looked lovingly at the dark head on her lap—"he used to feel he'd missed out because we weren't on your rent books and he didn't get to send you scampering with your tail between your legs."

"Yeah," came a snicker. "Benny boy stopped laughing, didn't he, when I shut him in the tater bin?"

The gun muzzle rested chill against my neck as I slid into the driver's seat. The Raincoat Man was the son of the wicked landlord of Crown Street and Magdalene was being kidnapped, with Ben and myself going along for the ride. The Raincoat Man got into the passenger seat.

"Move it, sister."

Please, Heinz, I prayed, do what you do best: stall.

While I fumbled with the key, Magdalene spoke. "I'd like to know, Reggie, why you never showed after luring me to the churchyard at dead of night?" She gave a sarcastic little laugh. "Did something better turn up?"

The damn motor throbbed to life.

Reggie pulled the brim of his hat low over his mean little eyes and stuck a home-rolled cigarette between his lips. "I dunno what the bleedin' hell you're talking about, which is because you's trying to confuse me. But it ain't gonna work." He twisted around and tapped ash in Magdalene's general vicinity. "I tell you I ain't stupid. Me dad's gonna get *that* through his skull when I pull this baby off." He tapped his chest with the gun.

We were through the churchyard gates, the stupid Heinz purring along as if newly minted from the factory. The breeze kept blowing my hair in my eyes. "Dad was all for putting the squeeze on old man Haskell when we got the chance to sell out all them scum-bag houses on Crown Street for a dozen times what they was worth. Some blokes wanted to tear them down and build a shopping arcade, but it was all nixed because that lousy little Shylock you're married to wouldn't part with his shop. The trouble with Dad is he don't think *big*. He made a couple of threatening phone calls and then got the wind up his pants when your coloured shop assistant rung back and told him, in that plummy voice of his—just like he was spouting poetry, to pack it in. Dad carried on like he'd been fixed with the evil eye."

Reggie shoved the cigarette to one side of his mouth and spat out the window. "Me, I was all for torching the shop but Dad said if I did, we was through. The arcade boys would smell a rat and call the whole deal off. It was me, the numbskull, who could see what he couldn't, that it didn't do no good threatening old man Haskell himself. The way to get to him was through his old lady. So I starts hanging about, watching you, letting him know that if he didn't sign on the dotted line his missus was like to disappear."

I stared straight ahead. "She disappeared all right, but at Mr. Haskell's instigation. You dithered too long, Mr. Patterson. My guess is that for all your brave talk, you were afraid of Paris, the Magnificent, afraid that he might step on you and not notice."

"No, I ain't." Reggie's eyes disappeared between lashless folds. "And I ain't afraid of no dogs." A scowl slid over his face like slime. "I just don't like the way they bark and set up the alarm. And in that buggering big house of yours, someone could creep up behind me and I'd have wasted me time."

I felt better but I was worried about Ben. I had to stay alive. I must take care of him. Keep Reggie talking. Try to get him to see the futility of his schemes. We were approaching The Aviary; there was the low buff wall, the gate, and the arthritic tree with its crippled branches supporting a huge bird's nest. But no sign of Mr. Digby.

"I suppose," I said to Reggie, "your plan is to detain us

until my father-in-law agrees to sell his shop to you and your father. But where does that really get you? The minute we are free he can cancel the agreement and stroll down to the police station."

Reggie turned a blackened smile on me. "No, he won't. Not if he's given his bleedin' word not to. Ain't it known from Crown Street to Buckingham Palace"—he flicked more ash at Magdalene—"that old man Haskell never breaks his word, not even if it breaks his heart?"

We were coming to a stretch of road I hadn't travelled before. The lighthouse rose up from a serene sea, the wind dropped. What better place to keep us prisoner than in a disused lighthouse? "Magdalene," I said brightly, "how long have you known, fully, what was going on?"

She sighed. "I suppose I'm not as quick as some. When I first came down here and saw Sid, I wondered if he might be the one, out to even some old grudge. I didn't figure out the truth until the night of the party at the restaurant. I don't suppose you remember, Giselle, but I was looking out the window, and I saw Reggie across the road under a streetlight, staring his weasel stare, and suddenly all was made plain."

The Raincoat Man tossed his cigarette overboard and scratched at his greasy sideburns with the muzzle of his gun. "I was halfway up the stairs of the bloody restaurant when two waiters chucked me out, the sods, otherwise I would have nabbed you that night."

"You wouldn't," snapped Magdalene. "I had my watchdog with me." She tapped me on the shoulder and Heinz's bumpers grazed against a jut of rock in rounding a curve. "Giselle, I know you won't understand why I didn't tell Eli how I'd finally seen through his pretense of being keen on Mrs. Jarrod. But after him being so strong and splendid in driving me away to the safety of the convent, I wanted him to go on thinking he'd spared me."

"I do understand completely," I said.

"What I don't understand is how I could have been so simple as to believe that he and Mrs. Jarrod were . . . you know."

"You mean because she was taller than he?"

"That, and Eli doesn't like pickled herring."

"What is this?" sneered the Raincoat Man. "Schoolgirl confessions?"

We ignored him. Magdalene sighed. "Just to make sure I wasn't going peculiar in my old age, I wrote to Paris and asked him to tell me, was I right—was I wrong? I got a letter back saying that Eli had decided to face up to the inevitable. Sometime this idiot was bound to get up his courage and kidnap me. So, best to get it all over and done with. Eli would pay the ransom, get me back, and then go to the police. They couldn't talk about idle threats then, could they?"

"Yeah! Well, the brain here outthought your old man."

I took another curve. The letter that, according to Roxie, had come for Magdalene from abroad must have been the one from Paris. Ben started to snore, which comforted me; the sound was noisily healthy. The same could not be said of Heinz's emanations.

Reggie's hateful currant eyes turned toward me. His dirty fingernails grabbed at my sleeve. "Why are you slowing down?"

"I have the thing floored," I pacified. The purr was still nice and even, but sleepy. We were coming to an elbow of land directly in line with the lighthouse. The Heinz slid a few more yards, then stopped. I gripped the steering wheel. "Sorry, Reggie, this is as far as we go. Something must have died."

"Something is going to die, sister, if you don't think again." His voice came silky quiet as his fingers closed around my knot of hair.

"You wouldn't kill us. You'd lose your bargaining edge."

"I could kill one of you."

"And then the arcade boys might decide not to do business with you." A gull winged it overhead. The scent of hawthorn on the grassy incline to our left and the distant swish of the waves made the place cruelly peaceful.

"Giselle, far be it from me to interfere," came Magdalene's plaintive voice, "but I think, for the sake of my son, you might start the car."

"Spoken like a first-rate mum." Reggie licked his scaly lips. "Benny boy mightn't love his wifey anymore if her nose came out the back of her head."

I explained and continued to explain until the message sank in that the car, not I, was the one playing games. Reggie sat picking his teeth and thinking, something clearly at which he wasn't too handy. At last he snarled, "You two out. Benny stays where he is."

To be preyed upon by wild dogs and the elements? Now

I had to stall. "What are we supposed to do—thumb a lift?" The last words came out in jerks. I was half out of the car. Reggie and Magdalene were already in the road and I was hearing the loveliest sound on God's earth. And, what was more, a sound that was endearingly familiar. Creeping toward us was the hearse. I recognized Butler, who was driving, but the other two occupants were strangers. Both wore leather riding helmets and goggles, but then I saw a flutter of lavender shawl and a beaded carpet bag being flagged out the window. Spitting fury, Reggie waved the hearse on. Perhaps he had forgotten the gun in his hand.

The hearse stopped. Nipping out of the vehicle, Butler glided around to open the other door, but Primrose was already trotting toward us, the ends of her shawl blowing in the breeze. "Ellie, my dear! Hyacinth and I are out on a scenic drive. How very pleasant encountering you! Surely this must be your mother-in-law, of whom we have heard *so* much. Have you also stopped to admire the view?" Primrose peered into the Heinz. "Why, poor Mr. Haskell! Carsick I see." Deliberately, she looked at Reggie and the gun. "Young man, were you never told it is rude to point?"

Snickering, Reggie chucked Primrose playfully under the chin with the gun. "Hey, old girl, was you born when brains was rationed?" He sucked in a fetid breath. "You got a choice. Get back in the death wagon with the other ugly sister, or come for a little walk and spend a naughty weekend with me. Only it won't be just the two of us, sweetheart, I'll have me other prisoners along."

Butler amazed me. He stood immobile in front of the hearse, his eyes fixed on the puffy little clouds, his expression one of mild amusement. It was Hyacinth in a Sherlock Holmes cape who now whapped past Magdalene, me, and Ben, still mercifully prone and oblivious in the back seat.

"How dare you!" She swept her sister aside and fixed her goggles on Reggie. "How *dare* you address my sister as sweetheart! I demand satisfaction, sir! And choice of weapons."

Her arm swung out in an arc, her hand cracked Reggie on the chops, her elbow caught the gun, sending it spinning over the cliff edge. It was probably imagination overload, but I swore I heard a small gulp from the sea.

* * * *

From the Files of The Widows Club

Saturday, 16th May

The Whist and Crocheting Groups both cancelled meetings on the evening of the above date, on account of several members not feeling up to light-hearted socialising as a result of the immensely disappointing cookery demonstration in the church hall. When it next meets, the Board will consider whether to withdraw our annual contribution to the Policeman's Benevolent Fund. It will also discuss whether the club feels it would be immoral to serve the recipe provided by Mr. Bentley Haskell at the Midsummer Potluck.

Also to be discussed at the next Board Meeting—1st June—is the matter of membership badges lost or misplaced by owners. Suggestions for penalties for this infraction will be voiced. In the past, offenders have been banned from participating in trips for a three-month period, but with the rising cost of badges, it is felt that this censure is insufficient.

23

"I always hoped I would get to meet the Raincoat Man." Primrose pushed her goggles up on her forehead as, with cowardice aforethought, Reggie decided against taking on four women bare-handed. Away he went, slithering over brambles and boulders to the flat land above the road, hurling down stones and threats.

"I ain't done for! I'll be back!"

"I shall pray for you," Magdalene called after him triumphantly. I would have cheered for her if my throat hadn't squeezed shut.

Butler coughed deferentially. "A very small world this is, madams. That cove . . . person is none other than Reggie Patterson; he and I were partners once upon a time in a pickpocketing h'enterprise."

"Really, Butler, you should be ashamed," reproved Hyacinth.

"Agreed, madam. I should have known better than to work with someone so incompetent." Butler flexed his fingers. "I'll see to your car, Mrs. Haskell. There's nothing I can't start, not h'even if the motor's missing."

"Where the hell am I?" came a drowsy growl from the back seat. It began to rain, a few drops at first, then a gauzy blur, like curtains blowing at the window. The Tramwells were talking to Magdalene, their exclamations of concern laced with professional excitement. Finally, the full horror of the afternoon's events clobbered me. I took Ben's hand, glad he couldn't see my face clearly. "We're on our way home, darling. There was a little accident with the pressure cooker."

Strangely, he looked more pleased than not. "Really! Well, you know what I think of those things. I've been having the most awful dreams, fraught with menace. I dreamed I was dying."

"You'll live," I promised fervently.

I was alone in the drawing room. Magdalene had led the Tramwells to the bathroom so they could freshen up. Butler was in the kitchen. And Poppa was with his son. Ben had insisted he was fine. His face and hands were only slightly reddened and sore from the steam, and his headache was negligible. Poppa had gone the colour of putty when he learned about the pressure cooker, and although he quickly rallied, saying that a mishap of that nature was preferable to rotten eggs being thrown by the audience, it wasn't hard to persuade him to take a little rest himself and keep his son company.

The women were back.

"Yes, Giselle does have everything nice and clean; my son won't have it any other way." As I got up from the sofa, Magdalene paused behind me and whispered, "These are your friends and this is your house, but you won't encourage them to stay long, will you?"

Both sisters heard, but gave no sign of taking offence. As we settled ourselves, Butler entered with a loaded tea tray.

"I can highly recommend the cherry cake," he informed the Tramwells. "Should anything further be required, kindly knock on the wall with the poker—this h'establishment lacks a bell."

As he padded from the room, Hyacinth adjusted her chair and drew out the familiar green notebook. "Where"—she flexed an orange-lipped smile—"do we begin?"

I handed out cups of tea. "Magdalene, the Misses Tramwell are private detectives. I want you to tell them about the Pattersons, after which they will have something to tell you."

Abigail watched from her portrait.

"My dear Ellie." Primrose clinked her teaspoon into her saucer. "Naturally, Flowers Detection will be delighted to do everything possible to assist Mrs. Elijah Haskell against the forces of evil; indeed, we regret that more pressing matters placed the Raincoat Man low on Butler's job list. As for . . ." she floundered, "I am not sure it is wise to discuss a certain organisation . . ."

"It isn't only wise, it's morally right," I said firmly. "Ben is Magdalene's only child and she nearly died three times having him. Besides which, I think she may unknowingly have the answers to some questions of mine."

"I don't know about that." On the edge of the seat, her feet tight together, Magdalene tugged at her cardigan. "And before I say anything about the Pattersons' persecution of Eli and me"—her eyes nipped from one sister to the other—"I do need to know if you charge by the hour. Otherwise I won't know whether to talk at a run or a walk."

Butler replenished the teapot twice during Magdalene's story. The Tramwells commented and exclaimed. They expressed sympathy and a willingness to assist, but I knew that their curiosity having been appeased, they were anxious to discuss Ben's close call.

"Magdalene," I said, moving to the edge of my seat so I could catch her if she swayed, "you face a very difficult problem. In fact, you face two. What happened to Ben at the church hall was no accident. It was a vicious attempt on his life."

Her screech brought an I-told-you-so look to Primrose's face. Out came the smelling salt bottle and at the close of the next minute Magdalene had a lavendar shawl around her shoulders, properly set for her hour of suffering. Throughout the horrible disclosures which followed, she resorted to the smelling salt frequently and was so silent I was afraid shock might have affected her vocal cords.

I took over the story from the Tramwells at the point where they entered Delacorte's to find me crouched over Ann's body.

"When I retrieved that note to Felicity Friend from Ann's bag and consumed it, I foolishly believed my involvement had ended. Admittedly, I felt a momentary alarm when I read a confidential in her column to Heartbroken, but I was confident it was a coincidence."

Magdalene's eyes closed. Was she praying for strength to forgive me?

"Completely understandable, my dear." Primrose's small papery hand closed over mine. "Your mind rebelled at the possibility of the unbearable. But it is apparent that the late Mrs. Delacorte had discussed with The Founder your avowed interest in joining the widows. What amazes me," she said with a tiny sigh, "is that anyone whom Mrs. Delacorte put up for membership should be accepted as a viable candidate. One must assume that your being known to The Founder stood you in good stead."

Hyacinth took up from Primrose. "We were duplicitous in saying that we were out on a scenic drive this afternoon. The confidential you mentioned, Ellie, did not escape our notice." Her voice was grave. "We, too, hoped it was a coincidence, but Flowers Detection leaves nothing to chance. Perceiving the grim possibilities of the cookery demonstration, we parked at the side of the hall in readiness for a quick getaway and, when everyone had gone inside, moved to stand outside the main entrance, where we could hear what was going on without our presence disturbing you, Ellie. I had brought along my grandfather's duelling pistol"—she patted the carpetbag—"and when the commotion commenced, we were about to charge to the rescue when the Raincoat Man burst around from the other side of the hall, barged against us without so much as an apology and went inside."

"An unsettling moment." Primrose crumbled her cake. "But after overhearing what he had to say, we thought it best to protect our cover and let him make the rescue. One does, at times, have to practise a professional detachment." Her face puckered. "I do hope you understand, Ellie?"

I took a slice—two slices, actually—of cake. "What I understand is that someone unknown fiddled with the pressure cooker valve and from behind the screen of steam a chloroforming hand was pressed against poor Ben's face." I stopped. Magdalene was crumpling. However, before I could touch her, she straightened, lips so compressed they disappeared. I continued, keeping a watchful eye on her. "And then came that awful Dr. Bordeaux. What sort of accident, I wonder, would have befallen Ben at The Peerless?"

"One can only surmise, of course, but one suspects he would have been sent spiralling down the stairs onto the marble floor or got tossed out of a window."

I reached out and took Magdalene's cold hand.

"Oh dear, yes." Primrose brushed cake crumbs from her fingers. "There would have been a distraught nurse sobbing into her starched handkerchief at the inquest, saying she had only left the patient for a moment, and when she got back, he was gone. He must have become disoriented waking up in a strange place and . . . thank you, Butler, I *will* have a ginger biscuit . . . . I doubt she would have been sufficiently composed to go on."

"But why? Why did it happen? Why did Ben get put on the widows' hit list? Ann said there were four stages to the application process. First, the heartbreak letter to Dear Felicity Friend; second, a telephone contact asking if you want your husband murdered"—Magdalene was going over the side of her chair again. Butler realigned her and I rushed on—"third, the confidential item in Dear Felicity's column delivering the message, *your application is approved*. Fourth, the initiation fee. But I was never contacted by phone, meaning Ben should have been safe."

The Tramwells weren't looking at me. They were staring at Magdalene, who sat there like a broken-winged sparrow. Somewhere in the house Sweetie howled.

"The voice didn't say 'Do you want your husband murdered?' " The movement of her lips made the rest of Magdalene seem abnormally still. "It said, 'Do you ever dream of having your husband murdered?' I thought it was Reggie trying to lure me out of the house in the middle of the night. I was told to bring money or jewelry and a signed note saying it was blood money and hide them in a statue in the churchyard."

"The dues." Hyacinth's earrings bobbed as she wrote.

Magdalene kept staring straight ahead. "I didn't know what to do. If I notified the police, they might capture Reggie in the churchyard, but what if he started shooting? How could I guess the voice was talking about murdering my son? Giselle hadn't thought to confide in me. His own mother the last to know! I still can't believe it. When I picked up the phone, the voice asked for Mrs. Eli Haskell . . ." Her voice wound down, and she stared at me. "Oh, I think I see . . . Mrs. Ellie . . ."

It was exactly the sort of bungle I might have made. Butler pressed a glass of brandy into Magdalene's limp hand. "I must be going senile," she sighed. "First the wrong convent and now this. I . . . I signed that note Mrs. E. Haskell." She reached into her cardigan pocket for a handkerchief.

"Nonsense." Hyacinth eyed her imperiously. "You—a woman stalked by an unscrupulous villain—pick up the phone to hear the word murder. What could you be expected to think? And to all proper-thinking people, Mrs. Ellie Haskell is an error of address, but"—a mild shudder—"*these* people don't think like us."

Magdalene held her nose and downed her brandy. "I have to blame myself. Perhaps if I hadn't come here, been such a burden, none of this would have happened." She set down her glass and squared her shoulders. "I have something to confess to you, Giselle, and, later, to Father Padinsky. I don't have any jewelry other than my wedding ring, so I took . . . stole your engagement ring. Naturally, I don't expect you ever to understand. . . ."

I stood and glared down at her. "Will you stop with this nonsense! That was a ring well spent if it saved Poppa's life, or if you thought it would. Now, can we stop talking about trivia, please, and decide how we are going to keep Ben from being murdered!"

Her eyes spun. When she revived, they gleamed with determination. Primrose signalled for Butler to fetch more brandy.

"My dear Magdalene, if I may so presume to address you, I do hope you do not think Flowers Detection is minimizing your personal plight, but kidnapping, whilst most annoying, is scarcely as onerous as murder."

"It would take a very selfish mother to put her own safety ahead of that of her son, and I am sure Giselle would not intentionally have given you such a view of me." Magdalene, hair wisping around her set face, was back in form. Primrose and Hyacinth made admiring noises.

Despair had me by the fetlock again. I stood up, drew the curtains against the gathering of evening, and spied a protrusion of tail over the edge of the bookcase. Reaching for Tobias, I buried my hands in his fur. Eyes on Abigail's portrait, I said, "It is clear to me what must be done to unmask The Founder and I am entirely prepared to face the risks involved. But in the meantime, how do we keep Ben safe? The widows won't fold up their weapons and go away. Remember Vernon Daffy? They tried and tried again until the third time was the charm."

Magdalene sat on the rim of her chair. "Far be it from me to interfere, Giselle, but if you insist . . . Why not phone up one of these wicked women and say, being careful not to give offence, that you've changed your mind. Say that Ben—oh, it breaks a mother's heart to think of the horrid things being said about him—has changed his ways, thrown Frederick over, so you've decided to keep him."

Primrose shook her silvery head. "I seriously doubt that backing out would be permitted at this stage. The risks to the club would be too great." She turned to me. "Indeed, Ellie, Ben must be hidden until all is safe once more. What a pity, Hyacinth"—she dimpled at her sister—"that we are not at Cloisters; the priest hole would be perfect."

Abigail's eyes smiled serenely down at me. "No more perfect than a dungeon." The Tramwells looked a little envious as I explained.

"I think we should explore the dungeons as soon as possible." Hyacinth rapped with her pen on the green notebook. "But first, Ellie, let us make sure we understand your plan."

Magdalene lowered her head onto her hands. "This will be Purgatory for my dear boy with his claustrophobia."

I couldn't answer her. My throat felt like straw. In attempting to save Ben's life, I knew I stood to lose him. Could he ever forgive me for this? If only I had talked to him, but the time for talking had been lost somewhere along the way.

"My plan is what you, Hyacinth and Primrose, hoped for all along." I let Tobias slide out of my hands. "Ann showed us the way. Can any of us doubt she got herself killed because she committed the unforgivable sin of asking The Founder to murder Bunty Wiseman so that she could make a play for Lionel? Therefore I must make a similar request. But what man shall I say I want at any cost, and what female stands in need of being removed from my path?"

Primrose watched me solicitously. "If Bentley hadn't been so charming, you and that handsome vicar would certainly have made a splendid couple."

"Rowland really isn't my type." I was remembering with a bitter pang that moment of emotional infidelity at Abigail's. "But—yes, I will telephone Mrs. Bottomly (I suspect from something Ann said that she is the president) and say that Ben has left me and ask her to put before The Founder my request that my cousin Vanessa be removed because she would make a terrible vicar's wife and I wouldn't."

"Oh delightful!" Primrose leaned back in her chair with a

contented sigh. "This should bring the same swift retribution meted out to Mrs. Delacorte."

Hyacinth folded up the green notebook. "The vicar is on holiday, but I see no reason to inform him on this matter. As I see it, the danger to Vanessa is nonexistent, but I suppose it would be courteous to inform her that her name is being used in this matter; an ideal time, perhaps, for her to leave the country." Hyacinth looked at me.

"At my expense, naturally."

"As for Ben's whereabouts, I believe that Flowers Detection can supply a credible fabrication to be put into circulation. We have in the course of our research discovered something interestingly unpleasant about Mr. Sidney Fowler." Hyacinth's lips formed a complacent crescent. "He is a bigamist."

Magdalene winced. "This will kill his mother. How . . . how many wives?"

"A lot," Primrose answered. "But, to give credit where credit is due, it would seem he came down to this obscure village and made a valiant attempt to fight his beastly urges. But Bentley"—she raised a finger at me—"all unwittingly, asked him to be best man at your wedding, Ellie, and at the sight of orange blossoms and bridal cake, old temptations must have flooded back. Mr. Fowler thirsted for the excitement of being once again a bridegroom. He put an advertisement in *The Daily Spokesman*. Perhaps none of his customers appealed or he didn't believe in mixing business with pleasure."

This was interesting, but Ben and Poppa might come down any minute. To move things along I said, "Sid told me that he had put a personal in the paper and had received a response from someone who seemed a soulmate."

"He most certainly did." Hyacinth's black eyes gleamed. "He heard from wife number one, Angelica Brady."

"Never!" said Magdalene and I together.

"We fear so." Primrose fussed with her curls. "Again unwittingly, Bentley sent Miss Brady some copies of *The Daily Spokesman*, and in one of them was Mr. Fowler's appeal. We have spoken to her and she likened the effect upon her to being drawn by an invisible cord. However, being a woman of the world, she did exercise some caution. She insisted that they hold to a use of code names and continue addressing their correspondence to post office boxes. Fear of disillusionment kept her from setting a first meeting, but with the cookery demonstration so apropos, it was arranged that they should each come to the church hall wearing a red rose." Primrose sank back in her chair, in breathless need of the fresh cup of tea Butler promptly handed her.

"And one or both of them told you all this as they rushed from the hall?" I didn't mean to sound biting, but how did Sidney's plight help Ben?

Hyacinth surveyed me. "Miss Brady put up at the Pebblewell Hotel last night and we engaged her in conversation; quite easily done—young people find it difficult to make a getaway when the elderly are persistent. And Miss Brady is a singularly sweet person. She confessed to us all about her early marriage and her acute distress upon discovering that her husband was leading not a double, but a quadruple life."

"No way round it, this will kill Sidney's mother." Magdalene was looking a little more perky. "Although there'll be those that'll say she brought it on herself, letting him get his own tea when he was little."

Hyacinth replaced the green book in the carpetbag. "When Miss Brady dashed out of the church hall this afternoon, she collided with us, babbling that her *amour de plume* was none other than her bigamist husband, Sidney. Scarcely had she fled between the gravestones when Mr. Fowler cannoned into us, babbling that he was going to grab a boat and head for France."

"We don't want to seem dim-witted . . ." Magdalene and I said as one.

Primrose gave a dimpling laugh. "My dears, Sidney disappears and Bentley disappears. Can you believe it won't be said that they have gone off together, to the chagrin of cousin Frederick?"

The sisters stood up. "Perfect, don't you think?" one of them said.

I could see a couple of flaws in the plan. Ben didn't deserve this. And what if Sidney was something worse than a bigamist? But there were bound to be holes in any other ideas produced. I looked at the clock on the mantel. Ben and Poppa had been upstairs for nearly an hour. It was time to explore the dungeons.

The Tramwells and I positioned ourselves on the spot next to Rufus. Magdalene, her face pinched, was assigned to twist the bannister rung, Butler, to depress the alcove ledge and send us on our way. If either man left his bedroom while we were down below, Magdalene was to stall him.

On our marks. The floor dropped away and my insides leapt into my throat. No sound from the sisters. Had they died of fright? A shuttering sound overhead. Then nothing but sooty blackness sucking us down . . . and down. . . . A light burst on, splintering the dark into hundreds of stars, and once again there was solid ground under our feet. Either by error or design, Primrose's hand had found the light switch. Was Abigail the one who installed electricity down here? I wished someone had installed an automatic air freshener.

"That was quite delightful." Primrose smoothed her curls and took a step toward Hyacinth, who had proceeded through a gothic arch and down some shallow steps into the main stone chamber lined with cells, the kind whence the sheriff was forever tossing Robin Hood. Each had a tiny grill in its door, enabling the prisoner to look out upon the focal point of the room—the rack. On closer inspection, this proved to be a reproduction. The walls weren't dripping and the chill was not unbearable. But the fustiness of the place lacked only the smell of hopelessness and fear. Hyacinth had one of the cell doors open and was urging Primrose and myself to come in and enjoy a peek.

Primitive but not punitive. I saw a narrow bed covered with a grey blanket riddled with moth holes, a stick table, and chair. Ideal sleeping quarters for guests who might otherwise have outstayed their welcome. Had such been Wilfred Grantham's thinking? We looked into several other cells. A few had the same narrow beds, others were empty, but one contained two beds pushed together. A grimy crystal vase stood on a handsome smoker's chest . . . exactly what I had been wanting for the study. The cell next to it had been fitted with all the accoutrements of a late nineteenth-century bathroom, including an oak-encased water closet. Hyacinth had out the green notebook and was murmuring to herself as she scribbled. "Pillow, sheets, blankets, electric kettle, tinned foods, fizzy drink, books, gallons and gallons of water."

"Ellie"—Primrose squeezed my shoulder—"I feel quite sanguine that Ben can be comfortable here."

Comfortable! My professional instincts might have been the teensiest bit inflamed by the romantic possibilities of the place, but Ben's claustrophobia would soon have him clawing the walls.

Hyacinth was looking upward. "No prison could be more secure. Not even the smallest window, only those pencil-like apertures close to the ceiling, which has to be fifteen feet up." She grasped my elbow and propelled me to the exit. "Let us depart, confident that your dear husband has no chance of escape."

It was going to work. A man at the complete mercy of his maniac wife.

Magdalene mashed into us as we stepped into the hall. "Someone is at the front door and I didn't want to let whoever it is in, not with you still down there." The floor slid into place. Butler penguined to the door and in swept Vanessa, all fox fur and gorgeous. What could be more propitious. Was fate beginning to smile?

"Ellie, darling! My, you look surprised! But when I phoned, I understood I would be welcome." She peeled off a glove and swirled it around. "Oh, I see you have other guests, but"—she dismissed the Tramwells and Magdalene—"surely they can entertain themselves while you and I talk about Rowland." Her eyes welled with tears, which may have been artificial but were nonetheless dazzling. "I want him, Ellie, and it is driving me insane that I can't buy him the way I bought this coat or . . . the way you bought Ben. So you—my only wholesome acquaintance—are going to have to advise me how I can sluff on the sort of attributes that will make me irresistible to him."

"You might," I said, "start with doing me a favour, one that should cost you little and gain you a trip anywhere you wish to go and save many lives."

"What kind of lives?"

"Male."

"Well, in that case"—she tapped me on the cheek with her glove—"*how* can I refuse! Especially when it puts you right where I want you—in my debt."

Somehow, I got through the rest of the evening. Ben and Poppa came downstairs seconds after Vanessa went out the front door. Butler made himself scarce. I discovered later he had gone to fetch the Tramwells' overnight bags. The sisters made rustling noises to the effect that they must be leaving. But Magdalene and I urged them to stay for dinner. The more voices, the more faces, the more hers and mine could get lost in the crowd. Ben was in excellent spirits. He was convinced the Hearthside Guild would never ask him to demonstrate again. His headache was gone, his burns superficial, and his hand kept touching my thigh under the table. Does chloroform have aphrodisiac aftereffects? Between dessert and coffee he came up with an excuse to lure me into the kitchen.

"Your friends are charmingly odd"—he drew me into his arms—"but let's not encourage them to stay late. I'd like an early night. And perhaps we can take a bottle of champagne up with us to celebrate being alive."

I dreaded going to bed. How could I lie beside him, knowing that in the morning I would send him hurtling into darkness? How long would it take him in his panic to find the light switch? What if his hair turned white within hours?

"I . . . I don't know about the champagne, Ben. I think I am catching your headache."

"You poor darling. You had a rotten scare this afternoon, didn't you? And Mum seems a bit off, too. She's back to hardly talking to Poppa."

When we returned to the table, Primrose brought out her ornamental brandy flask and demurely asked the gentlemen if they would take a drop in their coffee. They accepted, and while I was wondering why the ladies were excluded, both men flopped forward, their noses landing in their cups.

"Just a very mild sleeping agent, made entirely from the gifts of Mother Nature," Primrose assured us.

"I think you have overstepped yourself this time." I glared at her over the top of Ben's head as I struggled to hoist him up.

"It does look that way, doesn't it, my dear, but how could we get the dungeons all nice and cosy for Bentley, if he or his father are liable to descend the stairs at any minute?"

"Miss Primrose Tramwell is absolutely right, Giselle," said Magdalene as Butler appeared and lifted up Eli like a rug.

"Which bedroom, Madam?"

Magdalene said she would show him; they were gone no more than five minutes, then it was Ben's turn.

"Giselle," came Magdalene's voice; I couldn't see her because my eyes were a bit messed up. "Giselle, I have prayed and reached a decision; Eli must go into the dungeon with Ben."

"Oh, yes!" I turned and hugged her so tightly I almost toppled us. "What a brilliant idea!"

* * * *

We were all soon engaged in a flurry of activity. Ann had been murdered with such alacrity that we hoped I would not be kept waiting above a couple of days, but we wanted to be sure we provided enough provisions for Ben and Eli's imprisonment. While Butler was making one of his bucket-of-water trips, I unearthed an electric frying pan. Ben had to be able to cook.

"And what of razors and soap?" whispered Primrose. "I always think bearded gentlemen rather winsome, but I believe their morale remains higher if they can shave. And"—she dropped her voice—"don't forget fresh unmentionables."

I selected several books which I thought Ben had not read, including the Edwin Digby novels that I had not returned to Roxie. I was about to make a descent with them when I noticed Hyacinth's green notebook lying on the table. An idea broke into my mind, and I found her in the kitchen.

"Hyacinth, this journal provides a detail-by-detail account of your investigation, isn't that so?"

"Correct; it is a useful tool and one which I hope may one day become part of Primrose's and my memoirs."

"Let me leave it in the dungeon for Ben to read. I am going to write him a letter, but—"

Hyacinth put down the biscuit tin she had been holding and pressed her hands over mine. "Absolutely! Flowers Detection cannot properly thank you for what you are doing, but anything we can do to make things easier is done."

At last everything was in readiness. Two of the beds had been stripped and made sleepworthy with fluffy rose blankets and fat pillows. Now it was a matter of waiting for morning. Butler at dawn did offer to carry the drugged men downstairs and put them in the dungeons, but I wasn't utterly hardened; I couldn't have those sleepyheads wake to find themselves imprisoned. I'm a hands-on type. As my mother used to say, if a dirty deed's worth doing, do it well. Magdalene and I left the Tramwells and Butler in the drawing room to go upstairs.

"Ben, wake up! I have something you must see! A big surprise!" I had no trouble gibbering. I did have some trouble getting him to dress before coming downstairs.

"Why can't I wear my dressing gown?" His hair was rumpled, his face flushed like a sleepy child's. I wound my arms around him, clinging long enough to almost lose my nerve.

"All will be explained later."

"Oh, all right. But if this isn't something ultra special, you won't be my favourite wife anymore." He shook his head. "Must have been out of it last night. Don't remember getting into bed."

Magdalene also had some problems with Poppa, this being the first time she had entered his bedroom at Merlin's Court; but the four of us arrived in the hall on the heels of each other.

"Very good, now you two stand over there," I ordered. "That's right, next to Rufus. Close your eyes, close your mouths, and don't move."

"What is this? You have some hidden cameras?" Poppa straightened his bald spot. Ben shrugged, then grinned and spread his hands. Magdalene twisted the bannister rung, I depressed the alcove ledge . . . and the earth swallowed them up. Cries of horror included.

"Now, my dears, I know this is extremely hard on both of you"—Primrose pried my hands away from my ears—"so, Ellie, the sooner you telephone Mrs. Bottomly and get the chess pieces set up, enabling The Founder to make a move to murder you, the better."

Hyacinth frowned at her, then said brightly to me: "Have no fear that we will let anything of a final nature happen to you, my dear. We will remain in the house with you day and night, always at the ready."

Primrose settled Magdalene in a chair. "Rest assured, the presence of two seemingly"—a smile—"frail old ladies won't do anything to scare off a determined assailant. Also, we are not big eaters and do all our own hand laundry."

"And I shall h'endeavour to be of assistance in every way possible, madam." Butler picked up the handkerchief that had fluttered from my mother-in-law's hands.

I would need friends during this waiting period and later —when I was alone in the world. Staring at the phone on the trestle table, I thought, damn it, I am being selfish. Every minute wasted is a minute longer that Ben and Poppa are trapped in that hole. As my hand reached for the receiver, the phone rang. It was Bunty asking how Ben was faring after the accident.

"Fine."

"What did the police have to say for themselves? Cripes, Ellie, wasn't that detective a slug!"

"What? . . . Oh, yes." Amazing to think that the Raincoat Man had become an appendix. "Bunty, I'm sorry but I'm a bit short on time." The sisters were signalling frantically to me.

"Hold your horses," sang Bunty. "Just wanted to let you know there's a Follies rehearsal on Monday morning at eleven o'clock. You must be there because we will concentrate on your cake scene. Ellie, you're breathing awfully funny. Is something wrong?"

I finally read the sisters' mouths. "I'm feeling . . . I don't know what I'm feeling." A sob filled my voice. "Ben has . . . left. It may only be . . . temporary, but I don't want to talk about it."

"Marvellous!" Hyacinth enthused as I hung up. "No better way to fan gossip than to refuse to discuss something." She then dialed Mrs. Bottomly's number when my fingers refused to do the job, and wrapped my fingers around the phone.

"Amelia?" My voice sounded diabolically casual. "This is Ellie Haskell."

"Oh, what a pleasure!" I heard an edge of uncertainty in her voice.

"Don't worry," I soothed. "I'm not ringing to complain about yesterday, but wasn't it infuriating—that detective barging in just as things were looking so serendipitous?"

Her gust of relief almost blew me over. "What a splendidly understanding girl you are. Tell me, what can I do for you?"

"You can cross Ben off your list of husbands-in-waiting, I'm afraid. He's spoiled everything by leaving me, never to return, so his note says. He's asked me to send his clothes to Alaska."

"Good gracious, how frustrating!" A tremendous vibration as Mrs. Bottomly plonked herself in a chair. "And to think we had it all set to have him go out with a bang!"

"Yes, but I have learned a lot from this miserable misalliance." I paused to get my breathing under control. "What I should have done was to marry Rowland Foxworth."

"Indeed you should, my dear!" Vast, sentimental sigh.

"And I still can, can't I?" My voice slid into a blend of petulance and hope. "The only problem is my cousin Vanessa. She seems to have got darling Rowland infatuated, but if she were out of the way permanently, as in—"

"Mrs. Haskell, I cannot listen to such nonsense!" The receiver vibrated in my hand. "You can't realise what you are saying!"

"Certainly I do. I want Vanessa done in. What's the big

deal? I've paid my dues, and I don't want a refund; all I want is my money's worth. If I don't get it, I may say some things to the police that—" But the line was dead. Mrs. Bottomly had hung up.

Now the hardcore waiting began. We all avoided the hall because of the sounds we imagined below. A bitter pill to swallow was when Freddy pushed open the garden door as if nothing had changed.

"What's wrong with this house?" He lounged against the door jamb. "The drawing room windows are locked up tight as a safe, and who are these people? Leftovers from a party?" He flicked his plait of hair toward Butler. "Don't I know him?"

"You are correct, sir." Butler held the frying pan aloft on his fingertips. "I did a stint as a waiter at Abigail's. Now if you'll h'excuse me, I don't 'ave time to converse. My ladies get h'indigestion if they don't eat breakfast at the appointed time."

Freddy's darting eyes reminded me of a ray gun. "Hey! What's going on here? Even the doggywog"—he bared his teeth at Sweetie—"looks like it would go spewing if I pushed its belly button. Where's Ben?"

The Tramwells' faces had tightened. My mother-in-law's lips moved in prayer. Butler stopped slicing bread and tested the knife blade against his finger, eyes on Freddy.

Arms and legs extended, my cousin's body formed an X in the doorway. "I heard tell the pressure cooker backfired at the demo," he mused, "but most of the chitchat at The Dark Horse last night was about Sidney pelting into his shop, shovelling the lolly out of the till and crying, 'So long, it's been good to know you.' I do hope I didn't drive old Sid into a flit." Freddy's body sagged. "I'd decided not to sue, and I keep telling myself there's bound to be a simpler explanation, like he killed Mrs. Delacorte and the police were closing in."

I had to get rid of Freddy. Picking up a stack of plates, I shuffled them. "Afraid I'm not going to ask you in because . . . Ben has gone away for a few days and I really"—one of the plates slipped—"want to be alone."

Freddy yanked at the heavy chains around his neck, his eyes narrowing. "What's wrong, Ellie, old sock?" He made another move to push past me. Butler took a measured step forward.

"There's something going on here, but I know when to bugger off; I'll just stay for breakfast and—"

"Freddy," I said, "if you have any feelings for Ben and me, take care of Abigail's until he gets back."

I shut the door on him and leaned against it, trembling. I hadn't felt so abandoned since Dorcas and Jonas left. Where was the bride who thought marriage meant never having to say I'm lonely?

"What a truly delightful young man!" Primrose said. "Concerned, thoughtful—patently he did not like us at all. And now I do think we should get down to making plans; we can't continue to let the day slide away from us."

It was agreed that I should go to morning service at St. Anselm's. I usually attended so, if Mrs. Bottomly had been quick off the mark, it was a possibility that The Founder might try some not very funny business as I went to or fro or even as I knelt in prayer. Hyacinth would trail me with her duelling pistol at the ready. Butler and Primrose would stay with Magdalene. My mother-in-law was very distressed at having to miss Mass at such a time, but did feel that under the circumstances Father Padinsky would continue to give her a pass.

I went to church. I returned. No hand reached around one of the elms to encircle my throat. No car tried to nose me over the cliff. No whisper from bodyguard Hyacinth that we were being stalked. The day wore on with no one telephoning and attempting to lure me to a false rendezvous. Every time I forced myself to cross the hall to go upstairs I shuddered. Not a sound could be heard from below, but my head still rang with the tortured cries of Ben and Poppa as they descended into the stygian darkness of their prison.

Butler prepared lunch. Afterward we gathered in the drawing room and he gave the Tramwells what appeared to be an ongoing lesson in picking pockets. Magdalene and I sat and read, or pretended to. Dinner. Supper. I went out to the courtyard to fetch Sweetie in from her romp, but I wasn't tossed in the moat or shot through the heart. When the hall clock struck ten, Hyacinth rolled up her knitting, Primrose laid down her embroidery hoop, and Magdalene awakened from her nap.

"Ellie, should we not prepare for bed?" Primrose's eyes brimmed with the eager fear of a child playing murder in the dark. "I will conceal myself in your wardrobe, leaving the door agap, and Hyacinth will remain with dear Magdalene. Butler will be on the prowl." She turned to him. "Should you hear two screams at once, pray answer the loudest."

"Certainly, madam."

Lying between the silver grey sheets, I watched the shadowed pheasants on the wallpaper and counted the folds in the velvet curtains. What if all our hopes were in vain? What if The Founder did not act with dispatch, or at all? What if he/she decided to punish me some other way? Or worse, grant me a reprieve? Where could I hide Ben on a permanent basis?

Monday morning came. I was congratulated on having survived unmolested, but I sensed a growing impatience and began to wonder how long it might be before the others began to blame me, unconsciously, for my ineffectualness. When nerves are frayed, nothing soothes like a scapegoat.

Roxie stomped through the garden door at 8:00 A.M. She did a double take on seeing the Tramwells and Butler.

"What ho, Mrs. H., taking in paying guests, are we?" She dumped the supply bag on the table and began popping open the buttons on her burgundy brocade coat. "Stands to reason it will be twice as hard on me, weaving the mop between all them extra legs, but I won't charge you extra."

I was about to say that I really didn't need her today, but read Hyacinth's eyebrow signals. Should Roxie, perchance, be the one, she must be given free rein to push me down the stairs, choke me with the Hoover cord, or hit me over the head with one of Magdalene's statues. The sisters made a big production of sending Butler on an errand and saying they would walk in the garden and perhaps out onto Cliff Road, if Magdalene would accompany them. Minutes after the garden door closed, my hopes lurched when Roxie asked me to accompany her into the drawing room.

Since the curtains were still closed, it had a dim, unused look. "Over here, Mrs. H." Roxie's voice had an unmistakable gloat to it. "Now"—she flung out an arm—"if this isn't going to *kill* you."

An amazing calm enveloped me. My eyes followed her finger. Behold Sweetie, chewing on the leg of the bureau. Surprisingly, my heart and soul had not quite shrivelled away. A flame of fury leapt up in me. Thrusting open the French windows, I shoved a snarling Sweetie out into the garden. She might have remained planted in the flower bed had Tobias not shot out from under the bookcase and, like tabbied lightning, given chase.

"I'll put some scratch-cover polish on that bureau leg. I have some upstairs," I told Roxie. Out in the hall I listened to the deadening silence, then started up the staircase. I liked Roxie, but I wasn't prepared to pick and choose villains anymore. Let her be the one. I knew the polish to be in the kitchen so I was elaborately enticing her. No sound. I sat on the stairs and waited, maybe dozed. . . . A hand clutched at me, almost toppling me over backward.

"Rouse, my dear Ellie, I am most concerned," trilled Primrose. "Magdalene went chasing through the grounds after little Sweetie dog, who was being pursued by the pussycat. Hyacinth went after them, and a minute later I dispatched Butler to follow, because we cannot discount the possibility of that dreadful Raincoat Man being about. And the outcome, alas, does look bleak. None of them has come back. Admittedly, it has only been about ten minutes, and Hyacinth does have the duelling pistol with her, but I do think—as nothing seems to be ripening here—that you and I should attempt to locate them."

"No," I said, eager to do something. "You stay here. I know the grounds and the places where Tobias may have cornered Sweetie. If your sister and the others come back to the house and find us gone, they will panic. I'll be in no danger. The Founder isn't given to impromptu murder."

"Ellie, I think you should stay here and I . . . oh, dear me, no, that will never do; not if Mrs. Malloy is you-know-who." I was dragging on an old raincoat. Primrose's face crumpled. "I have an ominous feeling about this, my child."

Out in the garden I called out the string of names: Magdalene, Hyacinth, Butler, Sweetie, Tobias. No answering shouts, no rustle of shrubbery. It had rained earlier and the daffodils shone yellow under the fruit trees, which had blossomed overnight into fragrant canopies of pink and white. Birds twittered. Bees hummed. Everything was coming alive. Dreariness clamped down on me and, at last, the fear I had been waiting—hoping—for. Where were they? Three people whose current mission in life was to protect me wouldn't play silly games.

What was that scuffling noise near the iron gates? I began to run, feet skidding on gravel. As I drew level with the cottage, I saw Sweetie wriggle out from under the hedge and go hopping like a rabbit out onto Cliff Road. I raced after her.

She stayed barely ahead of me, but every time I was within reach of grabbing her, she would shoot ahead. Could it be that

Magdalene, pursued by Hyacinth and Butler, had chased her this way? And the little wretch had doubled back? Sweetie dodged into the churchyard; so did I.

"Magdalene! Hyacinth! Butler!" What was that? The moan of the sea? The screech of a gull? Or a voice crying out, "Here! Here!" Sweetie had vanished behind a tombstone, but the sound had not come from that direction. I ran up to the church steps and lifted the iron handle. The door was locked. A branch grated against a stained glass window and I told myself I had certainly imagined the voice. Hands in my pockets, I descended the steps. I would go home where doubtless I would find everyone returned safe and sound. A deepening of shadow against the east wall of the church hall caught my eye. I crept forward in time to see the delinquent dog make a dive toward the door, which was propped open. I couldn't go home without her, could I?

Memories of the aborted cookery demonstration crowded in as I stepped through that doorway. The place was thick with shadow and I could not find a light switch. Damn! I almost turned about and left, but a muffled noise convinced me that Sweetie was still in here, waiting to be caught. I felt my way along the wall, past the rows of chairs, stumbling into a table. At last. I was at the stage, hoisting myself up. Only a few yards now from a familiar light switch. My hand was on the curtain when I heard it again, unmistakably a human whisper. "Here . . . here . . ." A chill slid over me.

Something was wrong here. Something was missing. . . . And then it came to me. Bunty on the telephone telling me that there would be a rehearsal of the Aerobics Follies at 11:00 A.M. on Monday. Today. It must now be a few minutes one way or the other of that time. That's why the door had been open, but the hall should have been ablaze with lights and alive with the voices of my showmates. Instead, the emptiness and silence expanded until it seemed infinite. Almost. The whisper came from somewhere above me, or it might have been behind me.

"Here . . . Ellie."

Either someone, pretending to be Bunty, had phoned the others and cancelled the rehearsal, or—I desperately needed something to hold onto, like a large bar of chocolate, was I the only one Bunty had contacted in the first place?

This was the moment for which I had been hankering. The enemy was at hand. My support troops were otherwise occupied. I must hide, play dead; such was my only hope. I fought the urge to wrap myself in a fold of curtain—surely one of the first places The Founder would look. Forgotten was my conviction that life without Ben's love was meaningless. I wanted desperately to survive this character-building experience. When push comes to shove, life in a parrot's cage is better than nothing. I dropped to all fours and began crawling. My knees burned away the floor, until abruptly, my hands came to a full stop. Some obstacle was in their path.

"Here, Ellie . . ."

As the whisper came again, I frantically frisked the thing and felt a pinprick of hope. My cake. The one darling Poppa had made for me. If I could climb into it without making a breath of sound and draw down the wooden flap, I might be able to elude my persecutor until someone . . . say, the church hall inspector . . . came.

"Here, Ellie."

A thin hope against a dead certainty. The lid lifted silently; a blessing on Poppa's head for oiling the hinges. I was inside, huddled in a dark that was complete. I ordered my heart to slow down. If it kept up its present racket, it would either be heard or would set the cake walls to vibrating. The seconds stretched.

And then I heard footsteps and someone laughing—rather sadly, it seemed to me—before the hammering started. The hammering of my heart. The hammering of nails being driven into the carved icing of the cake top.

At first I struggled. If I could get my head back and my feet in kicking position . . . hopeless. Then I rationalized—there must be enough air in here to keep me in agonizing breaths for . . . minutes, after which my lungs and heart would explode. One second gone, two, three . . . Oh, God!

The horror seeped away, leaving me almost peaceful. I said my prayers. The Tramwells would rescue Ben from the dungeon and whilst he might not have been able to forgive me, had I lived, death would enshrine me in his memory, eternally angelic, eternally thin. The tragedy was that I was dying for nothing. The foul murders of the Chitterton Fells husbands would continue. The devilish Founder had escaped the snare. Stop it, Ellie. Focus in these last few moments on the good things. You could have died single. Instead you have known the great joy of loving Ben, and you know that what you have shared will enable him to go on when you are but a name engraved upon a stone. He will mourn for a while, and then one day some lovely young woman will admire the elegant way he holds an eggbeater, and you . . . you, poor fish, will be forgotten, except when casually mentioned as "my first wife." That apprentice wife who taught Bentley T. Haskell all the pitfalls of the first year of matrimony so he could avoid them the second time around.

It seemed I wasn't going to die at peace after all. Breathing had become an impossibility, but my lungs filled up with something more vital than air. Willpower. Ben would not have a second wife. I was going to scream if it was the last thing I did. I was going to tear this cake to shreds if . . . I don't think I had got past the planning stage, but such is the power of positive thinking that my prison was coming apart. Or was I dead and having one of those transcendental experiences?

"Ellie," whispered Ben.

I smiled seraphically. Heaven was every bit as wonderful as the prospectus claims. I was lying on a pillow cloud, and my beloved was present with me in spirit and coincidentally in the flesh, too. I blinked because the light had a sparkling brilliance, then weakly stroked Ben's hand. It felt almost real.

"Ellie, darling. You can't die. I don't care what your religion teaches, but I have it on the highest authority that there is no chocolate in heaven." He was kneeling beside me.

I struggled to sit up. "Ben, I think we are having a joint hallucination. I'm really in the cake and you are in the dungeon at Merlin's Court."

"No." He was rubbing my hands. "I got you out, thanks to Sweetie, who kept whining and chewing at the cake. And Poppa and I escaped the dungeons by means of a secret tunnel which exits under one of the beds. Poppa got the idea from reading about a similar arrangement in one of Edwin Digby's books. And, interestingly enough, our tunnel ended at the cellar of Digby's house. Highly convenient for old Wilfred Grantham and his assignations with the two sisters at The Aviary. Wonder if it dates back to smuggling days?"

Ben was talking as though he had been away for the weekend and wanted to share the details. I shuddered and hung my head. "That cake was hell, but I wasn't in it long and I don't have claustrophobia. . . . What I am trying to say, Ben, is that

I don't expect you to forgive me for the misery I have inflicted on you, locking you up, forcing you to crawl through that blackness, not knowing where, or whether it would end."

He leaned backward so that I had to look at him. "Hell was feeling the hall floor disintegrate under my feet. I was livid with you. I planned to murder you the minute I got out, but when I read that green notebook and realised that someone else was in all likelihood making the same plans, I didn't have time for claustrophobia."

I touched his face, so handsome, so concerned. "It was the same for me, in a way. When I became caught up in worrying about you, I stopped being frightened of food; I didn't have time to concentrate on not eating."

His arms entwined about me. "Ellie, don't be afraid now. We're going to the police; this monster—The Founder—will be stopped." His lips brushed my throat. "We've made a lot of mistakes, but what can we expect, we are only beginners. I don't suppose I'll ever understand you completely. I don't need to understand you to love you. All that matters is that I would have crawled through the centre of the earth to get to you and that I wasn't too late."

The moment was so fragile that I was afraid to say anything of what I felt, in case it broke. I cleared my throat and asked if Poppa was all right.

"Yes and no. Physically he's fine, but he's worried about how Mum's feeling and consumed by guilt because in the shock of being plunged into the dungeon he accidentally spoke to me."

"What made you look for me here?" I asked as Ben helped me to my feet.

"When we were racing up to the gates of Merlin's Court, Poppa and I saw Miss Primrose Tramwell; she was in a flap about everyone being missing." He touched his fingers to my lips. "It's all right, darling. Everyone is found. Poppa is with them. I didn't know where to look for you until we saw Sweetie coming along Cliff Road, and I clutched at the possibility you might have gone looking for her in the churchyard. When I turned that way, she ran back ahead of me and eventually in here to the cake."

I shivered, as much at owing Sweetie a lifetime of gratitude as the memory of what I had been through. She had probably only come in here to 'go'; so Roxie would claim anyway; but I would buy Sweetie a lifetime subscription to *How to Train Your Owner*. My mind began to whirl with questions. Had Ben and Poppa seen Edwin Digby when they exited in his cellar? What had befallen my comrades-in-arms? And . . . where was The Founder now?

Ben guided me to the door. "You have to get some fresh air, darling."

As we stepped onto the grass, my legs went pulpy, and the noonday sky seemed to tilt. The Founder could be behind any one of a hundred tombstones. I gripped Ben's hand tighter.

Mr. Digby was standing on the sun-dappled path, a gun in his hand, and my surprise was that I was surprised. Everything had pointed to him, but in his drunkenness he may have thought himself invincible. Mother was waddling around him in narrowing circles. I felt sorry for the goose. Mr. Digby's purplish fingers were pointing the gun, not at Ben and me, but at someone standing in front of an angel monument.

"Mrs. Haskell." His head moved an inch in my direction. "My abject apologies on behalf of my daughter Wren."

Ben and I turned in slow motion.

"No!" I exclaimed. "She can't be, she isn't . . . this is Jenny! Jenny Spender." I had suspected Bunty might be his daughter; she was the right age and admitted she used a nickname. Digby had said Wren was living with a man; gossip said Bunty and Lionel weren't really married. But, Jenny! Ridiculous! On second thought, maybe not. . .

Her eyes, those eyes which I had always thought too old for a child's face, drifted over me and fixed with the most chilling hatred on Mr. Digby's face.

"Jenny Wren." Ben stroked my hair back from my face. "Hyacinth Tramwell recorded all the clues in her little green book. That farthing, as well as the photograph in the pocket of the pin-striped suit you borrowed from Mr. Digby, suggested to yours truly that Jenny was the one. The farthing was the smallest coin in the realm and carried the symbol, on one of its sides, of the smallest British bird, the wren."

"She was such a tiny baby," Mr. Digby mused, "and she had given me that farthing in the happy days for a good-luck charm. It was easier to believe I had gone mad than to think of her grown evil. These past five years I have cowered in the bottle. But when you, Mr. Haskell, with parent in tow, burst into my house ranting about a widows club, I knew I had to pull the stopper, on myself, on my child." The gun wavered but he steadied it with his free hand.

Ben stared into the wedge-shaped face framed by the childish plaits. "The Founder had to be someone who could observe and listen unnoticed. A hairdresser? A solicitor? A secretary? A charwoman? All good possibilities, but what better cover than that of a child?"

Jenny smiled, her fingers gripping the angel's marble wings as if she would snap them.

"You were at Abigail's the night of Charles Delacorte's death," Ben continued, addressing her, "carrying a white plastic raincoat. How convenient! I suppose you walked into the office, smothered him, and wore the murder weapon off the premises." He paused. "Did you inherit your stage presence from your mother, along with your father's macabre imagination? Was she eternally youthful, like you?"

"I can't sing like Mummy," said Jenny in that dreadful childish voice, "but I do have her ear, as well as her great sense of timing." Her laughter went right through me. "I was able to phone all the ladies in the aerobics class—pretending to be Bunty Wiseman—and I cancelled the rehearsal. Then I rang her up, claiming to be Miss Thorn, saying the church hall wasn't available. A clever ploy, wasn't it, Mrs. Haskell," she twiddled with a plait, "to get us alone?"

Ben continued remorselessly, his hand tightening around mine. "Ann Delacorte recognised your mother as Sylvania, the singer on whom she had an almost schoolgirl crush, when she went to the Dower House that day with Ellie. That idea sneaked up on me when I read that the nanny called your mother Vania. And I'll wager the record being played was one of hers, from her heyday. The excitement caused Ann to turn faint—two thrills in one day, Lionel Wiseman and now the discovery of her idol." Ben shook his head. "Foolish Ann. She made a big mistake. She thought The Founder was pretending to be an invalid, not a child. And she was gripped by the sort of groupie closeness that gave her the confidence to go and ask a favour. That green car that slashed past you, Ellie, when you made your pregnant visit to The Peerless, I wonder if it was Ann's Morris Minor?"

"I really enjoyed killing her." Jenny's voice wasn't a child's anymore. It seemed especially evil that she should make such a pronouncement in this little place of consecrated ground. "I became quite expert at archery when Daddy here was doing research for his book, *Robin of Nottinghill Gate*. Simon tried to talk me out of retiring Mrs. Delacorte. He said it might stir up a panic among the widows, but Simon always comes around to my way of thinking. That's what love does—it turns people into fools. I rather enjoy watching the good doctor squirm for me the way my mother used to squirm for Daddy."

"Not true, Wren," said Edwin Digby.

"Yes, she did. She, the sparkling, glittering Sylvania, who had men reaching for her every time she stepped on stage and lit it up with her voice. She was ageless and she *loved* you, God only knows why, you ugly man, only to discover that you were trying to relive some adolescent passion with your secretary, the washed up, washed out Lady Peerless." Jenny took on Teddy's toothiness. "And because of you and your unfaithfulness, my mother, my exquisite mother, stuck her head in the oven and wasn't lucky enough to die. She became a husk. I can look in her eyes and call, but she isn't there."

Edwin Digby took a step toward his daughter and then retreated, the gun dangling in his hand. "Wrong, Wren! Your mother never really loved me. Her one passion was her career; she would never acknowledge she was married, even after you were born. She was obsessed with keeping up the aura of being unattainable. She insisted that I use the pseudonym Edwin Digby—in private life, to tighten the veil of secrecy, and you were kept hidden away with her childhood nanny."

He was a figure out of a vampire skit, with his twirled eyebrows and beard forked by the wind. "Teddy and I had been youthful sweethearts, but Sylvania demanded that I sever all ties with the past. Think what you will of me, all of you!" His eyes glared at Ben and me as well as his daughter. "Teddy is guiltless!" The words might sound as if they came from one of his books, but I felt drops of water on my face, that weren't rain. "She did not realise she would be working for me when she applied for the post of my secretary, ten long years ago. She had known me under my real name of Robert Burns, which—" his rheumy eyes were turned fully on Ben and me now, "I never used professionally, for obvious reasons."

"And you fell in love." Jenny (she would always be that to me) made the words sound like gutter ones.

"I swear there was no unfaithfulness. What drove your mother mad"—Mr. Digby's lips twisted—"was the idea of so unworthy a rival."

Jenny smiled mockingly. "You did not think it unfaithful to ask Mumma for a divorce."

I said, to be saying something, "The parrot in Teddy's office talks like one of your characters, Mr. Digby."

"A farewell present, Mrs. Haskell. Teddy was ever a bird fancier. I settled in Chitterton Fells to be near her, even though we had assured each other that all was over between us. I came to the Haskell wedding reception," the wind lifted his crinkly hair from his high forehead, "but too late, too drunk, to catch a glimpse. The first time I saw Teddy in all the years, other than to pass on the street, was at the restaurant soiree, the night Charles Delacorte died."

"Teddy saw your daughter there." I wrenched my eyes away from Jenny's smile. "Maybe she wasn't sure at first, but then the full horror must have hit her—that this was Wren," I inched closer to Ben, "grown frighteningly younger than when last seen. No wonder Teddy blundered into the office to escape and, instead, found a body. No wonder she wouldn't talk about that night. I don't suppose she suspected—do you Mr. Digby?—that Wren had anything to do with Charles's death, but I don't doubt she blamed herself, all over again, for the old tragedy and . . . the results to Mother and now . . ."

Jenny was still smiling. "I'm not mad and I do not consider myself a criminal."

Mr. Digby steadied the gun again. Mother trod over his feet, as he said, "I have not seen Teddy since that night."

"I imagine," Ben said to Wren, "that it was your father's latest pseudonym, that of Felicity Friend, that embarked you on your voyage of revenge?"

"It wasn't only revenge." Jenny's voice was wistful, a child's again. "I wanted to help other women whose husbands were betraying them. And when Daddy became Felicity Friend and I remembered that book, *The Merry Widows*—that sold three copies, it all became clear. I had expert medical advice from Simon, who yearned to suffer at my hands. I could kill off Daddy a little bit at a time with every other man whose death I staged and bide my time until I decided to bury him." Her eyes were on Mother, who was standing motionless with her wings spread. "You didn't like to refuse me, did you, Daddy, when I asked you to put the occasional message in your confidential column? I told you it was a little game I was playing. But you worried nicely about what it all meant—the dickybird brooches . . . the deaths, but Daddy's little girl was too big to go in the corner. And what you didn't see couldn't happen. What a weakling you are! Not even man enought to fight for your Teddy bear. I wish I could think she had read *The Merry Widows* and suffered accordingly, but even if she had—which isn't likely—I don't think her capable of taking the leap from fiction to fact. And such was your downfall, Daddy. You were ever so grateful (weren't you?) that I was looking after Mumma, and came to see you sometimes."

Jenny gave a childish giggle and addressed me. "I was at The Aviary the day you came, and he got the wind up, first that I might do something to tease you, and then that your charwoman had recognised him as Felicity Friend. I was so tempted to cheer him up by telling him I would kill her for him."

I drew closer to Ben. The rustling of the trees and Mother's feathers were for a moment the only sounds. "I should have guessed, with so much typing on his desk, when supposedly he hadn't written in years, that Mr. Digby was a prime candidate for the role of Dear Felicity. And I should have realised that the only reason to wear plaits that make you look too young for your age is because you are too old for them. I suppose that makes me rather stupid, but I really prefer that to being diabolically clever."

"Methinks the lady doth protest too much." Jenny stepped away from the angel. "And to think I thought you so guileless. I *liked* you. I really did. You gave me your wedding roses and I sent you some. But you figured out the way to trap me. Only it isn't going to work." She lifted up her arms and spread her fingers, as though pushing back the clouds. "It can't work because my dear Daddy wouldn't shoot me. He doesn't have the courage."

She stepped toward us. "I have nothing to lose, you see, because I have nothing to love. Mumma was gone a long time ago."

She kept coming. She was right. Edwin Digby couldn't pull the trigger. Closer, closer. Mother must have felt threatened, for suddenly her wings fanned out. Neck extended, she rushed toward Jenny, who turned her back and with an eerie, childish laugh, darted and zigzagged between the tombstones, arms outstretched. Maybe she didn't look ahead, maybe she did. It doesn't alter anything. She tripped and tumbled headlong into an open grave—the grave waiting for Ann Delacorte. And we were left standing in the wind-ruffled churchyard, listening to the gulls and the distant moan of the sea.

EPILOGUE

Primrose expressed my sentiments exactly. "I can have no sympathy for The Founder; but I am saddened that Jenny got lost somewhere in childhood, a place many of us like to revisit but do not want to relive, and that she is dead. Let us thank God her end was quick and trust that Mr. Digby is successful in persuading that friend of his at Scotland Yard that The Widows Club does exist. Although my strong feeling is that with its guiding force gone, the organisation may degenerate into a social group."

"I couldn't agree more." Hyacinth's earrings swung. "And now, my dear Prim, I think we should leave the charm of Merlin's Court for the charms of home and writing our report to our insurance company employer. Not, Ellie, that things haven't been entirely delightful here this afternoon with the constabulary buzzing in and out."

Actually I felt rather sorry for the police. They must have wondered whether they were coming or going. Mr. Digby and Ben had remained to keep vigil over Jenny's body while I raced home to report the accident, only to find uniformed lawmen spilling all over the ground floor of Merlin's Court.

Poppa and Magdalene occupied chairs of honour as they gave statements concerning the Raincoat Man (yes, our other villain had staged another kidnapping attempt). Hyacinth, Primrose, and Butler hovered in the background, supplying the occasional salient point. And lounging against a wall with a self-deprecating smile on his lips, was the hero of the hour, my cousin Freddy.

To return to the disappearance of Magdalene, Hyacinth, and Butler, it will be remembered that they had gone in pursuit of Sweetie and each other. And there they were, milling around the grounds near the gates, when Reggie, the Raincoat Man, slithered out of nowhere, yelling "Hands up!" He was in the midst of complaining that he kept kidnapping more people than he really wanted when Freddy stepped, unnoticed, out of the cottage.

My cousin had been harboring nasty suspicions about the Tramwells and Butler. He was certain they had Ben tied up and gagged and were keeping me and Magdalene hostage while they holed up at Merlin's Court until their boat arrived to take them to France . . . or something along those lines. He had been rattling his brain trying to think of some way to conduct a rescue without getting hurt himself when there he went walking smack into the bunch of them. Reggie's remarks suggested to him, as did the gun, that here was the leader of the gang. Feeling chuffed that his theory was right on, our hero stood for a minute, unseen, at the back of the group and was on the brink of fleeing the scene—to fetch help, as he tells it—when he remembered the chains he wore. Slipping one off, he tossed it around Reggie's neck, yanked until he could hear the villain's veins pop, then suggested that the gun be dropped.

Everyone (except Reggie) was ecstatic. But Freddy, unwilling to have the excitement peter out, voiced doubts that the Tramwells and Butler were innocent. Figuring Magdalene might be vouching for them under duress, he marched all of them, along with Reggie, into the cottage to telephone the police, which is why I couldn't find them when I went looking for my missing persons. Magdalene had just persuaded Freddy that Reggie was the only counterfeit in the group when she saw, through the window, Ben and Poppa running down Cliff Road, almost mowing down Primrose, who was searching for Sweetie near the gates.

Magdalene came out the cottage door. Explanations followed. The police arrived, Reggie was removed in handcuffs, and the decision was made to adjourn to the main house. Freddy didn't have any tea and the ladies expressed a dire need for its reviving qualities. Shortly thereafter I arrived with my news that Mr. Digby's daughter had fallen in an open grave, Ben had climbed in after her, and we were sure she was dead.

"An afternoon to remember, Ellie, old girl." Freddy crossed his legs at the ankle and inserted his hands in his pockets, studying his sockless feet.

"Yes," I said, "and you were marvellous. I'm sure I looked very ingenuous and wide-eyed. If my lids as much as flickered—I saw Jenny." A chorus of agreement arose from everyone. Ben was showing the last policeman off the premises.

"Don't say it," Freddy rejoined. "Don't say that line about everything I have is yours because, despite the vulgar tattle, I *really* don't want Ben. Sorry, darling"—he tossed back his hair—"I just don't think he is that cute. And this being the eighteenth of May—namely, my birthday—the date Jill and I assigned for renewed communication, I am off to see if she has come to her senses. It's begun to dawn on me, after watching your marriage close up, Ellie, that life doesn't have to turn into an old potato after tying the knot." He spread his hands. "There can still be the thrill of living on the edge."

"No one can guarantee you the perpetual enlivenment of murder," I felt compelled to warn, but he was gone. Minutes later we heard the roar of his motorbike.

Primrose sighed sentimentally. "Off to find his true love. And now, my dear Ellie, Hyacinth and I must also bid you adieu. It has been a pleasure and a privilege working with you and I do hope the opportunity may present itself again." She drew her shawl around her shoulders and glanced at her Mickey Mouse watch.

Hyacinth gathered up her carpetbag and rose from her chair. "Yes, Ellie, do keep in touch. And please spread the word to any of your friends who might be in need that Flowers Detection specialises in Crimes with a Difference." She shook hands warmly with my parents-in-law. "Good-bye, Mr. and Mrs. Elijah Haskell. I am glad that you may now return to your little shop in peace." As she came up to me, she whispered, "I do trust they will take the hint."

* * * *

To my dismay, it looked like they had. As I closed the front door on the Tramwells, Magdalene began filling her arms with statues of saints. "Well, Giselle, it looks as though you and Ben are about to be alone in your own home."

"Don't be silly," I protested. "You *can't* rush off this minute. We have to celebrate that we are all alive and that Ben and Poppa are talking again."

"Elijah and I are going to celebrate." I was close enough to see her face flush a dusty rose. "Unlike people of your generation, we want to do it in utmost privacy."

I grabbed St. Francis as he took a dive. "Are we talking about a second honeymoon?"

She looked at me, then began piling on more statues. "Eli and I never went on a honeymoon. We couldn't afford it, not that I minded. There are more important things in life, and I'm not the one to hanker for the little extras in life that *others* take for granted."

"Are you sure you won't stay here tonight?"

"Giselle." Sigh. "I don't expect *you* to understand Eli can be very difficult, but any woman can love a man who is easy. It takes a great love . . . a rare and radiant passion . . . as I read in that book of yours—*Marriage Made Easy*, to love the man who is often unlovable."

I didn't listen to any more. I went up to my bedroom and came back down with a tissue paper package. Magdalene reluctantly put the statues down on the trestle table and opened it up.

"A pink nightdress," she said.

"A pearl-pink nightdress," I corrected, "made from the gossamer wings of one thousand and one fireflies. Guaranteed to make you irresistible as long as you don't wear curlers with it or bedsocks."

She held it against her with one hand and touched her wispy hair with the other. "I must be truthful, Giselle. You weren't what I wanted in a daughter-in-law. It wasn't just the religion or your thinking I was a charwoman, it was you being so . . . tall and thin . . . and independent. I always hoped my Ben would marry someone . . . plump and grateful. But first impressions aren't everything. And I think we've grown closer these last trying days."

"You mean you began to like me a little better when you

no longer saw me as a pampered child of fortune?"

"Something like that, but not in those words." She stroked the nightdress. "I never thought Eli and I would have complicated my boy's life, or yours . . ."

"But you have," I said. "I've grown fond of you. Why don't you go upstairs and pack, and I'll make you a cup of tea. Oh, one thing . . . Because I was so nice and gave you the nightdress, how about leaving me St. Francis?"

"If you insist—Ellie."

"Thanks, Mum."

The house seemed nude without the statues and without the doilies and the crocheted covers on the cannisters and the patchwork rugs. Perhaps feeling their absence as well, Ben soon suggested we have an early night. On our way through the hall, the telephone rang. I was afraid to pick it up in case it was an outraged widow, but wonderfully, it was Dorcas.

"Ellie? Everything shipshape on the home front?"

When I could stop my joyous squealing, I said, "As of now, yes. Why?"

"Had the spookiest feeling all day that something was wrong. Got a letter this morning from one of the teachers at the Miriam Academy where I used to work. I'd written and told her about that girl you mentioned, Jenny Spender, who said she was a pupil at the school. But Evelyn, my chum, says there's no such kid. Never has been. Has to be a logical explanation, but haven't been able to shake this peculiar feeling of menace."

"Dorcas, it's all right. There was a problem with Jenny, which I will tell you all about when you get home. Which I hope will be soon. Because I miss you terribly. If you went away to be noble and give Ben and me time alone, forget it."

I could hear whisperings and then Jonas came on the line. "We'll be home on Saturday. Have the Ovaltine hot."

The air was filled with the lovely tranquility of twilight and apple blossom. I was lying on the bed wearing a rather fetching green nightshirt when Ben came in with a bottle of champagne and two glasses. His hand brushed my shoulder and then snapped on the radio. I started to tell him about the return of the wanderers when I became distracted.

"Ben, what is that music? It sounds like a knife on a sink."

Foam sidled down the bottle and a comma of dark hair fell

over his brow as he listened. "It's a violin solo, darling. Don't you like violins?"

"Yes," I said, "when they are lost in a crowd of trombones and flutes and other less screechy instruments." I took the glass he handed me.

"Why are you smiling?"

"Just happy." My fingers wove into his and I felt my soul being set alight by the emerald fire of his eyes. I looked down at my wedding ring and remembered, with regret, the diamond shine of my engagement ring.

"Now what are you thinking?" His lips touched the side of my neck and the horrible violins faded away.

"About Edwin Digby and Teddy. I hope they find happiness at last. I hope that Sylvania and the old nanny are well cared for after the investigations at The Peerless. I hope your parents are doing justice to my pearl-pink nightdress. We'll make Abigail's a success, not an overnight one, but the other kind is better."

"Here's to Happy Ever After, darling." Ben touched his glass to mine, and we crossed hands and sipped like lovers on the big silver screen. As I watched the golden bubbles dance, I thought with wry amusement of the girl I had been, the one who thought marriage was like a diet. If you followed the rules to the letter, it would be painless and you would be a winner. I reached out for Ben, wondering if I should warn him that the fat woman was alive and well inside me, that I knew enough now not to make any glib promises even to myself. Should I tell him what else these months of marriage had taught me? That there is no such thing as Happy Ever After, and that is the sadness, the splendour, the magic of real love.

From the Files of
The Widows Club

MEMO: To Mrs. Millicent Parsnip, Recording Secretary.

In view of the exodus from the community of the entire membership of our noble organisation, I request you burn all files lest they fall into unworthy hands.

Yours, in the hope that we shall rise again,

Amelia Bottomly,
President